D0371557

PULSE

Other books by Robert Cook

Cooch

Patriot & Assassin

PULSE

ROBERT COOK

A NATIONAL SECURITY THRILLER

This book is a work of fiction. Names, characters, businesses, organizations, places, events, and incidents are either a product of the author's imagination or are used fictitiously. Any resemblance to actual persons, living or dead, events, or locales is entirely coincidental.

Published by Greenleaf Book Group Press
Austin, Texas
www.gbgpress.com

Distributed by Greenleaf Book Group

For ordering information or special discounts for bulk purchases, please contact Greenleaf Book Group at PO Box 91869, Austin, TX 78709, 512.891.6100.

Design and composition by Greenleaf Book Group and Debbie Berne
Cover design by Greenleaf Book Group and Debbie Berne
Cover credits: Exterior of Mosque/EyeEm/Getty Images; clouds ©iStockphoto.com/upsidedowndog; electric lighting effect©iStockphoto.com /tolokonov

Cataloging-in-Publication data is available.

Print ISBN: 978-1-62634-247-7

eBook ISBN: 978-1-62634-248-4

Part of the Tree Neutral® program, which offsets the number of trees consumed in the production and printing of this book by taking proactive steps, such as planting trees in direct proportion to the number of trees used: www.treeneutral.com

Printed in the United States of America on acid-free paper

15 16 17 18 19 20 10 9 8 7 6 5 4 3 2 1

First Edition

For PJ, the love of my life

The most worthy of granting forgiveness are
those most capable of punishing.

Ali ibn Abi Taleb, son-in-law of the prophet Muhammed

ACKNOWLEDGMENTS

In my fledging career as a storyteller, there are many to thank for their support. First, there are my readers. Thank you for your support and the priceless word of mouth that you generate for the Cooch novels.

Once again, many thanks to those who made *Pulse* a better book with their critical readership and advice. Above all, I thank my marvelous wife, Paula, for her limitless patience and support. Particular thanks go to Judy Hamilton and Sally Krueger for their early, valuable insight. For things military and thoughts on national security, special thanks go to James Loy, Admiral, US Coast Guard (Ret), former Deputy Director of the US Department of Homeland Security, and to Thomas Fargo, Admiral, US Navy (Ret), former CINCPAC and submariner. Bob Bressler was once again my sounding board for all things electric, network, and Internet, and a great one he was. Michael Proctor was there for me from the beginning. Writer and moral support came from Art Allen, David and Gay Campbell, Bruce Coleman, Bob and Cyndi Elders, Tor and Susan Kenward, Rich Moore, and Wil and Karen Shirey.

A special nod to my editor, Michael Denneny, for tolerating a storytelling novice while doing a fabulous job with helping me say things better. The misses are mine, not his.

CHAPTER 1

TANGIER, MOROCCO

BUILT ON THE RUINS OF THE Roman city of Tingis in northern Morocco, a few miles across salt water from the looming mass of Gibraltar, lies the Petit Socco, the little square, at the center of the city of Tangier. It was once the pulsing heart of the ancient walled medina, beating with sophisticated Tangerines who gathered at Café Socco and others with broad terraces to see and to be seen.

The sophisticates have moved on, but the idle remain along with a few struggling writers, who hope for inspiration in the fading shadows of Paul Bowles and Ernest Hemingway. Ancient backstreets are narrow and dark; their scents are of offal and sewage. A few small shops and cafés remain along them, many with empty shells gaping in disuse. The ancient city has been passed by, with attraction neither for tourists nor for affluent Moroccans.

In the Petit Socco's southwest corner was a former stable, converted to a café to serve the locals. The faint, lingering stench was of animals past, deep in the grout and the swept dirt floor. Its windows were mere gaps in the walls, open to the elements. Stained Chinese copies of Persian rugs hung on two interior walls.

At the center of the café, two local men were seated at a small wooden table. The distinctive, rancid smell in the room came from a hookah, a water pipe at the table's center, loaded with local tobacco and shared by the two. The table's cut was a little better than that of the other furniture, and its occupants seemed by body language to be a cut above the other patrons. The shorter but larger of the two men had long, dark hair, tangled and dirty with a scruffy, dark beard; their body language said he was junior. He wore a green short-sleeved shirt. Huge arms stretched it at the sleeves; the vertical center vein on each bicep was prominent through the skin. One soiled leg was crossed over the other. His boots were scuffed and tied halfway. He was loud.

The second man was taller, smaller, older, and better dressed, with clean jeans and an ironed cotton shirt. His brown hair was well cut, and he wore brown laced-up oxfords.

Their Arabic accents were uniquely Tangerine, with speckles and threads of mangled French woven flawlessly into the patois. Speakers of classical Arabic often say, "Listening to a Tangerine speak Arabic is as listening to an Italian shoemaker speak Latin."

A young server hurried out with black ceramic mugs and set one in front of each man.

Another man walked into the room and took a small table in a dark corner of the small café, his back to the wall. He was dressed in the manner of a Moroccan city worker, with dark, loose pants and an off-white flowing shirt, open at the neck. It had just the vertical hint of a collar. The sleeves of the rough shirt were rolled to mid-forearm, exposing rough, gnarled hands below wide wrists. The forearms were huge, lumpy things wrapped in a tangled mass of distended veins climbing to rolled cuffs. His face was marked with a splash of tiny scars on the forehead, and an old, thin scar wandered down his cheek from a spot beside his left eye. A bump on the bridge of his nose suggested a fracture in the distant past.

He took a smartphone from his pocket. He held it in front of him in two hands, his thumbs dancing across the virtual keyboard. The thumbs were scarred and thick, with strange calluses at their ends, shaped perhaps to make typing easier. When the thumbs paused their dance, a few tiny black hairs showed, growing from their backs.

The server boy stopped beside his table. The man looked up and said in Bedouin-inflected Tangerine, "Tea. Two people." He slipped the phone into his pocket and glanced around to catalog the room. He liked to know who was where and a little more.

He heard the younger, loud man, who was facing the stranger's table say, "Oh ho, Youssef, a stranger in our midst. Maybe he comes to horn in on our business."

The other man, Youssef, responded more quietly, then glanced over at his table. He did a slight double take at the sight of him, then looked away.

The stranger watched them and listened.

Fellows, I hope you're not going to make trouble. I'd rather not be visible right now.

He held his left hand against his forehead and used his neck to push against the hand—hard—for thirty seconds or so. He then moved the hand to the left side of his head, then to the right, pushing hard against it. The dynamic-tension technique of the long gone Charles Atlas was still useful exercise for quick results. The neck began to swell from the extended effort.

"Maybe he'll buy us a drink or two, Youssef," he heard the younger man say and then laugh. "He seems to have a headache. Maybe I'll give him a bigger one."

Others in the café looked over at him, curious, then at the stranger.

Youssef swiveled in his chair and turned his head. He was smiling as he looked at the stranger.

The stranger fixed Youssef with a flat, unblinking stare. His neck was enormous, the thin shirt collar distended by bulging trapezius muscles. He extended his head suddenly from the neck, slowly blinked his eyes once; then brought his head back again, deep into the neck. His eyes never left the older man.

Youssef stared, transfixed for a moment. Then he turned his head and spoke to the other man, threw some money on the table, and started to stand. The younger man seemed outraged and glanced over at the stranger, ready to prove his leader too cautious. He stood and lumbered to the other table, his shoulders hunched to exaggerate his size and muscularity.

"So, my friend," he said, standing close to the table and facing the stranger. "You are away from home. You are not known here. My colleagues and I own this area for our business. First, you can buy me a drink, or I will hurt you." He dropped his left hand to the stranger's right shoulder to control any sudden moves. He could punch with his right. "Then you can tell me why you are in our territory."

An inner voice piped up from somewhere in the stranger's head, just behind his left ear.

"He doesn't seem to be armed. Sloppy walk. Weight is on his heels."

In a fluid motion the stranger reached up with his right hand. The big man felt fingers sliding up his left arm to the inside of the crook of his elbow and the thumb in the small hollow near the end of the elbow's bone. The stranger squeezed hard, digging with his thumb.

"Aargh!" the big man grunted as his elbow exploded in pain; the pain didn't recede. The stranger came easily to his feet, guiding the big man slightly aside, still holding the elbow and maintaining pressure with his thumb. They walked side by side to the older man at the central table, who was watching them. The big man had a newly stumbling, hesitant gait.

Youssef stared into the wide-eyed face of his big companion, his face contorted by a grimace. A grunting, moaning sound came from his lips.

"You should go now," the stranger said in a near whisper. He squeezed the elbow once again but much deeper. The big man went to his knees from the pain. He seemed woozy.

"You should kill them both. Kill them now, laddie. Now, so they won't bother you later."

The stranger released his grasp on the elbow and stepped back a pace. His flat, unblinking eyes were again on the smaller, older Youssef.

Youssef nodded and stood. He took the younger man by the arm, pulled him to his feet, and led him from the café.

The younger man stumbled as he tried to turn back. Youssef spoke to him urgently. "We don't have a gun. We'd need one for him, or maybe two. He's out of our league. If he proves troublesome, we'll deal with him using more than two unarmed men. I saw that look when I was in prison. It means 'I'll kill you for the sport of it.' Back off."

They walked through the open entrance, arguing.

The stranger, whose name was Alejandro Mohammed Cuchulain, sat back in his chair, relieved that public violence had been avoided.

'Gila Monster' is what my buddy, Brooks, calls that neck-stretching, hooded-eye look. He says it scares the civilians—seemed to do that pretty well here. Of course, I've practiced that look in front of a mirror a few

times. Sometimes with a little tongue flicker like a reptile, sensing, sometimes not. Flicker's good for Halloween.

"Nice to be with you again, laddie," Dain said in his mind.

"Dain. Welcome back. It's nice to know you're still watching and haven't jilted me."

Dain is my personal avatar, my schizophrenic fantasy or some such, who drove the shrinks crazy at the CIA's training spot, the Farm in Virginia. They seemed to need shrinks there for us CIA killers. Go figure.

Dain lives somewhere inside my head. He lived inside my father and his father before him. Dain is the Celtic voice of violence with a few centuries of experience. He helps out from time to time when things get ugly. He is alert for violence, if only because he seems to like it. Then again, violence provides the only time I feel a sparkle of inner harmony that is all of me; so it seems that I too like violence. Still, there is a time and a place to satisfy that need. Dain would rather not wait. His view is always immediate. He thinks it's safer that way.

Cuchulain stood as another man, dressed more formally in an ironed shirt tucked into cotton trousers, walked to the table. They shook hands warmly with a slap on each other's right shoulder. A second cup of mint tea was poured from the samovar.

"What a lovely choice of venue, Alex," the man said as he sat. "You look like a Bedouin thug seeking trouble. I actually saw Youssef Maki, the number-three Tangier drug lord with one of his muscle-bound goons walking out of this café as I walked in. You're lucky they didn't decide to have a little fun with a new thug on their turf."

"I'm a lucky guy, my dear Sino," Alex said. "Besides, I like places like this. I feel better when no one knows who I am or what I do. I'm Bedouin. I can better get to know my people here."

"Your people?" Sino ibn Nahir laughed. "You're an American, mostly. These are your adopted people at best."

"Even inherited perhaps. But they are mine, and I am theirs," Alex said. "I look like this because this is who I am much of the time. I'm not really a thug usually, just a Bedouin."

"Shall I call you Kufdani then or Alejandro Mohammed Cuchulain?"

"Alex will do as my name among us, as it has."

"No matter, I suppose," Sino said. "On to the business at hand. The king and his retinue continue to be stunned by our progress in mass adult education and job training, using those fancy phones of yours to project lessons anywhere there is a light wall or a bed sheet. Literacy is up, and we got a big second job from Boeing, assembling wings for their 787 airliner. They were quite impressed with how quickly our people came to acceptable productivity."

"Job training brings fast revenue, more taxes, and improving GDP numbers," Alex said. "Moroccans are good with their hands and are hard workers. But mark my words Sino; it is education of the masses that will bring the king the stability he wants. We need to educate the young. Better education of the populace leads to better jobs that pay more. Once this process gets rolling, it will take on a life of its own. If the king orders more training phones from us, the process will accelerate."

Alex raised his voice as Sino was distracted by a burst of loud noise from just across the room in an open courtyard. There was a group of roughly dressed local men sitting in a semicircle, most talking loudly. A few gambled with dice thrown against a wall. They drank from teacups, frequently refilled. Muslims don't drink alcohol publicly, after all.

Alex needed Sino's help, but didn't want to be obvious about it and had worked to find something mutually advantageous. He thought back to when they met. Life had a strange way of evolving.

Admiral Sino ibn Nahir, whom Alex called Sino, then a captain in the Royal Moroccan Navy, had attended the US Naval War College in Newport, Rhode Island, a few years back, at the request of the Kingdom of Morocco, and followed by an invitation from the US Departments of Defense and State.

Brooks Elliot was a student there as well in a slot arranged by a Colonel Mac MacMillan of the White House National Security Advisor staff. The admiral was Moroccan, Sunni Muslim, and an Arab—and consequently not often invited to participate in nonofficial War College social activity. Brooks F. T. Elliot IV was a navy reserve officer, a lieutenant commander who ordinarily would have been well down the pecking order in allocating coveted slots for the War College. Elliot was also a former Navy SEAL, a Rhodes Scholar, and the only son of the chairman of the Senate Armed Services

Committee. His US Navy personnel file had a large red stamp on it, CI for "Congressional Influence."

Few of the ambitious career navy officers attending were anxious to include him among their social activities. Mac had told Alex that Elliot wouldn't have been chosen for one of the few naval reserve slots at the War College if that red CI hadn't been on his folder and Mac hadn't given a hidden push, as Mac, that old CIA craftsman, sometimes did. Worse, Elliot had a sailing vessel, *Old Fashioned*, he moored nearby; it was worth more than most officers' homes. To sailors and naval officers, it was a fantasy boat with just the right numbers of features and gadgets—and it was well beyond any other student's budget.

Brooks and Sino had become friends, if only for the lack of other opportunities in the Naval War College's social world. They sailed on some weekends, the two of them managing a deep hulled, forty-eight-foot sailboat together. From a casual acquaintance, their friendship became closer over time.

Alex, who was Brooks's best friend of many years, had met the now admiral some time ago on a weekend sail from Newport, Rhode Island, to Boston Harbor and back, where he acted as the Moroccan chef and chief bartender. Alex had slowly developed a friendship with Sino as the three of them sailed and talked in the difficult coastal waters.

Sino had been appointed defense minister of Morocco several years later. He was a royal cousin

Nowadays, Sino and Alex met in Tangier from time to time to discuss intelligence findings and to get Sino updated on what Alex knew from his Kufdani trading network about goings-on in the Middle East and on how the events might affect the Kingdom of Morocco.

Alex was the sole owner of Kufdani Industries, an old, huge trading organization based in Tangier. One of Alex's ancestors on his mother's side had founded it, and Alex had inherited it from Grandfather Kufdani. It had trading reach across the Mediterranean, the Red Sea, and the Black Sea—and into southern Europe; various divisions handled specialty efforts in sectors such as agriculture and technology.

There was also a US component. Kufdani Industries was closely aligned with an independently owned hedge fund, Kufdani Capital in New York, which Alex had founded several years before.

Alex had proven useful to the Moroccan government in negotiating aid from the United States and international monetary authorities, as well as for his introduction of new educational technology that used recordings of the best teachers in many subjects, coupled with electronic student support. This technology was delivered to students at very low cost via a custom-designed smartphone, known as a Kphone.

Alex's role at Kufdani wasn't widely known in Tangier, since Achmed, a boyhood friend of Alex during his summers in Tangier, ran the operations of Kufdani and was its public face. Alex liked to move around society, listening. He was considered an authority on the history of Islam, based on his study of Islam in the College of Oriental Studies at Oxford University and since. He lectured frequently at universities across the Middle East and at conferences of Islamic scholars.

During their last meeting, Sino had asked Alex to consider what Kufdani could do to help solve the growing economic problems in Morocco. Within days, Alex took that opportunity to reply that he had an idea that could help the king solidify his voter base and cut Morocco's deficit, but the idea would be hugely controversial. He'd asked Sino to think about how to approach the king with such an idea, knowing that the question would reach the king's ear within the day.

"You got our king all excited with your talk of improving his voting reach," Sino said, "and on fixing our GDP somewhat on our way to Morocco becoming a power in the Arab world, of course. You pissed him off a bit with the mystery. So it's controversial. What?"

"It has to do with our Rif Mountains to the south and the Berbers there," Alex said. "We've looked into the opportunity more since we last met. A friend and I spent a few days there recently, looking around and talking to the locals."

"Those Berber outlaws in the Rif Mountains," Sino said. "They'd cut your throat for an extra ration of *kif.* They grow cannabis and sell it on the black market. I've been slashing and burning there for five years, and still it goes on."

"And how's that working for you?" Alex said. "Is our king pleased with your results? Are you?"

"He's really angry. I'm much more so. They have a half-assed farming effort that still produces ten billion dollars in illegal trade, and I don't seem to be able to stop them."

"And you don't get a dirham in taxes for it. We really should be taxing farm income."

"Alex," Sino said, "don't irritate me by reminding me of the obvious. That's cruel. We're worried about a popular religious uprising along the lines of the so-called Arab Spring. If it happens in Morocco, it may start in the Rif Mountains, if only because they're so innately rebellious there. I dread the thought of sending more troops in there. It's all steep hills and valleys, easy to defend and nearly impossible to police. The Berbers seem as nimble as mountain goats; that makes things worse. But what does any of that have to do with the king's voting reach and helping our sorry GDP get better?"

"I'm just a business guy," Alex said. "Kufdani Industries doesn't get involved much in politics, but some business things leap out at me when I look at the Rif Mountains and the Berbers there, in their little bounded and contained community. It's mostly business that can help improve the king's voting reach and the Moroccan economy. There are, of course, some politics involved. We've reckoned a way that may generate up to fifty billion dollars in trade that you can tax and we can exploit for profit. The farmers will get paid and be happy to vote for the king."

"Sounds like a fairy tale to me," Sino said. "What?"

"Give up on ripping out hectares of *kif* and replant the area you've destroyed."

"Replant it with what?"

"Replant with *kif*, of course," Alex said. "Let's call it '*kif*' rather than 'cannabis' or 'marijuana.' That's what the Berbers call it and what they know how to grow. But now we will offer them better farming methods, fertilizer from our potash stocks in the south of Morocco, training for their farmers, education for their people, and loans for their farming equipment. We know the market for *kif* is huge and lucrative, so the investment is solid."

"Are you crazy? Grow *kif* for profit?" Sino said. "We'd be thrown out of the Arab League. American leaders would stop all aid to Morocco and maybe attack us the way they did the Afghanis to stop their poppy production, even if that attack failed. I hope you didn't get the king all hot and bothered over a stupid idea like this."

"*L'audace, encore l'audace, et toujours l'audace*, my friend," Alex said. "It's audacity, always audacity, that will win the day. We Moroccans, of course, would only grow medical *kif* for the treatment of those suffering pain or other medical issues such as headaches. We would package it under government supervision and sell it after it has been taxed once or maybe twice. It's a medical service for society, from which there is a substantial sum as an incentive for us to grow and package it well. Call it twenty billion dollars in new trade for Morocco, growing perhaps to fifty billion dollars over a few years. And not coincidentally, happy farmers are farmers who vote to support the status quo."

"Audacity is indeed what would be required," Sino said. "I can see my execution in the future if I handle this idea poorly. I've known you long enough to be assured that you have figured most of this out and have designed in it a way for Kufdani to make a tidy profit. Tell me more, my stoner, my criminal."

"Here are the easy numbers for us Moroccans," Alex said. "We have a 160-billion-dollar GDP running a 23 percent deficit or so. Our public debt to GDP is over 50 percent. With audacity in place, we will generate an additional 20 billion dollars in trade early on, say over five years or so, with the jobs and increased local business that will inevitably arise. There is nothing wrong with this picture.

"Education of the masses is the secret," Alex said, "and it shouldn't take more than a generation to make an impact. The king will make a big deal of free education for the Berbers using those fancy Kphones you will procure from us for them to use and pay for them with Berber taxes. As with elsewhere in Morocco, Kufdani Industries will administer the education process for a fee. Kufdani will, of course, offer our services in the clearing and replanting of fields in the Rif Mountains. We may provide equipment for a share of the crop and education on farming best practices as a community service. Kufdani has an established trading organization that could distribute the product internationally and protect it from thieves."

Sino snorted. "One must assume that the profits would be enormous for Kufdani."

"One can but hope," Alex said with a grin. "But if so, we'll pay taxes to the king on the profits, and our employees will pay taxes on their earnings. The shopkeepers will pay taxes on what our employees spend with them. That's the way economies grow. We'll keep the region under control and promote the king's political agenda within reason. Most important, we'll ensure that the education of the masses there proceeds smoothly and broadly. It is that education process that will make the king's voting population the one he seeks."

"And how are we supposed to sell this narcotic travesty to the world, if I can sell the idea to the king?"

"I think we are out in front of the power curve for selling the idea of becoming a legal *kif* provider," Alex said. "Jamaica will soon legitimize its *ganja* farming and sell it to tourists. Uruguay has voted and passed legalization of marijuana production for medicinal purposes. Several states in America have done the same, and at least two have approved use of marijuana for recreational use as well. In Colorado, one of the recreational *kif* states, tax incomes are far higher than predicted. We must move quickly if we are to be the primary *kif* dealer to Europe. Purely medicinal *kif*, of course, at least for now."

"I am starting to like this idea, so I must be as crazy as you," Sino said. "What does the estimable Commander Elliot say about it? He's the Oxford-trained economist. A Rhodes Scholar yet and finding himself in the drug trade!"

"Sino, it was Elliot's idea, or at least that's what I'll tell the police if we get caught," Alex said, grinning. "Once Uruguay got started with the effort to legalize medicinal *kif* production, Elliot and I started talking about the Rif. Our situation there was summarized not long ago in an article in *The Economist*. The numbers are pretty compelling, if you do your homework. As far as providing better education and training there, beyond the ripple effect of the *kif* profits, there is also enormous evidence that educating the populace leads to a happier people. Happy people seldom revolt."

"Run the Rif numbers by me," Sino said. "I'm going to have to make a pretty compelling case to the king if I want to keep my job, even if I don't lose my head. Being a royal cousin has its limits."

Alex smiled and said, "OK, first there were 137,000 hectares of *kif* planted in the Rif. You destroyed 90,000 hectares of that by burning. That burning won't hurt the soil for the farmers; in fact, it may enhance it. It looks like the illegal farming generates six kilos of *kif* per hectare. With decent farming practices and support, we're confident that we can raise that number to ten kilos per hectare, which turns the trade volume from an illegal, tax-free ten billion dollars to maybe seventeen billion dollars taxable. Then we triple production as the replanted 90,000 hectares come online. The Berbers will get a better price in a managed farming environment. It's all written down. I'll send a copy to you by e-mail."

"I assume your e-mail will allow it to be forwarded and printed," Sino said. "The last e-mail you sent wouldn't allow that. I was afraid to give it to our computer specialists to decode for fear that my computer would blow up."

Alex laughed. "That e-mail was confidential between us, and you promised that you wouldn't forward or print it, so I ensured that. This one will be fine for forwarding and printing as a file, but it will have no mention of its authors."

"It's nice to be back in Tangier to see the people rather than the politicians in our capital," Sino said, leaning his chair back a bit against the wall. "Marrakech gets tiresome with its politics. Do you have any more information about the source of the student beatings that have been in the infernal news?"

"There have been several beatings of teachers here," Alex said. "And class attendance is beginning to fall a little with the warnings on violation of Sharia law that accompany the violence. The beatings are from several gangs, but we haven't found yet who pays them or gives them direction. One of the gangs is in the courtyard just across the room. I've been watching them for a while. They come here often."

"And here we are in harm's way," Sino said. "I think I'd rather not start trouble right now. What would you have me do about them?"

"Nothing in particular," Alex said. "I just want you to be aware that radical Islam is interfering with our ability to train our taxpayers for better-paying jobs and our children for a better life. Religion is also becoming more of a problem in Tangier. We are hearing that Iran's Quds Force is organizing the Shiites here for a more concentrated demonstration or even perhaps an attack of some sort. Quds is becoming a pain, with their international troublemaking."

A murmur and scattered applause outside the café in its courtyard again distracted Sino, and he turned his head slightly to observe it. There was a young man, a boy really, doing acrobatic tricks for a small crowd to rhythmic sounds from a small boom box playing traditional Moroccan music. Near him was a girl, who was a year or two younger, with a hat she held out for donations as she moved around the periphery of the crowd.

The boy was in front of the apparent leader of the group in the café when he fell to the ground on his back, then snapped to his feet with a sudden push from hands behind his neck. He then leaped into the air and did a forward somersault with his knees tight to his chest, releasing them just in time to allow him to land on the balls of his feet. Then he repeated the move with a back flip. Upon landing, his legs split to allow them to be flat on the floor with his palms down. He pushed his weight up, and his legs swung suddenly at speed in a circle under one raised hand and then under the other. Finally he pushed himself into a handstand, where he balanced first on one hand and then on the other as his sister moved around the crowd, shaking the money in the hat to get a few more coins.

"That boy's one hell of an athlete," Sino said.

"I'll say!" Alex said. "I've seen Olympic gymnasts who would have trouble with that routine. There's an American dance style called 'break dancing' that's close, but this kid is really good."

Just then a large, bearded man at the front edge of the crowd and in front of the boy in his handstand, reached out and shoved him. The boy landed on the dirt floor and slid a little on his left shoulder, ripping the flimsy cloth of his shirt sleeve. As the boy snapped to his feet, the man grabbed the young girl by the arm and pulled her to him and onto his lap. He snatched the hat from the girl's hand, spilling some coins to the floor.

"We have more money for drinks," he shouted, holding the hat above his head. "And I may have found a new wife. She looks to be about the right age to bear a few more sons for me. I just need to break her in a bit."

The crowd roared with laughter and applause as the girl struggled to reach the hat holding the rest of the money. When she failed, she leaned forward and bit the man on the bicep. With a roar of pain and anger, he cuffed the girl on the side of her head. The hat spilled more money to the floor. He bent and pulled his arm back, a closed fist ready to punch her.

She fell roughly to the floor as her brother reached her and punched the man's face. The man snarled as he drove his fist into the boy's left eye once, then again. He lurched to his feet and pushed the boy to the floor, then kicked him in the stomach. The boy rolled quickly away, but the man moved with him and kicked him again, this time in the right kidney just above the beltline. He dropped onto the boy's chest and put his knees on the boy's shoulders, then pulled a knife from his waistband.

"I think a notch in your nose would be a good thing. Beggars should not attack their betters, and their whores should not bite. I'll sample a free portion of her wares as well, I think. She will like having a real man."

"*The one in the green headgear, laddie. Gun on his left.*" Dain was still somewhere inside Alex's head, keeping his usual eye on the potential for violence.

"The skinny one, three to the right of the leader, has a small-caliber pistol in his left waistband, butt forward, in case you're armed," Alex said quietly to Sino. "I saw a suspicious bulge on your left calf as you walked in."

Alex came to his feet and dropped a five-hundred-dirham note on the table for the waiter. His face was transforming itself. The skin at the edge of his eyes was swelling, hooding them and highlighting the faint knife scar that furrowed through the wrinkled skin beside his left eye to his left cheek. The tiny scars on his forehead became more obvious as his face darkened. The sound of his breath whistling through his nose was becoming obvious.

"Stop," Alex said loudly as he walked toward them. "You have bested a young boy and beaten the girl child who is his companion. You seem to have stolen their money, or at least tried to. It should be enough. Crawl around the floor and pick it up; then go back to your home, to your pigsty."

"And if I cut you instead?" the burly man said as he came to his feet lightly, holding his knife low and against his body, blade up. "You stick your nose where it doesn't belong. I think I'll cut it off."

With a roar the man came for Alex, slicing up with the knife in his right hand, while his other hand poked at Alex's eyes as a feint and distraction.

Alex let his body open as his right heel slid back and behind him. His left hand grabbed the right wrist as it reached for him. Alex pulled the knife hand up and forward to turn the man, then drove his right hand under the extended knife arm, powered first from his straightening legs, then from his twisting body, and finally from his extending arm. Alex's target was six inches past the throat and Adam's apple of the bulky man, but his flat, extended knuckles were stopped short with an audible crunch as the windpipe broke and collapsed. With the follow-through from the neck blow tilting the man back on his heels, Alex swung his left foot under the ankles of his assailant and up, sweeping the heavy body in the air for a second. As the man landed hard, Alex spun toward the men still seated. They were gape mouthed and still. The fight had lasted less than five seconds.

The skinny man stood, reaching to his waistband. "You will die as a godless pig. You gave no warning!"

The hilt of a slim throwing knife appeared, buried in the man's throat, as Alex extended his arm in follow-through from throwing the blade that always hung just behind his neck.

A third man rushed Alex from his blind side, apparent only at the edge of his peripheral vision. Somehow, while barely glancing at his new assailant, Alex stopped the man with the heel of his left hand to the face just above the lips. Alex's hand spanned the man's face. With a thumb on the right eye socket and three fingers on the man's left eye socket, he squeezed the face between his hand, with a burst of energy dispatched from his core, his ki, and accompanied by a loud grunt.

"Hee-umph!"

As the thin bone around the eye sockets collapsed inwardly, blood shot from the man's face across Alex's wrist and partway up his forearm. Alex released his grip to allow the man to fall to the dirt floor.

Alex extended a bloody, dripping finger, with a piece of drooping, yellow gore clinging to it, toward the silent crowd. It moved to point at each of them as he spoke.

"Your kind is not welcome here," he said. "You make trouble for honest workers and their children. You have been warned," Alex said to the group.

There was a sudden uneasy silence in the room as each avoided staring at the extended finger, dripping blood more slowly to the floor.

'You," Alex said as he pointed at the boy, who still sat on the floor, gape mouthed. "Bring the girl and come with me. Leave the money behind."

After a moment the boy scrambled lightly to his feet, turned to the girl, and nodded. She grabbed the hat and a few coins near it, then ran to take her brother's hand.

Sino rose swiftly from his chair and led the way as they left the café. Then he turned away from the entrance and walked to a dusty Range Rover with darkened windows. It sat idling just outside the walls of the medina. Sino opened the back door, then the front, and sat in the passenger seat. He reached to an ankle holster for a compact Beretta 9mm pistol below his left calf, then looked behind his small group to the exit of the café.

Alex pointed to the inside of the car. The boy and girl scrambled inside, followed by Alex. The driver pulled away from the wall as Alex pulled the door shut.

"I was warned about you, Alex," Sino said, shaking his head. "Commander Elliot told me that you have a penchant for violence. It seems he was right. Tell me what just happened and why I was needed to be there alone. I could have brought a battalion of special troops."

"I didn't plan for violence, and what does Commander Elliot know?" Alex said. "I just wanted you to see one of the groups causing trouble for education and discuss plans with you for the Rif, as the king asked."

"I'd rather ask them some questions than be in the middle of a brawl. At least we should have gotten photos of them."

"I'll send you photos. I have some from my phone. You should look them up and question them about what other people are interfering in the king's work. Drop us here. We'll make our way."

Sino raised an eyebrow and gave directions to the driver. They slowed to a stop. "I assume you'll look after the children," he said. "You never cease to surprise me."

"I'll look after them, I suppose. I couldn't very well leave them there." Alex opened the door and got out. He beckoned the children to come with him. After a moment they scrambled from the car and stood by him, wide eyed. The girl clutched the hat with the remaining money to her chest.

The boy glanced down the street, deciding whether to try to grab his sister and run. The Range Rover pulled away and accelerated down the narrow street.

"Now is the time to run if you'd like," Alex said to the boy. "But if you come with me, I'll feed you and protect you, at least for a while." He turned and began to walk down the street. After a moment and a glance at each other, they ran to him. The girl's tiny hand disappeared in the gnarled, bloodstained paw beside her.

A short walk later, Alex glanced up and down the street at the passersby, then turned into an old shop that advertised antique maps in its front window.

An old man sat at the rear of the room by a corner table. There was a threadbare, ragged blanket on the table. The man's right hand was under it, holding an antique, side-by-side, eight-gauge shotgun loaded with number-two shot, with its butt against a beam to absorb recoil. Both hammers were back.

"Peace be unto you," the old man said to Alex and nodded to the children. "You bring young company. A first."

"And peace be unto you," Alex said. "They may stay with us for a while." He walked to a cabinet on the back wall and moved a book on its top. The cabinet swung away, revealing a tunnel. There were lights along its way. The walls were smooth.

"Come," he said to the children and entered the tunnel. They hurried to him and walked into a man-made tunnel, lit with bright lights. After a few hundred feet, there was an alcove carved into the tunnel wall with an electric golf cart in it and an electric charger attached. After a moment's explanation by Alex to the children of what it was, he unplugged the charger. They all got in the cart and drove away.

The tunnel was a minor part of a huge complex, the headquarters of Kufdani Industries, burrowed into the mountains over a hundred-year period. Its latest iteration was a high-tech fortress, with tunnels carved deep into the mountain on the southern border of Tangier.

Within a few minutes, Alex stopped the cart at another alcove with a large steel door in it. He got out and plugged another charger into it, then wiped his bloody thumb on his pants leg He pushed his thumb against a small pad on the wall. The door beeped and swung open. The children followed him through the door into a large room, then through another door to a small office.

An Asian man of some indeterminate age with a wispy beard sat on the floor with his legs crossed. He was dressed in a long-sleeved white robe, tied at the waist with a faded black cotton belt. He nodded to Alex.

"This is Tang," Alex said. "He will look after you."

Tang came to his feet in a fluid motion and bowed to the children. He glanced curiously at the ribbons of dried blood on Alex's left hand and arm and at the fading malevolence on his face.

"Feed them, bathe and delouse them, then find them some clothes," Alex said. "Bring them to me on my office balcony in two hours. If they wish to leave, take them outside and release them."

Tang bowed to Alex, still silent.

Alex turned to the children, who stood close to him, wide eyed, and said, "Tang will bring you to me when you are fed and cleaned. We'll figure out then what is next for you." He turned and walked through a steel door at the back of the small office.

Thirty minutes later, showered, shaved, barefoot, dressed in a pair of faded khaki canvas shorts and a white long-sleeved cotton shirt with the cuffs rolled twice, Alex walked from his quarters through his office to a large balcony overlooking the Tangier harbor. Sitting in a semicircle around a glass-topped green metal table were the four people whom Alex thought of as the varsity team. The newest was LuAnn Clemens, on her first visit to Tangier and getting up to date on recent team activities. Alex's best friend, Brooks F. T. Elliot IV, was grinning at him as he raised his beer glass. Elliot had the sloping shoulders of a serious swimmer and even in Tangier wore Madras shorts and a blue cotton button-down shirt, the classic clothes of a preppy, which he was. Elliot was well under six feet, maybe five nine or ten, with a shock of brown hair combed and parted with limited sartorial success. His sideburns showed flecks of gray, untended.

"It's a bit late, you are, and your face has the look of Cooch in trouble," Elliot said. "It's fading now, though. Trouble with my good friend, Sino? Are you going to jail as a dope dealer?"

"Not yet," Alex said with a grin. "But there was a spot of trouble with the locals we discussed. I sicked Sino on them. I ended up bringing two small problems back, but more about that later. Sino will take the idea back to the king. It may be a few weeks before we have a handle on whether they'll buy it or not. The idea of the king procuring more Kphones for the Rif went through him unnoticed."

"That's good," Elliot said. "I think you were right to ask us to focus on the Berbers as the next education target. That's a big, well-bounded group of untouched Moroccans for us to begin educating and converting to loyal, thoughtful subjects of the king, soon to have a mind of their own."

"And growing legal cannabis makes all the sense in the world," Alex said. "We get multiple birds with a single effort. First, effective primary education of the Moroccan Muslim masses will grow geometrically; second, the king gets more taxes; and third, the Berbers will be happy to have a more lucrative and even legal outlet for their crops."

Elliot turned to a notebook on the table in front of him. "I suspect that they don't care much about legal, but it could be lucrative for them. Right now, my friend, we have some more important things on our immediate agenda."

A large, bearded, dark-skinned man, Jerome Masterson, in a polo shirt and cotton slacks, nodded and turned in his chair to face Alex. For five years, Jerome had been Alex's partner in the CIA's Special Operations unit. He was a retired master gunnery sergeant in the US Marine Corps and a master sniper, whom the CIA had recruited some years before. He and Alex had become inseparable there, and their exploits were legend among special ops people around the world. He had an outlook on life that was often similar to Dain's. He had moved to Tangier several years earlier.

"The feces are starting to hit the flywheel back in DC," Jerome said. "They got Caitlin's latest prediction from her Emilie system. Surprise, surprise, Iran is about to complete their first nuclear weapon. They'll want you guys back there fairly soon, I imagine. I'll be busy on tactical planning, if things go as I expect. In fact, I'm busy right now. I expect to see Guns Epstein in the not-too-distant future."

A well-proportioned middle-aged blond woman in a polo shirt and cotton shorts nodded as she twirled a clear plastic swizzle stick in long fingers. "It always takes politicians a while to see reality staring them in the face," Dr. Caitlin O'Connor said. "The probability of Iran doing the radioactive big ugly, with a real live nuke in the hands of those religious crazies, has been going up for many months. They're paying attention now. I hope there's enough time."

O'Connor was a Caltech-trained computational physicist who had won a MacArthur Foundation genius grant at age twenty-three. Since then, she'd been working on developing software that could absorb and process vast amounts of information, then infer probability conclusions from the mass of data found in hundreds of newspapers and thousands of intelligence documents, satellite photos, intelligence reports, shipping data, and so forth, that were fed daily into the maw of her system. Caitlin's innovations in predictive analytics had stunned the professionals at the National Security Agency with their accuracy.

Brooks turned his head to LuAnn and said, "I guess we're sort of responsible for the change in assessment of Iran's nuclear plans. A while ago, Muslim terrorists destroyed our Kufdani office in the Yemeni port city of Aden, killing thirty-seven of our people, including eleven children attending preschool there. Alex went over there to check the damage and figure out whether it was safe to rebuild. Jerome followed in a Kufdani freighter, bringing supplies and some protection."

Alex nodded and said, "Two bad guys were in Aden, watching the office rubble to see who showed up, I guess. Anyhow, I got drug darted, kidnapped, and taken to a spot inland, where they started to ask me questions very unpleasantly. For openers, I got this there." He held up his left little finger to LuAnn. It was missing its top joint and was scarred over.

LuAnn held up her right little finger. Its first joint was missing.

"Hell, I thought you rode rodeo. That's where I lost mine, on a bad rope wrap that left my fingertip between the rope and the saddle horn with 1,300 pounds of steer about to hit the end of my rope. Yours should have been a bit more unpleasant if it was just for openers."

"I got to Aden by boat a few days later and went looking for Alex," Jerome said. "I figured out where he was and between us we captured Alex's interrogator, but first the guy got himself snake-bit by a saw-scaled viper when he hid from us in a stone closet. He babbled in his pain about the Shiites soon taking over the world and a new caliphate arising. The venom killed him before long, so we took his computer and some files back with us. Caitlin found some interesting data in that computer before it went to NSA."

"Yeah," Caitlin said. "In the computer's trash bin of deleted files, there was a draft press release from Iran that told of an impending nuclear attack on Israel, with instructions as to how and when to deploy the masses of radical Shiite Islam to attack Israel after the nuke hit. That disclosure was a very big deal for Emilie and for the US government."

"When Caitlin fed that press release into her Emilie system," Alex said, "the probability of Iran nuking Israel started to go up quickly. I'm not sure what all Emilie glommed on to in her further analysis, but it moved the danger needle for the US intelligence community."

"There were a bunch of different addressees on the draft press release. They all got watched more carefully after the find," Caitlin said. "Emilie can really suck up specifics on data when the NSA knows who to target. Probabilities of Iran having a completed nuke and attacking Israel with it started up in a hurry."

"Iran was clearly planning an attack, not just talking about how much they hated Israel," Brooks Elliot said. "The idea of tens of thousands of Shiite warriors, including Hamas, Hezbollah, the Islamic Jihad, and the rest of that scum, swarming Israel's borders got the US's attention. War planning at DOD was stepped up a notch."

LuAnn nodded. "I can see why everyone was more concerned," she said. "That sounds like a very big deal."

The intelligence function of Caitlin's computer system, named Emilie, had arisen almost accidentally, as O'Connor struggled to devise and encode a system to handle the large quantities of data needed to improve the management of corporate America. Emilie was now the most important intelligence system in the US government. Sales to corporate America were only recently coming to fruition; early costs had proved too high and capabilities too low for most of profit-conscious American commerce. But the US government had far less sensitivity to costs, was willing to fund capabilities to meet their needs, and soon discovered O'Connor's Emilie.

O'Connor had also designed an enormously powerful smartphone several years before, dubbed the Kphone. The Kphone had more than one hundred times the computing speed of the most advanced smartphone and had access to vast memory. Among its other functions as the user interface of Emilie, the Kphone used the capabilities of the Emilie product to present lessons of many different types from a recorded library of great teachers. Emilie kept track of student progress and provided electronic student support based on any given student's progress and apparent problems and needs. The student support was a work in progress as Emilie adapted to various levels of student needs.

"It sounds like there's a heightened level of concern in Washington, at least," Brooks said. "Mac called a bit ago. We may be asked to pitch our view of the Iran situation to the president. Mac sounded positive about our offering Alex in a role as a facilitator inside Iran. So we should probably make plans to get back there sometime in the next day or so, if and when they call. There is a longer, detailed call planned for tonight."

"Once the US is convinced that Iran is about to deploy an operational nuclear weapon," Alex said to LuAnn, "The US is going to have to act in some way. If that action is a military response, we think there's a decent chance that we could help start a civil war in Iran and avoid committing US ground troops there. That's what we want to pitch to the president."

Jerome snorted and picked up his glass, shaking his head.

"Are you losing patience, Jerome?" LuAnn said.

"My patience never runs out," Jerome said. "I'm patient for a living. I'm a sniper, remember?"

"How could I forget?" LuAnn said. "But what do you think of the chances for success?"

"This whole idea, this fantasy, is just stupid enough that it might work," Jerome said. "Lemme see now, we attack Iran because they're about to deploy a nuke. We kill a zillion of their people and destroy their navy and air force. Then we send in our man Cooch here to fix it and get them to start a civil war because we don't want get our US boots bloody on the ground. We want them to like us now, and play nice. Seems simple enough."

"Sarcasm doesn't become you, Jerome," Alex said.

"Bullshit, Cooch," Jerome said. "This is some complicated shit that you're up to. Remember Murphy and his law. He's liable to bite us right in the ass."

Brooks laughed. "We're trying to find allies in our quest, Jerome. You should be supportive."

"Yeah, supportive. I'm going to be the one lying on his belly six hundred meters out, watching through a Swarovski scope as five thousand ragheads with guns chase Cooch if you fuck this up."

"Good point, Jerome," Alex said. "As usual, I'll expect you."

Jerome raised his right hand and gave Alex the bird. "Yeah and as usual, I'll be there. I don't have to like the odds though."

"Before we wrap this up," Alex said, "I want to discuss the two small problems I mentioned at the outset. They are standing just inside the glass behind you, with Tang." He waved them in to join the meeting. Tang slid the door open and led the two children out, then went back to stand behind the door as he slid it shut.

"Welcome," Alex said in Arabic with the Tangerine accent, "I am Kufdani, and this is my office and company complex. These are my friends, whom you will meet in a moment. What are your names?"

The boy spoke quietly, in a shaking voice. The girl bounced on one foot and then the other, not making eye contact.

"I am Karim. This is my sister, Salima."

"Where are your parents?" Alex said. "Why were you on the streets, working and begging?"

"Our father died many years ago," Karim said. "Our mother died several months ago. We had no food and no relatives to feed us, so we work for food. We sleep in empty shops. Today we had more food than we can buy in a week with what we make."

Caitlin stood suddenly and started to move to the girl to comfort her, but Salima ducked and hid behind her brother. Caitlin stopped short and considered her actions. She shrugged and returned to her chair, slightly embarrassed for her outbreak.

"This is Dr. Caitlin O'Connor," Alex said with a grin. "She seems excited to see Salima; that may be the most important thing that ever happens to Salima. The big man with the beard is Sergeant Masterson, and beside him is Mr. Elliot."

He looked at the boy and said, "Karim, Salima, you have had time to consider what you would have us do with you. Would you like to stay for a time, to see how you fit in?"

They looked at each other, then nodded vigorously.

Alex smiled and said, "That's fine. We are to be gone before very long for a few days, perhaps a week or more. You will stay with Tang and do what he asks. Be patient with his Arabic. He so seldom speaks that his language skills are weak. Sergeant Masterson will be available if you need him and may pay some attention to Karim. Salima, you should speak with Dr. O'Connor before we leave for the United States."

O'Connor nodded enthusiastically. Alex beckoned Tang to return.

When Tang again stood in front of Alex, he waited silently.

"This is Karim. His sister is Salima," Cuchulain said in English to Tang. "They will be staying with us for several weeks, perhaps longer. Arrange the suite next to yours for them. Spend time with them and observe. Dr. O'Connor will talk to Salima when she has an opportunity."

Tang nodded. He beckoned to the children and walked through the door, Salima's hand in his.

"We're heading back to New York tomorrow," Elliot said. "LuAnn has work that can't wait. She can use some help. We'll see the rest of you back in the land of the round doorknob."

CHAPTER 2

THE WHITE HOUSE OVAL OFFICE

"OKAY, COLONEL MACMILLAN," President Roberts said. "You once told me that your job is to figure out a solution to difficult problems that may not want to see the light of public scrutiny. You used, as an illustration, the possibility of the Israelis attacking Iran in the middle of our night without warning. Is there an update to that scenario on the table in this potential Iran confrontation? Talk to me like an international thug. Show me some original thought."

"If I'm an international thug, Mr. President, there are at least two more—North Korea and Iran," Mac said. "It's their thuggery that we need to anticipate and counter. First, the press release and the other information from the computer captured in Yemen have been analyzed by the CIA and NSA and matched to other intelligence. Both have concluded that the Iranians will detonate a nuclear burst over Israel that won't kill a lot of people, but rather destroy their infrastructure. The weapon will be used soon. They are likely planning to use an Electro-Magnetic Pulse as their primary weapon as a byproduct of the nuclear blast. It's called EMP.

"Let me use the United States as an example of what may happen. Israel, for perspective, is about the geographic size of New Jersey. EMP charges can be shaped to geography—the smaller the footprint, the greater the energy. Israel could take a pretty devastating hit.

"Back to the US an example," Mac said and leaned forward in his chair. "If Iran or any other power manages to detonate a single nuke of megatonnage size high over Nebraska, there would be an electromagnetic pulse, an EMP, that would cover our nation ocean to ocean, from the Pacific to the Atlantic. That would be an unmitigated disaster particularly in the Midwest. Israel is more likely to be Iran's target, with perhaps worse, more focused results."

"Tell me about why it would be a disaster here and then relate that to Israel and don't tell me any fairy tales."

"I'll give you facts, Mr. President," Mac said, "that are easily checked with our military and with our scientists."

"These are facts that would surround a potential nuclear detonation over our Midwest at high altitude, right?"

"Yes, sir, a megaton-level blast, however unlikely that might be. Perhaps we can put a probability on that event, but I can't individually. It's a lot more likely than most would guess. Current US technology has allowed a lower altitude and a shaping of a nonnuclear detonation electromagnetic pulse, wherever it's used, but we don't know that any other country has yet developed this technology.

"First, the EMP pulse would probably last on the order of a millionth of a second but be enormously powerful. A megatonnage blast would create a pulse that would permanently fry all unprotected circuits and silicon in the continental United States and lower Canada."

"I doubt that statement can be taken literally," Roberts said, "but it sounds bad enough. Go on."

"During the nuclear tests in the Far East about fifty years ago, a nuclear test burst over Bikini Atoll turned out the lights in Honolulu twenty-five hundred miles away. Every lightbulb in the islands had to be replaced. That was many years ago. The technology is now far more sophisticated and powerful.

"So today, if there was an EMP burst over Nebraska, nearly every modern car in the country would drift to a halt, forever disabled. Almost every modern truck, every train, every phone, and every computer in the area from the West Coast to the Atlantic Ocean would be ruined. There would be no electricity to power pumps for drinking water, to run hydroelectric dams and control their valves. There would be no streetlights, no refrigeration. Airliners in the air would stall and crash immediately; river traffic would be without propulsion or protection. Anyone with a pacemaker would die quickly. A successful EMP attack against the United States would end life as we know it."

"I think you're bullshitting me, MacMillan," Roberts said. "Why haven't I heard of this other than in passing, buried in reports?"

"As with my speculation about Israel," MacMillan said, "I imagine you haven't asked and haven't focused on it. You're a busy man. I used a very large bomb in the US in this example to try to match the smaller nuclear burst impact on such a small state. President Obama chose not to enable the technology to destroy a ballistic missile in its boost phase when it is most vulnerable. President Bush ignored advice for dealing with North Korea's EMP capability. James Woolsey and Peter Pry wrote an op-ed in *The Wall Street Journal* in the spring of 2013. It was entitled 'How North Korea Could Cripple the US.' You may recall that Woolsey was a CIA director and well thought of; I liked him. Peter Pry was on the Congressional EMP Commission. They mentioned most of the salient facts surrounding an EMP attack on the United States. Woolsey and Pry were focused on North Korea, but now Iran is close to having the same capacity as North Korea. They wrote another *Journal* op-ed in the summer of 2014—same topic. It's a very big deal. The time to deal with the EMP threat is not after the event."

"I'd nuke anyone that did that to us," Roberts said. "Right back at them."

"That's your call, Mr. President, and I'm thankful it's not mine. Retaliation might make Americans experience a bit of schadenfreude, but our world would be changed forever."

"You're just a bundle of joy, Colonel MacMillan," Roberts said. "Maybe the nickname Colonel Doom would be better for you. I thought I was going to hear about an unconventional solution to our immediate problems in Iran. Instead you present me with a nightmare you say is possible."

"I gave an example of EMP use against us in this country, Mr. President," Mac said, "and I used a megatonnage weapon in the example, a huge bomb. Things would be harsh for us with a weapon that size over Nebraska, but only a few countries have the delivery systems and technology to make that possible. I suspect they would be just as harsh if much-smaller Israel suffers an EMP from a smaller weapon and a shaped burst. We think Iran has developed that weapons set.

"I said I'd next do an assessment of the possible impact in Israel. First, Iran has nothing approaching a megatonnage weapon. Theirs is likely to be about the size of the Hiroshima nuke in yield—2 percent of a megaton. Second, Iran doesn't want to destroy the infrastructure of neighboring states. This is an operation against the evil Zionists.

"We think it is likely that they can shape the blast to cover most of Israel without impacting Syria, Jordan, Lebanon, and Egypt too much. They think there will soon be borderland available to be awarded as recompense if too much damage is suffered by any of the bordering states."

"Go on, Colonel MacMillan," Roberts said. "How will it play out?"

Mac leaned forward. "Israel is tiny, as I said, with about the geographic size of New Jersey, so it's far easier to cover with a directed blast than the United States. Israel has enemies on every border salivating to entirely destroy their society. Even a crude nuclear blast will destroy most of the power systems in the country. As I said, we have reason to believe that the Iranians know how to design a weapon for energy over blast, to shape that energy to focus its devastation. Beyond the information on the captured computer, we have determined Iran has alerted the Shiite terrorists around Israel that they will soon have a chance to defeat, and loot of course, an underarmed Israel—troops are moving slowly toward Israel as we speak. Israeli phones won't work, cars won't run, and the other problems I mentioned in the US example will be in play. When the lights go out in Israel from the blast, tens of thousands of men will attack across Israel's borders. It will be fairly even hand-to-hand combat, the last thing Israel wants."

"Have you read those analyses, Colonel MacMillan?"

"I have, Mr. President, but I think the press release draft tells much of the tale. It talks of not killing the Jews but putting them into slavery. That implies use of a weapon that maximizes gamma rays in its nuclear blast, designed to maximize EMP damage rather than blast damage. If the only thing that is killed in Iran's attack is Israeli infrastructure, the Iranians will claim 'no harm, no foul.' I can hear it now, 'After all, wars are simply wars and the Israelis have been fighting and oppressing

Muslim patriots for years. This time they lost.' Iran has talked publicly about nuking Israel," Mac said. "They released an animated video in early 2014 that showed a nuclear burst over Israel."

"I just might stuff that press release up Iran's nose," Roberts said. "You talk to all your spook friends and come up with suggestions, Colonel MacMillan. General Kelly will keep our friends at DOD informed. I'll listen carefully to anyone with an idea or a solution, but it is Iran that is a problem, not EMP. Keep that in mind."

"Yes, sir."

The President turned to General Kelly. "You're my National Security Advisor and a retired Marine four star. What's your advice on all of this?"

"My advice is to keep the military rolling on plans for dealing with the Iran threat. They could just as well hit us over the Gulf of Oman. We'll worry about EMP later and hope there's time."

"Maybe I'll put a warrior in as the chairman of the Joint Chiefs," Roberts said. "The head of special ops might be good."

"I'd advise against that, Mr. President," Kelly said. "General Moore is a bit stiff, and I know you don't care for his personality, but he's very smart and a fantastic staff officer. He has a Chicago PhD and a reputation as our best planner. That's what we need right now—a planner."

"I'm skeptical," Roberts said. "I think we need a tough guy."

"Consider World War II, Mr. President," Kelly said. "Imagine if Patton, a tough guy, had been supreme commander in Europe in 1944 rather than Eisenhower, who was considered the best staff officer of his time."

"Huh," Roberts said. "Patton would have kept us rolling into Russia. I guess we'd have been in a war with Russia in a hurry after pissing off both Churchill and Stalin. That would have been a bad thing."

"Indeed. Both Hitler and Napoleon found that chasing Russians across Eastern Europe is a fool's errand," Kelly said. "Any attack on Iran needs an Eisenhower, not a Patton. The job demands careful planning and coordination among all the services."

"And you think an air force general is the man for the job?"

"I think General Moore is the man for the job," Kelly said. "The fact that he's air force is incidental. And Moore's tough."

"Really," Roberts said. "I wouldn't have guessed toughness, but he got promoted ahead of a bunch of other air force officers, so I suppose he is. OK, gentlemen, General Moore it remains. Defense seems to be deep in planning mode, so keep an eye on them."

Kelly and MacMillan rose to their feet, nodded to Roberts, and walked from the room, both distracted by the to-do lists being constructed inside their respective heads.

The following day
The White House
Situation Room

Secretary of State Harriet Colaris scurried into the Situation Room ten seconds before the hastily called, limited-access national security meeting was to begin. She wore a black linen suit, with the top cut long to soften her profile. It was wrinkled from wear. Her blouse was off-white, freshly ironed, and laundered. There was a pencil sticking out from her thick, blond, unruly hair just above her left ear. She looked tired. She spoke to the president, nodded to the others in the room, and took her seat.

"Good morning, Madam Secretary. It seems that we are about to be engaged in yet another war, this time with Iran, and again not of our choice," President Roberts said. "There are few strategic options, but in the past you have had strong opinions, solicited or not, about our military ventures. We want your advice before plans become public."

Sitting at the long table in the Situation Room were the president at the head of the table and Secretary Colaris at his right. Also at the table were General Patrick Kelly, National Security Advisor; General Richard Moore, Chairman of the Joint Chiefs of Staff; Blanche Baird, the Secretary of Homeland Security; and Sherman Goldberg, Director of National intelligence, responsible for the entire US intelligence effort. Senior members of the intelligence community and the various chiefs of staff of the armed forces sat in chairs behind the table, ready to address questions or concerns in their respective specialties.

Secretary of State Harriet Colaris had spent more time trying to help or fix the Middle East situation than her past two predecessors. She'd been quite visible in her efforts and enjoyed wide popular support in the United States. Her advice had consistently been to minimize the use of ongoing force; to avoid commitment of ground personnel to Afghanistan and Iraq beyond special forces troops to train the friendlies, if they could be identified; and to efficiently kill the enemy. She was generally believed to be a dove. She'd been proved more right than wrong over the years. The president was concerned that strong dovish opposition from her in the Iran matter would be a barrier to his nomination for another term, particularly if any action taken was less than successful.

General Kelly stood and summarized the probabilities of the Iranian situation for the group and the secretary. "The bottom line, Madam Secretary, is that we believe Iran will launch a nuclear attack on Israel within the next several weeks. There may be an EMP weapon in play, and North Korea has demonstrated capability to engage if they so choose. Those two nations are in touch daily."

Colaris leaned forward in her chair and looked around the room.

Secretary Colaris was quiet as she gazed at the president. The silence became uncomfortable in the room as she folded her hands under her chin, then sighed. She said, "The fact that the United States sends a woman to deal with the Arab world has become an inside joke among them. They snicker that it's appropriate; I'm a metaphor for our country. They comment among themselves on the growing size of my behind despite my sartorial camouflage. Our policy is considered flabby and feminine. They are confident that we don't have the courage of our convictions and are easily controlled, given a firm hand by them on the reins of policy and our response. You've probably read the same transcripts that I have."

Roberts began to speak, but Colaris held up her hand. "That was a preamble, Mr. President. Do me the courtesy of allowing me to pursue a spontaneous, albeit considered, reply to your surprise request for my support in what was a presentation of options. It was neither a plan nor a recommendation."

Roberts frowned, then nodded and leaned back in his chair.

"So, as I see things," Colaris said, "We have lost all of our wars during the past fifty years or so, when those wars are viewed in terms of accomplishing our national security and political objectives. In waging those failed wars, several hundred thousand of our citizens have been killed or maimed. That history of failure tells me we should consider updating the way we fight the wars we choose to fight.

"General Kelly, you're our national security advisor. Why haven't we responded to threats to our men and women in uniform more forcefully?"

"Madam Secretary, I think we have done quite well at responding to those threats under the rules of engagement we follow," Kelly said. "If you have specifics, we will certainly consider changes to help protect our troops in battle."

"Well, specifically, I think you're a bunch of sissies," she said. "The rules of engagement in force don't do us any good, and we are still killing our young men and women as a result of them."

Kelly flushed; the scar on his forehead showed white. He said, "The rules of engagement are a political phenomenon, not a military one. We work for you civilians. That's the way our system works. You make the rules—we follow them."

"Ah, then," Colaris said, "our rules of engagement are at the heart of our problem, are they?

"We publish our rules of engagement, the internal rules under which the United States engages in combat for the world to see. In them, we enable the enemy by letting them know that we won't target their schools and hospitals, that we won't shoot at innocent civilians. That's noble of us—we want to be viewed as humane and caring. The enemy responds to our nobility by deploying their weapons in hospitals and schools, where they are safe. We've seen them marching children through minefields or in front of attacking infantry to get them safely closer to our lines so that they can kill our citizens.

"We send you, our best and brightest officers, to the best graduate schools in the country at government expense. You draw full salary and benefits while you're there. We pay to move your families to be with you. Most of you got paid to go to college at one of our military academies, while most of our students today take painful loans to get a mediocre education. We pay a fortune for you to be trained in strategy and tactics at the Naval War College and a bunch of other places like it. You get to study and discuss in depth masters of strategy like Thucydides, Sun Tzu, Carl von Clausewitz, and Baron Antoine-Henri Jomini to prepare you for a role in setting strategy. You have time to consider longer-term options, as few politicians may, for lack of time.

"Yet here you are, all apparently fans of that old Prussian, Carl von Clausewitz. You think warriors should leave the politics to the politicians and fight the wars the politicians define. You just leave all the decisions to the politicians and fight the wars as best you can, comfortable with that arrangement. How's that working for us? If it's not working well, who's trying to fix it? Has anyone in our military leadership considered arguing forcefully for a change in our rules of engagement? I think another of those old strategists you studied, Baron Jomini, said it's your duty to do just that.

"You have shown yourselves to be masters at winning battles, but you haven't won the wars. Since Vietnam, perhaps Korea even, we have not won, really won, a war. Is it too comfortable sitting here in all of your uniformed splendor to consider that? We face an existential threat if the Middle East goes nuclear.

"I don't like this fluid situation you present one more time," Colaris said. "Let's consider massive changes to our rules of engagement. Let's rethink how we approach war. It's time to use some of this damned miracle technology our taxpayers spend tens of billions of dollars on each year. It's time to demonstrate that there is a limit to our patience. I'm certainly at the end of mine. If the Iranians get and use a nuclear weapon, the party is over for us as a political force in the Muslim world, and there would be no hope for reason to prevail in the Middle East within the next hundred years or so. We will have wasted tens of thousands of American lives and trillions of hard-earned American dollars for naught. Every Tom, Dick, and Hussein is going to want—and get—a nuke, once Iran shows one. The world will become a vastly more dangerous place. Plus the Israelis will be demonstrably unhappy and add enormous fuel to the proliferation fire. One would guess this will happen sooner rather than later."

She sat, red faced. She pointed a finger at Moore and Kelly and shook it. "You find a way to kill those godless bastards who run Iran. Emasculate those sons of bitches. There are good people there who will take control if we give them an avenue. And you don't get to use a nuke. That's my political view on the situation."

Secretary Colaris sat back and folded her hands under her chin, then picked up her head, leaned forward again, and said, "I'm tired of this nice-guy crap. It doesn't work and gets our young men and women killed while we are viewed as fools and weaklings. I have seen nothing in your scribbling I can support. Go back to the drawing board. Use your expensive educations to apply history's lessons of war and strategy with acceptable politics to our environment of hegemonic technological advantage. Redefine the damn rules of engagement in our favor. Teach your buglers to play 'No Quarter'; they've forgotten how by now. Minimize my tears over the lost lives and maiming of near children. This is State, out."

She sat back once again and picked up some papers, the roots of her hair damp from perspiration. There was quiet in the Situation Room.

The following day
The White House
Oval Office

"Welcome back, gentlemen," the president said to Patrick Kelly and MacMillan. "I assume you have solved my problem and that we can tell Secretary Colaris that she needn't be concerned. If so, I am confident she will support whatever it is that needs to be done."

"Defense is making good progress in their planning but lacks specific guidance for an attack," General Kelly said. "We have a suggestion, Mr. President, that may lead to a solution to the rules of engagement problems Secretary Colaris so forcefully articulated."

"Do tell. It's about time."

"Our Emilie intelligence system both predicted the ending completion of the Iranian nuke and found new evidence of their expertise in designing and shaping a nuclear charge. Emilie is administered by the team of Elliot, Cuchulain, and O'Connor," Kelly said. "You've met both Elliot and Cuchulain. Colonel MacMillan is our primary interface to them. Their technology, Emilie, is run by our national intelligence executives, as you know."

"Uh, huh," the president said. "Maybe I should make Elliot secretary of state. His father would like that, and Colaris might be happy. What the hell do those three have to do with anything?"

"Cuchulain is our strongest Arab ally, and he is a capable Islamic scholar," MacMillan said. "He could be useful in that role. He's also scary smart, as is Elliot. Neither is nearly as smart as O'Connor, of course, but both are capable and well read. All are patriotic Americans."

"And?"

MacMillan again leaned forward in his chair. "And they'd like to meet with you for longer than a few hours. They'd like a full day with you somewhere remote to present their ideas and work them out with you. They say the smaller the crowd, the greater the chance of figuring something out."

"Let me check my calendar," Roberts said. "I'm confident that I have one whole day with nothing to do. My job is easy enough that I can do that, wouldn't you think?"

"We talked to all of them for quite a while last night by secure phone," Mac said, ignoring the sarcasm for which Roberts was noted. "They have worked through some new thinking on old, accepted strategy,"

"General Kelly?"

"I think you should do it, Mr. President. Secretary Colaris's derision has everyone riled up, to the point that new options are being sought all over the Pentagon. That's a chance for you to get enthusiastic support for a new approach to strategy and tactics. This situation screams for your leadership. We need a new paradigm for dealing with the Middle East before it blows up. In my opinion the Iran situation is leading to a battle that, if lost or bungled, precedes a conflagration across the Middle East. We need to win that battle decisively to prevent a very broad and long-lasting war."

"I'll consider that meeting and let you know. That's all, gentlemen."

Three days later

Camp David, Maryland

The Marine helicopter that routinely carried the president did local duty for guests who were invited to Camp David, albeit without the designation of Marine One, which meant the president was on board. The five now on board were Elliot, Cuchulain, O'Connor, Kelly, and MacMillan. As the high-tech helicopter slowed to a near hover to drop to the landing pad by a swimming pool, the scope of the presidential retreat became obvious to the passengers.

In a fenced and heavily guarded area of about 120 acres that was once a World War II Office of Strategic Services training site, there were a number of cabins and support buildings in view. The cabins were named for trees growing on the property; most cabins had hosted notable guests. There was one cabin named Maple, another called Poplar. In all there were at least fifteen named cabins. The men aboard had been assigned to Poplar. Caitlin was to be in Dogwood, with Roberts's chief of staff and her assistant. The president was the only person permitted to use Aspen. Less obvious were the bowling alley, the theater, and other facilities designed to amuse powerful people at leisure. Deep beneath Aspen lodge was a tunnel of six miles or so leading to a hardened mountain fortress called Site R, where the president would be rushed in an emergency.

Most guest cabins had sitting rooms, fireplaces, and advanced communications facilities usually found only in the most secure government facilities around the world. Over the past fifty years, many powerful leaders from governments around the world had spent time at Camp David.

The cabins were rustic board-and-batten over a layer of Kevlar on steel studs, with fireproof asbestos shingles on their roofs.

Alex and Brooks quickly settled into Poplar. Mac and Kelly took a little more time. When the tardy men came into the sitting room, Elliot said, "Pillows all fluffed, gentlemen? Shall we be off to Laurel cabin to meet our host?"

In Laurel, a conference table was set with chairs for eight.

"I've been getting opinions from my key advisors," Roberts said, "on what to do about the news that Iran is far closer to having nuclear weapons capability than we believed earlier, partially as a result of conclusions drawn by Dr. O'Connor's Emilie intelligence system. I've been led to believe that the group of you may have a new perspective. I hate the idea of going to outsiders for thoughts, but you have some unique credentials. General Kelly and Colonel MacMillan tell me I should spend some time with you, so here you are.

"Mr. Elliot, you are the man with the background to represent our views to the friendly Arab community on how we think we can help transform their society. Dr. O'Connor, you are the author—or perhaps the progenitor—of the Emilie intelligence system that leads us to these startling new conclusions about Iran's capabilities and intentions. Mr. Cuchulain, you are the one perhaps most likely to have a handle on the thinking of our Arab allies and its genesis. Among you there may be a viewpoint I haven't considered. Mr. Elliot, would you care to lead this discussion?"

"I'll at least try, Mr. President," Elliot said, leaning back in his chair. "I think this discussion has to be framed in the light of a number of different perspectives. First, there is the overarching issue of allowing Iran to get a nuke and the consequences of that. Second, we need to look at the way Iran, its leaders, and its allies are viewed by the key players in the Middle East and their citizens, colored by any action options we decide we may want to consider. Third, we must consider that Israel may decide that violent, unilateral action against Iran is their best option and move precipitously to execute that option without much advance notice to us. Finally, any plan of action that fails to consider all these options in various blended forms that leads to a conclusion is dangerous and shortsighted."

"Maybe you should run for office, Mr. Elliot. You seem to have all of the answers."

"I don't even have all of the questions, Mr. President," Elliot said, smiling. "But we should be able to delve into a few of the questions today without wasting too much of your time."

"Dr. O'Connor," the president said, "do you support Mr. Elliot's observations? You seem to have been indirectly responsible for the need for this meeting with your Emilie product's intelligence conclusions."

"What Brooks said is the synthesis of a great many available and existing independent and dependent variables. I haven't tried to get my mind around all of that, but Brooks is capable. What Emilie, my intelligence product, does is take vast amounts of data we collect and reduce it to a series of inferences and probabilities that certain events will take place. The more data we get, the better chance that events can be predicted accurately. There is a high-probability prediction on the table."

"If you don't have an opinion, Dr. O'Connor, why are you here?"

Caitlin flushed as Alex glanced at Brooks, who wore a faint smile; his right eyebrow was raised. Caitlin often didn't deal well with issues of her relevance.

She shrugged. "I suppose it's just because I'm a lot smarter than the rest of you. If there are logical inconsistencies buried in what you say, I'm likely to find them before they occur to others. I'm also part of this team. That's part of what I bring to this table."

"Is this meeting the goal of the team?" Roberts said. "If not, how does that goal relate to what we are doing here?"

Caitlin frowned and sighed. "We digress from the goals of this meeting, which Brooks summarized crudely, but I'm happy to give an answer as to relevance, if a bit terse due to time constraints.

"Crudely, the team goal is to transform the Middle Eastern Muslim culture by applying the lessons of the Enlightenment to life there using modern technology as a catalyst for transformation. As background, the cultural environment today for Muslims in the Middle East is enormously similar to that of the pre-Enlightenment period in Western Europe, beginning in the late sixteenth century. One of the most prevalent similarities is in the power structure employing a controlling and demanding theocracy for repression of popular education and repression, particularly of women. Effective mass education provably leads to a more thoughtful and productive society. Improved education of women leads to lower rates of procreation and thus greater family wealth—again statistically provable. At some point of progress, families will worry more about protecting what they have than punishing those who have more.

"As to the situation at hand, Iran is in the way of progress toward team goals. By destabilizing the Middle East, they are threatening the gains we have made. They must be stopped for our gains to be consolidated and moved forward."

President Roberts gazed at her, bemused. Elliot and Cuchulain looked at him with interest and faint grins.

"Got it," Roberts said. "I'm not to pursue any conflict our national security may have with team goals."

Caitlin nodded. "There are none at the moment."

"And now, Mr. Cuchulain," the president said, with a hint of a smile and shaking his head slowly. "What are your thoughts as to the attitudes of the leaders in the Middle East toward the Islamic Republic of Iran and how those attitudes arose?"

Alex smiled at Caitlin and collected his thoughts. "It's easy to get caught up in the political structure of our Middle Eastern allies and to attempt a solution to the current Iran problem, which is suboptimal, at least for the moment," Alex said. "In my opinion, it is the religious structure of the Middle East that should drive our response and planning over the immediate term. The two dominant forms of Islam are the Sunnis and the Shiites. Islam in the Middle East is about 80 percent Sunni, at least in its leadership. Iran is vastly Shiite, and Iraq has a majority Shiite population. Bahrain, home of the US Fifth Fleet, is largely Shiite with a ruling Sunni leadership that Saudi Arabia has assisted in suppressing Shiite protests. Hezbollah, Hamas, Islamic Jihad, and the other violent splinter groups are mostly Shiite, with the notable exception of al-Qaeda and the Islamic State of Iraq and Syria, ISIS, both of which are radical Sunni. The dominant Sunni population and leadership provide an opportunity for us to gather support for any effort we make to control Iran. Sunni governments are afraid of their Shiite population rising up against them. The whole situation in Syria is increasingly polarizing the Sunni/Shiite schism and has allowed the birth of the Islamic State of Iraq and Syria, ISIS, that is acting up over there."

Alex took a sip of his water, then leaned forward.

"I believe any action on our part against Iran that gives cover to the Sunni-dominated governments will be very well tolerated. On the other hand, any action by Israel against Iran will be viewed, at least publicly, as oppression by the Zionists against Islam and cause at least the beginnings of coordinated hostilities against the Jewish state.

"I am a unique creature in this equation. For the first time in modern history, the United States has an Arab business and Islamic thought leader who is respected in the Middle Eastern power structure and has the best interests of both in mind.

"In summary, I think our plans will be well advised to consider this view of Islam."

President Roberts chuckled and again shook his head slowly.

"I once again find you facile in your presentation, Mr. Cuchulain, and your opinion of your importance in geopolitics arrogant and questionable," the president said. "What about the oppression of the masses by the various rulers who happen to be Sunni?"

"I am Sunni, as is most of Morocco and its king, Mr. President, but considering legitimacy issues of Sunni monarchies is a problem for another day. Today we worry about Iran and its potential nuke. That problem is fully enough for us to deal with right now, in my opinion. To devise a plan to democratize a vast swath of power and money is to destabilize the Middle East while dealing with Iran's nuclear plans. That seems unnecessarily dangerous and ambitious to me."

"We'll not reach any firm conclusions tonight," Roberts said. "I'm just gathering information, so you needn't worry too much just yet, Mr. Cuchulain. I suppose I understand the thinking of your team, but I'm troubled by the foundation of this thinking regarding Iran's goals and actions being wrapped up in the enigma of Dr. O'Connor's Emilie creation. At dinner, I think we should investigate that. Perhaps you would all be so kind as to excuse me for an hour or two, so that I can catch up on what's happening around the country and around the world. Dinner will be at seven. Cocktails are at six. You may start without me. I'll be along."

Elliot smiled as he stood. "We'd be delighted, Mr. President. We've summarized much of what we have to say. We'd like to help if we can."

Alex and Caitlin rose beside him and said with a nod, "Mr. President." They walked to the door, opened it, and went out. It closed firmly behind them.

Dining Room

Camp David, Maryland

The long wooden table was set with starched white linen and Riedel crystal. The china had the presidential seal on large plates and small. The flatware wasn't notable but functional. Pine-paneled walls held photos of presidents past and their Camp David guests of note. A low wood fire flickered in the corner fireplace.

Dinner had been served, and the last of the wine was being poured. Mac had brought Dancing Hares, a domestic red wine blend that was Alex's favorite. It proved popular; three hares, holding front paws and dancing on their hind legs, were etched around the bottle, causing curious comment. A bottle of Favia sauvignon blanc was nearly empty.

There were eight around the table, chatting casually with their dining partners on either side. President Roberts sat at the head of the table. Elliot was at the president's left, and Sheila Molyneaux, the White House chief of staff, was on his right. Alex was beside Molyneaux, who'd entirely ignored him. The National Science Advisor, Dr. Phillip Ashbury, was beside Elliot, followed by O'Connor and General Kelly. Mac sat beside Alex.

Roberts took a deep sip of his wine and turned to Mac. "Good choice on the Dancing Hares, Colonel MacMillan. I've not had it before. I'll keep it in mind for a state dinner. Enough small talk," he said. "I'm still interested in Dr. O'Connor's self-declared mental superiority. Dr. O'Connor, can you net out for me how you got so smart, as you claim to be? I am now almost a believer, after comments from my national science advisor."

"I may be able to do that," Caitlin said. "I didn't get to reading Leibniz until I was ten or eleven, but I read Isaac Newton a few years earlier."

"Age ten or eleven?" The president smiled. "I guess I'd rather hear how you got to be smarter than the rest of us. There was a Rhodes Scholar in the room when you claimed that. He didn't object or seem surprised."

"How true," Brooks said. "I've learned."

Caitlin smiled absently. "We dated at Princeton a thousand years ago, but I don't mean to say Brooks is dumb, Mr. President," she said. "He got a late start, but he's actually quite clever."

"Continue relating your childhood learning adventure, Caitlin," Brooks said. "I find that story fascinating."

"It's more than a little different from my childhood story," Alex said.

"Early childhood is a blur for me," Caitlin said. "I remember events and conversations at four or five, but not life as a preschool child. My father is an astronomer. He's well thought of in that bunch and happy in his role. My mother is a professor of probability theory and a bit of a Leibniz scholar. She calls herself a statistician. Early on I showed some good insight into arithmetic and algebra and was reading pretty well, so they decided to have some fun and see what they could create from who they'd created. They worked with me."

"Anything worth memorializing for a way to teach our kids today?" the president said.

"Well, there is one thing they did that changed everything in my life," Caitlin said.

"What's that?" the president asked.

"They gave me books, and we talked at dinner a lot about the way the authors, some of the early guys, did math," Caitlin said. "It was mostly Bacon, Galileo, Hook, Boyle, and Newton. But the books were in Latin, and I struggled a lot until I got a handle on written Latin; the good news is that math has no mother language other than itself. I finally got through Newton's *Principia Mathematic*a, where he summarized what was going on in mathematics up to that point, before discovery of the calculus."

Brooks was grinning as the president said, "So that was the secret that changed everything? Newton's book? It was that good?"

"Ha! I caught you with that one," Caitlin said, acting smug. "My parents kept me from learning the calculus until I was ten. That was the secret."

"Mr. President," Alex said, "Caitlin feels that the foundation she had in math, before the shorthand of the calculus was available, is the key to her success today. It allowed her to see what used to be possible in solving problems and what became possible with the discovery of the calculus, along with an approach to breaking problems down to their smallest, solvable elements."

"It's simple," Caitlin said. "Isaac Newton, with the newly discovered calculus, allowed problems to be reduced to simple models that could be solved and proved mathematically. Its effective use is an essential tool for the modern scientist. Newton took mathematics from an abstract, pure science to an applied science. He enabled the ongoing agenda of the physical sciences."

"You're starting to lose me again," the president said, shifting uncomfortably in his chair. "You were telling us how you got so smart."

"Oh, yeah. It's mostly about my head start in calculus," Caitlin said.

"I handle calculus like Herman Melville handled English. The rest of you learn calculus in high school or college and will thus utilize only schoolboy calculus. Your insight into science is as effective as schoolboy French employed while discussing Rousseau in a Paris salon. Even if our intelligence grew at the same rate until adulthood, I had deep knowledge mass by the time I was ten. Think of it as the magic of compound interest applied to effective intelligence. If you start with more principal and grow it at the same rate as others, you end up with a total far greater than those who started with far less. I'm capable, so I probably grew it faster than most, and here I am."

The president turned to his science advisor. "Is this bullshit?" he asked.

"It's not bullshit, Mr. President," Ashbury said. "She's a bit of a legend for her intellect. Her assessment of the rest of us may be a bit harsh."

"So that's how I got to be smarter than the rest of you," Caitlin said and picked up her wine glass. "I got started earlier."

"I never heard that story before," Ashbury said. "It makes things a bit more clear."

The president glared at him.

Ashbury shrugged and said, "Dr. O'Connor made much of her reputation in the shadow of Richard Feynman, the physics Nobel laureate. She would sit, as Feynman did, in an elegant presentation of some advanced physics concept. Then after the applause subsided, she'd say, 'What an elegant concept and proof! Bravo! But why not do it this way?'

"She'd then reduce the math in the proof to something far less complex and far more elegant. It's just that she seems to feel calculus and quantum mechanics in her soul. As she said, she got a big head start on the mathematics that underlies most scientific thinking."

Roberts shook his head and said, "Enough. Dr. O'Connor is clearly the smartest person in the room, among some smart people. That's one piece of this puzzle I understand.

"I'd like now to extend the approach I have chosen to look at this problem from a number of different angles, by splitting our group once again. Ms. Molyneaux will meet with Mr. Elliot and Mr. Cuchulain in the Cumberland Room, through the door on my right. Ms. Molyneaux has issues of morality, politics, and votes she wants to discuss. I'll pass the time right here with General Kelly and Colonel MacMillan. Dr. O'Connor, you may join the men with me. Please excuse us, Dr. Ashbury. I appreciate you taking the time to meet with us."

Ashbury nodded and stood, then nodded to his tablemates, walked out of the dining room, and turned left, on the way to his quarters.

"Coffee is available. Ask the steward for dessert if you want it." The president pointed to a yellow telephone. He turned an impatient gaze to Cuchulain, Elliot, and Molyneaux.

The three moved quickly into the Cumberland Room and closed the door. By the window was a small table with a good lamp, a modern desk chair, and a small Hewlett-Packard laser printer at table's edge. Four traditional stuffed chairs consumed the rest of the room; they were upholstered in a dark plaid and positioned around a small coffee table. A bar was set up against the back wall in a corner. It had various bottles of whiskey arranged against its back and a small refrigerator below.

Sheila Molyneaux was in her late thirties and dressed in what could be called "government casual," with dark slacks, cotton shirt, and an old blazer over brown deck shoes. No socks. She was perhaps five foot eight and had ten or fifteen pounds of extra weight on an athletic body, with small streaks of gray beginning to show in her brown hair and light stress wrinkles around her eyes. Molyneaux was widely known as both a flaming liberal and an outstanding thinker. She was widely credited for assembling the technical talent it took to get the Internet presence that got Roberts elected and for having an uncanny sense of the left-leaning voting electorate.

Alex and Brooks remained standing until Molyneaux sat down, then took a spot on either side of her.

"Well, now, aren't you the gentlemen?" she said with saccharin sweetness. "Do you suppose that's a common trait among warmongers?"

"It's going to be one of those sessions, is it, Ms. Molyneaux?" Brooks said with a slight smile. Alex was silent, his face neutral.

"It most certainly is," she snapped. "If you think I'm going to stand by and let you railroad this president—my president—into starting yet another war, you're crazy."

"What would you have us do?" Brooks said. "I must have missed your response to Secretary Colaris's comments on the rules of engagement and sissy officers."

Molyneaux flushed and said, "If you weren't copied on comments, ask the president."

"I don't want to see your comments, Ms. Molyneaux. I want to help us figure out what makes the most sense for us to do as a nation. We'll then so advise the president."

She turned to Alex. "And what do you care about what our nation should do in these circumstances, if you're even capable of that kind of thought? You're an Arab. You'll worry about your own."

Alex smiled. "We all do ultimately. Self-interest is why we all ultimately do what we do; I suppose we're wired that way. We're making a very big bet on that trait with our education efforts. But as for my caring about our nation, Ms. Molyneaux, let's compare credentials. I was a serving United States Marine for eight years. I was wounded eleven times, or maybe it was twelve, in the line of duty. I was raised by a father in a wheelchair who had the Medal of Honor and no functioning legs. He was second-generation Irish. My mother is a Bedouin who taught math at the local community college in Audley, South Carolina. My thinking skills are the best I can manage, given my history. And your credentials, Ms. Molyneaux?"

She gazed calmly at Alex and then at Brooks. "OK," she said. "The introductions are out of the way. I've read your biographies, and you've read mine. Let's get started. For now, call me Sheila.

"I have several problems with what I heard recently about plans in Iran, but the biggest one is that people in our government are proposing that we look at starting a war rather than responding to an immediate threat. Is that being proposed?"

"I certainly hope so," Brooks said. "But my opinion about whether or not to start a war with Iran is not being solicited."

"Then why are you here?"

"We're here to discuss intelligence received and processed that leads us to believe there is an ironclad—or nearly so—case that American casualties will be minimized and American interest best served if we proceed in a certain direction in the face of an imminent threat."

"You guys are dangerous," Molyneaux said. "You make an intellectual case for a course of action that, in terms of international policy, is both immoral and suicidal. That's a very bad thing. If implemented, it would sink this president. That's not going to happen on my watch. I shall oppose you with every fiber of my being."

"The way we see things," Brooks said, "is that we must find a way to keep Iran from radioactively igniting the tinder that is the Middle East."

"And to do it," Alex said, "without massed boots and armor on the ground."

"That is a conceptual oxymoron," Molyneaux said. "It's never been done that way. Of all people, experienced killers like you two should know that. If it were possible, we wouldn't have gotten bogged down in Iraq and Afghanistan. It's not as if old farts like the two of you will be called to Iran to die."

"True," Brooks said. "The real issue is whether we'd be better off with a nuclear Iran and what that would mean for regional stability in the world's largest source of oil."

"That's total bullshit," Molyneaux said. "The real issue is whether or not Iran is within sight of having an operational nuke and whether they would use a nuke if they had one. The negotiations with Iran are going well. We have Iran wanting to negotiate away their nuclear weapons capability to get the crippling sanctions on them removed. The American public is behind those negotiations."

"And if they are playing us for more time and fewer sanctions until they complete their nuke?" Elliot asked.

Molyneaux shrugged. "The president and I know your opinion as to the correct courses of action. If we don't go that way, what? And when?"

"I guess we'll see," Alex said. "A nuclear arms race in the Middle East might get a tad ugly. My Muslim colleagues often do suboptimal things while under the conviction that paradise awaits them. Dinner tonight notwithstanding, mushrooms can be particularly ugly if rising above cities. The air becomes foul for all of us."

Elliot stood and said, "We've pretty much said it. We'll await the president's decision as to a course of action."

Molyneaux nodded and stood. "You know what I'll be saying."

"We do," Alex said. "I hope we brought some light to your end of the debate as you did to ours."

The three of them walked down the hall and turned in separate directions. Molyneaux was anxious to get back to work. Alex and Brooks were anxious for a glass of port and some relaxation.

IN THE DINING ROOM the president was being a politician as Mac and Kelly relaxed, charmed. There had been more alcohol consumed, and Roberts had told more stories from the campaign trail and Molyneaux's incredible nose for public opinion. Caitlin sat in her chair, busy on her Kphone and ignoring them. After a soft knock, Elliot stuck his head in the room. "Do you need any of us right now?" he said.

"We'll find you if we need you," Roberts said. "But on second thought, Mr. Elliot, please join us. Ms. Molyneaux and Mr. Cuchulain can go about their business for now. Perhaps they'll discover they are soul mates."

"As you please, Mr. President," Elliot said and turned to murmur to Alex. He closed the door and walked to his old place at the dinner table. Caitlin stood and left the room, still focused on her Kphone.

"Gentlemen," the president said, "I'm troubled that we are asking a young man, Mr. Cuchulain, an American who is newly an Arab, to do things that would challenge the most seasoned diplomat, Arab or not. You can't just send a man into a hostile country to incite a civil war from a cold start in the midst of a shooting war. That's just not realistic. The stresses on him will be enormous. Between the three of you, perhaps you can give me some comfort that he may be able to step up, without losing his temper or his composure, to the stresses he may find. He has little formal training for this kind of thing, and we have no sense of his mental stability under stress. Help me understand this man and how he will react to stress."

"I don't know much of him in his early years in the corps, Mr. President," Kelly said. "He operated well below my pay grade and was detached to the CIA. I saw him in violent action only once, and that was recently."

"And?" Roberts said. "Is he still competent, or has a life of the mind and business atrophied those skills?"

Kelly chuckled. "Not long ago," he said, "Cuchulain, MacMillan, Elliot, O'Connor, and I were on Elliot's fancy sailboat, *Old Fashioned,* anchored in an inlet on the Chesapeake Bay. Cuchulain was doing a Moroccan food event of his own design; he's a competent chef. The boat was bouncing around a little from passing speedboat wakes. We were sitting around a table, talking, when three men popped over a stern rail, carrying weapons and informing us of a holdup and bonus unpleasantness to come for O'Connor. I was stunned and thinking furiously about alternatives. Cuchulain killed the three men in ten seconds or so, then killed a fourth who was a latecomer to the heist. Interestingly, the latecomer turned out to be Spetznaz, a Russian commando, on a diplomatic passport, who was freelancing."

"Ten seconds?" Roberts said. "That has to be a fairy tale."

MacMillan smiled. "It wasn't more than fifteen seconds for the first three. He's the best I ever had in my CIA group, and he hasn't lost more than a half step in the past ten years. Cuchulain was a legend in the Special Forces community; he was called Cooch there."

"How does someone as articulate as he is get to be a stone-cold killer?" Roberts said. "It doesn't compute."

"I've heard him asked that question," MacMillan said. "He responds Socratically with the same question about Sun Tzu, Hannibal, Alexander the Great, and even Rene Descartes, who twice spent time as a mercenary. He claims it is only in the past two hundred years that politics and combat became so separated. He can go on for an hour about that topic. I think he's a tad sensitive about it.

"My response to your question is more immediate, Mr. President," MacMillan said. "All of my CIA Special Operations people were smart; we tested for it. Cuchulain is spectacularly smart, particularly in quantitative things, but I didn't recruit specifically for his kinds of smarts. Perhaps I should have. He knew more about tactical explosives than any man alive at the time he was active. We still use some of his designs; his design premise was 'thoughtful lethality.' He had time to study broadly, and he used that time well.

"When he and his partner, a world-class Marine sniper, were on a mission that had big waiting times; they often used that time to study warfare and small, unit tactics. They'd discuss Jomini and von Clausewitz and that whole politico-strategy crowd, then be ass deep in a firefight a day later. He took classes at William and Mary, and he chose quite an eclectic set of subjects. Cuchulain and I sat and talked for hours in the evenings after dinner. He has one hell of a broad-reaching mind. I'd say he knows more about Machiavelli than most professors who teach the period when he lived. As far as his mental stability under stress goes, he has probably spent more time with shrinks than any politician alive; he's stable and lethal when under stress. We tried to figure out what made him tick so we could replicate it. He should have been dead a long time ago."

"And did you succeed in figuring that out?" Roberts asked.

"We found a lot out but not that."

"Jesus," Roberts said. "Why Machiavelli? Most people think he was a monster."

"I'll leave that question for him to answer, Mr. President," Mac said. "But Cuchulain says the poor man was misunderstood. 'Machiavelli was just a realist,' he says."

"It sounds like he should be put away, General Kelly," Roberts said with a grim smile.

"I've heard a lecture at the Naval War College where the professor admired Machiavelli's thinking," Kelly said. "The political environment is entirely different now than when the Borgias were in power in Florence, but some things never change."

Roberts opened his mouth to speak, then shrugged and nodded.

"Or not," MacMillan said. "Maybe we're just living in a golden age brought on by our employment of the military hegemony Secretary Colaris so forcefully described in the Situation Room."

"OK, enough of that," Roberts said. "Tell me a Cooch story from when he was active and working for you. Show me why he should be trusted under stress or at least why he is admired by some, like the three trained killers in front of me."

MacMillan leaned back in his chair, then got up, walked to the wooden cabinet, and poured another glass of Dancing Hares for himself. He raised an eyebrow at the president, who nodded and jerked his head toward the decanters. Mac reached for a low highball glass and put two ice cubes from a bucket on the sideboard in it; then he poured two fingers of Laphroaig malt scotch over the ice, walked back to the table, and handled it to Roberts. He sat down and leaned back in his chair. "Brooks," he said, "Why don't you tell the story of how you and Cooch met?" Brooks shrugged and nodded.

"I was assigned to a SEAL team and Cooch was assigned to us from CIA Special Ops as a combat demolition specialist. We went into Halat, a beach town in Lebanon a few miles north of Beirut, on a mission to kill a guy named Abu Nidal, who was planning a big mission against the US. Nidal and his planners were in an apartment building in a four-building complex. Intel said the only troops were in that building, so Cooch was going to blow it up after we did our shooting and got whatever plans and documents we could find. It turned out that there were armed bad guys in two other buildings—lots of them.

"I was the 'escape shooter,' at the high water level of the beach. I was dug into a dune with an M14 rifle and a nightscope all bedded down and stable, ready to provide protective fire if our guys needed it as they ran back to the boats. I'm watching through my rifle nightscope and see Cooch with his vest lit up in infrared the way we do, running toward me and throwing timer grenades, hustling back to the boats.

"By this time, shooters are boiling out of two buildings with AK-47s shooting away at my buddies and they are setting up a machine gun on the roof of one building. I'm blazing away at the pursuit.

"So, Cooch drops beside me, looks downrange, and blows the first building as soon as the last of the SEALs clear it. It was cool—he blew the roof straight up then collapsed the sides all at once. Just then I got shot in the shoulder pretty bad—couldn't shoot.

"Cooch grabs my rifle and continues in the 'escape shooter' role, dropping guys right and left and killing the machine gunners on the roof before they could get set. When the last SEAL clears my position on his way to the boats, Cooch picks me up in a fireman's carry and sprints about 120 yards and dumps me in an inflatable boat, in front of a corpsman. I weighed a bunch, since he didn't stop to get me out of my vest and ammo before he picked me up and ran for the boats."

Elliot picked up his wine glass and said to the President, "I'd have bled out in another few minutes, but that's less important than the fact that Cooch did his job, then took over the escape shooter's job, and was the last man to clear the combat area—a dangerous situation. Prudence says he should have just run back to the boats without me. He had done enough."

"And the conclusion I am to reach from this exciting story?" Roberts said.

"He's a mission guy. He focuses on the mission," Elliot said. "Beyond that, making good decisions while people are shooting at you is notoriously difficult. He made three of them in a row. Cooch handles stress well."

"Anything to add, Colonel MacMillan?" Roberts asked. "Another story? Something more recent, more personal?"

"Let's take one you know about from a few months ago," Mac said. "At an early stage of the aborted terrorist Cowboys stadium mortar attack where you were present a few months back, Cooch was in a cantina near the Texas/Mexican border with six Mexican gang members protecting some Arabs they had escorted across our border. He wanted to see if he could identify the Arabs. It turns out that one of them was a known terrorist in Iraq, identified a few years before. Cooch passed as a Mexican, but the protection leader wanted trouble and sent his biggest man to make it. Cooch killed the big man a few seconds later, then walked out unharmed."

"The lesson there?" Roberts said.

"Cooch passed as a Mexican with less background than he has as an Arab scholar. He handled the situation with no more violence than was necessary, given there were civilians in the cantina and no reason for him to take more risk than he had."

Roberts looked at MacMillan.

"The lessons are?" Roberts asked.

"Cuchulain is experienced under pressure," Mac said. "He thinks and acts well there. He understands it. He supports the mission and supports it well. He doesn't rush into violence. That's the lesson."

Roberts sighed. "At least Cuchulain is ruthless and thoughful under stress. I'll think about it some more."

He stood and walked from the room.

THE FOLLOWING MORNING ANOTHER of the president's helicopters took off for Andrews Air Force Base with Cuchulain, Elliot, and O'Connor aboard. They landed a short while later in suburban Maryland, just south of the District of Columbia.

A ground crew unloaded their luggage, then escorted them to two waiting staff cars. Brooks was going to Reagan National Airport for the short hop to New York on the Delta shuttle. Caitlin and Alex were taken on a longer ride to Washington Dulles, where they boarded a flight on an Iberian Airlines 777 for the nonstop to Madrid, with a good connection to Tangier.

CHAPTER 3

MOROCCO

IN TANGIER, ALEX SAT IN A padded chair in his office across a small table from Tang, his martial arts instructor of many years and a close associate, who chose to stand. Tang had no friends to Alex's knowledge, but he had proved to be extraordinarily loyal to Alex over the years and seemed a friend.

Tang had the gift of movement. He knew where every part of his body was at any given point in time and had control of it. Tang also had the gift of proximity sensing. He could detect the presence of animate things before he saw them simply by sensing, perhaps feeling, their presence. Alex had studied and developed that skill intensely for nearly a decade at the Farm and for many years since. He still had primitive sensing, compared to Tang.

When Alex left the CIA and the Farm after eight years, Tang stayed behind, only to be called to follow several years later when Alex moved to New York and later to Tangier.

For the past year or so, Tang had worked with Caitlin when she was in Tangier; she had a taste for the martial arts and violence. Tang said she would have been adequate had she started studying with him as a youth, as Alex had. A determination of adequacy by Tang was tantamount to an unqualified endorsement by anyone else's standards. Recently, Tang had been working with Karim, the boy Alex had brought to him, assessing him at Alex's request. Alex had to make a decision about what to do with Karim. Tang's observations would be a key element of that decision.

"I'm pleased to see you, Tang," Alex said softly. "You have been busy."

"Busy is good," Tang said. "We must return to your studies. You have been gone for several weeks and have no doubt become slow and sloppy in your movement and insensitive in your perceptions."

"My trip was useful," Alex said. "Thank you for asking."

The edges of Tang's lips twitched under his wispy beard. He nodded.

"Have you reached any conclusions about Karim and Salima?" Alex said.

Tang nodded slowly, his focus flat on the unadorned wall, contemplating.

Alex waited.

"There are problems," Tang said. "Karim is as yet unable to focus acceptably. Salima is not a candidate for study with me."

"Then I'll have Caitlin worry about Salima or place her with a Bedouin family. Tell me about Karim. Does he have promise? Does he have the physical skills to study with you?"

Another lip twitch by Tang. "He does have promise. How often and how long may I have him?"

Alex smiled to himself. He'd just heard a plea from Tang to keep a student. That was a first and an interesting start to Alex's day.

"We'll see how he progresses. Tell me about where he is today."

"Karim is physically weak, which limits his ability, but he has an extraordinary connection from his mind to his body, a useful skill. He moves very well and is surprisingly limber. He is only beginning to hear his inner voice direct him, as I said earlier, but shows good progress."

More accolades. Interesting. For Tang, an inner voice is what keeps the body moving as trained, rehearsed, and directed, while the intellect considers future moves as it watches the world around it unfold. I wonder if a Dain will show up for Karim. Dain has been a comfort and an asset for me. He showed up slowly, incrementally, as my proximity sense grew. Dain has more of a personality than one would expect; he was also a subject of great interest to the CIA shrinks.

"What shall I do to help?" Alex said.

"We should allow him to observe our interaction," Tang said. "I will teach him about power growing from his core. You should begin to teach him about strength from the core, the way you developed it. It is unlikely that he will develop the hand strength you have, so we will seek another advantage for him if he continues to develop. Perhaps he will become adequate with a knife, something you failed to do, other than to throw one well, a skill a chimpanzee can master. I will attempt to grow his awareness."

Alex nodded. "Thank you for your observations, Tang."

Tang nodded. He had been dismissed.

"Send Karim to me. Karim and I are likely to return to you in less than thirty minutes for some work."

Tang bowed slightly, turned, and left the room.

Ten minutes later there was a soft knock on the door.

"Enter," Alex said from his desk chair. The door opened, and Karim entered, clad in a loose shirt and baggy pants, tied at the waist with a white cotton belt. He bowed slightly and stood still, waiting, as Alex looked him up and down.

"You and your sister are well and treated acceptably?" Alex said. Karim nodded.

"You are both content?"

Karim shrugged, then nodded.

Alex smiled to himself. Tang's loquaciousness was rubbing off. From an open desk drawer, he removed the hat the girl had retrieved when they left the café. The coins were still in its bottom.

"I am considering what to do with the two of you. I can put you with families who will care for you, if they are paid and I check on them. I can release you to return to your former life with some funds to get started and a new music player to replace the one we left behind at the café. Or you can stay here. If you stay here, you would both be my charges. I will provide food, education, shelter, and protection. You will work with me and do my bidding. Salima will stay with you and find a place in our family, perhaps with Dr. O'Connor. Do you have a preference among these choices?"

Karim nodded. "My sister and I have been discussing what is going to happen to us; we don't like not knowing. Tang has given me skills that may protect us if we are told to go back to our previous lives. We would both prefer to stay here, if given the chance. We will do work as we are told and try to please those who control our lives. We would like to keep our picture phones with the lessons, if that is possible; there is much of interest to both of us in those phones. I will earn the money to pay for them, and you may keep the money from Salima's hat from when you brought us in."

Alex smiled. "I'll keep the coins as full payment for the picture phones, which we call Kphones. You may return the hat to Salima." He dumped the coins on the desktop, counted them, and swept them into the drawer; then proffered the hat to Karim.

"You may address me as Kufdani, Tang as Tang, Jerome Masterson as Uncle, and Caitlin O'Connor as Doctor. You will both stay in the apartment beside Tang, as you now do, and continue to eat with the staff in the cafeteria. You will not discuss your lessons or your life with the staff, but you should be pleasant to them. You are not to go to town without an escort designated by Tang.

"You may stay for the foreseeable future as long as you perform as you are directed. Be respectful to your elders and your teachers. Do what is asked of you, even if difficult and not clearly of any immediate benefit. Do not brag or speak inappropriately. You are far behind your peers in your learning of book things and things Arabic, so you will have to be diligent if you are to catch up acceptably. Your Kphones are to be used first as learning devices and only secondarily as devices for amusement. Treasure them. You will learn to speak and write English, then other languages. I expect it will be difficult for both of you."

Alex gazed at Karim. "Do you understand and agree for both you and your sister?"

Karim straightened. "I understand and agree for both of us, Kufdani. We will make every effort to please you."

"Good. Let's go meet with Tang and set things up with him."

The boy became wide eyed. "Am I to spar with you? Tang said you have a gift. I am anxious to learn it."

Alex smiled and said over his shoulder as he walked to the door of the office, "Not today. Tang and I will spend some time with a form of sparring to freshen my skills and demonstrate what is to come; then you and I will discuss exercise and strength. First, you build your strength. Perhaps then we will spar."

Tang's "lesson room," as he called it, was five meters square with both walls and floor heavily padded. There was a smaller room just beyond, dark with the light from the lesson room splashing an irregular pattern on a smooth stone floor. Alex raised an index finger to Karim to hold him and walked through a door at the end of the lesson room. He returned a few moments later dressed in loose pants and shirt, similar to those Tang wore.

Alex walked to a spot in front of Tang, sat cross-legged in front of him, and closed his eyes. Tang slapped him across the face but nearly missed because of a sudden backward movement of Alex's head. Tang's left hand followed in a blur, but a hand movement from Alex knocked it slightly off course. It was a miss. Suddenly, Tang struck with both hands, then with his feet. More landed than not. Alex tried to counter each strike, either with movement or blockage by his hands and arms, but many blows landed. After many seconds of continuous strikes and blocks, Tang stopped and said, "Enough."

Alex opened his eyes and stood, then bowed. Tang bowed in return.

"You have been too long in the crucibles of corruption," Tang said. "I can smell the alcohol from your pores and the smoke from your surroundings. They destroy your perception."

Alex bowed again, beckoned to the wide-eyed boy beside him, and turned. They walked through a door at the far end of the lesson room and Alex flipped on the light. There on the floor were a number of exercise objects. There were several steel balls with handles on their tops, each larger and apparently heavier than the next. Various pulley machines with steel plates on them sat unused around the room. In the far corner, there was an area with a dark-blue padded mat on the floor. They walked to it.

When they stopped, Karim turned to Alex and said, "I expected you to spar with Tang and show me how to do the fighting that Tang is trying to teach me. Instead, you closed your eyes and Tang hit you often, but many blows were blocked by you. How do you do that, and why did you close your eyes?"

"It is the training that I do now with Tang, after I learned to spar," Alex said. "It is important that you learn how to sense danger and its source. I am still learning to sense movement and am not yet proficient.

That is the hardest thing to learn, and starting early is quite important on the path to mastering that skill. I want you to build that skill while you learn the physical moves. Tang tells me that you move well but need to build your strength. I know some simple exercises that I will demonstrate for you that will help build your strength."

He pulled a blue half-sphere object from the wall. It had an inflated half ball on its top and a solid, thick, black plastic base with handles at either edge. He pointed the curved base against the floor and let the flat, hard black surface wobble until it was level under his hands.

"This is a Bosu ball," Alex said. "They come in different sizes that you should investigate as you become comfortable with the drill I will show you. Smaller is more difficult."

In one motion, Alex leaned from his waist to grasp the handles of the Bosu ball then went into a handstand on it, legs together and toes pointed. His feet swayed slightly, and his arms flexed as he adjusted his weight to keep his balance stable on the round, inflated base.

As he adjusted to the unstable base, Alex said, "This is the starting point for the most elementary of the exercises. It may take you several months to get it right, as it did me. There will be other increasingly difficult exercises when you master this one." He lowered himself very slowly until his chin was just above the black plate; then he pushed his arms to full extension at the same pace. As he slowly lowered and raised his body in the handstand, the Bosu ball quivered and moved with only his shifts in balance to keep it steady. He did ten slow repetitions, the second five with his eyes closed; then he gave a sudden push from the bottom position and spun in the air to land on the balls of his feet. He opened his eyes and gestured to Karim.

Karim looked at the strange ball, then leaned over it, grasped the handles, and went into a handstand on it for a moment. He then lost his balance on the strange rounded surface. He allowed his legs to fall and came to his feet. He tried a second time with the same result, but it took a bit longer for him to fail. On the third try, he was able to maintain the handstand. His legs swayed with the change in direction on the half ball, and his arms quivered with the strain, but he held the handstand until Alex said, "Enough. The rest is hard and will take time."

Karim let his legs fall as he swung to his feet and stood in front of Alex. There was a strange curiosity in his eyes.

"You have much to learn, but you are young," Alex said. "Tang will be your teacher in these physical things and, most importantly, in the sensing. I will help when I am in Tangier. Your Uncle Jerome will teach you to be invisible and to deal with enemies by working with others. Above all, you will work with your Kphone on your studies as defined by me, Doctor, and Uncle Jerome. You and Salima are well behind where you should be to prepare you for life."

Karim bowed slightly from the waist as he had seen Alex and Tang do and said, "As you command, Kufdani."

Alex turned and walked to the door. Karim turned and looked again at the Bosu ball, then stepped to it with determination. Alex turned his head to watch him; Karim closed his eyes and concentrated. He opened his eyes and swung into the handstand on the Bosu ball; he seemed more comfortable now.

CAITLIN WAS BACK IN the office beside her apartment in the Kufdani complex after getting things on the right path in Algeciras and catching up in Tangier. Her short blond hair was combed but wet. Salima sat across from her, also damp headed.

"That was a good swim, Salima," Caitlin said. "You have been practicing while I was gone. I'm happy about that."

Salima beamed. Keeping Doctor happy was very important to her. She liked this place, with its unlimited food and its warm, safe place to sleep beside her brother. She also liked being the only person allowed to use Doctor's pool in her absence as the occasional reward for doing well in her studies.

"You must learn to focus in your studies," Caitlin said "You are not catching up the way you must, particularly in mathematics and the sciences. Study the material, then go to swim and think about what you have read while you swim. When you are able to do that for long periods, you will learn faster."

Doctor spoke to Salima only in Arabic. The Arabic that Kufdani and the others used was without the Tangerine inflection Salima and

Karim had known since infancy, but it was increasingly understandable. Both Salima and Karim had taught themselves to read Arabic years ago, which proved helpful to both as Caitlin ranged for the best way to teach them. The English on Salima's Kphone was easy to follow and practice. Salima would speak to her phone, *her very own phone*, in English to learn the words and their accents. Her phone would tell her when her accent was strong and praise her. When she made a mistake, the phone would correct her in an understanding voice. Strangely, Salima felt that she and the plastic phone were nearly becoming friends.

"I'm having trouble with algebra now," Salima said. "It was easier after the arithmetic, then hard. It's now harder still."

"You must see the equations as little friends who have things to tell you," Caitlin said. "At first they are all strangers; then you discover that they are cousins of each other and friends of yours. You can't rush their story, so perhaps we should allow them more time. Thinking while swimming allows the story of the equations to unfold slowly. I'll have a look at the lessons on your phone to see whether we should take a little more time for the story to be told. It's only been a few weeks. You can always catch up on the other science; it is mathematics that is the queen of the sciences."

"I will do better, Doctor. I will make you proud."

"I know you will, Salima," Caitlin said. "If you are steady and hardworking, the light will come on for you and show the way to related new things that are fun. When it becomes fun, learning becomes easier. Your English is getting better, your Spanish is acceptable, and your other work is coming along acceptably. I'm considering taking you along when I next travel to Spain."

Salima bounced up and down on her chair, thrilled at the prospect. "I have never been to Spain! Will Karim come, too?" Salima jumped to her feet and began to run around Caitlin, singing an Eastern melody with nonsensical lyrics.

"Perhaps," Caitlin said, smiling at Salima's enthusiasm. "I'll discuss it with Kufdani. But first Kufdani and I have to deal with a few problems in America."

CHAPTER 4

WASHINGTON

MAC CALLED TO TELL ALEX that the president wanted to talk to him again, one-on-one, on short notice. Alex was on a plane from Morocco that day, changing planes at Charles de Gaulle in Paris for a flight to Washington Dulles International Airport. Both flights had been without event—the finest kind.

Alex walked from customs at Dulles International to the long, clunky people mover that would carry him from the long, rectangular building that allowed Dulles-bound airplanes to dock away from the small main terminal. After a few minutes, there was a hiss of air, and a door opened. He entered the famed Eero Saarinen building, the original Dulles Airport, with a leather garment bag slung over his shoulder, his only luggage. Alex didn't expect to be in Washington for more than a few days. He kept clothes and other necessities at his apartment in New York.

Alex walked outside the terminal to the line to hire a cab. Cabs were a monopoly at Dulles, owned and managed by a group of Persians. Most of the drivers were Persian refugees or their offspring from when the Shah was overthrown in Iran. Alex enjoyed listening to the radio banter in the Persian language, Farsi, as they sped down the limited-access highway through the Northern Virginia towns of Reston, MacLean, Falls Church, Arlington—and finally came to the Roosevelt Bridge across the Potomac.

The Kennedy Center was immediately on his left and the Lincoln Memorial on his right as they entered the District of Columbia. After flinching at the eighty-five-dollar taxi fare, he handed the driver a hundred-dollar bill, shouldered his bag, and walked into the lobby of the Hay-Adams Hotel on Sixteenth Street, just across Lafayette Park from the White House. There was the usual set of protestors about, some camped in shabby tents and others with signs that proclaimed their outrage about one thing or another. The stele of the Washington Monument rose above the White House, a pencil balanced on a wedding cake.

He walked across the small lobby to the reception, quietly examining each of the men sitting at small tables around the lobby, reading. There were none of interest to him. He checked in, went to his small room, and opened his computer to check the latest news. A few minutes later, he was in his bed and asleep.

THE FOLLOWING MORNING ALEX awoke early and went for a run up Sixteenth Street to Connecticut Avenue, then to Fourteenth Street; then he turned toward the National Mall. He had a look at the Washington Monument, Abraham Lincoln in his memorial, and Mr. Jefferson by the reflecting pool. Cars streamed across the Fourteenth Street Bridge to the city, their occupants ready to begin another day in service to Uncle Sam.

The bulk of the Pentagon was visible across the Potomac River, shrouded at the bottom in ground fog. He turned and picked up his pace to run past the west side of the White House, then up Seventeenth Street past the gray mass of the Old Executive Office Building beside Lafayette Park. Then he went back to the Hay-Adams for a quick shower. All the while, Alex's well-developed proximity instincts, in combination with a complaining Dain, warned him about people with weapons watching him from rooftops.

"They're watching us through gun scopes, laddie. I hate this feeling. Still, I'm glad they are on our side."

Forty minutes later, Alex walked across Lafayette Park dressed in a gray suit with faint-green pinstripes, a white shirt, and a green silk tie.

He presented his credentials to the uniformed secret service officer at the pedestrian gate to the White House.

A few minutes later, a badge around his neck with a blaze-orange V for Visitor, Alex sat in an upholstered chair in the Oval Office across from President Roberts. His chief of staff, Sheila Molyneaux, sat in a chair beside the president's massive live-oak desk, made from the revolutionary-era hull of "Old Ironsides," the USS *Constitution*. After quick greetings, Roberts got to the point.

"Mr. Cuchulain, you're here once again because your country appears to need you, and I need to be entirely comfortable with you. I've come to grips with Dr. O'Connor's intellect and her related role in our national security. Mr. Elliot claims no special place in any upcoming operations other than offering to be available as an advisor. You're my loose end.

"General Kelly and Colonel MacMillan have convinced me that I should consider you for a role in upcoming events. That's just what I'm doing today, *considering*. My chief of staff, who is noted for the qualities of both her intellect and her instincts, says such a role being set is a dangerous precedent and that you are a dangerous, homicidal man."

Molyneaux glared at Alex from her chair, a notebook perched in front of her and a felt-tipped pen clutched in her hand. There was another pen sticking in her hair; this made her what Brooks called "a belt and suspender" type who didn't allow herself to fail. She wore dark cotton slacks, a button-down white blouse under a blazer, and thick-soled, black leather lace-up shoes.

"I have yet to be accused of homicide by any government, so I'll do what I can, Mr. President," Alex said. "What can I do to help you?"

"You and some others think you can walk into an Arab country and have influence on the choice of a new government in the midst of our attack on them. I'm troubled that I'm contemplating reliance on a notorious killer who happens to be an Arab sheikh but the son of an American hero. I want to get to know you a little. We're never going to be friends, but I need to know how you think and how you view things over there right now. If I decide that I can live with having you involved, I'll have you briefed on ongoing plans evolving at Defense so you can interact intelligently with them."

"What would you like to know, Mr. President?"

"What do you know the most about, beyond the possible conflict at hand?"

"I know about education, technology investing, small-business operations, small-unit tactics, the martial arts, and tactical explosives, from most recent to the distant past. I'm also a credible Islamic scholar with a graduate degree in Islamic studies from Oxford. I speak and read most dialects of Arabic and Farsi."

"Which of those skill sets drives your thinking, Mr. Cuchulain?"

"Education on a path to reform thinking in the Middle East, Mr. President," Alex said. "That's not changed since we met at Camp David, nor will it."

"That's one of the things that bothers me. Almost anyone with a brain will tell you that your goals to quickly transform Muslim society are so unrealistic as to be laughable."

"Then I'm going to die a ridiculed, embittered old man, Mr. President, but that's what drives me."

"It seems more likely that you'll first be killed in a firefight, given your past."

Alex shrugged. "I've come to believe that if I was going to get killed in a firefight, it would have already happened. To address the education question, Mr. President, it will be technology that enables such rapid progress in educating the masses, and it will be technology that enables a successful effort in Iran by me, if there is to be one. I know quite a bit about technology."

"I'm also skeptical, of course," Molyneaux said, jumping in, "but let's bring this discussion back to the matter at hand. Why is this threat from Iran a situation you've stuck your Sunni nose into?"

Alex sat for a moment, considering his reply and Molyneaux's behavior. *Let's see. I'm Irish and Arab, a former Marine and a killer. Could she be trying to piss me off to terminate this discussion before it starts? Of course she is. This is not the moment for an angry response.*

Alex leaned forward with a relaxed focus, intense but unthreatening.

"Because Iran with a nuke and a delivery mechanism for it is an existential threat to us and the free world," Alex said. "One level of thought below that existential threat is that Iran, with a credible nuclear capability, will destabilize the Middle East for decades. Sunni nations will scramble to get nuclear capability once Shiite Iran demonstrates it. Any influence we have enjoyed as a country and a world force for good will be massively reduced."

Molyneaux's face darkened. "What possible contribution can you envision that would help us deal with this existential threat you fantasize?"

"I can establish a back-channel link with Iran through my Arab connections and my work as an Islamic scholar. How that would be used will depend on the plans Defense makes up. I can provide back-channel links to the Sunni nations that maintain good relations with Morocco. I can establish a good link with the government of Morocco, which is our best friend over there."

"Oh, really? Morocco? Just when did that become a known fact?" Molyneaux said.

"I forget exactly, but it was around 1777 when we were in a bit of trouble with the Brits. Morocco was the first country to recognize our new government."

"For political reasons, no doubt," she said sarcastically.

Alex smiled. "No doubt," he said. "Some things never change."

Roberts glared at his chief of staff and said, "Is this little pissing contest over yet?"

Both Alex and Molyneaux were silent.

"Fine, children," Roberts said. "Shall we move on? Let's get to the moral issues involved here. I understand, at least as much as I'm going to right now, the risks to my popularity and my legacy.

"Ms. Molyneaux and I have been having a discussion about the morality of the United States interfering in Iran's sovereign environment in a violent manner and the domestic consequences here of a massive attack, such as the one the Defense Department is planning as a contingency. I've invited her to join us as we discuss that issue. Are you comfortable with that discussion, Mr. Cuchulain, or should I instead invite Mr. Elliot?"

"I'm comfortable with Ms. Molyneaux joining the conversation; it's your call. Elliot is the philosopher, but I can talk the talk."

"Ms. Molyneaux was a Marshall Scholar," Roberts said. "She studied at the Sorbonne in her earlier days. She has an informed opinion."

Alex nodded. "I read her dissertation on Voltaire. Quite impressive."

"You did what?" Molyneaux said as her head snapped up. "Oh yeah, know thine enemy. I should have guessed."

Alex smiled. "And what did our government files reveal on Alejandro Mohammed Cuchulain, Ms. Molyneaux?"

"OK, let's get to it," she said, ignoring his question. "There is a groundswell of opinion in our government that seems to be asking the president to attack a sovereign state on nothing more than speculation, to attack Iran for the greater good, as defined by the state, with untold consequences. I don't come close to buying into that view."

Molyneaux leaned forward for emphasis and said, "Voltaire concluded that Christian factions always seek domination—using the state. Each religious faction then becomes either prey or predator. It seems to me that this cabal consisting of you, O'Connor, and Elliot is proposing just that. You want us to impose the Christian view of society on those who won't play the Christian game."

The president's head turned to Alex.

"And here I am an Arab. Go figure."

"That's part of what I can't figure out," Molyneaux said. "Or at least I'd like to hear what you have to say about it."

Roberts smiled faintly and again turned his gaze to Alex. "Indeed Voltaire said that," Alex said. "But what if Christianity was a just a metaphor for the state, the combination of the French Catholic Church and its government, as he was describing it way back then? Voltaire's lessons are certainly valid in the Middle East. The state there is a theocracy that imposes its will and views upon the people. Anyone who claims infallibility when interpreting Voltaire hasn't read him. And you have."

Molyneaux shrugged. "What if it *was* a metaphor? You are still proposing that we impose our will, our way, on another sovereign society by using military might."

"In turn," Alex said, "you are proposing that a single nation's sovereignty—Iran's in this case—trumps the sovereignty of all nations in a region and their collective populace, ultimately around the world. I'm puzzled about how to figure that out.

"Ms. Molyneaux, we disagree. You and I are on different sides of the long debate that has been going on endlessly since Aristotle or before:

what is the package of knowledge, culture, and government that best serves the needs of the larger populace? That debate doesn't involve itself except by implication on the short term of political actions on people's lives and deaths."

"That's bullshit," Molyneaux said. "And what do you know of Aristotle?"

"Not much. Less than I know about Voltaire, which also isn't much. I know a bit more about Thucydides, since I'm more interested in the politics of power than Aristotelian thinking. I say that given the Enlightenment changed lives for the better, how do we facilitate its lessons across the Middle East in hopes of accomplishing the same?"

"Net it out for the problem at hand, Mr. Cuchulain," Roberts said. "We're starting to spin our wheels."

Alex sat back in his chair and was silent for a few moments, then said, "The problem at hand is that Iran has developed an existential threat to society and may or may not use it. There's the bet. They have promised to remove Israel from the face of the earth. That's an oft-repeated fact. Now they are about to have that capability. This is not the time to rehash tactics but rather to decide what we must do to preserve society as we know it and how. It's the politics of power one more time.

"It may be that negotiations will solve our problem," Alex said. "Perhaps not. But with which option are our gains greater and our losses lower? How do we measure the probability of success of the course we choose?"

"Those do indeed seem to be the issues at hand, Mr. Cuchulain," Roberts said. "I don't think you and Ms. Molyneaux are going to agree on these issues or the action required, so let's move on.

"I'll take the next step, Mr. Cuchulain. I'll direct that your clearances be updated and that you be briefed on the current plans in the Department of Defense, but I have made no decision. I hope you bring something of value to our table. It's hard to imagine you stepping into Tehran out of the blue and influencing a sovereign government to do our bidding."

Roberts came to his feet behind his desk. He reached across to shake Alex's hand.

"Thank you for your time, Mr. Cuchulain," he said.

Alex walked with Molyneaux out of the Oval Office. As he heard the door click closed behind them, he stopped on the way down the hall to the exit and turned to face her.

"Why don't I buy you a drink or dinner? We can talk about things we agree on."

Molyneaux snorted. "And why would I want to do that?"

"Well, the sympathy vote would consider that I flew a zillion miles or so for this meeting with the president. It's over, and the evening is young."

"And if I don't buy the sympathy hit?"

Alex grinned a boyish grin that lit up his face. He looked almost handsome but for the scars on his forehead and down the left side of his face, and his slightly misshapen nose. His eyebrows were bushy, lumpy, and unattractive.

"There's always the intellectual challenge," he said. "You're an expert on Voltaire and could use that to challenge my views on the long debate. I could become your devotee after a few drinks and some conversation."

"Too much trouble, a fool's task, and I don't need an ugly devotee," Molyneaux said. "You might even be a Nazi. Any other bullshit reasons for me to spend any more time listening to you babble from *Mein Kampf*?"

"Jeez, you're tough," Alex said. "Well, I could help with your expletive vocabulary; it's tiresomely limited. I've learned hundreds of scatological expletives I could teach you for use in vocabulary at work to give your spoken word more color and pizzazz. Plus, I was a hired warrior. You get to go out and pick the mind of a government employee who was a cold-blooded killer and who is stupid enough to discuss those things with a pinko government bureaucrat."

"Are you rich?" Molyneaux asked.

"I am."

"Good. I'm meeting a friend for a drink; she might be charmed by that. You're welcome to join us. I buy, rich boy, so don't pig out."

"Even better," Alex said. "As I may have mentioned, I'm available."

Molyneaux stood with her hands on her hips and glared at him, then guffawed. "I gotta get my coat and put some stuff away. Clyde's in Georgetown. Thirty minutes."

Alex grinned that same grin, then turned and walked toward the uniformed secret service officer at the green steel desk by the exit. As Brooks had taught him, when you have the order, don't negotiate further. Discourse with a woman blocking the path to world peace was a potentially useful venture. Well, maybe not world peace, but the exigencies of the times might be well served. Unchecked, she well may be a problem for the team's plans. So many opportunities are missed by looking for only the sure thing.

ALEX WALKED NORTH ALONG Pennsylvania Avenue and then M Street, past Wisconsin Avenue in Georgetown, to the door of Clyde's, a well-known watering hole. He pushed gently through the crowd of well-dressed men and women, who were nearly spilling out the door. There were a dozen or more varied groups; there were six groups of just men, one of women, and the rest were mixed. More than one of them was gesticulating with a wine glass or a waving hand in the air to describe a point.

He'd always liked this place. It was dark wood and mirrors, with a long, brass-trimmed bar down the south wall and a foot rail of brass. The walls were hung with old prints and tapestries. A number of small tables were arranged along the north wall, all filled.

At the back of Clyde's, past a partition, were a number of small dining rooms. Someone had been thoughtful enough to provide some sound cushioning in the ceiling and on the walls, so a small table could talk comfortably and quietly.

He stepped up to the hostess stand behind a couple and waited for them to be seated. After a few moments, the perky hostess, wearing a gray polo shirt with the Georgetown bulldog printed over the shirt pocket, said, "Hi. Reservation?"

Alex smiled at her and hung both hands over the top edge of the hostess stand. He watched her stare at the expanse of them, with their gnarled fingers, wide wrists, and distended veins sticking incongruously from crisp white French cuffs with silver eagle cuff links, at once delicate and patriotic.

"I don't know about reservations," he said quietly. "'Molyneaux,' maybe for two. We'd like to make it for three."

She frowned and began typing and looking at her reservations screen. "I have a reservation for a Molyneaux on the wait list. It may be a while."

"I've made it harder for you by changing it from two to three. But maybe three is easier."

The left hand hanging from the edge of the hostess stand shifted, and the big numerals on the corner of a twenty-dollar bill peeked out between the thumb and forefinger almost magically.

She looked up at him, then back at the twenty. "I don't know," she said and looked around at the crowd, then back at Alex.

Alex glanced at his right hand where the corner of a fifty appeared. His friend and tutor, Tang, had a thing about finger dexterity. He thought the illusions of a magician were useful, if practiced, and healthy for the hands of some. Hands were Cooch's secret weapon; they could be so much more than a blunt-force instrument. He liked to keep them supple.

"Maybe something in the back," the hostess said.

"That would be marvelous," Alex said as he tucked the fifty beneath her ledger.

"What is your name?" she asked with her pen poised. After a moment's hesitation, he said, "Just write 'Cooch.' You have the women's names."

She nearly giggled as she led the way. As with women named Gay, Alex's nickname had become something of a joke over the past several years.

In a small room with tables and decor faintly reminiscent of New Orleans's French Quarter with green wrought iron abundant on table legs and chairs, Alex now watched Molyneaux and another woman, older with a wool wrap and a plaid scarf thrown around her neck, walk through the entry behind the hostess.

He stood as they sat down, one on either side of him. As the hostess walked away, Molyneaux turned to him and said, "I understand that you canceled my reservation and made it for three, rather than two. Then you jump the line for tables somehow, and we now have a table. You may be the most infuriating man I've ever met."

Alex turned to the other woman and said, "Hi, I'm Alex Cuchulain. Thanks for including a lonely Marine in your group tonight."

"Oh, screw you, Cuchulain," Molyneaux said. "How the hell did you get this table?"

"I'm rich. I thought that's why you invited me, so I could ease your path without the burden of receipts and congressional inquiries as to your leisure and entertainment practices."

Molyneaux threw her hands in the air. "I need a drink."

"I thought you'd never ask. Peddling my wares is thirsty work."

The other woman stuck out her hand and said, "I'm Brigitte Malley. I understand that you know something about education. Don't often find rich folks who do."

"Ain't it the truth?" Alex said. "Mostly we send our kids to private schools and cry porcelain tears as our teachers' unions destroy our public education system with their greed and their votes. I'm glad I'm not a public school teacher. Teaching seemed like a fun profession before the unions took over."

"Sheila hasn't shared how the two of you met," Malley said.

After a glance from Molyneaux, Alex said, "I was peddling my wares to Ms. Molyneaux today at the White House. I wasn't altogether successful."

Malley raised her eyebrows. "I've heard that getting an appointment with the president's chief of staff is difficult. Particularly for someone peddling their wares."

"I'm rich," Alex said. "And I have powerful friends. And you, Ms. Malley? What is it that brought you and the powerful, articulate Ms. Molyneaux together as friends? What is your involvement in education?"

"It's Dr. Malley or Brigitte. I teach at Georgetown. Education is one of my interests. Sheila and I once studied together briefly. And you, Mr. Cuchulain?" Malley said. "How do you spell that name? The hostess said you were Mr. Cooch."

Alex spelled the name and said, "It's pronounced Coo-hull-an. There was a moment's struggle up front with the spelling. Thus my conversation with the hostess Ms. Molyneaux mentioned."

Malley nodded. "Ah, Cuchulain, the legendary Celtic warrior. Are you a warrior?"

Alex grinned. "I am, he said modestly."

Malley raised her eyebrows again. "In your head or in your life?"

"Both, actually."

"Molyneaux, what the heck is this?" Malley said. "Where did you get this guy?"

Molyneaux giggled. "I told you. Isn't he awful? I spent a couple of hours today trying to right his twisted mind, but he's incorrigible."

"And rich. Don't forget rich," Alex added and wiggled his lumpy, bushy eyebrows at Molyneaux.

Three glasses of house chardonnay, three glasses of water, and a basket of chips showed up. A black folder with the check was left at the table near Alex. Alex pushed it near Molyneaux and took a big drink of water and a sip of his wine.

"I feel like I'm dealing with an unruly student," Malley said. "Let's reduce the problem, as they say. May I gather some basic information from you, Mr. Cuchulain?"

Alex grinned that almost boyish grin at her. "It's Alex," he said. "And you may. My life is an open book."

"Well then, give me a thumbnail of your life."

"Born and raised in Audley, South Carolina. Marine Corps at sixteen, discharged at twenty-five, college, work, graduate school, hedge fund. Took over maternal grandfather's business in Morocco. And here I sit."

"Combat?"

"I was never assigned to a combat unit in the Corps."

"Ah then, I believe then that you're what is termed a REMF."

"But I'm cute. That counts, and REMF is just another pejorative acronym that slights both the contrition and the contribution of those serving in the rear."

"Say what? Contrition?" Malley said, holding one hand up.

"Indeed," Alex said. "They are sorry to be in the rear but perform an important, even essential, role as best they can. Competent staff egos flourish in the garden of good combat support. They should flourish; anyone with a brain knows the importance of competent military staff. Machiavelli, von Clausewitz, and Jomini were staff officers, as was Eisenhower. Descartes, on the other hand, was a warrior."

"What's a REMF?" Molyneaux asked. "And what the hell are you talking about?"

"REMF is an acronym for Rear Echelon Member of the Forces, I believe," Alex said. "Or some such. It refers to those patriots laboring away from the violence in a war zone."

"What you are is insufferable," Malley said. "Tell me about your education. I'm a snob that way. Try to impress me, warrior man."

"Carnegie Mellon in electrical engineering and computer science, Oxford, a little business stuff at NYU."

"MBA?" she asked.

"Sadly, no. Too stressful," Alex said.

"College at Oxford?"

"The College of Oriental Studies."

Molyneaux interrupted with a snort. "He fancies himself an Islamic scholar. Don't get him started."

"Hold on here," Malley said. "He ain't a warrior, apparently. I want to delve a bit into what else he ain't. An Islamic scholar? I may have neglected to tell you, Mr. Cuchulain, that I teach modern philosophy. I'm quick. And I'm supposed to be baiting you, while Sheila giggles at your humiliation. You must have pissed her off today."

"It wasn't hard."

"She has that reputation," Malley said. "Now a tiny test for our budding Islamic scholar."

Alex held up his hands, palms out. "Hey, I never claimed to be a budding Islamic scholar." After a moment of mildly stunned silence, he said, "I'm the real deal."

"Uh-huh," Malley said, "Well then, which of the Islamic intellectuals do you most admire?"

"There are many, but I particularly admire Al-Farabi from the tenth century, I suppose, if one ignores medicine. He is held in high regard at Oxford; I share that regard."

Malley gazed at Cuchulain quizzically. "And why do you suppose that he is held in that high regard?"

"Al-Farabi wrote a marvelous treatise on Plato's *Republic* that ended with an Islamic spin. He claimed that the flaw in pagan teaching and thought is that it ignores God, Allah in this case. It was nicely done. Al-Farabi was known to Islamic scholars as the 'Second Teacher.' Aristotle was the 'First Teacher.' This was during the Dark Ages in the

West, I might add, when Europeans were slobbering around campfires and fighting over raw meat."

"What did Al-Farabi have to say that is of use today?" Malley said.

"Enough of this crap," Molyneaux said. "What I want to know is why, oh why, O Islamic scholar, do you Muslims hold female virginity in such high regard?"

"We fear comparison," Alex said.

Malley coughed a little chardonnay onto the tabletop as she laughed.

"Hold it," she said. "OK, Sheila, let's be civil now. This guy might be a keeper. It's shallow fishing for cocktail companions you've brought me 'til now. And I'm the resident cocktail widow."

Molyneaux frowned openly, while thinking this was the sort of fun conversation she once had at the Sorbonne.

"Give me the next thought level down on Al-Farabi," Malley said. "Something useful today. If you get this one right, I may keep you."

"Oh, joy," Alex said. "But I'll tell you what Al-Farabi said in his final synthesis. My opinion of why he said it and whether that's what he really said is a topic for another day. Arabic is a language of great nuance."

Malley shrugged and nodded. "Fair enough."

"Al-Farabi wrote that the isolated individual couldn't acquire all the inner perfections described by Allah by himself without the aid of others. He later said that to achieve those inner perfections, every man needs to stay in the neighborhood, each responsible for the other, more or less. That's a message of modern importance from a tenth century Arabic scholar. We Arabs must cease our petty conflicts and work, each with the other, to advance Islam in the eyes of Allah. Specifically, this schism between Sunnis and Shiites is an abomination in the eyes of Allah."

Malley clapped delightedly. "Bravo! You could teach this shit."

Alex smiled at Molyneaux and said, "I have."

"It's getting late, and I have work to do," Malley said. "We'll talk education another time perhaps. I'll let the two of you get to know each other. Call me the next time you're in town, sonny. I love good talk. You can buy, rich boy."

"Oh, no," Molyneaux said. "You're my ride. You're not going to leave me stranded here with Mephistopheles." She looked at the bill and dug in her purse for money.

"I think she likes me," Alex said. "It must be my money."

"Can you imagine the two of you together?" Malley said as she stood and pulled on her wrap. "Christ, I could sell tickets to listen."

"Not in my lifetime," Molyneaux said. "Puke."

"I'll walk you and the lovely, powerful, and articulate Ms. Molyneaux to your car," Alex said. "She can hit on me another time."

THEY LEFT THE RESTAURANT and turned south to walk to Thirty-First Street. There were two DC police cars with flashing lights pulled to the curb across the intersection. Four policemen were visibly frisking two young men who leaned against the wall of a bank, palms against the wall, their feet positioned well out from it. A policeman's black-shod foot was planted just inside each foot, ready to sweep it and the suspect's balance away if the need arose. There had been a recent rash of muggings in tony Northwest Washington and a consequent uproar among the merchants, students, and residents. The police were responding.

Malley's car was parked in a big lot beneath a fancy retail mall, located a few doors north of Clyde's on M Street and extending south behind it to Thirty-First Street. As they walked from Thirty-First Street into the belowground, covered parking, three young African-American men approached them. They were wearing dark hoodies and pants that sagged precariously around their buttocks. Cuffs were puddled around partially laced high-top sneakers.

"*Careful, laddie,*" Dain piped up from his subconscious.

Alex eased a step in front of the women as the men stopped and spread to form a pocket around them. The leader was perhaps eighteen years old and moved well. He held both hands up, palms out, to stop them.

"How about a few bucks for the poor, folks?" he said. "We needy."

A second man, a few years younger, bigger, and without the grace of the leader, stood just behind him and said, "Yeah, really needy, mutha fuckas." He had his right hand lightly tucked into the pocket of his hoodie.

The ever-watchful Dain piped up again. *"The second one, laddie . . . just behind. Probably not heavy enough for a gun but something. Right jumper pocket."*

Alex let his legs bend a little and shifted his weight.

"There's no need to be harsh, my good men," Alex said. "Here's a twenty. That should help fill your needs." A twenty-dollar bill appeared, extended between the fingers of his left hand, the arm extended slightly.

The sudden appearance of the bill in Alex's hand, apparently from nowhere, startled the leader. He looked into Alex's face and nearly recoiled. It was the flat look of an alley cat watching prey. No emotion, no fear. Nothing. Breath began to whistle through the man's nostrils.

"OK, my man. This is your lucky night," he said and took the twenty. He was ready to bolt.

"No fuckin' way, mutha fuckas," the second man said and pulled a knife from his pocket. He used his thumb and wrist to throw open and lock the blade as he stepped forward and pushed it at them. "Give us all of it. The watches, the jewels, the cash. Now!"

Alex's extended left hand snaked out to grab the hand holding the knife. The blade sticking out looked insignificant in front of the bulk of his hand. Alex dispatched a surge of energy from somewhere at the center of his lower stomach, his *ki* that was the repository of his power, to his hand in a fierce squeeze. He felt small bones break. His head turned slowly to look at the leader as the younger man screamed from the pain.

"You should go now," Alex said softly, and released the second man's hand. The leader turned and ran, the third man a step behind him. In a moment the second man followed, holding his right hand in the other, yipping with pain at each step.

"Goodness," Alex said. "They weren't very pleasant, were they?"

Molyneaux's eyes were wide as she clutched her purse to her chest. Malley was breathing hard; he could see her pulse thumping at the side of her neck, but she was under control. He looked at her as his face slowly transformed from lethality to civility, the eyes once again becoming friendly and benign.

"Warrior, huh?" Malley said. "SEAL? Delta?"

Alex shrugged. "CIA Special Ops as a serving Marine."

"Got it. You were never assigned to a Marine combat unit."

"I never was. Most don't figure the rest out. You must be a service widow."

"Yeah, he flew C-130s out of Hulbert mostly. He ran out of airspeed and altitude simultaneously one day a few thousand miles from here almost twenty years ago."

"Good bunch. I'm sorry."

Molyneaux blew out a long breath and said, "I'm shaking like a breeze-touched aspen. What just happened here?"

"Why, our new best friend here just saved us from an expensive and perhaps painful encounter with some of DC's finest citizens," Malley said.

"What the hell did you do, Cuchulain?" Molyneaux asked loudly.

"I applied the least amount of force necessary to protect our status quo and way of life, Ms. Molyneaux, just as I proposed earlier to you in a larger context. Granted, it was less important here, but still immediate."

Alex squatted quickly to pick up the knife from the ground where it had fallen. He looked at it and closed it, then pushed with his thumb to start the blade out of the handle, then threw it open with his wrist. It locked again.

"Nice knife. It's a William Henry. I wonder where our articulate assailant picked that up. Probably not at the shop in Santa Cruz."

He closed the knife and handed it to Molyneaux. "Here's a memento of our recent social encounter. Think of the circumstances around its use, or not, when you see it. I remind you that I first negotiated, then partially capitulated, then finally acted as needed before things got ugly. Further negotiations seemed useless and perhaps even hazardous."

"Give it a rest, asshole," Molyneaux said. "I need to get out of here."

Alex bumped lightly into Molyneaux as they walked and slipped the knife into her purse with a subtle motion of his hand. Malley dug in her purse and handed him a business card as she reached a beat-up Volvo.

"I think you've been dismissed," she said.

"Indeed I have," Alex said, turning. "And seldom has it been done with such grace and elegance. It's humbling to see an attractive grown woman grovel with gratitude. I think she likes me."

Molyneaux raised her middle finger to him and got in the car.

"Until next time, Dr. Malley. Good evening, Ms. Molyneaux."

Alex turned and walked toward the exit. It should be a pleasant walk back to the Hay-Adams.

Next stop New York for a few days, then back home to Tangier, with a stop in Spain. His frequent-flier miles should get him an upgrade to first class. Waste not, want not. Caitlin would fly first class regardless.

CHAPTER 5

THE FOLLOWING DAY NEW YORK

ALEX SAT AT A TABLE FOR FOUR in the rear of an Italian restaurant named Angelino's on Third Avenue in midtown Manhattan, waiting for Caitlin and their lunch date, Sarah Hamilton, a materials scientist at New York University. Before she came to work at NYU, Hamilton had gotten her PhD at the materials science lab at MIT. The topic of this year's Kufdani Capital annual ideas lecture was "The Societal Promise of Materials Science."

Sarah and Caitlin had been roommates at Princeton for a time and still saw each other frequently. Caitlin was a regular at Hamilton's NYU lab when problems were being mathematically formulated and were thus subject to Caitlin's magic in describing them concisely and elegantly. There was a touch of arrogance in her descriptions—the students liked that. After all, she was Caitlin O'Connor.

Alex had met Sarah several times with Caitlin at lunch. Most of their discussions had been about the past and about old friends. Hamilton was fairly recently divorced and with two kids newly in boarding school; the tangled emotions of that experience had taken a lot of lunch time to explain. She had a dry wit and was clearly very bright. Alex liked her.

Caitlin came through the restaurant, all blond and stunning and turning heads, chattering to Sarah behind her, who was a little shorter than Caitlin's five nine. Sarah was more square, easy on her feet, with a body more like a good soccer midfielder than a swimmer. She had brown hair pulled back and wore minimal makeup. Glasses hung around her neck on a thin gold chain.

Alex stood as the two women came to the table and sat on either side of him. As they took off their wraps and settled in, Caitlin said, "Christ, I could have been trampled out there if I hadn't been with my favorite jock, Square Shoulders here. These New Yorkers are nasty."

"Heck, then make them vanish," Hamilton said. "You can do everything else. Except swim well, maybe."

Hamilton had twice been an all-Ivy field hockey player at Princeton. Caitlin had failed to get all-Ivy honors at swimming there, despite three years as a varsity swimmer.

"Vanishing people is against the law," Caitlin said and stuck her tongue out at Hamilton. "If you hadn't taken so many blows to the head, you might have been a physics jock today."

"You're right. God save me from that," Hamilton said with a short laugh. "But I do worry some about the head bangs, given what's going on with concussion research in the National Football League. I had two or three in college. You ever had any concussions, Alex?"

"I've had a few," Alex said. "But I don't worry about things I can't change. I imagine NFL linebackers get hundreds of them over the course of a career. That's more than I've had by far."

"So, Alex," Sarah finally said, "I'm happy to give the materials science talk to Kufdani Capital but fill me in on the gestalt of what you're trying to do on behalf of the firm and why. What have you seen among our materials science magic that excites you and, again, why?"

"Kufdani Capital makes money from technology investing to reinvest the profits in our education endeavor. We're interested in what technology or product we can find as a paradigm breaker to make more money," Alex said. "An example is the firm in Utah that you mentioned earlier with the new nanocapacitor-loaded paint. That product could be huge in Africa and the Middle East. Almost every town of any size has a mosque; every mosque has a dome. If we start painting mosque domes in Islamic green or gold that happen to have a film of nanocapacitors within the paint, we have enabled a system for Internet connection nearly everywhere we choose without building communication towers in the cities. We could then do the city-to-city hop with satellites. That's a huge cost winner and has good social implications as well. We may make a profit while enabling the common good."

"Oh ho," Hamilton said. "I see a Kphone in your fantasy. Suddenly, everyone in the Middle East is connected and has access to a good phone that teaches, and maybe sneaks in some politics. Of course, knowing you, they only find out about the teaching part later. First, you make the Kphone essential and ubiquitous; then you expand its horizons and those of its users. I love that phone, by the way."

"Thanks for doing that Kphone video series on materials science careers," Caitlin said. "It's surprisingly popular."

"You're welcome," Sarah said. "I use it from time to time now. It's good to be able to point a talented student at the magic and the money of a materials science career. Computers are so yesterday."

"I certainly agree with that yesterday observation," Caitlin said, "but they're really handy for their memory and for their speed. It's just that computers have leapt from a role of innovation to the role of a tool kit for innovators. Emilie couldn't do what she does without enabling technology, but the innovation is fundamentally in predictive analysis. What that predictive analysis provides, in the form of my product, Emilie, is a foundation for innovation similar to what computers used to do. For example, we're doing education support by understanding the student more deeply and predicting, with high probability, the lesson support he or she needs to be successful."

"I think we've gotten off the track you queried, Sarah," Alex said. "You're right on the sequencing of the Kphone introduction; slow and steady is the key. Ask me something else."

"No need, I guess. I get it. Getting an enabled network out of a bucket of paint that someone else will apply, maintain, and protect is enough. Even to a geek like me, there's a profit pony there."

"There is," Alex said, "but step one is to make sure companies with ideas we like get funded and are decently managed. Kufdani Capital is good at that."

Hamilton looked at her watch. "Yikes! I have a postdoctoral seminar in an hour. We need to wrap this up. Fun lunch, though, but more for Caitlin and me than for you, I suspect."

"I like to listen to the two of you," Alex said. "We'll do more business another time or at least talk about it."

"Caitlin told me that you're a squash player," Sarah said. "If you're ever looking for a game, I'm your girl. Partners are hard to find around here."

"I'd love that. I'm not getting much exercise lately," Alex said. "Let me know when you want to play."

"How about tomorrow morning? I belong to a club with courts in the basement of my building. There are nice locker rooms with lockable lockers for your street clothes. We could have breakfast afterward and talk a bit. I have a fairly light day tomorrow until the Kufdani meeting at two."

Hamilton took a pen and business card from her purse and scribbled on it. "Seven o'clock. Here's the address. I'll leave your name at the check-in. There are exercise machines if you want to come early, but I'll see you at seven. They open at five thirty."

"I'll see you then," Alex said.

"Don't expect any mercy, muscle man. I like kicking executive ass."

Alex grinned and picked up the folder with the restaurant bill. "None expected, none given; it's a deal. Thanks for the time today."

"I'm going to bolt with Sarah," Caitlin said. "I'd like to sit in on her seminar. It's a math thing, and she thinks I may have something to offer, if only star power. I'll see you tonight at Bouchon Bistro with the team. Seven thirty."

The two women walked, still talking, through the restaurant and out the door. Alex paid the tab and stood. A few hours at Kufdani Capital of talking to the CEO and the senior people would be pleasant. He'd spent a few days there with the younger, more junior people several months before in preparation for this annual meeting.

THE HUDSONIC ATHLETIC CLUB was clean, bright, and underground, near Columbus Circle on Manhattan's West Side. Even at six thirty in the morning, young people were seated near the juice bar talking, with small white towels draped around their sweaty necks.

Alex checked in and was shown to the men's locker room, where wood-textured lockers were numbered side by side. Their locks were self-service, with a four-digit code of the user's choice that was erased with each unlocking.

Hamilton ended up winning, three games to two.

They walked from the squash court to the lobby and its juice bar. A few minutes later, they were sitting at a small table drinking freshly squeezed carrot juice.

Hamilton gazed at him as she set down her plastic juice glass. "Are you and Caitlin an item?"

"I guess not, ah . . . a personal item very often. We're close in business."

"Do you see women, ah . . . personally, other than Caitlin?"

"I do, but seldom—more because of availability and convenience than anything else. Take you for example. You're a hard body— smart, single, and sexy. I thought about trying to snuggle up a bit to check the temperature."

Hamilton smiled. "And?"

"And I decided that you and Caitlin are close enough that it might piss her off if we got involved a bit or more. I can't afford that. Her contributions are vital to what I do—to my life's work that we've discussed several times. Without Caitlin's Emilie, we would be underfunded and underperforming in education."

"Interesting," Hamilton said. "Did it occur to you that I would check with Caitlin before I saw anything of you, given that neither she nor I is looking for a spouse?"

Alex grinned a boyish, almost mischievous, look. It transformed his face. "It didn't occur to me. Did you check?"

Sarah smiled. "I did."

"And?"

"She had no objection and even offered procedural advice. She's kinky that way."

"Did she now? Guess it's OK then for me to hit on you a little."

"A bit late for that, isn't it?" Hamilton said. "I think I just backed into you, hitting hard."

"Let's plan to have lunch. Maybe breakfast," Alex said.

"I live in this building. Why not shower at my place? I'll do breakfast, then we'll figure out the rest of the day."

"What a marvelous idea," Alex said.

In a short time, the elevator stopped after a few moments, and the door opened. They walked down a softly lit hall and entered one of four apartments on the sixteenth floor. The foyer was adjacent to the living room with a kitchen just beyond. Sarah pointed left and said, "There's a spare bedroom over there. Drop your stuff and come back to the kitchen."

Alex went into a small room with a queen-size bed and a small shower and bath. It was impersonal, with no evidence of teenage visitors. He dropped his gym bag and hung his street clothes in the small closet. He then walked back across the living space to the kitchen and sat at a small table beside a Viking gas stove in front of a window with white wooden slatted blinds. Hamilton walked in and poured a glass of water from a bottle in the refrigerator, then another. She handed one to him.

"I'm going to get out of these sweaty things and jump in the shower," Sarah said. "Since there's a water shortage, you may want to help me conserve." She grinned, then turned and walked back into the master bedroom.

Alex heard the shower start. He walked into her bedroom and saw her sweaty clothes in a pile on the floor. He stood on one foot, then the other, to get rid of his sneakers and socks. His wet gym clothes joined hers on the floor in a pile. He took a half step toward the sound of running water, then stopped, stepped back, and bent at the waist to fold his sweaty clothes, then hers. The shoes went side by side evenly against the wall.

In the shower Sarah stood with her back to Alex, the water cascading down her back. Alex stepped into the shower, then soaped his hands. He stepped up behind her, then pulled her gently against him. He began to soap her thoroughly. He started at Hamilton's neck, then moved to her shoulders, kneading the exercise-induced lactic acid from the deltoids. Her lats were next. Fifteen minutes later he was at her waist, working on her hip flexors. She took his wrists and moved his hands up.

Sarah finally turned and pressed her soapy body against his. They kissed for the first time. Her mouth was open and her tongue active.

As the kiss deepened, she took some soap from her body and reached for him.

"Goodness, gracious," she said. "All for me?"

"Uh-huh," Alex said. "We can stop anytime you choose."

"I've had two kids—Lamaze. It will be fine. Girth is a good thing, taken slowly. Caitlin tells me you know about slow. Surprise me."

Alex flexed his legs to stoop and put his arms beneath her thighs, then lifted her and put her back against the shower wall.

After a few more kisses, she said, "You're just going to hold me up in the air against the wall?"

"Uh-huh," he said. "Your move."

"Aha."

She grinned around the kiss and reached. After a bit of trial and error, she settled down and brought her hand to his neck and smoothed the hair from his eyes.

"And now?" she said.

Alex flexed his arms a little, curling her up a few inches and then down.

"Now you get to decide the optimum amount of movement," he said. "For as long as I can hold out."

"My word. That was certainly a good start," she whispered in his ear as the water pounded over them. "A little more would be nice and a little bounce."

A few minutes later, she whispered in his ear, "Right there! That's perfect." She panted in his ear. "Oh my God. It's been so damned long."

LATER THEY STOOD OUTSIDE the shower, drying themselves. Hamilton glanced down at him. "It somehow sticks out at me that you seem to have missed some of the passion."

"The morning is young," he said, smiling. "And I'm an optimist."

"That was quite a sensation, there against the shower wall. Just how often did you curl my 140 pounds in there?"

"It was a lot less than 140 pounds with your back against the wall, taking some of the weight. I curled things more than a few times, I suppose; but it was indeed my pleasure."

Sarah giggled. "Caitlin didn't tell me about that experience. It's a fabulous first. Do you have a scientific name for it?"

"A colleague decided some time ago that it should be called the 'Cooch Curl.' She liked the double entendre."

"Cooch Curl it is then," Sarah said with a grin. "Cooch Stretch doesn't alliterate. Do you have any more tricks?"

"Well, you bring out the best in me. We'll see. What advice did Caitlin give you?"

Hamilton grinned lazily. "Let me see if I can recall some of the specifics," she said. "Caitlin said that if you had a single strong point, it was patience. She also mentioned that you were quite versatile and thoughtful. I guess I've seen versatile already today."

"It's always comforting to know that your lovers have clinical discussions about your sexual performance."

"Uh-huh. You're doing well thus far; don't give up now with the midterm and final exam in sight. In a fit of optimism, I turned down the bed earlier. I also put some music in the player. I'm going to go do girl things. Turn it on and crawl in."

THE MIDMORNING SUN SHONE through the slatted blinds as Alex finished the scrambled eggs, fluffy with herbs and shaved Asiago cheese, Sarah had prepared. He sat in a T-shirt and boxer shorts at the kitchen table, his hair still damp from his second shower.

Sarah sat across the table in a white terry cloth robe, sipping her coffee.

"I can't recall ever hitting on a man so directly," she said. "You'll do, though. Well done, my good man."

"Does that mean we can have a semiregular squash game? That would be super."

"Super? Super? I can't recall, like, an adult, like, using that word," Hamilton said, smiling, "but it would indeed be super, so yes. I'm going to be sore all over from slamming into you on the squash court just to get a few extra points, but the ultimate result was indeed, ah, super. Do you happen to scuba dive?"

"I do," Alex said.

"Let's consider that sport as a somewhat less competitive and painful endeavor sometime. I don't know how much you weigh, but running into you is like running into a tree."

Alex grinned. "Super. 'It will let us branch out,' the tree said. Let's keep it in mind."

Sarah gazed at him over the Irish-green rim at the top of her white ceramic mug. "That might be too much togetherness, though. I'm going to have to think about it. This little encounter of ours was a test run for me. I was field-testing Catlin's feminine wisdom."

Alex shrugged and smiled. "Why wouldn't you? Seems prudent to me."

"You're supposed to be offended that I used you."

"Aha," Alex said. "Why?"

"Why, indeed?" she said. "You're a bit of a strange man; you're a little too easy to trust. You're a little too easygoing. You're different to the point that I'm mildly uncomfortable with any relationship beyond the occasional extended and rewarding squash match, at least until I get to know you better. Tell me more about Alex. Tell me about the significant others who haven't worked out. Who do you have on the hook right now, waiting to hear what you're going to do?"

"Are you thinking about the two of us beyond the obvious? On a path to get serious?"

"God, no," Sarah said. "Perish the thought. I'm not over the pain of the last one and not yet thinking about the next one, and I'm certainly not leaving my kids to move to Tangier to live with some pony-peckered Arab. I just want to know someone a tad better than I know you before I spend two or three days in a shack in a beach village with him, screwing his brains out after diving all day."

"There's no one," Alex said. "There has never been anyone. I thought I was starting down that road with Caitlin, but she didn't like that idea."

"Marriage and babies and stuff? With Caitlin? Jeez, Alex."

"Yeah, what *was* I thinking?" he said. "For me, it was more about monogamy and commitment than babies and marriage, at least early on. For her it was just a nonstarter. She didn't bother with making rejection palatable."

She again picked up her coffee mug. She sipped and put it back on the green woven place mat and smiled.

"Subtlety is a tool Caitlin seldom uses," Hamilton said. "She wouldn't want you to misunderstand. Sarcasm, on the other hand, in all its ugly, edgy little flavors and nuance is something she does spectacularly well. Still, she kept you around."

"Yeah, thank God. Her work is essential to our education efforts. In her spare time, she uses me to scratch her horny itches."

"You poor baby. There are more than a few guys who would sign up for that duty. My ex was one of them, I think. Or he tried. She wasn't in exclusive company, though."

"Huh. Caitlin is more loyal to her friends than one would guess, I suppose," Alex said. "And I'm handy fairly often."

"And you are one great, multifaceted lover. I suppose you know that by now. Good lovers are hard to find these days. I guess they are always hard to find but more so as I age. Fewer men apply, even as I get pickier. My ex was good in bed. That's one of the reasons I married him, but that charm faded for him after the kids came along and he found newer models, tightly constructed, to appreciate his skills. Bingo. Single mom."

"Multifaceted, huh? That must be a Princeton description. I've had to overcome my shortcomings, you might say, but I'm a little surprised that Caitlin passed me over to you for a test ride."

Sarah laughed. "She's generous that way. She even gave you references."

Alex rolled his eyes and laughed. "OK, now you have to tell me. I didn't know about that."

Hamilton leaned back in her chair and stretched her arms over her head.

"First, she had to convince me that having a sexual relationship, just for the sex, with a man you don't know well can be a worthwhile endeavor," she said. "Caitlin makes a good case that emotional attachment just gets in the way of a good orgasm, particularly if such attachment is an unwelcome intruder.

"The fact that we've been together in meetings several times with Caitlin gave me a good vibe about you—but, still—you know. She just said she had field-tested several lovers for suitability, but you were a good one—a big, athletic man who knew that speed was the bane of fulfillment. I thought she was talking about your height and weight, but lo and behold I look down, and there's a one-eyed, two hander staring at me in the shower. That's a little scary at first."

Alex grinned again. "Yeah, I know. The Cooch Curl was created to help deal with that."

"Cooch Curl—I'll remember that. I'm not sure I know anyone else who has the arms to do that. Your biceps were like blue-veined cantaloupes when we finished. Or at least when *I* finished. Caitlin also told me to download that *Cool* album I was playing," she said. "I didn't know I liked Bob James and Earl Klugh that much."

"Caitlin, in her everlasting quest for precision in her life, calls it 'the oral artistry of the background beat,'" Alex said quietly. "It's the background beat as they run through the jazz. It's always nice to have a distraction for your focus on an intricate and complex journey like that. When you finally notice where you are, upon subtle but building insistence, the pleasure's often a little more intense. Good for me, good for you. I hope you enjoyed it."

"You couldn't tell?"

"I thought you were just having bad dreams and clenching your jaw from time to time."

"Of course you did. I was worried about ripping your ears off."

"Always look for the guy with the pistol-grip ears. At least you didn't say Gee and Haw like the farm girls do."

"I'll remember that. I'm actually getting horny again. I really must remember to send Caitlin roses."

"Maybe you'll invite me back when I'm in town, before we get around to the scuba trip, if we do."

"Oh, yeah, Mr. Ed. I'll invite you back. If you could make that thing vibrate, you could be on *Oprah* and *American Idol*. You're a single mom's dream."

"Uh-huh." Alex grinned. "I swell well, I don't tell, and I'm grateful as hell."

"Enough already," Sarah said. "Let's talk a little more about you."

"What's to talk about? I'm not very complicated. I mostly just work."

Sarah shrugged. "Your work seems to be going fine. I don't want to talk about that. This talk is different. It's about this void in your life. No mate, no kids, no serious relationship ever. That doesn't bother you?"

Alex leaned back in his kitchen chair, sighed, and gazed blankly at the ceiling. "It bothers me a lot, and it bothers me often. It's part of the topic two or three nights a week at three in the morning, when I wake up sweating and I have to deal with my subconscious. There's no place to hide when you're alone and wide awake in bed at oh three hundred hours. It has to do with my commitment to this Muslim education thing and doubts about making it work. I end up seeing myself in my sixties with no kids, no mate, and the education thing failing. A life wasted by taking too much on, to the exclusion of other important life things. It's scary."

"You obviously decide each morning to continue down the path you're on," she said. "You were some kind of commando, Caitlin told me. You have a fascinating set of scars on you. Does that come back to haunt you at night? The fear, the killing?"

"There's a story behind every stitch but no," Alex said with a smile. "I was a serving Marine for over eight years, most of the time assigned to the CIA Special Ops unit. I got a lot of shrink time back then and learned to deal with all that to the point that I don't think about regrets. I learned to use personal fear to my advantage and to view the killing as part of the job."

"Eight years? How did they keep you for eight years? That seems a bit above and beyond."

"I liked it, maybe loved it, for a while. I wanted to be there. It's still what I do better than almost anyone; I like that. When I was twenty-five, I left the Marine Corps and went to Carnegie Mellon for electrical engineering and computer science degrees. Until then, the CIA gave me a life where I could be good at what I did and still have time to sit around and think. I was valued. People paid attention to me and sent me to school and training. I learned a lot about stuff and about myself."

"You went there when you were seventeen years old? What about high school? What about your parents?"

"My father was a Marine, a legend in the Corps. He had the Medal of Honor from an event in Vietnam and a wheelchair that came with the Medal. We lived in South Carolina on his disability pay and fifty bucks a month for the Medal, plus what Mom got for teaching math at the community college. I got into some pretty bad trouble with the local law, and Dad called a friend in Washington to bail me out of the problem. Part of that bailout was me enlisting in the Corps. A friend of my father ran the CIA Special Ops unit and many serving warriors are detailed to the CIA, so things just happened from there. It was a good eight years. Dad died a few years ago."

"Your mother? Siblings?"

"Mom lives in Spain, near Gibraltar, with a sister. She's Bedouin; I inherited Kufdani Industries from her father. She married my dad while he was stationed at a US naval base in Spain, and she was teaching there. I have one sister, who teaches eighth-grade math in New Jersey. I see her a few times a year, but her husband isn't crazy about me being around their kids. Hard to believe, huh?"

"Hard to imagine," Hamilton said. "There's nothing intimidating about you. You're short, skinny, and stupid. You're afraid of your own shadow. You're a failure in life and a lousy lay, needledick."

"Yeah," Alex said. "I'm trying to cope."

CHAPTER 6

MANHATTAN
UPPER EAST SIDE

BROOKS, LUANN, CAITLIN, AND Alex walked up several flights of stairs to the top-floor study of Elliot's brownstone, a long-held home away from home. The building seemed small from the street, but was deep and had four floors and a basement. The study was a dark-paneled room with windows on two sides overlooking the neighborhood. There were four maroon leather easy chairs positioned around a small table.

A middle-aged man stood erect by a wall, his right hand clasping the stump of the left in front of him from which protruded a stainless steel prosthesis that looked like a lobster's claw. He wore a white shirt, dark trousers, sensible shoes, and a gray apron with a subdued logo of the Navy SEALs embroidered high on the left chest. The stippled walnut grip of a compact Kimber .45-caliber pistol peeked above the waistband just behind his right hip.

"Hey, Cooch," he said. His accent declared him to be a New Yorker from one of the five boroughs.

"Hey, Jimmie," Alex said. "How's it hanging?"

"Can't complain," Jimmie said. "'I haven't had to kill anyone today,' like the ugly cowboy guy said in the movie with Billy Crystal. Life's pretty good, actually."

Jimmie turned to Brooks. "Are youse having cigars tonight?"

"Let's ask the ladies. Caitlin?"

"A cigar," Caitlin mused. "Let's see; they stink, they're expensive, and they are bad for your health. If I can't have a joint, I'll have a cigar. LuAnn?"

"I'll skip the joint, but a cigar sounds just fine. Daddy and I smoke them from time to time and there's cognac over there as an accompaniment."

Jimmie turned to a large wooden humidor on the sideboard, raised the lid, and lifted the box. Various lengths and thicknesses of cigars lay within it. He turned to LuAnn, who studied the selection then pointed to a medium-sized cigar in the middle of the box.

"A Montecristo Number Three. I haven't seen one of those for a while, maybe because they're illegal. That's for me."

"If it's good enough for LuAnn, it's good enough for me," Caitlin said. "I'll have one too."

Jimmie turned back to the sideboard and lowered the box, then picked up a brass end cutter and snipped the ends from two cigars. He plucked a large kitchen match from a chrome cylinder by the humidor and struck it, then began to warm the cigar with the flame as he turned it to avoid scorching its outer wrapper. After a few moments, he blew out the match and struck another, then handed a warmed cigar to LuAnn. She held it to her mouth, while Jimmie put a flame to its end. As she drew on the cigar, she turned it slowly. In a moment there was an even coal at the end of the cigar, burning smoothly. Jimmie repeated the lighting ritual with Caitlin as Brooks took drink orders.

On the bar was an empty bottle of 1963 Dow's vintage port; its contents had been decanted into a wide crystal bottle standing beside it. There was a half bottle of 1990 sauterne, Chateau d'Yquem, opened and ready on the bar beside the port, with appropriately sized and shaped Riedel glasses standing beside them. Brandy and an assortment of light and dark whiskeys stood ready against the bar wall in thick, stoppered crystal decanters. Silver name tags were draped on thin chains over each bottle's shoulders, lest a sniff didn't disclose its contents. A rack of various crystal glasses stood to one side, waiting.

"Here we are for the umpteenth session of the Velvet Salon," Brooks said as he sat. "Our group has expanded by 25 percent with the addition of the love of my life, LuAnn Clemens."

Caitlin made a slight, silent motion of hand clapping. LuAnn smiled and nodded.

"Here is where we find out what is going on in each other's head and discuss said goings-on," Elliot went on. "It's all on the path to figuring out how our little group of five can change the world, or at least be an active catalyst to that end.

"Our absent member, Jerome Masterson, has declined our invitation once again, to stay in Morocco and prepare for Iran's attempts to end life there as we know it. Jerome believes that a Shiite attack on Kufdani in Tangier is inevitable. Whenever it happens, it won't be pretty for them with Jerome planning the defense. His rejection was accompanied by words to make it easier on us. It was something profound like, 'You people can sit around and get shit faced while you pretend that you've solving the problems of the world and sucking down some sort of legal or illegal, foul-tasting smoke. We figured out what to do a long time ago. Now it's time to get off our dead asses and do it.'"

"Hear, hear," Alex said.

"How charming," LuAnn said with a grin. "Eloquent."

"That's my Jerome," Alex said.

"So, to the topics of the day and their nuance," Elliot said. "How did it go with Molyneaux and Roberts?"

"A little worse than we thought it would," Alex said. "The president was basically working a salon-type discussion between me and Molyneaux, with him as moderator. Molyneaux is coming down hard and negatively on dealing violently with Iran. She has an interesting argument."

"She's right?" LuAnn said.

"I'm convinced she's wrong, but who knows?" Alex said. "We'll know more in twenty years."

"Did she discuss any triggers from Iran for an all-out war, like launching a nuke?" Brooks asked. "We could use that."

"Nope," Alex said. "It may not have occurred to her, but I suspect she views that kind of thing as merely tactics. She wants to argue national policy and doing what is right."

"There you go. We want the same thing," Elliot said. "And then there is the matter of votes and public perception. She wants to protect the president's legacy. The shorter view dominates her thinking."

"That seems about right to me," Alex said. "We have defined the battlefield between her and us on this one. The president is the referee and ultimate decision maker. He's working us."

"As well he should," Brooks said. "He's the commander in chief, facing what we claim to be an existential threat. Roberts should use every good mind available to help him with the decision. He has no doubt consulted others for opinions."

"Agreed," Alex said. "You've done your own consulting and research. You also have the best and most informed mind among us to synthesize the theses and antitheses playing out as they swirl around Armageddon. We're support on this one. We'll carry your water when we need to, as I did today, but we need to win this one with the president. You have the intellectual conn."

"Yeah, I agree on being a support troop," Caitlin said. "I can't reduce this kind of complex problem like Brooks does, and I'm a smart fucker. It just doesn't compute. There are too many dependent variables, and too much bullshit. But I like where he ends up."

"I can't do it as well as he can, either," LuAnn said. "That's why I keep him around."

"Full stop, segue," LuAnn said. "Brooks said you had cocktails with Roberts's chief of staff. Tell us about that. I heard she's a ballbuster."

"She is that. But I sort of like her," Alex said. "Seems like a pet cobra. Cute, moves well, but deadly."

"Aha," Caitlin said. "Did you fuck her?"

"Caitlin!" LuAnn said. "Behave."

"It's OK, LuAnn," Alex said. "I assure you that Caitlin's interest is purely prurient. She's kinky that way."

O'Connor raised her middle finger to him. "I'm kinky in general, asshole, as you well know. Lucky you, among others."

"And articulate you are," Alex said. "Molyneaux, the chief of staff, had a cocktail date with a friend, a Georgetown professor, late forties/early fifties maybe, walks well, good body. Her name is Brigitte Malley. I think Molyneaux invited me along so I could get my arrogant, intellectual ass handed to me by Malley in critical conversation. Molyneaux was unhappy with my arguments during our time with the president."

"Go figure. Why bother with the cocktails?" LuAnn said. "You had your say."

"Molyneaux is the voice of the opposition in dealing with the Iran threat," Brooks said. "The better we know her, the better our chances of being successful in dealing with her and perhaps even bringing her to our view of things."

"She's a Voltaire junkie," Alex said. "And a good one."

"Yeah, I read her paper," Elliot said. "She has a good mind."

"What's with the Voltaire argument?" LuAnn said. "He's just one of many back then, right?"

"Voltaire might be the smartest of them," Brooks said. "At least when you read the reviews."

"They had reviews back then?" LuAnn said. "Who would take the time to handwrite such a thing?"

"Reviews back then were often essays concerning the author's thinking and style," Brooks said, "rather than specifically about some piece of his work. One essay sticks out in my mind. It was a short and sappy, blubbering piece of sycophancy. There was superlative after superlative, ending with the word *perfect*."

"OK, tell me," LuAnn said. "What suck-up wrote this piece that attracted you so?"

"Goethe," Brooks said.

"Aha," LuAnn said.

"Aha, indeed," Elliot said. "Comments like that from a towering intellect make one search out Voltaire."

"I've read a bit of Voltaire's stuff," Caitlin said. "I tire of the endless nuance, but his mistress, Emilie du Chatelet, is my idol, so I suffered through some of it. I work by reducing problems to their smallest solvable elements; Voltaire doesn't lend himself to that."

"Thus the name of your product—Emilie?" LuAnn said.

"Yeah," O'Connor replied. "Emilie fucked her way across Europe with her boyfriend, Voltaire, while her husband, a count, was off fighting one noble battle after the other. In her spare time, with a sixth-grade education, she translated Isaac Newton's mathematics for the masses."

"Quite a girl," Alex said. "But how Molyneaux uses the arguments of Voltaire to foil us is the issue of the day."

"Foil us?" LuAnn said with a smile. "Oh, curses on that dastardly soul."

"I'm getting bored," Caitlin said. "What about the Voltaire lady and her friend at Clyde's?"

"The other one, Malley, is an air force widow. I like her. I'll look her up when I am next in Washington. And no, Caitlin, I don't plan to fuck her either. I might even fix her up with Mac."

"Wow," Brooks said. "She's that good?"

Alex shrugged. "I liked her quite a bit; you would too. Her guy flew 130s out of Hulbert."

"I love those guys," Elliot said. "She was likely married to a warrior."

"Mac is one of those—a warrior," Alex said. "That's one reason that he ran the Farm for twenty years. It's slim pickings for women out there for Mac, given his job. Worse, or maybe better, he's very polite and very picky about his companions. There have been several former first ladies who have allowed Mac to escort them to events, because he can hold his own anywhere and be a decorated Marine colonel or a savvy, articulate conversationalist. It's worth a dinner and some talk to see if there's a fit. Mac did his graduate work at Georgetown. He might know her. She might even be useful to us."

Caitlin grinned and said, "You just couldn't let that 'useful to us' tail gunner alone, could you?"

"I think it's best if we let Mac's love life rest for now," Brooks said. "He's a busy man. Maybe we'll fix him up when this Iran mess is over."

Alex smiled. "Yeah, I'm just reminding everyone how important this whole thing is."

"You don't think we know?" LuAnn said.

"I imagine you're like me, considering what stays in the front of my mind. Important stuff gets crowded out by the everyday flow of being. It will slip out of my consciousness unless goosed. So, on that bet, I talk out loud when I am talking to myself."

Caitlin laughed. "So, goose you, goose me. Don't really care if you don't like it."

Alex leaned back, took up his port glass, and raised it. She did the same with her half-empty glass of sauterne.

"God, do they do this shit all the time?" LuAnn said to Brooks. "Just like we do, sort of?"

"Pretty much but only here in the Velvet Salon," he said. "We all do it. You will too, I imagine."

"To the topic at hand," Brooks said as he turned to look at Alex. "Any progress with figuring out how to get to Molyneaux and have her see things more the way we do?"

"Maybe," Alex said. "I got lucky. We got jumped by a trio of hoods on the way from Clyde's to the parking lot to get Malley's car. I had to break a kid's knife hand. While Molyneaux was dealing with her adrenaline rush, I told her that the situation was a real-world illustration of the utility of applying the appropriate amount of violence in an appropriate situation to maintain the status quo and liberal civility."

"And she said?"

Alex laughed. "Something rude. But the encounter and its resolution may have struck a chord with Molyneaux, emblazoned in her memory by fear."

"OK, I got it," LuAnn said. "It's all about making the president's advisors, and thus the president, buy into your view on the Iran situation, as long as it takes you to do that and as tedious as it may become. This really doesn't have anything to do directly with education and the Enlightenment ideas. It's about getting Iran out of the way of all of that and how."

"Pretty much," Brooks said. "We can't continue our education progress if there are nukes going off all over the place. Nukes would ruin the educational ambience. We're looking to Alex to lead the way in solving the little nuclear problem the Iranians have so cruelly put in our path to reforming education in the Middle East. Alex and I disagree sometimes on solutions to be implemented and how. This will be his show."

"Aha, conflict," LuAnn said. "Disagreement. Strife among us."

"Indeed," Brooks said. "It's mostly in a discussion of tactics in the evolving Iran situation where we disagree."

"Uh-huh," Alex said. "We know where and what the problem is. We use whatever we must to solve it. Lies, deception, excessive force are all good tools, if needed. This is the gospel according to Jerome Masterson, honed while bullets flew overhead."

"Alex is more a student of Machiavelli than Plato," Elliot said. "He is a student of the politics and application of power."

"A useful set of skills and thinking just now," Alex said. "Remember what Hitler said after World War II."

"What was that?" LuAnn said.

Alex grinned. "'Next time, no more Mr. Nice Guy.'"

"Boo!" Caitlin and LuAnn said in chorus.

"Enough," Elliot said. "It's getting late, and LuAnn and I have a full day at Kufdani Capital tomorrow, as do you."

"I'm looking forward to tomorrow," LuAnn said as she stood. "I've been busting my ass to make money for Kufdani Capital to fund our educational fantasy. Now I get to see a little more of what makes Kufi run."

Manhattan

West Side

In the seventeenth floor of an office building just off Forty-Second Street in Manhattan, Kufdani Capital housed fifty-three employees, mostly business analysts with an MBA from a good school with hopes of making a reputation in the lucrative investment-management business. Kufdani paid relatively high salaries rather than share its incentive fees, as many successful firms did. But its reputation was good and its management fair, combined with a national reputation for investment thoroughness and excellence. There was a surprisingly large number of former military officers among the analysts. Women were overrepresented as well.

The workers were on a single floor. There was an open working area with partitions between desks and a few small conference rooms scattered against the walls. On one end was a window-walled large conference room with a long table and five chairs, plus a spot without seating. A "bragging" wall had been created on the long wall across from the windows. On it were announcements of investments made by Kufdani Capital, mergers and acquisitions of complementary companies, and sales of Kufdani investment companies to others. Initial public offerings of Kufdani companies were featured prominently.

At each annual meeting, the finances and performance of Kufdani

Capital were reviewed, investing strategy going forward was discussed, and a speaker was hired to present new technology that was deemed likely to affect future investment decisions.

For the first time, there would be a short review of the four companies LuAnn Clemens actively supervised on behalf of Kufdani Capital. Caitlin O'Connor would give her annual status update on the direction and capabilities of the Emilie product's technology.

Around the table, with Kphones plugged into computers in front of them, were Alejandro Mohammed Cuchulain; Brooks F. T. Elliot IV; Dr. Caitlin O'Connor; LuAnn Clemens; Kufdani Capital's managing partner, Richard Fellini; and the guest speaker, Dr. Sarah Hamilton of the NYU Materials Science Laboratory. A large screen had dropped from the ceiling at one end of the room to be used for presentation graphics, if needed.

The investment emphasis of Kufdani Capital was technology, with a bias for products and services valued by the Department of Defense, the Department of Homeland Security, and the US intelligence community. Richard Fellini, the managing partner, was an Annapolis graduate with an MBA from the Sloan School of Management at MIT, all on the government's nickel. He was also a former Marine officer who lost both legs just below the knee in Iraq due to a buried IED, an improvised explosive device, during a patrol there. A number of severely wounded men and women were among the Kufdani employees. Their heads worked fine, their bodies not so much.

In the Kufdani conference room, Caitlin glowingly introduced Sarah Hamilton. There was a short discussion about the firm's interest in materials science, with the capacitor-laden paint as an example. Hamilton went further as she speculated on paint containing the equivalent of solar cells or photovoltaics.

"We may be painting solar cells onto our houses soon from paint bought online," she said. "If we can model it, we can make it. Tesla's factory in Fresno, California, is a stunning example of pairing the power of robotics with new materials and ideas. If you haven't seen that promo flick on YouTube, you should."

Hamilton's presentation was succinct and precise. She built a case, slide by slide, on the big screen at the end of the room, projected by her Kphone, that any future investment tsunami was more likely on the side of materials science against computing technology as the next big thing; computers and software would be in a support role. At the end of her presentation, there was a vigorous question-and-answer session.

As she stood and gathered her few papers and her purse, she said, "There it is, folks. You do the finance; we do the ideas. It was fun. Thanks."

She left the room behind applause.

"OK, folks," Fellini said. "Let's take a twenty-five minute nature break."

He looked at the assembled group and nodded to the group of three men and a woman, who had been invited as a result of their materials-science investment mission. They were assembling their various equipment, preparing to leave the room.

Fellini pushed his wheelchair back from the table. "It takes some of us longer for a nature break than it used to."

When they reassembled after a half hour, there were just the principals. LuAnn looked around the room and said, "I love all of this new, groundbreaking technology stuff. I had another useful day. I see some of it with the companies I oversee. This is all wonderful, but Brooks and I are looking for cigarette-manufacturing companies, for crying out loud. Maybe buy one; maybe buy the equipment. To support growing and selling dope from Morocco? There is so much more we could do with our money.

"Has anyone thought this through? If so, I'd like to hear about it in some depth. It seems to me that we are risking this whole majestic, world-saving endeavor that I've signed up for over an iffy chance to make some money selling dope from the Middle East."

Alex chuckled. "It ain't a little bit of money," he said. "It's tons of money, if we play it right. It's tons of money now and tons again when we sell it. I won't see another business opportunity this big in my remaining life. And the risk profile is really good—at least fifty-fifty with most of the venture money happily put up by the Moroccan government. I think we should go for it."

"It's the long view," Brooks said, "and what should happen in order for us to accomplish our transformation mission. We have a population where we can test our Emilie tools for the education of children; we've proven them for adults. That's really where we are going. The fact that we can make money in the Rif doing just that is a bonus. We strive to create a thinking population. We're doing it first in the Middle East."

"This whole effort relies on our social contract with the Muslims," Alex said. "We're telling them that if they play our game, they will be better off—and their children better off still—than they are today."

LuAnn picked up her water and sat back in her chair. Then she shrugged and said, "Got it."

Fellini said, "It's six o'clock. Let's call it a day."

Brooks stood. "That works for me," he said. "It was a good day."

"Thanks for coming, all," Alex said. "Caitlin and I are heading to Spain tomorrow, then back to Tangier."

Each gathered belongings and drifted to the door, some talking, some quiet.

CHAPTER 7

IT WAS LATE AFTERNOON WHEN ALEX and Caitlin stepped from their rental car to a long, low building painted a dusty yellow. It was at the edge of the sprawling Spanish city of Algeciras, a busy port on the Bay of Gibraltar. The building was owned by Kufdani Industries and was the seat of its Education Technology Division, where the keys to Emilie's teaching technology resided and its development efforts were planned and executed. Minimizing per-student expense was one of the tenets of Emilie's technology-enabled training, with support to be delivered electronically based on the progress and "reputation" of the student.

Emilie kept track of the "reputation" of each of its users, whether for intelligence or education. She knew various parts of each user's "identity," such as name, personal information, passwords, thumbprints, voice prints, and typing speed. For education users she knew much more. She knew past courses taken and performance on them, speed of learning on several different axes, and the ability of a given student to do given work at some speed. Together, all these components and many more constituted the reputation of the student. It was by that reputation that student support requirements were determined and delivered electronically, specifically for each student. It was also by reputation, including any or all of fingerprints, retinal scans, and passwords, that keys for secure messaging were generated using a cryptography algorithm Caitlin had designed using quantum physics. Security was about the identity of a sender and recipient; from there the encryption was unbreakable. First, know the players with complex certainty, then make sure that others don't read their thoughts.

Kufdani's education efforts had thus far been far more successful with adults than with primary school students, a fact known only to a few within Kufdani Industries and to none without, or so they hoped.

The Education Division leader, Hala, had moved to Spain from Tangier earlier after a terrorist attack at Kufdani's facility in Yemen widowed her. In Algeciras she went to work in Kufdani's education technology operation. Hala had shown particular skill in critical analysis, gained in an honors program at a small university in western Pennsylvania. Her critical thinking complemented and enhanced the management skills she'd learned in an MBA program completed at IES in Madrid several years earlier, funded with a loan from Kufdani Industries. As a result of both skill and ambition, Hala rose quickly to the top of that division and was now its leader.

Hala's influence on Kufdani's education technology evolved in the area of student support. It was Hala who discovered and documented that some students, especially the younger students who were the target of much of the thinking of Elliot and Cuchulain, needed motivation to study, and guidance. Some adult supervision was needed.

Caitlin had tasked Hala to find a cost-effective solution to the need for adult supervision of children in training. This was to be the first of several top management meetings between her and Caitlin since Hala was promoted. She walked into the room, wearing a floor-length dark dress and a green hijab, a long scarf wrapped around her head and neck. There was a small, round glass-topped table and six chairs around it, each with a brightly colored, woven cotton cushion as padding. Hala sat in a chair next to Caitlin and looked at her expectantly. There was an empty chair between Alex and Caitlin.

"You said you had developed some ideas to get the student support we seem to need," Caitlin said. "Talk to us."

"These ideas don't much involve Muslim men," Hala said, "so they may not be popular."

Caitlin frowned and glanced at Alex. He shrugged.

"Go on," Caitlin said.

"I have done some early development on a path to enlisting the support of Muslim women in our education efforts. This is a source of support that is nearly ideal, given that many Muslim women work in the home and have discretionary time.

"There is a movement among devout Muslim women such as myself. It is called the Piety movement or *da'wa*. It brings Islam to the women of the faith without much of the chauvinism and questionable dogma prevalent among Muslim men today. There is an excellent book, *The Politics of Piety*, that discusses much of the early movement and it's where I first learned of it."

"What about Sharia law?" Alex said. "Its precepts are often seen to be firmly against many roles for women that are routine among most of the world's peoples."

"A good question," Hala said. "We in Piety view Sharia law as something we can support and see it not as a restrictive tool of a state-supported agenda, but rather as a guideline for discourse concerning moral and ethical concepts and the pursuit of them under Allah."

"That works for me," Caitlin said. "But how do we apply all of this to teaching children? It is the effective teaching of children we must achieve with the use of Emilie, with the use of electronic teaching methods. But now it seems we need people in the mix."

"Indeed we do," Hala said. "Personal student support and guidance are far more relevant for children than for adults, as we have found. This method I propose is to bring student support to the local level through the use of the women of Piety. The Piety movement has been growing quickly. With the teaching of our young entwined with the teachings of Islam and women within it, the use of adult women to support the education of children is a natural for the Muslim world."

"And how do we bring these women to your idea of providing support for educating children?" Alex asked.

"We provide support through the teachings of Allah as recorded by Mohammed in the Quran," Hala said. "I have identified a number of teachings that can be used to motivate women to do as we ask and as Allah asks. We must also use Emilie to teach and train the women to do the support as we ask and in the way we train them."

"Aha," Alex said. "These women are adults. Emilie knows how to train adults and keep track of their progress."

Hala smiled and said, "Precisely. I'd love to try teaching an Emilie course for them."

"You should," Alex said. Caitlin nodded absently.

"How do you feel now about targeting the Berbers as our first large effort with children, as Alex suggested earlier?" Caitlin asked. "I understand they can be difficult."

"The Berbers care about their young and very little about inconvenient orthodoxy," Hala said. "No one recruits suicide bombers among the Berbers. I take that as a good sign."

"And how do you plan to implement performance to accomplish your goals?"

"As we go from village to village, discussing the Piety Movement and recruiting for it, we will discuss the teaching of children as an act of piety, of service to Allah. We link the Piety Movement to the common good and thus to our goal. Recruiting for Piety becomes easier when a benefit for children is tied to our movement. We will learn as we do."

Caitlin shrugged. "I don't care much about women's movements in any religion. This seems just one more feminist drill, where men are the bad guys and let's find something to occupy our time until we have enough membership so that we can become shrill. Don't lose sight of our objective—the kids. Walking around in a long dress and that head scarf you are wearing is just an admission of your subservience to men."

Hala bristled. "The hijab is no more a statement of admission of subservience than wearing a crucifix around your neck announces your support for the principles of the Spanish Inquisition or Christianity's three hundred years of persecuting witches. The hijab is a display of pride in being a woman in Islam. Nothing more."

"And the long dress?" Caitlin asked.

"Ah, the long dress," Hala said. "The infamous Muslim long dress in all its forms—the dreaded chador with only our eyes peeking out. How could we conform to that? I think often about gender issues and how they manifest themselves in different societies.

"The Quran provides that men and women are created equally. Of course there are broadly publicized problems in gender relations in Islam. Christianity of course has none of these. But the Quran, the infallible word of God, is clear about gender equality—it exists. He also calls for modesty.

"I don't wish to display my body for all to see. When I play tennis, I dress appropriately. When in a business meeting in the US, I dress differently than I do here where I wear what is comfortable.

"I suppose if I was liberated I would wear an open top with an uplift bra pushing the swell of my breasts with cleavage abundant. I would wear tons of makeup, and high heels to accent my bare legs. As I succeeded and grew in stature, I could be more subtle in the way I acted to attract men. But I ask myself which of these two groups of women is more liberated in their thinking. Is it those who expose all facets of their physical being in the most sexually seductive way that society can contrive? Or is it those who dress for the task at hand without willing thoughts of the distraction of sex?"

Caitlin shrugged and nodded. "Makes sense to me. But it's still a better deal to be a guy, all things considered."

Hala smiled. "But, all things considered, we play the cards we're dealt as the Americans say."

"The two of you comparing culture notes is marvelous conversation," Alex said. "But it seems likely, obvious probably, that Hala will be better received in the Rif in her traditional dress than in her tennis outfit. Right now it seems we have a possible solution to a potentially vexing problem. The solution involves reaching out to Muslim women. We should encourage and fund Hala in her passion for Piety and in tying support for early childhood education to the movement. It seems perfect."

Hala nodded. "Allah be praised."

Caitlin nodded agreement and clapped silently.

"I'll be working with you to adapt the education model in Emilie to this new role for student support," Caitlin said. "I'll be in Algeciras until the middle of next week. Can we spend a few hours together?"

Hala's face brightened and she said, "Absolutely!"

"We've made progress in getting the king and the government to look more positively at the Berbers, particularly in the Rif Mountains," Alex said. "That should make things a little easier as they buy and provide Kphones to the populace as we teach."

He stood and said, "I have a few things to do here in Algeciras, and it is getting late. Perhaps we can meet for dinner later to discuss things further."

Caitlin gazed at Alex for a moment, then looked at Hala. "I'm whipped from the flight and the time change," she said. "I'll leave you two to it."

Hala's face flushed, and she said, "I have children and obligations at home. I won't be able to make evening meetings for two, now or ever."

Caitlin smiled. "On second thought," she said, "I may be able to make just one drink. Shall we say in two hours at our hotel?"

Alex grinned. "Two hours it is."

He turned and walked from the small conference room.

ALEX'S MOTHER, MARIA, HAD lived in Algeciras since not long after his father's death. They had met there many years before, when Gunnery Sergeant Michael Cuchulain had been a Marine at the nearby American naval base. The locals used Arabic and Spanish nearly interchangeably, and Morocco was a short, inexpensive ferry ride away, so there was a large population of Muslims. Maria had two sisters who'd settled there long ago. Their girls were grown and gone. The sisters now cared for young children of Kufdani employees during the days; Maria helped them from time to time.

Maria and Alex sat at her kitchen table, drank tea, and had small cakes she had made earlier. They talked about Alex's sister and her children, who had recently been to Algeciras to visit, and about Tangier and Alex's efforts there. They talked briefly about Mick and Audley, South Carolina, where Alex had been raised.

Finally, Maria spoke of the future.

"When are you going to get married and have children, Alejandro?" she asked. "You are not getting any younger."

"No prospects yet," Alex said with a smile. "But I never stop looking."

Maria gave him a strange smile and said, "I help my sisters from time to time with the day care for the young children of your employees."

"Thank you for that," Alex said. He knew Maria had more than enough money. He made sure of that and had provided watchers to ensure her security following Mick's death, just as her father had done before him. Maria seldom made idle talk, so he waited.

Maria stood and walked to the teapot on the sideboard, then poured more tea for Alex and her.

"There are two new children at the care center," she said. "A boy and a girl. They belong to your new manager here, a woman who was widowed not long ago."

Alex shrugged and waited.

"I had occasion to change their nappies yesterday. Both are strapping, young children. The boy is causing comment among the adult workers there."

"Oh?" Alex said.

"Yes," she said. "A breeze came through when I was changing the boy. He got an erection, as infant boys often do in a breeze; then they urinate straight up in the air. Two of the women nearby noticed and called the others over to witness. They began to giggle at its size. It was the thickness of my thumb. There was also a birthmark on his lower stomach in the shape of an inverted comma."

Maria raised an eyebrow as she gazed at him. "Am I likely to see more of these among your employees?"

Alex flushed purple for the first time since he was a youngster. The birthmark was the giveaway. He'd been with Hala three different times in Tangier just after she was widowed. It was at her request, and they agreed to keep the encounters a secret between them. Hala hoped to mitigate the pain and loneliness of sudden widowhood with a martyr's children, apparently successfully. His dinner request earlier was a chance to inquire about the success of their endeavor. Hala's rejection was either a rejection of any further sexual activity or a rejection of his interest in the results, or both. Caitlin's grin at the time had been her comment on the former, Alex guessed.

"It's unlikely," he said.

"Why don't you just marry her?" Maria said. "She is young and attractive."

"There won't be more, Mother," Alex said. "And please don't comment on your speculations."

"At least I know you are capable," Maria said with a little grin. "And I have something to amuse me while I wait for you to find your true love. As the Americans say, 'Little acorns to giant oaks.' Don't make me wait that long. There will be talk."

She turned and walked from the room.

CHAPTER 8

WHEN ALEX GOT BACK TO HIS hotel, he walked into the bar. Caitlin was sitting at a corner table, drinking a glass of rioja, the popular Spanish red wine. Her thumbs were on her Kphone, dancing a staccato blur. She grinned at him as he walked up, then she pointed to a chair at the table. He pointed at Caitlin's wine glass and nodded to the watching bartender, then held up two fingers.

"I've been thinking about you since Hala shot you down at the office," she said as she dropped her Kphone into her purse. "Perhaps I can assuage your needs in a bit, and you mine, after you ply me with alcohol."

"Assuage," Alex mused. "That sounds kinky."

Caitlin laughed. "I certainly hope so. I wouldn't waste my time on the mundane. You can tell me about Sarah and you in New York, playing the beast with two backs."

"As usual," Alex said, "I'm not telling you anything about that kind of thing."

"Yeah," she said. "You're a shit that way. No worries, though. I talked to Sarah. She talked and talked. You were a hit . . . something about a pony-peckered Arab, as I recall. And now I get to repeat what she told me step-by-slow-step while you act it out. I want to know about this Cooch Curl she was so enthusiastic about."

"I can't do this without music," Alex said. "I'm an artist."

"I downloaded the music to which you last performed. *Cool* with James and Klugh, wasn't it?"

Alex grinned that grin. "Among others," he said. "I'll make do, as artists must."

He stood and offered his arm. "Shall we?"

CHAPTER 9

TEHRAN
ISLAMIC REPUBLIC OF IRAN

ALEX CUCHULAIN WALKED FROM HIS plane to the international terminal of the Imam Khomeini International Airport, where a short line of foreigners stood waiting for Iranian immigration to decide whether to admit them. Kufdani, as Alex was known in the Muslim world, was to give a series of lectures on Muslim life prior to the Sunni/Shiite split in philosophy in Islam that had begun not long after the Quran was revealed. That split was still an issue with the devout on both sides, each believing Allah had blessed exclusively their conflicting views.

Alex's sponsor was Jahan Ghorbani, a professor of Islamic history and philosophy at the University of Tehran, with a strong bias to the Shiite view of Islam. There were several impartialists among Islamic scholars, who believed and espoused a view of Islam that had Sunni and Shiite views and policies devoted to a peaceful, if wary, coexistence. Many considered Alex to be the preeminent Islamic scholar among them.

An immigration officer dressed in mismatched dark clothing manned the immigration desk, with a sergeant of the Islamic Republican Guard behind the four immigration desks, sitting on a high-backed chair and looking bored. Alex presented his passport. The customs officer looked up sharply; it was a Moroccan diplomatic passport reserved for religious leaders, its holder not subject to inspection of person or luggage. He looked over his shoulder at the Republican sergeant, then asked in Farsi, the melodious language of Persia and in its latest national iteration, Iran, "How long do you plan to stay in the Islamic Republic of Iran?"

"I'm not sure," Alex answered in Farsi. "A month, perhaps six weeks. I am to deliver a series of lectures at the University of Teheran on the philosophy of Islam."

The approaching Republican guard spun at the mention of philosophy and returned to his chair. He'd heard enough of that at training.

"You have luggage?"

"Yes, of course. I am here for quite some time."

The immigration officer stamped his passport and handed him a card. "Show the customs inspectors this card. They will let you through on a diplomatic basis without inspection. You may stay no longer than six months without renewing."

Alex walked with his hand luggage to baggage claim. In a few minutes, two green canvas suitcases and a large box rolled from the baggage cart to the moving belt. Alex plucked them from the belt and set them on the marble floor. He looked around for a porter, then for a luggage cart. Neither was obvious. He reached in his hand luggage and pulled out a long, webbed belt and wove it through the two suitcase handles and the one on his hand luggage; then he adjusted the length so that it became a shoulder strap. He dipped to get the strap on his shoulder, picked up the box, set it against his hip, and stood.

He walked past the customs line and began to walk out of the terminal when a Republican customs officer, standing in front of three tables with agents going through luggage, stopped him.

"You carry your own bags," he said. "Do you not trust the Iranian citizen to protect your bags from theft while you look for a porter?"

Alex grinned and said in Farsi, "Trust Allah but tie your camel."

He showed his immigration card and was waved through with a laugh. One of the most popular Arab proverbs had been perfect for the situation.

Alex fee-haggled for a few moments with a thin, scruffy-bearded cab driver, who offered his prized thirty-year-old Citroën for hire and wore the bush jacket popular with fans of the former president, Ahmadinejad. Alex soon had a taxi deal for the ride to Tehran. The driver wrestled

Alex's luggage into the trunk; then they were on their way down Route 7 on the thirty-kilometer trek to the center of Tehran at nine o'clock on a weekday morning.

There was a loud swarming, buzzing around the cab and a cloud of black smoke. That swarm held some of the seeming thousands of 250cc, two-wheel motorcycles, a few buzzing perilously close to the Citroën's fenders. Black smoke spewed from tail pipes of motorcycles that seemed to range in age from old to ancient. At the edge of the highway, there were similar motorcycles flowing seamlessly single file. Most had a veiled and chador-clad woman on the seat, with several children seated here and there, looking straight ahead as she drove and managed her blowing chador, seemingly oblivious to the swarm and its danger of collision.

The driver threw up his hands and said in Farsi, "These women are all crazy. Look at them, kids hanging everywhere. They have no idea of the dangers."

"Keep your hands on the steering wheel, please," Alex said in the same language. "It is *my* safety that concerns me, not that of a few women and children minding their own business."

"You are safe," the driver said. "I am a highly skilled driver, making a living so that all of my family may live a little better. My wife does not ride a motorbike and risk the lives of our children."

"There are many women riding motorbikes out there beside the road," Alex said as he leaned forward and looked to his right. "Why would they do that? At least some of them know it is dangerous, yet they cruise serenely."

"It is all they know, maybe?"

"Indeed," Alex said. "Perhaps their husbands have no job, want no job, and beat them and their children. They are on their way back to live with their mothers."

"Some of them, perhaps. Not all of them. Many of them may deserve a beating."

"There was a German writer, a man named Nietzsche, who said something like that. But I think it was one of his characters talking."

"It's no secret. Even a German might know that a good beating from time to time is good for a woman and helpful for her obedience in the service of Allah."

"Perhaps," Alex said. "But now I must rest." He leaned back and closed his eyes.

THE TAXI DROVE PAST the four modern arches of the University of Tehran's main entrance gate and finally arrived at the university address Alex had provided. As the taxi came to a stop beside a low, flat, two-story building, Alex got out of the cab, paid the driver, and helped him extract his goods from the Citroën's trunk. When the bags and the box were on the curb, the driver jumped in his cab and drove off with a wave. Alex once again got the webbed strap from his hand luggage and was weaving it through handles when a voice behind him said, "Even a Sunni should not have to manage his luggage alone. Let me help with that or at least have one of my strong young students help."

Alex turned and grinned at his good friend Jahan Ghorbani; then they embraced. There was a husky young man with Ghorbani who rushed to pick up the two large canvas bags. Alex passed his hand luggage to Jahan, picked up the box, and put it on his hip.

"Lead on, my friend," he said.

Jahan's apartment was on the top floor of a blocky, two-story white building in need of paint, which stood nearly hidden for its ordinariness. On its first floor was the oldest classroom building on the campus. It was used daily by the Department of Islamic Philosophy. On its second floor was a large storage area at one end and Jahan's apartment on the other, provided in recognition of his station as the department chairman and his stature as a Shiite thought leader and philosopher, although the Shiite powers in Qom had registered their displeasure with Imam Ghorbani's reluctance to endorse all their radical views by ensuring that nothing new was provided to his department, including modern quarters for its chairman.

They climbed two flights of stairs and stood in front of a door with aging, flaking paint. Jahan pushed the door open and gestured to Alex to enter, completely ignoring the young man who was sweating heavily with the two large canvas suitcases in his hands. Alex looked around. There was a large room that appeared to serve as a living room and reception and dining area. Books and papers were stacked here and there, and a long wooden dining table was covered with stacks of magazines and papers. Whiteboards stood on wheeled wooden frames in front of chalkboards still covered with dusty white ramblings in Farsi and Arabic. A small kitchen was against one wall with a gas stove and a large white ceramic refrigerator which wheezed and coughed quietly. A long wooden counter with four padded stools separated the kitchen from the rest of the great room. There were four doors just beyond the dining area, with eight wooden chairs stacked beside one door.

"Please go into the second door on the left. That will be your residence while you are a guest of the university," Jahan said as he finally glanced at the sweating young man. "Put the bags in there, Ali. Thank you for your help. That will be all."

The sweating young man smiled and nodded at Jahan, then dropped the two bags inside the room and scurried for the exit door. Alex took his hand from his pocket. A tip was apparently not appropriate.

"Thank you," Alex called as the young man closed the door behind him.

The large room had been partitioned with four large bedrooms. Each had an en-suite bath, with a large ancient tub and a sink beside a toilet with a wooden seat. There was a wall-mounted, brown ceramic flushing tank on the wall behind it, armed with a pull chain. In the room Jahan had assigned to Alex, there was a handsome wooden desk and a swivel chair against one wall and a window with sheer white drapes, open to the breeze. Alex swung the box from his hip to the floor just outside the room, beside a whiteboard.

"Very nice, Jahan," Alex said. "This will do nicely. I look forward to spending time with you. I am pleased that I will share your living spaces for a time."

Jahan smiled, pleased with Alex's comments.

"I'll give you some time to get settled in, Alex," he said. "I'll be here when you are ready. Your first welcoming presentation is in four hours in the auditorium just across the street. There will be a reception for Imam Kufdani following your remarks."

ALEX STOOD IN FRONT of an audience of three hundred Shiite students, clerics, and scholars. He was met with applause.

"It is a rare opportunity for a Sunni Islamic scholar to address such an august group of Shiite Islamic scholars and thought leaders. I spent many hours deciding what to say and how to say it. I asked myself what Allah would have me say and do.

"Let me say first that I sometimes tire of the endless scholarly interpretations of Allah's word in the *hadith*, specifically the writings since Mohammed's death that reflect on meanings of Allah's words to our way of life. None of us may doubt the *hadith* of Gabriel, for example, but interpretations of other *hadith* are not so clear. The *hadith* for Sunnis and Shiites differ and increasingly diverge.

"I sometimes awake in the wee hours, sweating and afraid. I feel the burden of being unworthy of Allah's grace. I wrestle with what I have read in one *hadith* and then another with different views. I seek knowledge and comfort.

"I remind myself that Allah's word is literal, with seven meanings from the most obvious to a meaning known only to God. The Quran was sent from heaven to the prophet Mohammed as a guide for humankind. It was revealed, not created, and thus not subject to change. Mohammed's life is given as an example of purity.

"Let me quote one line from the Quran that has comforted me in these times and may be worthy of your consideration. I will comment on this in a manner that has given me comfort.

"The Quran, Chapter 2, verse 256: 'There is to be no compulsion in religion.'

"Many Muslims feel we must impose by force our religion on the other Abrahamic religions, the Jews and the Christians. Perhaps my arguments against such a course of action against infidels would be controversial in the eyes of Allah. But where are the lines in our Quran that say that we may kill other Muslims over issues of leadership while Jews and Christians prosper?

"While I am with you as a lecturer and fellow Islamic scholar, you may expect that I will speak of the problems I have in understanding what I know and what I wish to know. This is one example for my brief comments today. The issue for me is the stark clarity of Allah's words. How else may I understand the simple line: 'there is to be no compulsion in religion' than in its literal interpretation?

"Many Islamic scholars, and likely most of you, know the Quran better than is likely for an amateur such as I. What I know well is business and its intricacies. I often find it comforting to think of my issues within Islam in terms of the metaphor of business. I will do that briefly today and more extensively this month while I am with it you, discussing scholarly things such as gender issues and our obligations to our children.

"We are all thinking adults. We think for ourselves, while easily mouthing the dogma required for easy assimilation in our societies. A metaphor is a useful thinking device to examine sensitive issues while avoiding the attention of our dogmatic, more radical contemporaries. We are just talking about business.

"So, there are two brands in Islam; the Sunnis and the Shiites. We are killing each other over our differences in views about our brands. Our arguments are ones of leadership, dating back more than a thousand years. Given different leadership in each of these brands, and many years of sometimes violent contention, our brands have diverged and dogma has emerged for each. For the first 500 years or so from the death of Mohammed in 632, we Muslims were able to work together without much bloodshed as our differences grew. Each century since the thirteenth has increased the animosity between our Muslim brands and lessened our abilities to compete and grow on the world stage. The competing Abrahamic brands of Christianity and Judaism have prospered for the most part, at least recently. It is worth considering why they prospered. I'm sure Allah is watching. I am not sure he is happy with us.

"The Christians had a major split in their religious brands called the Reformation. It roiled the Christian world for three hundred years beginning in the fifteenth century, but little of that discussion was violent. The wars and violence over the split between the Roman Catholic Church and the Protestants ended in the seventeenth century with the Peace of Westphalia. Following that peace, we know of the Enlightenment, the industrial revolution, and the other blessings of society that were their world for the 350 years following their religious truce. We Muslims were left behind. Why?

"Could we be in disfavor in the eyes of Allah, our one and true God? Have we ignored his literal, eternal, revealed word, one line of which is 'there is to be no compulsion in religion'?"

As he ended his lecture, Alex said, "Better to allow the faithful to live productive and peaceful lives as in the Golden Age of the eighth to thirteenth centuries, when Shiites and Sunnis lived together in common service to Allah. Great things happened then. Now we kill each other to no good end. Should we not instead study Muhammad's history until the year 632 and the infallible words of the Quran revealed to him for the twenty-two years before his death? How would Muhammad feel about slaying thousands of Allah's children in a quarrel about whether his successor in Muslim leadership is Shiite or Sunni, while the infidels prosper?

"I submit to you that the violence we show today to our fellow Muslims is an abomination in the eyes of Allah. We shall talk of these things further."

Modest applause met his conclusion, suppressed perhaps by Republican intelligence officers standing by the doors at the back of the auditorium, each with his arms folded in front of his chest.

After the lecture and sparsely attended reception, Alex walked with Jahan from the auditorium back to their quarters. They entered the apartment, and Jahan gestured to a padded chair by a tattered wooden desk. Jahan walked to the small stove in the kitchen behind the desk and set an old white teapot on the burner; then he fussed with some tea bags and two green ceramic mugs as he waited for the water to boil.

"You were good and quite articulate in your reasoning tonight," Jahan said. "Your scholarship remains impressive. Your thoughts may have some influence here at some point, but Tehran is a long way to come from Morocco for a single lecture. I hope the discussions we will have over the next few weeks will prove fruitful, and our scholars better informed as to the history of Islam. The attendance at your reception was disappointing; our secret police are not a trusting group, and many hesitate to come to their attention. Perhaps your time would have been better spent at a convention or a meeting of some sort a bit closer to your home and with a more welcoming crowd."

"I'm delighted to be here, Jahan," Alex said. "I've wanted to spend more than a few minutes with you for quite some time. When we spoke in Cairo during the council on Islam last year, government thugs were so numerous around you that it was uncomfortable to talk. Here we can explore our differences. I am concerned that Islam will continue its violent divisiveness to the point that we destroy each other and leave the world to the pagans. Your country seems to be leading the efforts for the Shiites."

"And the Saudis for the Sunni," Jahan said sharply from the hot plate as he turned and brought two mugs of tea to the desk and sat on the second padded chair. "I believe their ill-formed view of Islam has made the most trouble for our world thus far. Iran has picked up the leadership mantle for the Shiites since the accursed Shah was overthrown and religion came back to power in Persia."

"Indeed, Jahan," Alex said. "Of course, your war with Iraq was unfortunate, but you seem to have gained some power there in the past few years, since the Yankees attacked again, then left."

"There are many Sunnis and many Shiites in Iraq today," Jahan said. "It is not yet clear to me which faction will prevail now that the Great Satan has deserted them."

"I don't see why we can't just live together peacefully, but enough of that talk," Alex said. "Let's talk about happier things, like education. My company has made great strides in adding technology to education. Let me show you one example, with my commentary as a Sunni scholar, from the conference in Istanbul two years ago."

Alex picked up a pair of scissors from a green ceramic jar on the desk and walked to the large box he'd brought with him. He cut it open and pulled some thick metallic padding from it and set it aside; then he pulled a Kphone from the box. He removed another and set it aside, then put the padding back in the box.

"It is this phone that we use for training. It was developed by one of our people and is quite powerful."

Alex keyed the phone several times, then looked for the best blank wall to project images where both could see. He chose a clean whiteboard and moved it into place against the wall, then adjusted the image to the space.

A professional-quality image showed on the white surface. It was of the conference on Islam philosophy in Istanbul in the spring of the year before last. The voice-over in classical Arabic gave a flowery introduction of Jahan, who then gave the classic argument for the supremacy of the

Shiite religion, tracing things from the first split in personalities and the resultant arguments that had lasted for more than a millennium.

As the credits ended, Jahan turned to Alex and said, "That's simply marvelous. That is one of the best lectures I've given. I've often wished I had a copy. May I make one from your recording?"

"I brought a box of these smartphones, all video capable," Alex said. "Take this one." He tossed the phone underhand. Jahan fumbled the catch, and the phone hit the floor. Ghorbani's look of dismay was nearly palpable as he picked it up and looked at the keyboard.

"It's a tough little phone, Jahan, and easy to operate. Now, push the letters *DE*, the 'return' box, and point it in the general direction of the whiteboard."

Jahan used a forefinger to poke at the phone three times.

The same video was shown with an English translation. "Oops," Alex said, grinning. "Push *DA* for 'display Arabic.' Or *DF* for 'display Farsi.'"

"I'm stunned," Jahan said after a few more pokes at the keyboard. "Who did the translations? They're quite good, if a bit formal."

Alex laughed. "No one. The computer system does it once the digital video is entered. It doesn't do as well with analog recording translations."

"How do you make this thing work?" Jahan asked.

"The easiest thing to do is talk to it," Alex said. "Push the question key and ask your question. Try asking 'Muslim children training—general.'"

Jahan asked the question in Farsi. On the wall began the first of a three-hour series that introduced Islam to children in Farsi. The first video discussed the concept of Islam from AD 632 until the eleventh century. The Quran was introduced, and the early history unfolded. Islam dominated the world. The next two videos discussed Shiite and Sunni Islam, one video for each. The narrator was only a voice in each of the videos; he wasn't identified in the credits. His name was Kufdani, a Sunni Moroccan.

"What a masterpiece this smartphone is, Alex," Jahan said. "If I had the budget, I'd get one for the entire faculty. Well done, indeed. But how did it know to answer in Farsi?" he asked. "Is it just because I asked in Farsi?"

"Like most new smartphones, this one has a GPS, a global positioning sensor, to determine its location. If you're talking to it from Tehran, the odds are you're asking in Farsi and will first get the answer in the same language—Farsi."

Jahan grinned at Alex and in Arabic said, "Muslim children training in general."

The presentation came up with the introduction in Arabic. Jahan said, "Stop" into his Kphone. "All of this for worldwide education? I know you're rich, but this is an enormous project."

"We got a lot of development money from the US military," Alex said. "They use it to train their troops, particularly the officers."

"So your time as a US Marine wasn't entirely wasted," Jahan said. "You have contacts to help you get contracts. That's the way it works in Iran, too."

"We compete for most of our contracts. Things have to be affordable."

"Do you have a specialty for your training of the US military? Such as guns, airplanes, or something?"

"We do," Alex said. "We specialize in intelligence training for technology-based ground combat support."

"Goodness," Jahan said. "That's a mouthful. I don't have a lot of interest in that kind of thing. But I have invited my brother, Dahir, to dinner tomorrow evening. He will certainly enjoy the video demonstration of Muslim thought. He's quite a curious fellow. He is a lieutenant colonel in the Republicans and teaches urban warfare and tactics at our Imam Ali military academy."

"I look forward to meeting him," Alex said.

CHAPTER 10

A MAN'S LEFT HAND extended from a green uniform jacket with a starched white cuff showing. The hand was darkened on its back by the sun; a crescent of white skin showed on the second finger behind a simple gold band. The hand jerked back and up. Suddenly, ragged red lines showed across its back. The hand shifted; it jumped again and became more stained as red was speckled across its back and tiny lumps joined the kaleidoscope. They were gray and red, shaped like tiny pieces of mushroom. Another shift, then again; two more shots sounded.

The hand that gripped the 9mm semiautomatic Makarov pistol hung still. The Makarov was placed in a shined holster on the uniform belt of a lieutenant colonel in the Republican Guard of the Islamic State of Iran, called the Republicans by most Iranians. He closed the flap above the pistol and came to attention, then rendered a crisp salute to departing souls.

At his feet were the bodies of four men, shot by firing squad at the directive of the commanding general of the Republicans by the grace of Allah. Their bodies had been cut loose from the posts that held them erect before they were shot, but their hands were still bound behind them. The coup de grace by the colonel in command of the firing squad was a formality.

"Sergeant, dismiss the men," he said. "Assemble the burial detail."

The sergeant saluted, and the ten men of the firing squad snapped their rifles to the salute position, looking over the bayonet stud on

Kalashnikov barrels, held vertically. The colonel saluted, nodded, and strode through the sun-mottled dust for the portal that was the exit from the prison's execution court.

Outside he walked down a cracked concrete path to his personal car, a black, dented 1994 Subaru Outback and raised the rear deck lid. He took a towel from a green plastic basket on the right side of the car and wiped the detritus of violent death from his hands with an expression of revulsion. He removed his holster belt, took the Makarov from its holster, and wiped it clean with the towel. He set it on the deck of the Outback; it could be properly cleaned later.

Until 1991, the Makarov had been the official handgun of the Soviet Union for forty years. Many of the armaments Russia discarded ended up in the hands of the Iranian army, along with more modern weapons to repel attacks from the air and sea.

He removed his uniform blouse carefully, then dabbed at the remains of human beings still staining its left sleeve and placed it on the floor of the Subaru. He closed the deck lid and got in the car, then drove down a crumbling street and went past the prison guardhouse, returning the salute of the guard. After a half kilometer or so, he turned into a small residential street on the outskirts of southern Tehran, near the Republicans' military academy. It was housing for the senior officers of the Republicans who taught there. With its identical mates, his two-story town house formed a hollow square, a full city block on each side, five units to a side. The front door was unlocked.

He hung his uniform blouse in the tiny foyer and walked to the kitchen. Two young girls and an attractive middle-aged woman with gray-streaked, brown hair, pulled back and pinned, were sitting around the table, papers scattered in front of them. The girls had pencils in their hands as they looked up.

"Good morning, my love," his wife, Yasmin, said as he leaned over and gave each of the girls a kiss on the top of her head.

"Good morning, Daddy," the girls chorused.

"Good morning, ladies," he said and walked toward the small guest bedroom. In a moment he fell to his knees and grasped the cold porcelain lip of the toilet bowl and began to retch. A few moments of silence later he began again.

Darya, the elder of the girls, said, "Daddy has been sick a lot lately. We're scared."

Yasmin smiled wearily. "He'll be OK, I think. Sometimes his job is very hard."

A few moments later, he emerged with his face damp from a quick rinse. He pushed fingers through thick black hair.

Yasmin glanced at him, concerned, and said, "Outside for a little play now, girls. That's enough study for a few minutes."

The girls grabbed their sweaters and ran for the back door to play in the courtyard surround in the middle of the square block of officers' quarters.

"You seem even more distraught than usual, my love," she said. "Did something go wrong?"

"No, there's not much that can go wrong with an execution that isn't fixed immediately. This one was bad because Jimeh was among the executed."

"Oh, no!" Yasmin said. "All from those trumped-up Islamic purity charges by our favorite general, Masaud Nikahd?"

"Nikahd claims a pure heart, but he was quite upset when his offer to arrange a marriage between their children was refused. Jimeh's arrest came not long after that, and the charges seemed questionable, as do most of the Islamic purity charges brought these days."

"Mark my words; you're going to be on his list," she said. "You've crossed him too often."

"I suppose," he said, "but I'm the only competent trainer in urban tactics available around Tehran. Plus I drive up to the headquarters compound to do his dirty work, like the executions. I'll worry about it some other time."

"When you start to worry, worry about me, and the girls too," Yasmin said angrily. "Darya will be old enough, in the eyes of Iranian religion as practiced today, to be betrothed when she reaches age twelve; that's in two years."

Dahir Ghorbani shook his head. "Now there's an ugly thought." After brief consideration of another trip to the toilet, he walked to the rack and picked up his uniform blouse.

She came to him as he turned for the door and went into his arms. He held her and stroked her hair, troubled once more.

YASMIN STOOD AGAINST THE doorjamb and watched Dahir walk to his battered car, squaring his shoulders. He had classes to teach.

She had been an Islamic literature major at the University of Tehran. It seemed a century ago. Yasmin had worked as a research assistant only until her marriage after a two-year engagement. The virgin marriage of a twenty-six-year-old woman was of great interest to Tehranian society. She was viewed as ancient, perhaps of dubious character arising from negative influences associated with her useless education. This talk was mostly from women. Their husbands were fully aware of political risks. Yasmin's father was a man of influence in Iran, and Yasmin was his fourth daughter. The eldest son was to take over the family business soon; he had a close relationship with his siblings.

Yasmin published her final paper on the works of Avicenna, a major player from the eleventh century in the history and philosophy of the Shiites. In her spare time as a homemaker, she developed a following among the faculty at the university as she read and wrote about Avicenna.

CHAPTER 11

BRIGADIER GENERAL NIKAHD WAS at his desk. His aide, Lieutenant Latifpur, who stood facing him, had recently returned from the execution court. Nikahd's office was in a small two-story building in a Republican headquarters compound.

"So, how did our dear Lieutenant Colonel Ghorbani handle the execution today?" Nikahd said. "Did he show any emotion over the loss of his impure friend?"

"He was professional, as usual. He again saluted the dead."

"Yet another demonstration of impurity, I'm afraid," Nikahd said. "Whatever are we going to do with him? Do you have suggestions, Lieutenant Latifpur?"

"Colonel Ghorbani is seen as a good officer and is well liked by his students. He speaks well and seems quite clever."

"Ghorbani is all of those things," Nikahd said. "I like him as a person. He is capable. We were schooled at the Imam Ali Academy together. But he is not pure, despite his military education. He either misunderstands or chooses not to support our holy mission. Allah frowns upon him, as does the ayatollah."

"Are you thinking of Ghorbani as a candidate for charges?"

"Of course," Nikahd said. "He befouls our young officers with his attitudes about Islam. Our holy word, the Quran, is to be obeyed, not discussed."

"He has voiced these attitudes?" Latifpur said.

"He has not that I have heard, but his heart is not pure."

"Shall I prepare 'purity' charges against him?" the lieutenant asked.

"No," the general said, smiling. "At least not yet. Allah has infinite patience. We must be patient as well, as I plan Colonel Ghorbani's continued service to Allah."

"Shall we remove him from his teaching role at Imam Ali Academy?"

"Of course not," Nikahd said. "Ghorbani has a gift for urban tactics and teaches it well. As we pursue our holy mission, we will soon annihilate the Zionists and reclaim our stolen land. The Great Satan may again choose to attack a nation of true Islam. If so, Iran will be the target."

Latifpur waited as the general's face flushed, and he stood and began to pace the room.

"What have you heard from Fallani?" Nikahd asked.

"Just the usual monthly report," Latifpur said. "He thinks he may be getting close."

Nikahd paced more quickly with abrupt turns. "If the Yankees come, we will slaughter them in our streets. Ghorbani will be promoted to lead this holy effort as a tool for Allah's victory. If he survives—Allah be praised—we will deal then with his impurity and that of his attractive wife and their two lovely daughters, who are being led down a path of moral destruction. There is hope for his women. If we lose Ghorbani, they will be easy to place."

Nikahd chuckled. "Of course, there may be some education required of them. Their thinking may have been corrupted by Ghorbani."

CHAPTER 12

ALEX KNEW QUITE A BIT ABOUT Dahir Ghorbani. He was potentially very important to his team's effort in one of the team's best scenarios. His connection to Jahan and thus to Alex was essential to their plan. If Dahir Ghorbani wasn't suitable for the scenario as outlined, Alex would try the next-best scenario as determined by the team.

Caitlin had been tasked to have Emilie find some match for Iranian officers with a combination of military background, religion-hindered promotions, liberal education, and thirty-four other factors that were thought essential to the team's plans. E-mails and the flow of Iranian society over the Internet were extracted from telephone and Internet records, led by a massive effort on the part of the NSA and the CIA. Others labored with magazine articles, newspapers, and receipts—collected and digitized.

Emilie had ultimately been fed the vast data flow of Iranian society for the past two years. She was going to crunch that information to a purpose. Fourteen hours later, she spit out her first pass from the mass of data. Caitlin glanced through it and keyed a button to copy the file. She made a few changes to the search criteria and set Emilie off on a second pass on the data.

Four hours later Emilie presented a list of Republican officers who were most likely to be qualified to lead a revolt in modern Iran. There were two groups of eight, several hundred miles apart, with no apparent contact between them. The group in Tehran was thought to be the better first choice for discussion, if only for convenience. There had been many extracted e-mails within the Tehran group, some nearly subversive. They had many dinner receipts that matched those of the others in the group. The group had been meeting for several years, with only one new member recently recruited. Dahir Ghorbani was thought to be second in thought command of this potentially subversive band.

"I'M HAPPY TO SHOW your brother a few of the military training videos on the capabilities of US forces," Alex said to Jahan. "They are public information. I don't see why I can't show them to your brother or anyone else. This training has been a very good business for Kufdani in America."

"Well, I don't want you making a sales call on him or anything," Jahan said uncomfortably.

"You're safe," Alex said. "We're booked up for several years on the military side and spend all our incremental time and money on public education. I'm as happy to talk about world affairs."

"So would he. He said he'd come around six," Jahan said. "There should be adequate time for discussion before, during, and after dinner. You've seen the larder. Does your offer to be the chef still stand?"

"It does," Alex said. "It's time that you ate some real Moroccan cuisine, so I may shop a bit."

"Moroccan cuisine? An oxymoron, I believe."

"Ha!" Alex said. "The altitude and the smog in Tehran have no doubt ossified your taste buds. I shall reawaken them. I'll prepare and cook while you use your new Kphone to educate your Muslim brother on modern Muslim education. Plus you can show him your best work in Istanbul. He should be proud."

"We've always gotten along famously," Jahan said. "He was younger enough that I became a bit of a mentor to him—until he decided on a military career, that is, for what reason I still don't understand. We had quite hostile words about that."

"It sounds like you are past that," Alex said. "Good. Blood must stand together. I'm fine with showing some of the military training as well. It sounds like he is in that business."

"Aren't you afraid that you'll tell more than you should about US capabilities, in the event that the US and Iran engage in battle?"

"Jahan, if there is a face-to-face conflict, it will be a bloodbath, not a battle. The United States has combat-hardened forces in vast numbers and complete military and technological hegemony. It would be really ugly."

"Perhaps you underestimate Persia," Jahan said slyly. "The United States has lost a great deal of public support during two Iraq wars and the one in Afghanistan."

"Indeed," Alex said. "They will no doubt come at their next ground war from a different perspective. That would be a fun conversation with your brother. He's liable to be right in the thick of it."

Jahan nodded thoughtfully, then went quiet. Alex sat patiently, comfortable with the direction of the conversation.

"Dahir was a rising star at one point early in his career," Jahan said. "I was certain his career would skyrocket. He taught 'The History of Eastern Thought' at the academy until he was found to be insufficiently pious, a not-unusual indictment under those idiots in Qom."

"I'm looking forward to meeting Dahir," Alex said. "Maybe I'll get two good Ghorbani friends out of this trip, rather than just the one I have now."

In the morning Alex was up early and sat alone at the old desk to make a list of ingredients for dinner. He went down the stairs, walked out of the university grounds, and looked for a shop with good fare. As he walked, he noticed that almost every shop that didn't sell food had a talisman in its window to ward off the evil eye in a surprising acceptance of pre-Islamic Iranian superstition.

There were hundreds of pharmacies, clinics, doctors' offices, and stores with guaranteed herbal remedies for any affliction that might occur. Hypochondria was a national affliction. Huge displays of condoms were displayed at the entrance to pharmacies, apparently ignorant of the approved national denial of non-procreational sex in any form.

In one of the most polluted cities on earth, the drivers of hundreds of buses, trucks, motorcycles, pale-orange and green taxis, and private automobiles seemed to believe that sounding their horns would clear the air and that they were entitled to occupy solely any space where they pointed their vehicle.

Alex pushed past a small crowd on the sidewalk and suddenly encountered another. He was bumped roughly. The nudge didn't move Alex much but it alerted his senses, and Dain's. He sensed a close mass on his center right.

"Right hip," Dain said. Alex's right hand was already spiking toward his hip pocket, adjusted midway to a spot six inches behind his pocket as his training kicked in. His hand closed around the forearm of whoever was there. The hand pulled back and something dropped from it, then Alex closed his fist around the wrist as the arm pulled back.

Alex turned the wrist to the outside and up, twisting the wrist and elbow and then straining the bones already being squeezed and bowed in the man's wrist. He spun his head in both directions, looking for evidence of organized violence, as the Farm called it—one must ensure it's not a competent crowd of bad guys. There was no one of note.

A boy, about fifteen, dark with long hair and ragged clothes, hung by his wrist at the end of Alex's upraised arm. He was screaming with pain. Alex let up on the pain a bit and sensed another body behind him, low.

"Mass behind, laddie."

He leaned forward to see a hand reaching to the ground for his fallen wallet as he held the boy's wrist. He pivoted on his hips and stomped the hand with his right foot as it grasped the wallet, then brought the foot forward with his core muscles and ki. Alex then drove it back into the chest of the man behind him whose hand he had stomped. The crowd fell down as he hit them.

Alex ducked lower and brought his balance to center then swung his right foot back under him with a quick bump of the wallet to his left hand. He stood up. The boy was still under control, still grimacing but no longer screaming. Alex's holding hand was again in the air. The boy was staring at Alex, furious in the midst of the pain.

An old lady glared at Alex. Her head and body were wrapped firmly in a chador.

"Let the boy go, you evil man," she shouted. "Why are you torturing him?"

Several others took up the cry. Soon there were fifteen or more, shouting at Alex.

Alex raised his left hand and lowered his right arm to his side, but kept the pressure from his grip on the boy's hand.

"Of course I'll let him go, if that is what you want," Alex said loudly. "He's a pickpocket. You saw me pick up my wallet. He won't come back for me, but he just may find one of you an attractive target. What will you eat when he steals your money?"

Alex released the pickpocket's wrist and stepped back. The boy's eyes were curiously large.

"Drugs, laddie. Be careful."

The boy's left hand slid into a side pocket and came out with a knife. It snicked open as he lunged for Alex's stomach, stabbing. Alex shifted his body and batted the blade aside, then brought his weight over his left foot and kicked the boy's kneecap with his right, dislocating it.

Alex turned to the crowd, pointing at the knife on the ground beside the howling pickpocket. "First he picks my pocket and then tries to kill me when it didn't go well. I don't know what Sharia law would say is a good punishment, but I'll leave that to you. Allah is watching. Are you sheep?"

He turned and walked away through the crowd. He had shopping to do.

Behind him there was a roar as the crowd confronted the boy.

Alex smiled to himself as he walked. He felt no sense of guilt for enabling the boy's fate.

We're all sheep when we're in a flock. Flocks exist for gathering together to defeat or discourage wolves and other predators. I just pointed the flock at someone else. That was fun.

Alex bypassed two supermarkets, dodging vehicles that ignored any niceties of traffic as they apparently tried to run him down. Finally, he found a butcher's shop with fresh vegetables displayed on tables outside its door. After thirty minutes of haggling, he left the shop satisfied and returned to the apartment with two bags of groceries.

DAHIR STOOD, LEANING AGAINST a whiteboard. He held a small red ceramic cup of thick, steaming coffee, made with hard-to-find Iranian beans. Nescafé seemed to be the preferred coffee choice in Tehran, but Alex had found local beans.

Dahir smiled at Alex and said in classical Arabic, "I've been looking forward to meeting you. Jahan says nice Islamic, scholarly things about you, for a Sunni at least. Jahan also tells me you were a US commando."

"At least I was a US Marine for eight years. I liked the life. But I hadn't been to college, and I was twenty-five. So I left the Marine Corps."

"A key decision," Dahir said with a wry expression. "At that age everything in life you do going forward is driven by that decision."

"Agreed," Alex said. "My father, as a US Marine, had their highest medal. I was entitled to an appointment to any of the US military academies. But I chose not to go that route."

"Do you have regrets?" Jahan said.

"No regrets."

"I think I would miss the camaraderie of my brother officers," Dahir said, ambling across the room, then pouring another splash of coffee into his cup. "It would be hard for me to keep a sense of mission if I were a civilian. The inevitable backstabbing would bother me too."

He picked up the small pot and raised an eyebrow in question.

Alex nodded, held out his cup, then said, "That is indeed what bothered me most in civilian life, that lack of a sense of, and a dedication to, some mission. The backstabbing was usually done by the small minded and is just a fact of civilian life."

"And what did you do about tolerating that?"

"I put up with it for as long as I had to," Alex said. "I found other things to worry about, until I could start my own company."

"Making what?"

"Making informed investment decisions mostly. At the university I studied electrical engineering and computer science, and I discovered that I didn't want to work in that industry either. So I ran investments for others in high-tech stuff mostly. That's where I found the company that makes this smartphone and the software that drives it."

"Enough of this biography drivel," Jahan said. "It's time for you to start cooking. I'm hungry, and Dahir has to drive home tonight. We'll look at the phone later. Maybe we'll play a video then."

Alex moved behind the wooden counter to the stove. He wanted to get the Kphone idea into the head of Dahir; intelligence videos could come later. He stepped to a cabinet beside the refrigerator and picked up a tagine, a two-piece cooker with a deep, round ceramic base and a conical, vented top, fired in a deep-green color. He'd loaded it with lamb and vegetables while Jahan was getting dressed. It went to sit on a medium flame on the gas stove. He picked up a turnip and began to slice it.

"Jahan, why don't you put your Istanbul talk on for Dahir? I think he'll enjoy it. I'll work away on your culinary education."

"That's a marvelous idea," Jahan said and stood to walk to a counter drawer. He pulled his Kphone from it. He looked at the screen while he walked back to his chair and stumbled on the edge of the carpet, nearly dropping it.

Jahan sat in his chair and poked at the Kphone screen with his forefinger. The image from the Istanbul conference came on the wall, then adjusted itself for focus as Jahan set the Kphone on the side table, pointing at the wall.

Dahir looked at Jahan who leaned forward, intent on the image and smiling. He sat back in his chair to watch. He didn't often see his big brother this excited. Questions about technology could wait. He turned and glanced at Alex, who gave him a big, almost conspiratorial, smile. Jahan was proud of himself.

After the video finished seventeen minutes later, Alex had the cheese course ready to serve. Slices of various Iranian cheeses, sliced vertically, were arranged on a plate with pickles and turnips between them. Jahan and Dahir sat on stools near the kitchen counter. Mint tea was poured into fresh cups.

"Well, Jahan, I'm proud of you," Dahir said. "That was a wonderful presentation. I'm sure you got great applause."

"At least the Shiites liked it," Jahan said with a grin. "The applause from the Sunnis was lukewarm. Except for Alex, who was quite enthusiastic."

"Tell me, Alex," Dahir said after he swallowed his first bit of cheese and pickle. "Do you keep up with the geopolitics between the United States and Iran?"

"I try," Alex said. "I still have friends from the old days, and we meet and talk from time to time when I'm in the States. It's often about the situation with nukes in Iran."

"Without getting into the issues around Iran executing its sovereign prerogatives in power generation, do you and your friends have an opinion about how the United States will react to our efforts, if we are successful?"

"We do," Alex said. "We're convinced that the United States is going to attack as soon as they determine that an Iranian nuclear weapon is imminent. They can't live with you being on the doorstep of holding 264 kilos of enriched uranium, or whatever the amount is, as the world press alleges. The Israelis are far less pleased about that slowly opening enrichment portal. I'm told they're not even sure where it all is hidden. You can believe that or not."

"That's outrageous," Jahan said. "The Yankees wouldn't dare attack us without just cause. That would be immoral!"

"Ignoring that, I'll grant that the Yankees have a big first-mover advantage," Dahir said, "but there is still the problem of the United States putting boots on the ground in Iran. That will be unbelievably bloody. I teach the 'Urban Warfare and Tactics' program at our military academy. I know about how to make a fight bloody. From what you say, the American public will be unhappy about that carnage, given your experiences in Iraq and Afghanistan."

"True," Alex said. "I can't imagine there is much American public support for another war with US boots on the ground. They're going to have to find another way. They seem to be trying."

Dahir laughed. "And what, pray tell, might that effort be?"

"There are rumors in the Sunni world that the Yankees are talking to the Saudis about them and their close Sunni allies doing an invasion and the US providing intelligence, artillery, air support, and ground-troop support. The powers in Morocco are not very happy about that possibility but perhaps resigned. The Saudis will expect support from all the Sunni-led nations, since they're trying to be our thought leader. It's about the bomb Iran is developing and what it will do to further destabilize the Middle East from an already-unstable spot in the eyes of the Yankees. The Saudis have expectations of broad Sunni hegemony."

"And how would that work?" Dahir said. "We can slaughter Saudi troops in our streets even more readily than US-trained ones. Our Quds Forces would be frantic at generating internal strife among the Shiites in Sunni countries, and there are many unhappy, oppressed Shiites in the Sunni-led Muslim world."

"Good point," Alex said. "I don't know, of course, but I imagine the Yankees would try to provide combat support from their fleet and their air forces at a minimum. Intelligence gathering would be a US priority in helping the Saudis."

"That will be a problem in Iran," Dahir said. "There are few lovers of Sunni Islam in Iran. And even fewer of us love the Saudis. No one will talk."

Alex shrugged. "They might not need the Shiites of Iran to talk. Intelligence has been modernized for the battlefield, even if not for politics and espionage."

"True," Dahir said, "but gathering intelligence and information is a very slow process. And, as one of your people said, 'No good plan survives the first contact with the enemy.'"

"I think it was von Clausewitz or maybe Helmuth von Moltke the Elder," Alex said, smiling. "I've also heard that everyone has a plan until they get a good punch in the mouth."

Dahir said, "I believe that was your pugilist and philosopher, Mike Tyson."

"Indeed it was," Alex said, "but a good observation still."

"Let me serve the lamb and vegetables," Alex said. "Maybe we can find something more pleasant to discuss once we have eaten."

Alex put a woven rush trivet on the table, then moved the tagine to it. More mint tea was poured, then Alex removed the conical top to the tagine with a flourish. "Voilà!" he said. "Tangier in Tehran."

Fragrant steam rose from the tagine, and Alex pushed it around as he waved the towels he'd used to hold the hot tagine. The smell dominated the room and brought smiles and silent hand clapping from Jahan and Dahir. The lamb had been placed on the bottom of the tagine and cooked from contact with the flame-heated ceramic base and a small amount of vegetable stock for braising. The vegetables had cooked in the steam generated in the process and vented as needed as a result of the hole in the tagine's conical top.

"Wherever did you find a tagine in Tehran, Alex?" Jahan asked after sampling both the lamb and the vegetables.

"Actually, I saw several," Alex said. "This one was made in Iran, so I got a good price. I'll leave it with you when I depart so that well-prepared food is within reach, should you choose to go that route."

"It's delicious," Dahir said. "Well done, Alex."

Alex stood and refilled teacups as the brothers finished their dish.

Dahir picked up his napkin from his lap and wiped his fingers and then his lips. "We were talking about combat intelligence earlier. You mentioned that technology had helped the process. Tell me more."

"If you're interested," Alex said, "I have training videos we have done for the US military that illustrate just that topic.

"My company, Kufdani, has a contract with the US military to provide training films to accelerate the effective use of new military technology in a combat environment. I have access to some videos we created. I shared a few with your brother, such as his noble effort in Istanbul. I'm happy to do the same with you. There's one that is an introduction to urban intelligence gathering and rapid reaction you might like. They are all public information, if seldom mentioned among civilians, and difficult to buy."

Dahir looked a little startled, then grinned and said, "By all means. One should gather intelligence wherever it is offered, particularly about urban warfare."

"This is the second edition of the video. The first was used at the US Army's Command and General Staff College in Kansas, where young field-grade officers are introduced to complex command. This second edition is designed as an introduction for combat unit commanders on the ground. This unit will emphasize the need for unity of command, with senior commanders always in the action loop."

Alex thumbed his keyboard a few times, pointed the Kphone at the wall, then sat back.

The video opened after the credits by showing five unmanned aerial vehicles, or drones, taking off from a small airfield. The narrator began with the obvious, discussing drones, their assets, and their capabilities. Next a large city was shown on the immediate horizon. There were some fires burning and few lights.

Dahir smiled. "Tough target, Alex. There are snakes hidden everywhere down there. And they have brains and leadership. This must be a very good training exercise, if the students you hope to train are to be effective."

The video continued to roll. The narrator talked as a satellite feed was sent to the drones, marking points of most obvious concentration or problem on the right side of a split screen of a Kphone. The drones shifted slightly in the air and diverged, each directed to a specific zone.

The narrator continued. "Often a drone, armed solely with the highest-quality electronics, is flown as a lead, but the availability of satellite data in this case is superior. For purposes of this video, assume that your drone pilots are in Missouri, as many are. Others are in places like the fleet headquarters in Bahrain. There is a longer but predictable delay in voice communications if distances to the pilot are large and must bounce from a satellite."

A city street appeared, first empty, then showing up in a fluorescent green from the drone's low-light cameras.

The narrator spoke again. "The transmitted image is showing up on the company commanders' screens and handsets right now." The image cut to a short glimpse of a Kphone in someone's hand, with the image showing beside a city street map.

The screen view moved from one drone to another until a military staff car was seen, driving along a city street. The drone pilot apparently decided to follow the car. It finally stopped. Two men in combat uniform hurried out of a building. One opened the door for the other; they got in, and the car drove away. Before the car moved, the drone camera greatly magnified the building number and the staff car. The drone pilot had taken a picture of the scene in telephoto.

"Why doesn't it shoot its Hellfire missile?" Dahir said. "Our Quds officers say its effect is simply devastating. As you know, our Quds Force is our liaison to freedom fighters such as Hezbollah and is legendarily effective."

"The drone is perhaps more valuable unseen," Alex said. "It has only one Hellfire. The intelligence gained may be more valuable than the few casualties a Hellfire could cause."

"I think you're anthropomorphizing your drone," Dahir said with a smile. "Do you give them names?"

"I don't know a lot about drones," Alex said, "so I guess I am. The Yankees don't give each one a name, from what I understand. Still, we just read the script and logic for the training film."

The narrator said, "This may be an important car. There may be a high commander in it, based on the actions of the others. Watch how more data is gathered." The screen showed camera movement.

The address of the building showed on the screen as well as the license plate and markings of the staff car. There was a decal on the left rear bumper with some obscure lettering and the number three, written large, in the middle of the decal.

The half-screen display opened to say, "Lieutenant General Rodney Klinger, Commanding, Seventh Aggressor Corps, Bio available. Car assigned to Major Diego Donuttin, aide-de-camp to Klinger."

The narrator said, "We want to watch this car for a while. It may lead to something more interesting before we kill them. Hold on. We're getting new uploads."

All the drones but one turned to a new sector, alerted by satellite to new movement and heat on the ground. On the screen in a few moments, a large body of armor and troops is seen gathering in an open field.

A higher authority made a decision concerning the staff car and flashed it on the screen. The first drone launched its Hellfire and destroyed the moving staff car in a bright flash that obscured the picture for a moment; then the burning hulk of the staff car came into view. The drone then resumed its street search from a wider angle to pick up part of the surveillance load from the diverted drones.

"Well, Dahir," Alex said, "that answers your question about Hellfire deployment. I've been told that was a realistic depiction of the staff car posthit."

The other four drones spread out to monitor and assess the newly discovered troop concentration. A call to the US Navy's orbiting fighter bombers was shown, together with the grid coordinates of the massed forces. "ETA four-zero seconds" was the reply shown on the screen, and an image of three F/A-18 jets was shown as they dove toward the target, one after the other.

After a few seconds' delay, a massive amount of ordnance was shown impacting on the massed forces.

"That would be quite a bit of assistance to the Saudis if it works as shown," Dahir said. "And I suppose I have no reason to believe it would not. There would also be a brutal amount of assistance to the Saudis from the US Navy and the US Air Force. That could be very ugly for us."

Alex nodded and said, "They are quite capable and battle hardened."

"I don't think anyone on our side has looked at this sort of thing as realistic," Dahir said. "I don't know quite how to bring this up to my superiors without infuriating the religious leaders and being accused of treason."

Alex sat quietly, thinking about how to turn the direction of the conversation to his advantage.

"I wonder if anyone within the Republicans would believe all of this from an introductory training video anyhow," he said. "I don't want to be showing this from a jail cell. I'm here to spend time on discussions of how to unite Islam but not in prison. Perhaps you should bring together a few of your trusted Republican officer friends for a dinner like this and get their opinions of how best to alert your authorities."

"I wonder what reaction I'd get on the potential Saudi involvement," Dahir said quietly, almost to himself. "That situation would demand a lot of planning to avoid a total bloodbath. In a situation like this, I can't imagine that the Saudis would take many prisoners."

"The Saudi thing is speculation on my part, based on the Sunni rumor mill," Alex said. "I don't imagine you'll get much traction there. I also don't think you have a lot of time."

"You know a lot for an Islamic scholar," Dahir said. "What's in it for you and Morocco? What is your agenda in all of this?"

"I am Muslim and Sunni. I was a US Marine, as was my father, so I know something of battle and I still talk to those with whom I served, some of whom have been promoted several times since then. I am a citizen both of Morocco and the United States. I have studied Islam in depth for many years, as has your brother. We Muslims once had science and technology beyond the wildest imaginations of anyone in the West when we all worked together for several hundred years, beginning in the ninth century, not too long after the Quran was revealed.

"Roman Catholics and the ex-communicated Lutherans who broke off with the Catholic Church after a thousand years or so now coexist with little public animosity. We Muslims should be able to figure out how to live together as well or even better. Roman Catholics and Lutherans and Buddhists coexist happily with Jews, to the benefit of all of them. It is we Muslims who have petty, violent quarrels and get left behind. Allah may not be pleased, nor Mohammed, with our performance as Muslims."

"That's religion," Dahir said. "This is politics you describe."

"Of course it's politics I describe. I'm proposing that we get religion out of politics, at least to the degree that my king has begun to do."

"Enough," Dahir said with a grin. "I just came for dinner and to meet a friend of my brother. I wanted to see if Sunnis really have horns."

"Do you feel better now?" Alex said with a laugh.

"Actually, I feel a bit gored," Dahir said. "In any case I may take you up on bringing a few colleagues to dinner, if I can convince my esteemed brother, the professor, to be the host."

"Your esteemed brother, the professor, would be pleased to be the host of such a dinner," Jahan said, "provided you bring the food, or at least pay for it. A dinner for eight or ten is beyond my budget by a considerable amount. However, anything I can do to help prevent the slaughter of thousands of Allah's children, whether Shiite or Sunni, is time well spent."

Dahir stood and thanked his brother for arranging the dinner and Alex for the cooking and entertainment. Then he left the room, wondering what the Yankees were really thinking in Washington.

CHAPTER 13

THE WHITE HOUSE SITUATION ROOM

GENERAL RICHARD MOORE, THE chairman of the Joint Chiefs of Staff, stood in front of a large screen that showed the deployment of US forces in the Middle East. It was a screen crowded with military symbols depicting the level of force that had been assembled. Around the table sat each of the Joint Chiefs of Staff: Harriet Colaris, the secretary of state; General Patrick Kelly (USMC, retired), the national security advisor; Blanche Baird, the secretary of homeland security; Sherman Goldberg, the director of national intelligence; and the leaders of the CIA and the NSA.

"We are as prepared as we can be, given that we don't know when, or if, we will attack," General Moore said. "There is new intelligence from the Emilie system, and now supported by an NSA bird in geostationary orbit over the Shiite holy city of Qom, that an Iranian Air 757 has been diverted to a newly constructed air strip a bit south of Qom near the village of Fordo, their main plutonium-enrichment facility. There is a high probability that it is the delivery vehicle for an Iranian weapon, probably targeted at Israel. The probability of them attacking Israel has gone up one more time."

"But not a sure thing, of course," President Roberts said.

"No, sir," Moore said. "In our business there are few sure things. The decision will be yours, as it should be. You are our commander in chief."

"How much leakage of plans do we have?" Roberts asked.

"None yet that we can see," Moore said. "But it's just a matter of time. Allies will have to be told at some point. The Israelis are quite nervous, but they have been brought informally into the loop, as we discussed earlier. I suspect that if we do not move soon, they will. They were getting active when we decided to give them an informal heads-up to put them on hold."

"Any word from Cuchulain?" Roberts asked.

"No, sir," Kelly said. "He has accessed the training videos we edited several times, so one must guess that he is working away."

"I wish him the best of luck," Colaris said. "Try not to kill him unnecessarily. Our plan is outrageous, depending on an Arab civilian to minimize US casualties. But I asked for new thinking, so here we are. I like it. There doesn't seem too much downside for us, only for our Arab emissary."

"Any sense of timing from the Iranians?" Roberts asked.

"No, sir," Moore said. "Our best guess is merely 'soon.'"

"OK," Roberts said. "We'll delay DEFCON 3 for a bit. The cat will be out of the press bag once I call that."

He stood and walked from the room.

The Pentagon

Arlington, Virginia

In the late afternoon following the latest meeting with President Roberts, General Richard Moore sat in the conference room adjacent to his office in the E-ring of the Pentagon, looking at an image on the large screen in front of him, dropped from ceiling over the long table. The battle plan for attacking Iran ran to hundreds of computerized pages. Moore was working on the summary plan, trying to figure out what they had missed. Neither was on paper.

"Let's run this through one more time, Josh," Moore said to the air force colonel across the table from him. "This time at fifty thousand feet. Then let's talk about your end of things. I've trained all my adult life for this engagement, and I still don't want this war. But we have it. What matters is what we do when von Clausewitz's proverbial first shot is fired and the plan breaks. When it breaks, our response will make or break the offensive in terms of our losses. We simply can't afford big losses."

Colonel Joshua Kim was the special deputy assistant chief of staff for plans. The personnel slot he occupied hadn't been in existence six weeks before. A navy two star with responsibility as strategic liaison with the Pacific Fleet had abruptly been sent to work for the commander in chief in the Pacific, CINCPAC, in Honolulu for a few months. Kim, a colonel, was filling the slot.

Josh Kim had graduated second in his class from the Air Force Academy, where he was a varsity wrestler. He'd been offered the traditional postgraduate education opportunity for top military academy graduates and had enrolled at Princeton for a master's degree in Near Eastern studies under Bernard Lewis. When he completed that study, he was sent to North Dakota to command a battery of ICBMs lying still under wheat fields and ready to deliver Minuteman ICBMs upon command, each with ten independently targeted megaton-level nuclear warheads. While there, Kim had authored a plan for real-time warhead targeting worldwide based on various given situations, with targeting coordinates developed and staffed. Plans were changed and Kim was noted as a player in the profession of arms.

A Marshall Scholarship for a year of study at King's College, London, followed, where he studied strategy under Lawrence Freedman, thought by many to be the premier academic strategist working in the Western world. When he finished and was ready to return to duty, Kim's utility as an officer was in question by the Air Force personnel assigners, given that he'd spent more time away from active service than in. He was assigned a slot in the Pentagon, working on war plans kept but seldom used. It was a low-prestige slot, where any promotion opportunities would be based on unusually strong work. Within two years, Kim had developed a computerized system that allowed battle plans to be critiqued and updated in a few weeks rather than the months' long duration normal until that time. After a series of glowing efficiency reports, Kim was sent to Colorado Springs to work in a huge tunneled cavern beneath the nearby mountain and to help with efforts to plan the offense and defense of a cyberwar in space and on the earth.

Kim was given an accelerated promotion to major, as his work and his intellect became more widely known. He moved jobs again but this time Kim only went down the road to the Air Force Academy, where he taught for three years and began to publish works on strategy—some classified, some not. The Council on Foreign Affairs began to notice Kim after two particularly stirring essays on the teachings of old masters such as the Chinese legend Sun Tzu, applied to the modern battlefield.

A series of assignments after his role at the Air Force Academy cemented his reputation as one of the air force's finest minds in the application of violence in support of political objectives. Kim was of the informed opinion that political aims and organized violence were sleeping buddies.

When the immediate Iran affair heated up, Kim quickly became special assistant to General Moore, the chairman of the Joint Chiefs of Staff. He wasn't an aide, although there was a colonel's slot assigned to Moore for that purpose. Kim had served as an aide when Moore was a brigadier general, so they knew each other well. Kim was awarded an accelerated promotion to lieutenant colonel largely as a result of his work with Moore. He was the intellectual alter ego to Moore, who was thought to be the top executive intellectual in the armed forces. Kim's new job was to plan for things going wrong in the execution of the attack on Iran. Kim had published widely and argued that damage suffered during glitches in battle could be mitigated if a myriad of alternative solutions could be planned and staffed in advance.

"Take it from the top one more time, Josh," Moore said. "Walk me through the first forty-eight hours. What are we missing here?"

Kim nodded and began to key his computer as the image on the big screen changed. "We'll probably have the element of surprise in our favor. We must hit what we want everywhere during the first few hours of the battle, but we must above all swarm the Gulf with weaponry and mass. The key differentiating weapon we have is the portable use of non-nuclear EMP, the Pulse. We plan to use it everywhere we need it.

"First," he said, "we must secure the Straits of Hormuz and the safety of our fleet. The Iranian Corps Guard has twenty thousand men and more than a thousand small attack boats. We don't know precisely where all of them are, what armaments they have on them, their speed, capability, or their ability to coordinate an attack under duress. It may be ugly. The American public doesn't want to see another bloodbath of US troops and will likely be vocal if this battle goes on for long or if the fleet is taking unacceptable losses. We should be more worried in the early phase about the Corps Guard, the radicals, than of the traditional force, the Republicans. Surrender is more likely with traditional troops than with radicals.

"Next, we know of three nuclear enrichment sites. They must be gone in the first few hours; I'm comfortable that we can do that. We don't know what else they are hiding. We will be aggressive about learning what we can about other nuke spots.

"Third, we must make them blind and deaf. We'll Pulse their key communications and Internet facilities, then bomb them. There are rumors that they have built facilities in deep tunnels around their key communications complexes and headquarters. We'll shoot Tomahawk Pulse missiles into those sites before we hit them with bunker buster bombs, the new AGM-130C model. Anything they bring up will be hit again.

"Fourth, we must take out the Corps Guard leadership as deeply as we can. We have grid coordinates on many of their training facilities, including the headquarters building in North Tehran. The leadership in the city of Qom should go first, together with their fancy Internet control facility there. The strike on Qom should be coincidental with the attacks on Fordo and the other two nuke enrichment sites. In Qom, we will hit the Internet center. All of their leadership is bunched close to it. They've probably tunneled, and our plans make that assumption.

"Our air force and navy have to strike early and hard. We'll see what Iran has in the way of ground-to-air stuff from the Russians and hope they are not S-300s. And if they are, we hope they're not hardened for EMP against our Pulse.

"The tricky part of this, other than what we don't know and don't know we don't know, is to keep the Republicans largely intact, while we destroy the more radical Corps Guard. This whole plan is dependent on creating a civil war environment the good guys can win. Of course, we don't know too much about who the good guys are and are not. For that we depend on the White House and their communication with assets on the ground. That is a scary scenario given the lack of control we have."

"I'm told that Israel is or will be on board with what we're doing," Moore said. "What about the others?"

"That's a problem," Kim said. "We'll provide a flash message to the Sunni nations, warning of coordinated hostilities by the Shiites that are imminent. They may not have time to react well."

"The price of operational security, I suppose," Moore said. "We need to make sure that our base in Bahrain is secured, but the rest are on their own for a while. We should give Bahrain an hour or two early notice and use our troops to reinforce their perimeter."

"Noted, sir," Kim said. "I have my alternative plans done and staffed as best I can. If we call on someone to act, they'll know the target, the communications protocols, and our perceived risks of a given tactical action. There will be armed drones cruising above the known Shiite locations in Bahrain to provide extra security for our base there.

"If it can be done, sir, I'd like access to this Emilie product that is providing so much of the foundation intelligence for our plans. That's a big *if* in our planning. I don't have a need to know who we have on the ground now in Iran, but I need to know more about this Emilie product and its capabilities."

"I'll look into it," Moore said. "The NSA holds on to that like a mama bear holds a threatened cub; she's ready to attack at first movement. The president has named a special assistant to advise him who is said to know a bunch about the Emilie product and its utility. Maybe you can meet with him."

"Really?" Kim said. "A civilian, I assume."

"Indeed he is, and he's a doozie," Moore said. "He's a former SEAL. He's also a Rhodes Scholar and the son of the chairman of the Senate Armed Services Committee. His name is Brooks F. T. Elliot thc umpteenth."

Kim whistled through his teeth. "Damn, boss. He might have some oomph down this road we are on. Can you pull some efficiency reports from his days in the navy? That would be some interesting reading. I'll find a way to get to this Elliot guy."

"I don't see why not," Moore said. "This isn't the time for political niceties." He gathered the few papers in front of him. "Until tomorrow we're as ready as we can be. Let's try for a few hours of sleep. The balloon is going up soon. We won't get much sleep after that."

CHAPTER 14

NORTHERN TEHRAN
OFFICE OF THE COMMANDANT
CAPITAL REGION
ISLAMIC REPUBLICAN GUARD

DAHIR GHORBANI SAT ACROSS A small table from Colonel Abu Tousi, an old friend and classmate. Tousi commanded a full brigade defending Tehran, consisting of five battalions of armor and infantry with attached artillery. It was thought to be the best-equipped brigade in the Republicans inventory.

"So, Dahir, did that beautiful wife of yours leave you for an imam?" Tousi said with a grin. "Or what brings you out slumming with real troops? You made it seem urgent that we meet."

"It may be urgent, maybe not," Dahir said. "I went to dinner at my brother's place at the university last evening. He has a houseguest for a month or two. The guy's a Sunni Islamic scholar from Morocco doing lectures on Islamic philosophy. His name is Kufdani."

"If this is an invitation to a lecture on Islamic philosophy, Dahir, I'm busy that night."

Ghorbani laughed. "This Islamic scholar happens to be a former US Marine who got rich by inheriting a trading company from his grandfather in Tangier. I checked our intelligence on him. He was in the CIA's commando unit and was quite well thought of there, even if most of the talk about him is probably hyperbole. His former boss at the CIA, a retired Marine colonel, is now working in the White House."

"You think he's a spy?"

"I don't," Dahir said. "He's been out too long. Since then he's been to a university and built a business. He has a graduate degree in Islamic studies from Oxford. But he has some disturbing insight into Yankee thinking and some very interesting US military training videos his company did under contract. The worst of it is rumors of the US allying itself with the Sunnis, led by Saudi Arabia. The US provides fire support and intelligence, the Sunnis provide boots on our ground. It occurred to me that the Sunnis outnumber us Shiites by about four to one."

Colonel Tousi leaned back and stared at the ceiling after Dahir finished his brief description.

"That's a very ugly scenario, that Sunni hegemony thing," Tousi said. "Do you think it's real?"

"I have no idea," Dahir said. "But you should see the training videos the Americans use to train for fire support. I was stunned."

"I wonder if the Yankees will really attack, whether Iran is nuclear capable or not," Tousi said.

"If they do, we are going to take horrendous casualties," Dahir said. "Our only decent shot at a win is to close the Straits and make public opinion and high oil prices hostages to a settlement."

"Do you think so little of Persia?" Tousi said with a grim smile. "Our fearless leaders in Qom say that Allah will protect us."

"Is that the same Allah who is telling the Sunnis he will protect *them*?"

Tousi chuckled. "Tell me about this former Marine, Kufdani, with the training videos."

"There is quite a bit on the Internet about him and some of his colleagues that our intelligence people found," Dahir said. "His best friend seems to be the son of the US Senate Armed Services Committee chairman, who is quite a powerful man. Kufdani has been reported to have a romantic and professional interest in a noted physicist; he has invested heavily in her company. Her company is reported to have several contracts with the Yankee intelligence community. Kufdani is unmarried."

"Is his company real?" Tousi said.

"Yes. Kufdani Industries has seventeen thousand employees across twenty-six countries. It is a Middle Eastern trading organization of note. A Tangerine boyhood friend of Kufdani's is its managing director, but Kufdani owns the firm and is active in its planning and oversight. It has a US presence that arose from a business that he built in the United States, Kufdani Capital. He inherited Kufdani Industries, the trading business, then merged the two."

"That's a real company," Tousi said wryly. "Anything else?"

"Kufdani is rumored to have close ties to the minister of defense in Morocco," Dahir said, "but I haven't been able to confirm that. When he was discussing the Saudi-led Sunni element, he mentioned that Morocco had been approached to provide support for the Sunni effort against us. I suppose the rumors of ties to Defense there give some credence to his opinions on the US options.

"As perhaps an aside," Dahir said, "Kufdani is a noted promoter of primary and adult education for the Muslim world, using technology as a catalyst and manager of efforts. The technology developed for the US military is apparently also useful in a civilian training role. Morocco was recently awarded a second large contract for assembling wings for the new Boeing 787 airliner, based on training results gained using the educational technology. The device used to show the films to me seemed to be just a small smartphone, but there may be more technology."

"Let's have a small dinner with our un-pious colleagues tonight," Tousi said. "We'll discuss things. See if you can get the dinner with this Kufdani fellow set up soon."

"We'll have to decide how far to let this word out," Dahir said. "I'm not anxious to be identified with anything that smacks of defeatism or realism."

"Nor I," Tousi said. "I detest attending executions, even if you are presiding. I'd like attending mine even less, standing beside you. We'll draw some conclusions after we meet this Kufdani fellow together and see these videos that disturbed you so."

"I'll set it up and see you at dinner tonight for some prep work, my friend," Dahir said. He stood, gave a casual salute, and walked from the office.

Two days later

Tehran

Dahir drove to the University of Tehran and to his brother's apartment with five other field-grade officers, led by Colonel Tousi. Alex served barbecue chicken livers as both an appetizer and a meat course for dinner. They were a favorite street food in Tehran, and he'd found a good butcher shop for them. Alex had done the chicken livers with ingredients also bought in the local markets, blended in a special Tangerine sauce he'd learned from his mother. They were a hit and helped start the conversation.

In his pre-dinner remarks, Dahir related to the others Alex's revelation of a possible Sunni attack on Iran, with the full force of the US military in support. Alex was busy cooking and listening.

"Are you sure of this, Kufdani?" Tousi asked. "Or is this fantasy?"

"I'm not sure of it, sir," Alex said over his shoulder from the stove. "I'm just relaying rumors that make sense, and a little gossip from Morocco that seems to support the rumors. The Americans don't want to go through the public bloodshed of another invasion by US ground troops."

One of the other men, a major named Fallani, said, "Do the Americans really like you Sunnis that much? Or is there another reason for this proposed sacrilege?"

"I know for certain that there is no love for the Sunnis, except perhaps for their oil," Alex said. "Al-Qaeda is radical Sunni and brought down two buildings in New York, as you know. The Saudis continue to shelter and fund al-Qaeda, and now ISIS, very quietly. The Americans have long memories."

Alex carried a serving platter of heaped chicken livers to the crowded table, set for eight. As everyone was seated, Jahan and Alex brought platters of vegetables and bread. There was a silence as each helped himself from the platters being passed. Teacups were refilled.

"Shall we view the video that started all of this discussion?" Dahir said when the serious eating crowd slowed their efforts.

"As I mentioned to you earlier," Alex said, "I have the senior version and the junior version that Dahir watched the other night. Let me show the introductory version used to train and advise the more senior of the battlefield commanders."

Dahir shrugged and looked at his brother officers, one of whom said, "How about both?"

"OK, let start with the senior version," Alex said as he slipped his Kphone from its holster, "since all of you are more senior than the training targets for the first video. Together, they are about seventy minutes long."

He pointed the Kphone at the blank wall and started the first-edition video. It was in the same format as the second edition but with a larger canvas to paint the war. It showed forces and problem areas, punctuated with on-call video and satellite images. Attack plans were shown as forces moved around the Kphone images to mass for an attack. In a sudden burst of movement, the attack began. The remainder of the video was dedicated to how to deal with unanticipated problems of the battlefield. When air superiority was achieved, plans morphed quickly to take advantage by massing enormous amounts of bombs and missiles on the aggressor's key forces.

There was silence in the room. The Republican officers looked at each other as the credits ran to the end of the video.

"And here's the more tactical version," Alex said and began a repeat showing of the video shown earlier to Dahir. "They are probably better shown sequentially."

The group watched the drones operate and the consequent fighter-bomber support.

"Are you here to negotiate for the Yankees or the Sunnis, Kufdani?" Tousi said. "If not, what is your role here?"

"I am not here to negotiate," Alex said. "I am here as a guest of Imam Jahan Ghorbani to do scholarly work on the history and philosophy of Islam. Besides, I rather doubt there is time for new negotiations. When I was flying in a few days ago, the sea around us was crowded with US warships with more on the way. The sea lanes looked like rush hour."

Dahir glanced at a middle-aged major two seats from his left, who was in the intelligence business; he shrugged and nodded.

Dahir looked at the head of the table. Tousi was looking directly at him.

"Imam Kufdani is perhaps the leading scholarly advocate of cooperative efforts by Shiite and Sunni to live and work peacefully together in

Islam," Jahan said, "and to get radical religion out of politics. He is here at my invitation and brought a video presentation of a speech I gave in Istanbul on the philosophy and history of the Shiites as the true believers. It is available on the fancy phone that he brought, if you'd like to see it. I have one given to me by Kufdani. I am competent in its operation."

"Another time perhaps, Imam Ghorbani," the colonel said. "At the moment, I'm more worried about survival than religion."

"What are our options, Kufdani, in your opinion?" Tousi said. "Even if we win, this will be a costly war for Iran. There may be a way to enter the negotiations with this new information."

"The Yankees won't want to see a whole new set of negotiators, even if you could convince your leaders to re-engage. More likely you would lose your heads or your commands," Alex said. "It seems to me that the Yankees just want Iran to stop developing nuclear weapons and are willing to try a new powerful set of tactics to accomplish that."

"Even if we came up with something, how would we propose it?"

"I might be able to find someone to listen and pass the word," Alex said. "But I suspect that it's a bit late to try that, even if you could start an idea without getting yourselves, and me, executed."

"We will talk among ourselves," Tousi said. "If we come up with any new ideas, we may ask you to try your contacts with the Americans."

"That's fine with me," Alex said. "I'm here to teach and discuss how to make Islam a more positive force for all. This talk about preventing a Muslim slaughter is interesting but beyond my skill set. For the sake of Islam and its innocents, I'm happy to act as an advisor in this matter, although I bring no formal authority."

Alex looked up at the ceiling and was quiet for several moments. This could be a good window for planting seeds for future conversations. He leaned forward and lowered his voice.

"Kufdani Industries, my company, did the training film you just saw. We do a fair amount of that kind of work with our US affiliate. I showed it to you to illustrate the intelligence capabilities you may face and the rapid, bloody impact they may have with a US-supported Sunni invasion of Iran. I imagine the Saudis will first target your Quds violent outreach capabilities to minimize troubles with the Shiites elsewhere around the Middle East, or ask the United States to do the targeting. In the areas where Republican forces co-locate with Corps Guard forces, there seem likely to be major casualties for any force showing armor or massed infantry. You Republicans have more heavy weaponry than the Corps Guard and seem likely to suffer disproportionate damage."

Tousi glanced at Dahir and raised an eyebrow. Neither had considered that possibility in quite that way.

"You may want to consider pulling some of your forces away from Corps Guard controlled locations and dispersing them," Alex said, "to live to fight another day, if I'm right. If I'm wrong, what did you expect from a Sunni Islamic scholar?

"The rest is up to you. Each of you may want to take one of these smartphones I brought for Jahan's use. Jahan's video is quite wonderful, and you may want to watch that as well. So I have set three videos to play anytime you want to review them or show them. Push the shift-I key for an index of other videos to watch, such as Imam Ghorbani's marvelous talk on Shiite wisdom and some early training videos for Muslim children. If you talk slowly in Farsi to the questions key, the phone will do what you want. It's quite capable.

"Telephoning someone takes a bit more setup because these phones use a US satellite network, and your phones are probably using Tehran's network, but I could make the Kphone work like a two-way radio among you, if you'd like. It's quite secure in its messaging. There's no reason to be obvious."

The dinner broke up, with the Iranian officers muttering among themselves as they walked to the door to leave, each clutching a Kphone.

CHAPTER 15

FORDO
ISLAMIC REPUBLIC OF IRAN

JUST A FEW HUNDRED KILOMETERS south of the city of Tehran, in Northern Iran, lies the Shiite holy city of Qom. The city is the largest center for Shiite scholarship in the world and is a significant destination for pilgrimage.

Between the two cities is the mountain village of Fordo, which houses Iran's newest underground facility for the enrichment of uranium. It is thought impregnable to bombing and thus a strategic asset. The Fordo facility is within an area surrounded by double strands of wire fencing. There are guard towers rising every twenty-five meters along it. Inside the fence are several large administration buildings. They surround six steel-and-concrete portals leading to a cavern dug deep into the mountainside. Each portal is ten meters wide and five meters high. The cavern has been reinforced with walls and ceiling of a special, porous polymer concrete that was designed to yield and absorb force, then repair itself within a few hours. Its thickness is more than 150 feet and was applied layer by layer beneath a hard rock mountain that rises nearly nine thousand feet above it. An electrical hum pulses the air in the cavern as vast rows of spinning centrifuges slowly enhance uranium to a density needed for a nuclear weapon.

In the largest of the administration buildings just outside one of the closed portals, ten men were seated around a long table in a conference room. The leader was a small man with dark hair and an unkempt black beard.

"It is a glorious day for our Islamic republic," he said. "The first of our weapons is complete and ready to be used against the Zionists. General Ashin will discuss its deployment."

General Ashin, a tall man with a neatly trimmed beard of brown and gray, was dressed in the uniform of Iran's Corps Guard. He stood, picked up a small black device from the table beside his papers, and walked to a tall white projection screen. An image of the Iranian flag appeared on it, as a sitting subordinate engaged the computer projection. General Ashin nodded to the president and the ayatollah, the religious leader of Iran and a power in all of Shiite Islam. He stood to the side of the image and pressed a button on the small handheld device. A new image appeared, an official document with the current date. It was a short memo marked TOP SECRET that announced the completion and imminent deployment of the nuclear weapon to the top ranks of the Iranian leadership across the country.

"As we have reported to you," General Ashin said, "we have not yet accomplished the miniaturization technology required to mount the weapon on our Sajjil-2 solid fuel missile. However, we finally have a small weapon fully assembled, as the president said. We pronounce our world leadership with its use.

"It is possible to deliver this weapon effectively using technology we have already developed and an existing delivery mechanism. The nuclear yield of this weapon will be equivalent to about five thousand tons of TNT, similar to the weapon the infidels used to destroy Nagasaki in World War II, but with only a fourth the destructive energy of its blast. Our scientists have refined the use of phased array antennae as part of the weapon that will precisely focus the remaining energy released upon Israel. The well-known result of this energy being released and directed is to destroy the electrical infrastructure and electronics of the target. Every civilian car, every telephone, every civilian computer will fail to function as a result of this electromagnetic pulse directed from our weapon."

"What about their military?" the ayatollah said. "They will surely counterattack."

"No doubt they will, Your Holiness," the general said, "unless we can keep them busy doing something else."

"Will this pulse granted to us from Allah destroy the Zionists' military?"

"Probably not, Holiness. The Great Satan has given them the means to protect and shield their godless military. The trucks that support them will likely be inoperable. The food that feeds them will not be delivered and so on. But they are likely to be militarily capable."

The ayatollah leaned back in his chair. "Then we must prepare our forces and our people for attack."

"Indeed we must, Holiness, but Admiral Armeen has made preparations that you should hear." General Ashin walked back to his seat as he handed the small image-control box to the approaching admiral.

"As a result of your long leadership in the purity of our Shiite cause, Ayatollah," the admiral said, "we have many allies to help us with our cause."

The ayatollah smiled and nodded. "Allah smiles upon us and gives us strength. The reinstatement of the caliphate is inevitable. How will we be helped and by whom?"

"The Zionists are surrounded by Shiite patriots, Ayatollah. In just a few days, the Zionists will not be able to call their reserves to duty. There will be no working phones to alert them and no operating cars to carry them. Their forces will be in shambles. We believe that much of their radar and alert electronics will survive but will have no electricity to power it. The pumps that deliver water to their people will fail."

Each member of the group was now leaning forward, listening intently.

A map of Israel and its surrounding neighbors appeared on the screen. The admiral used a laser pointer to illustrate his points.

"At our alert the forces of Hezbollah in Jordan and Syria will mass. The people of Palestine will pick up their weapons and bring their rockets and mortars from hiding. The Islamic Jihad will mass at the border with Egypt, and all will attack an Israel without electricity, trucks, or running water. The fighting will be man-to-man, with no technological advantage for the Zionists. It seems unlikely that their military will have time to plan or execute an attack on Iran. The Jews who survive will be our slaves. Their goods will be forfeit to us."

"And how will we deal with the forces of the Great Satan poised to strike over our waters?" the ayatollah asked.

"Plans are still being finalized, Your Holiness, but we will make it in their interest to accept a fait accompli. They think we don't yet have even one special weapon. The shock of its use will make them wonder how many we have and where. They will worry about their soil and not ours."

"Praise Allah," said the ayatollah. "Return of the caliphate is within our reach."

CHAPTER 16

ROME
FIUMICINO INTERNATIONAL AIRPORT

JEROME MASTERSON SAT IN A small café at the edge of the walkway in Rome's international terminal three. He had a double espresso in front of him. The coffee on the short flight from Tangier had proved to be undrinkable.

An Italian official propped open a set of doors and a line of people hurried from the customs and immigration area, most holding only hand baggage needed for a short visit, to avoid the hassle of baggage inspection. A stocky man with giant biceps stretching the sleeves of his short-sleeved shirt spotted Jerome at the table and waved, then headed toward the table.

Jerome stood as he approached, and they shook hands warmly.

"Guns, my man," Jerome said. "You look well. Still spending a little time doing curls in the gym, I see."

Seymour Epstein, known to many as "Guns" because of his outsized biceps, grinned at Jerome. "They'll turn to ugly fat if I don't spend a little time working on them. Besides, I do my best thinking in the gym."

Epstein had spent many years in the United States as the undercover senior operative for Israel's spy agency, Mossad, while teaching electrical engineering at a university in New York. From time to time, he'd been useful to MacMillan and covert US operations, on loan as an electronic surveillance expert. As Alex had once said, "Get Guns. He could bug a bald head from across the city."

Epstein's posting back to Israel had come as a result of a promotion. He was now the number-two man at Mossad.

"So, Jerome," Guns said. "Long time, no see, and now I get a cryptic message from Mac that I should meet you here. And here I am. One learns that Mac seldom makes frivolous use of others' time, let alone his own. I have a return flight in three hours. Shall I cancel it?"

"Nah, this is fairly simple," Jerome said. "Switch on your magic conversation stopper, and I'll tell you a story. Mac thinks it would be better coming from him through me, an informal source, rather than from some State Department puke with national security leaks as a key part of his career plan."

Guns pulled a small device from his pocket, fumbled with it, and set it on the table beside the saltshaker. No one in the surrounding twenty meters would be able to make a recording of any sort while it was enabled. Mobile phone transmissions would be garbled in the cocoon of white noise.

"And how is our inestimable friend Cooch doing in life?" Guns said. "Married? Babies?"

"Cooch is good," Jerome said. "The education effort is taking good shape. Kufdani Industries is growing and healthy, and Caitlin's Emilie product is bringing it tons of money from the Feds. So far nothing exciting in the family way for Cooch, or Caitlin for that matter. I thought they might become an item, but I don't think Caitlin is in that market."

"Too bad," Guns said. "It's a shame to let her genes go unforwarded, particularly paired with someone like Cooch. We could have a patriotic, homicidal genius."

"We already have one in Cooch, but I hear you," Jerome said. "Still, he's only that way when he's stoked. Most of the time he's almost normal."

"I'm disappointed that he didn't come along on our little coffee klatch in Rome here," Guns said. "Mac didn't invite him?"

"Cooch is in Tehran. He sends his regards."

Guns was silent for a moment. "Is he? Now why would he be visiting ground zero just now?"

"You'll recall that your leadership got a plea recently to hold off on making Iran an active ground zero for just a bit?"

"How could I forget?" Guns said. "The agreement on our part wasn't nearly unanimous. Iran is very, very close to having a weapon or two. We can't allow that."

"Nor can the United States allow that," Jerome said.

"Tell me something new and exciting," Guns said.

"The United States will attack Iran in the next week or two, zipper down, balls out."

"My, oh my," Guns said. "That *is* something new and exciting.

"What, pray tell, can we do to help with this noble endeavor?"

"I think the United States can handle that end of things, but there are a few things we should discuss. Thus this little coffee date."

"I'm all ears."

"Cooch found a computer a bit ago. He actually confiscated it from a dead, snake-bit Yemeni Shiite who had no further need of it. In the files that had been deleted but not erased, there was a record of Iran soliciting support from their informal allies in the aftermath of a forthcoming EMP attack on Israel."

"I assume you mean their informal allies in the form of Hezbollah, the Islamic Jihad, and scum like that."

"Indeed I do, with a little Hamas support," Jerome said. "It seems that your folks are unlikely to have much in the way of effective arms after a small nuke EMP attack."

Guns was again silent, pensive.

"And?" Guns said. "Mac didn't ask me to fly to Rome for that. What?"

"So, Iran is encouraging them to mass at your borders and await Iran's attack, then swarm over Israel with thousands of armed fighters to take their land back from the accursed Jews. There was a draft press release on that computer that was illuminating."

"That would be most unpleasant for our people," Guns said. "Is there any indication of when this may begin . . . this massing of the allies?"

"There has been movement detected by our satellites for the past several weeks. Small groups are making their way to Israel's borders. Some are armed, others are not. We don't have a trigger or a code for that event, but it seems that it will happen reasonably soon. We're working on it. We do happen to have a code that will be sent to initiate the attack."

"And who do we trust to send the code to them—or not?"

"Why don't I just give it to you?" Jerome said. "Who better? If we don't use it, you can. For humanitarian purposes, of course."

Guns grinned. "Who better, indeed? What will Mac think about that surrendering of the code?"

"I don't think he wants to know about that. I think he wants deniability, if it should somehow leak that you conniving Jews had gotten the code. You got it from a deep cover operative, didn't you?"

"The thought plickens," Guns said. "I got it from a skinny, circumcised mole with thick glasses, working in Iran's war-planning department. Do you have more?"

"I could have sent the code to you by FedEx or secure e-mail, Guns. Of course I have more."

"You were always a devious, thoughtful son of a bitch," Guns said. "I want to hear it."

"Suppose, just suppose," Jerome said, "that the code was sent just as the United States attacked Iran and that the lights all over Israel went out at once ten minutes later."

Guns's face lit up.

"Yeah," Jerome said. "Thousands, maybe tens of thousands, of radical Shiites would swarm your borders from all directions but the sea. They'd be thinking about murder, loot, and pussy, just as invaders who flung the chunk thought about those things."

"We could let them in, then slaughter them," Guns said.

"Think a little further about this, Guns, although I know you'll do just that when you get home and talk to a select few of your folks."

"Like what?"

"Like keeping all your arms under control for thirty minutes and fighting them with tanks, rifles, and machine guns. No fighters, no helos, no artillery other than mortars, no technology until thirty minutes have passed."

"Why?" Guns said. "I'm not sure we can hold them with just small arms. They might overrun our positions. We should just kill as many of them as we can once they attack."

"Step back, Guns. Think of this as an opportunity that Sun Tzu would salivate for, that Thucydides would appreciate, that would cause Machiavelli to chuckle, and Jomini and von Clausewitz to do a high five."

Gun's face was blank for a minute or longer as he stared into a wall decorated with fake ivy and Italian kitsch. Jerome waved to the waiter and raised two fingers to get more coffee.

"I get it," Guns said. "We have an opportunity for a decisive engagement in Machiavellian and Jominian terms. We have the political and fighting elite of our enemies attacking us all at once. We'll never have a group of them come together like this again."

Jerome grinned. "Yeah. Kill them all. Let the first wave attack into a decent defensive field of fire, with no Israeli helos, artillery, or tactical air in sight," Jerome said. "Give it thirty minutes, then cut the artillery, attack helos, and your air force loose after the Shiites commit their reserves. I imagine you know where their key headquarters are, if you decide to communicate violently with them from the air. For them, let there be only martyrs—no man left standing. Don't kill the moderates hiding in their homes; just scare the shit out of them and leave them in uncontested power. I suspect you may have no more than twenty-four hours for this gig, before the pinko press goes crazy at the slaughter. Leave their infrastructure alone, or you'll have to pay to rebuild it."

Guns shrugged and nodded. He'd been with Jerome on several joint special operations. His wit and wisdom about ground-combat tactics were legendary.

"Makes sense," Guns said. "As you say, we may never have this chance again. But the UN would have a shit fit. We'd get thrown out. Too many dead for political acceptability."

"Bullshit," Jerome said. "You were attacked in the dead of night without warning. The press release talks about driving you back to the Stone Age and making you slaves. Use it. They just kept coming, and you just kept shooting. Be hurt and confused."

"That press release is old news. 'That dog don't hunt' in the vernacular you once used on me in your cruel criticism of one of my brilliant ideas."

"That may be why you're talking to me today in Rome rather than

Mac and General Kelly on the secure phone link," Jerome said. "The United States will attack Iran's communications centers in Tehran and Qom in the first few moments of the war and put out their Internet lights. The very same press release may come out from them—released by us, of course—within seconds after that. How would they deny the press release without a means to communicate to the world? How could you Israelis read that release and not be hurt, confused, and lethal?"

"What else will the United States be doing?" Guns asked quietly.

"They'll be trying to keep the Straits of Hormuz open. No mean feat, I'd guess."

"I imagine both sides will get to try out all sorts of new technology," Guns said. "It will be bloody."

"What do I know?" Jerome said. "I'm just a retired Marine. But I think it will become clearer to all that it's not nice to tug on Superman's cape. US military misfortunes in Iraq and Afghanistan may fade in the world's collective memory."

"What happens to Iran?"

"That's Cooch's job at first. We'll see. If he fails, there's going to be a million Iranian dead in a big hurry."

"That should take the world's attention away from Israel for a while, if it happens."

"C'mon, Guns, think about it. Iran declared war and attacked. Use that fact. It won't last long, like you said."

"You're right again, Jerome," Guns said. He put his hands behind his head and tilted his chair back, pondering.

"I can probably sell all of that," he said. "What else?"

"The goal here is to minimize needless Israeli casualties," Jerome said, "while maximizing political advantage, I assume."

Guns laughed. "I wouldn't have phrased it quite that way, but how could that not be the goal? Some, but not nearly all, political power flows from the barrel of a gun, if only because it creates political advantage."

"I talked to Cooch a little by phone before I took off for this meeting. He has some ideas."

"I think you two are fucking with my head the way you always have," Guns said. "What? What the hell does Cooch think we should do?"

"Cooch said, 'Why don't you figure what you were always willing to give up to the Palestinians in the end, including maybe the Golan Heights? Give it all up very publicly to the UN to give to what remains of the Palestinian government just after you've kicked the shit out of the Palestinian radical force.'"

"Cooch has a dirty, devious mind," Epstein said. "I like it. I probably can't sell it, but I like it. What else did he say? Give me the bad news."

"Cooch talked to Elliot recently. He said that Elliot is now a special advisor to the president. Elliot told him that the president is pissed about all of this and will be looking to take some spite out on Israel after it's over, because you sort of caused the Iran nuke problem by being the target. He's worried about showing balance in the affairs of state. This is your chance for a riposte that will make Roberts look good and perhaps be far less pissed at you."

"It must be nice to be able to read the president's mind," Guns said. "But if anyone can do it, Elliot can. I'll float that trial balloon. Let's just see what happens."

CHAPTER 17

THE WHITE HOUSE

GENERAL PATRICK KELLY SAT ACROSS from President Roberts in the Oval Office. He'd been asked to give the president an informal update on the rapidly evolving situation in Iran.

"The Iranians have a large team working on the 757 that has been diverted to the airstrip beside Fordo. The general consensus among our intel folks is Iran will launch their attack within seventy-two hours. They have alerted their forces and are preparing for something ugly."

"Damn," Roberts said. "What do you recommend? I can't think of a good reason to assemble another meeting in the Situation Room. We know little new, other than more precision, but still it's a guess about the timing that was predicted earlier."

"I'd say it's time, Mr. President," Kelly said. "NSA intercepted top-secret communications among them that make it clear they have a weapon and a plan to use it. As you know, we have intercepted and decoded the message the Iranians will use to alert their guerilla fighters from Hezbollah, the Islamic Jihad, and those bunches of radical Shiites to attack Israel and God knows where else. We should release that alert at the time of the first strike by us. Israel is ready, and we'll alert the other nations that may be hit by Shiite fighters."

Roberts nodded, looking troubled. "God help us all. I'll give the order to execute Operation Fallen Timber in one hour. Let General

Moore know. Ask Ms. Molyneaux to come in. We have domestic planning to do. I suspect Iran isn't going to take this lying down. Come to DEFCON 3."

"Yes, sir," Kelly said as he snapped to his feet, then turned and walked from the room.

CHAPTER 18

TEHRAN

ALEX LAY IN HIS BED, THE WINDOW open to the sounds of student life below, second-guessing things once more. The students were passing by on their way to or from something exciting or at least different. They seemed happy. They seemed normal enough and thinking that things could be worse or better. They discussed and argued about the complicated ballet of Iran's security. Fun talk, late at night.

He could feel in his bones that the battle was about to be joined. Lives would be changed forever. He needed to renew his efforts to see that things in Iran changed for the better, all things considered. There would be some pain—relatives lost, brigands enriched, as always.

Alex's mind wandered to the job at hand and the US plans to get that job done.

The strategic bet looked pretty safe. The United States could eliminate the nuclear threat and destabilize Iran, thus reducing their influence in the Shiite world. They could be left to fight it out. The tactical bet in this engagement was with some combination of Corps Guard and Republicans.

If the plan to destroy Iran's ability to communicate worked, Alex thought things could go well. Effective command and control structure is fundamental to the conduct of successful modern warfare. Without the ability to adapt quickly to an ever-changing battlefield, a force has little opportunity to defend itself effectively or to plan and execute counterattacks. Modern communications facilities are the backbone of effective command and control. Modern war planners consequently target enemy command and control facilities at the earliest possible moment, even as they deal with weapons that can ruin their efforts.

Alex considered the psychology of warfare and how it was morphing quickly. In the second Gulf War, when the US attacked Iraq and Saddam Hussein's forces over the possible possession and use of weapons of mass destruction, "shock and awe" was the term used for the early stages of the attack. Also called "rapid dominance," its objective was to use overwhelming power, dominant battlefield awareness, and spectacular displays of force and military prowess to overwhelm the enemy's perception of the battlefield and destroy the will of the enemy's leadership to resist the attacker. During the earliest stages of the first battle, the enemy was to perceive that resistance was futile in the face of the technology and might displayed.

Civilians seemed to think that a war was something thought up on a Friday and executed on Monday morning. Alex knew that General Richard Moore's planners and those of the various Joint Chiefs had been working nearly nonstop for three months to get the initial attack right, with no assurance that it would be used. Ships had been loaded with the appropriate supplies and weapons and were steaming to the Middle East or were already there. There wasn't room for all of them at once.

It was clear to Alex, Brooks, and most of the US military that much of the danger to US forces was from the Corps Guard Navy, in the south of Iran, where they guarded and threatened the Straits of Hormuz, a global chokepoint for the movement of crude oil; seventeen million barrels passed through there daily. There were several large Iranian installations with radar and surveillance stations coupled with docks and boat-maintenance facilities; large mine-laying ships were stationed in these. Modern Russian surface-to-air missiles protected them. There were also surface-to-surface missiles that sophisticated communications could direct toward the US fleet or its headquarters in nearby Bahrain.

The briefing for Alex by the war planners in the Pentagon had been fairly technical. They were troubled by the hundreds of small boat docks and hiding places along the long coastlines near the Straits of Hormuz. A single speedboat could carry a modern Russian torpedo or surface-to-surface missile with the power to destroy a five-billion-dollar nuclear carrier with more than five thousand US sailors aboard. Some of these boats were said to be stored in hidden two- or three-boat structures that had been hardened against EMP attacks using Russian technology.

In the initial stages of the US attack, beyond addressing the nuclear weapon issue, Josh Kim's planners decided to direct every available asset at the Corps Guard Navy in the South and Iran's telecommunications infrastructure in the North. A major portion of the plan was that Iran would become blind, with no telephone, Internet, or other electronic forms of communications with their forces or their allies. The purpose of a series of directed EMP attacks along the coastlines was to cripple the trucks, tractors, generators, pumps, and communications infrastructure for more than three hundred miles of coastline and a swath of land running several miles inland.

ALEX AWOKE TO THE vibration of his Kphone, a notice that someone had texted him. He sat up in his bed and pulled the Kphone from its holster on the nightstand. The text was from Mac. There were just two words on the screen.

Fallen Timber

He smiled to himself. This was likely to be one of the more interesting days of his life. He thought he would hear from some Iranians within twenty-four hours.

The target list for Tehran, when he had last seen it, was fairly short. The three buried nuclear enrichment sites were to be hit first, followed by a massive attack on the Persian Gulf. Internet centers were high on the list but would entail relatively few casualties. There were plenty of other targets, but none were in the center of Tehran where Alex lay in bed. Iran's South would get warm fast.

CHAPTER 19

FALLEN TIMBER PLUS FIVE MINUTES

THREE VIRGINIA-CLASS ATTACK submarines were making seven knots about twenty-three miles from the coast of the Gulf of Oman, south of Iran and the Straits of Hormuz. Commander Jared Fargo, captain of the USS *California*, sat in the filtered light of its Combat Information Center, the CIC, watching the status board on the twelve BGM-113 Tomahawk cruise missiles loaded in *California*'s vertical launch tubes, energized and ready to fire.

These unique Tomahawk missiles were designed to create an electromagnetic pulse without the nuclear explosion ordinarily required to trigger the enormous burst of energy needed to create the Pulse. They used a coil wrapped in an explosive shell and shaped to create an implosion. An electric charge passed through the coil just as the ring of explosives detonated. An extremely powerful magnetic field would be created for an instant which would destroy electronics and electricity-generating equipment just as efficiently as the EMP of a nuclear burst but with far more precision of targeting.

"I think we're going to ruin a few days ashore if any of them need electrical power or a computer, XO," Fargo said to his executive officer. "And a few more at sea."

"About time, Captain. I never did much care for the way we spend a couple of billion dollars on boats like this, then never get a chance to help out with the ass kicking."

"Well, at a million or so dollars a copy for these flashbulbs in our missile tubes, we're going to do some serious damage. Our sneaky little fish will also likely bring their own price. The Kilos are a bonus."

The display to the left of the missile-status board lit up with a message. "I have a launch order. Confirm Whiskey, X-ray, Juliet five four two." The launch order came from the Fifth US fleet high command.

The XO reached for a keyboard and tapped a few keys. "Captain, confirm Whiskey, X-ray, Juliet five four two."

"Open outer doors on torpedo tubes one, two, and three," Fargo said. "Do we have a good fix and computed solution on the Kilos?"

The Iranians had three modern diesel-powered submarines, Kilo models, purchased from Russia. They usually cruised near the US fleet, listening and waiting for orders to attack it with their Russian torpedoes. There had been strong rumors that the Iranians had received several dozen VA-111 torpedoes from Russia; powered by liquid-fuel rockets, they were very hard to detect or defeat once up to speed. The VA-111 exits a torpedo tube at fifty knots and accelerates quickly.

The Kilos hoped to surprise the US carriers in the event of a US attack; they were thought to be too quiet to be detected, but *California* had been following them effortlessly for the past four days.

"Targets at three thousand to five thousand yards, Captain. We are locked on and tracking. All are barely maintaining headway at three knots. Computed solution is set."

"Very well. Match sonar bearings and shoot."

The US torpedoes were new and stealthy. They came to power as a small rush of water from *California*'s open torpedo tubes shoved them out. They ran silently at moderate speeds, driven by an Integrated Motor Propulsor which incorporated a radial-field electric motor, thus providing closed-cycle propulsion that was silent, wakeless, and depth independent. Communication by *California* with each torpedo was by a broadband acoustic signal. Guide wires were obsolete. When each of the torpedoes was within one hundred meters of the computed location of its assigned target Kilo, the activate signal came from *California*. They went to full power and pinged once for their targets. They found them immediately. Each accelerated toward two hundred miles per hour, avoiding in a cloud of tiny bubbles much of the friction that is the enemy of underwater speed. A device at the nose of the torpedo generated an "air envelope," which allowed friction to be minimized.

All three Kilos came to full power and released a noisemaker to confuse the US torpedoes. There was no time. Just before the detonation of 250 pounds of high explosive on the Kilos, the propellers of both a Russian and Chinese nuclear submarine spun as they accelerated to flank-speed. The turbulence around the propellers from the sudden acceleration became obvious on *California*'s sonar. They had reacted to the noise and the sonar ping in classic fashion, releasing a noisemaker to confuse incoming torpedoes and making a hard-knuckle turn right to hide under that noise as they dashed away from the target. Each foreign sub came directly for the two other Virginia-class subs as expected, and a single loud ping from US attack sonar greeted them.

The American subs' torpedo doors were open, and target calculations had been made. The message was clear. It said, "We know you are there and we are not shooting at you. If you were the target, you would be as dead as the Kilos." The Russian and Chinese subs quickly slowed and again became silent when it was clear the torpedoes hadn't been directed at them. If either had been detected opening its outer torpedo doors, it would have been sunk immediately.

The sound of a radio antenna being released to float to the surface happened quickly. The Russians would send a warning notice to the Iranians of their loss, then notify their own leaders. A tiny, powered homing device called Voicebox rose from the sail of the *California*, driving to the surface toward the Russian transmitter's antenna. At the beginning of the next Russian transmission, Voicebox would release an electronic charge right next to the Russian device to fry its circuits. It would be quite some time before the Russians figured out what had gone wrong with their well-tested transmitter, which Iran relied on for reports and early warning and which planners at home in Russia relied on for updates.

The basso groans and sighs of the Kilos breaking up were loud on *California*'s sonar speakers. It was easy to think of the men dying inside the collapsing Kilos. Fargo thought they should hear it for a few minutes for perspective. Then it was time.

"Ripple vertical tubes one through twelve, fifteen second separation. Now," Fargo said.

The *California* shuddered as the first Tomahawk was launched from its tube in a rush of compressed air. It cleared the surface, and solid-propellant engines ignited as its wings unfolded. It lifted toward one of twelve targets along the Iranian west coast. The Corps Guard Navy threatened the fleet. It was first on the target list, and the *California* had the honors. At 550 miles per hour, the Tomahawks would reach their targets in about twenty minutes.

"I imagine things are about to get a bit warm ashore, Captain," XO said.

"I certainly hope so. For sure I wouldn't want to be sitting on Iranian radar right now."

"The way we configured the Tomahawk phased-array antennas, I wouldn't want to have my homework on a PC either. Ninety square miles isn't a lot of spread for the kind of pulse we're delivering."

"I'll say," Fargo said. "It's way cool that the geeks figured out how to change the shape of the blast pulse, using phased-array antennas. It would be nice to avoid frying the Saudi oil-pumping empire sitting next door by a few hundred miles or so. I suspect the Iranian oil business up north is about to come to a temporary halt, compliments of the Air Force."

"Yeah, a fried generator will do that to a diesel pump," the XO said. "It would be nice to avoid ten-dollar gas at the pumps, too."

"There is that. My Corvette would be on the market in a hurry if it cost me two hundred bucks to fill it. It's close to a hundred right now."

Farther north and beginning ten seconds later, two additional sets of twelve Tomahawks ignited their burners as they came bursting from the sea, one at a time. Each began to fly to the location programmed in its computer. Some were radar sites; others were military and commercial targets along the long Iranian coastline.

Tomahawk cruise missiles had been around for thirty years without much visible change. Beneath their covers, however, they had been enhanced to be sufficiently accurate that they could fly through a window one meter square at a terminal velocity of over one thousand miles per hour. The power of their EMP blast had been refined and expanded. A Tomahawk could chug along at up to six hundred miles per hour for a thousand miles. Tonight's targets weren't that far away. The first thirty-six of them would radiate the air with a short Pulse of enormous power, hungry for copper and silicon, rather than burst on the ground.

South of Iran
Gulf of Oman
USS George H. W. Bush
Fallen Timber plus six minutes

Turning into the wind on the Gulf of Oman two hundred miles from the Straits, the nuclear-powered carrier USS *Bush* prepared to launch aircraft. Lieutenant Darius Wallsky, USN, call sign Bingo, saluted the ground officer visible on the flight deck at the front right of his EA-18G Growler, the electronic warfare version of the F/A-18. He pushed his helmet back against the headrest and inhaled. The steam catapult slammed his plane down the deck surface of the *Bush*. The Growler reached a speed of 162 miles per hour in less than two seconds and lifted from the deck. Wallsky banked left to keep his Growler outside the carrier's path in the unlikely event that the Growler failed and crashed. He shut down the afterburners and climbed to refuel high above the Gulf of Oman; afterburners were thirsty beasts.

The nuclear carrier USS *George H. W. Bush*, otherwise known as CVN-77, was the tenth and final Nimitz-class, nuclear-powered carrier built. It had been commissioned in 2009 after six years of construction. *Bush* carried a crew of more than five thousand men and women. Among others, there were 110 cooks and 180 food attendants. It was a small city dedicated to delivering air power from wherever it sailed.

Wallsky had been flying this mission for four months. Even though he knew where each of Iran's twenty-one fixed radar locations was on a map, his Growler knew much more. Each mission would detect the radars of Iran's Corps Guard and note their locations as the Growler's state-of-the-art electronic warfare equipment listened and calculated locations, then assigned GPS coordinates to them. Onboard computers did target allocation among Growlers. The Iranians hadn't yet been exposed to the active side of the Growler, even after hundreds of missions had been flown. Bingo hoped tonight was his active night.

"Bingo, this is Sierra." His control at *Bush*, call sign Sierra, was early with his call. Wallsky settled back in his seat.

"Sierra, Bingo."

"Bingo, execute Fallen Timber. I say again, execute Fallen Timber."

Bingo's data display lit up with a confirming message, and his face with a grin.

"Wilco, Sierra. Executing Fallen Timber." Wallsky turned toward his targets and dove to a preassigned launch altitude, then leveled.

With four seconds between launches, six AGM-88F Advanced Anti-Radiation Guided Missiles dropped from their wing rails and ignited. Each of the fourteen-foot-long, eight-hundred-pound missiles had a speed above Mach two and a range of one hundred miles. A separate target had been programmed into each. Bingo's targets tonight were bunched near the border of the Persian Gulf and the Gulf of Oman in southern Iran. Bandar Abbas and islands nearby held key radar units that monitored the US fleet. There had been a Growler launched from each of three US carriers—the *Bush*, the *Abraham Lincoln*, and the *George Washington*. The *Bush* launched two. Their targets were the radars that controlled the defenses of the Islamic Republic of Iran and the people and equipment surrounding them. Each had its own set of targets.

There were at least four mobile radar units staffed with junior Iranians. The Corps Guard posting for a truck-based unit that was always moving was unattractive due to its long stints away from home and its poor food. The second Growler from the *Bush* had missiles that would lock on a moving radar pulse and follow it to within ten feet of the last signal before detonating. It was listening and waiting for the first salvo of AGM-88s to hit. If the mobile units were going to go active, they would do so soon.

As the last of his missiles launched and accelerated beyond Mach two, Bingo lit his afterburners and accelerated straight to the sky in a noisy vertical climb.

If that doesn't get their attention, Wallsky thought, *nothing will. Come on, truckers, light up your radars.*

Aboard *Bush*, the last of the mission's F/A-18 Super Hornets launched and climbed to their aerial refueling stations. The first flight landed, refueled, rearmed. They launched again and turned for the coast, waiting for a signal to accelerate and execute their mission. Two other nuclear carriers in the Gulf of Oman, the *Abraham Lincoln* and the *George Washington*, were carrying out their own orders in support of Fallen Timber.

Fallen Timber plus fifteen minutes

Sirens blared from a radar alert as Iranian sailors ran to their boats at the Bandar Abbas complex ashore, which dominated Iran's electronic surveillance of the Straits of Hormuz. The doors to the hardened dockage began to swing open to allow their boats to depart. Trucks were moving to the docks with missiles and mines to be loaded. Lights came on across the complex as emergency preparations began and the Growler's missiles started to arrive. One radar installation was above a large office building, slightly elevated for a better signal path and a better view of the Persian Gulf for the building's tenants. The missile detonated ten feet from the radar's dish and sprayed the area with 150 pounds of directed fragmentation steel.

Sparks exploded behind the remaining twisted frame of the small power station beside the radar. The roof of the building heaved once, then groaned from the concussion of the blast and the weight of the radar installation as twisted steel beams rubbed against one another. The smoking mass fell through one floor before it stopped amid a group of desks crowded together. People ran for the door.

The nearby islands of Tund, Qeshm, and Kish had their own radar installations and were subjected to similar harsh attention. A little to the north, Kharq Island lost its radar capability. Its largest building caught afire and most of its small population perished.

The submarine-launched Tomahawks arrived from ten to fifteen minutes after the Growlers attacked to ensure that the concussion and shrapnel of the Growler blasts would not interfere with the Tomahawks' guidance, as the cruise missiles flew at 550 miles per hour toward their targets.

South of Tehran, the holy city of Qom and the small village of Fordo were blanketed with close-range, directed electromagnetic pulses from Tomahawk missiles launched earlier by the stealthy B-2 bombers. Trucks, support equipment, and the everyday conveniences of life were suddenly still. In the hospitals pacemakers became dormant, and dialysis was suddenly impossible. Surgeons felt their way from darkened operating theaters, leaving their patients to die on the operating table. Ventilators, medical and industrial, didn't ventilate. The city was dark.

Fallen timber plus six minutes

A stealthy B-2 launched a cruise missile not far from Fordo.

The Tomahawk's phased-array structure was shaped electronically to direct its entire pulse at three S-300, advanced Russian-sold ground-to-air missile batteries protecting the Fordo installation. The pulse spillover from such narrow targeting was intense for one hundred meters around the burst. Just outside the door of the complex, near the town of Fordo, there were generators that powered the support equipment for the infrastructure that produced bomb-quality uranium essential to the construction of a nuclear weapon. Most of the infrastructure that supported the equipment and personnel in the cavern was external to the cave. The Pulse fried circuits and a few brains in the laboratories nearby. Fatalities were an unplanned bonus with the Pulse, but they happened when humans were close to the center of an electromagnetic pulse. Even if the S-300 sites were pulse hardened, the trucks and equipment so necessary to their effective use were useless forever. Drones were soon to hover to deliver devastation to any newly enabled radar.

Josh Kim had methodically calculated the incidence of fatalities arising from a powerful nearby Pulse using both parameters from a test of the Pulse in Utah and theoretical mathematical calculations from physicists under contract to the Department of Defense. His computer model allowed planners to vary the strength of the Pulse and its shape, just as the Tomahawk allowed. In the Fordo attack, Kim's work showed full fatalities among the crews of the S-300 installations. Most slept in unprotected barracks, waiting to be alerted to reinforce the S-300 sites. Once air force battle planners examined those Kim calculations they were used, freeing up assets for other violent work. There were thought to be many more S-300 missile batteries active in Iran.

Two minutes after the initial pulse, the first of a pair of AGM-130C rocket-assisted, precision-guided bombs arrived at Fordo. They were launched by the Air Force's lead B-2, which had flown a stealthy, hazardous path over the Iranian border to get in position. Both AGM-130Cs were bunker busters, the second launched forty-five seconds after the first. In the crenellated hills surrounding Fordo, there was a crease in the mountain range just above the uranium-enrichment facility. It cut by 540 feet the distance to be penetrated to a still-impossible 8,500 feet of mountain rock and concrete below it.

There was a roar, and vast chunks of rock and dirt were flung into the air as the first AGM-130C detonated its special two-thousand-pound warhead deep into the crease. Rocks rolled down the steep hillside as the debris settled. Suddenly, the second rocket-powered bunker buster launched by the B-2 accelerated into the crater left by the first. There was a second detonation far below. Inside the vast cavern of spinning centrifuges, the floor shook slightly but the automatic shutdown wasn't triggered. There was a fine powder falling from the ceiling. The special concrete was slowly sealing the created cracks. Above, a giant hole opened in the crease of the mountain. Dust settled into the crater after the successive failed attempts.

In the cavern men ran to clean the dust from the priceless centrifuges lest they become fouled. There were smiles and nods among them. The cavern had held as the ayatollah had promised. The internal generators continued to provide power after the initial Yankee bomb attack. They were safe from the infidel's bombs and protected in the arms of Allah.

Fallen Timber plus nine minutes

Four hundred miles away, another three US Air Force B-2 stealth bombers banked lazily, carving giant circles in the air fifty thousand feet above the eastern Mediterranean Sea, waiting to be useful. Autopilots were set to conserve fuel, and electronics actively scanned the empty sky. Each had a single weapon in its bomb bay and had been on station for three hours, having refueled twice since it left Missouri. This was their third deployment from the air base in Missouri.

Suddenly, a message appeared on the secure data screen mounted just above the lead pilot's left knee. Major Clyde Bransfeld flicked the autopilot off and turned east as his onboard computer loaded and checked the new data being sent against the store of data in the B-2.

The weapon in each of the B-2s' bomb bays was new and untested in combat. It was a GBU-57 MOP, a guided nonnuclear Massive Ordnance Penetrator. It weighed thirty thousand pounds and carried an explosive payload of fifty-five hundred pounds. It was about seven meters long, with wings for steering, and held the best electronics the United States could devise. The MOP was supposed to penetrate to a depth of four hundred feet before it detonated with something over five thousand pounds of precisely directed high explosive.

The failed bunker-buster bombs with their custom-designed two thousand-pound warheads had paved the way for the MOP by creating tiny cracks in the natural armor of the mountain and the reinforced concrete below. The concrete's sealant took several hours to fully repair itself; today it would have only several minutes.

Major Bransfeld, in the lead B-2, flew toward Forto. The other two B-2s armed with MOPs turned to attack two other installations where Iran had enrichment facilities. All had recently been visited by AGM-130Cs launched from companion B-2s.

In the hills above Forto, the massive hole created by the earlier smaller bunker busters had a new visitor. A delay fuse mounted in its tail allowed the MOP to penetrate deep into the blast hole before detonation in a shaped, directed charge focused beneath the detonation point. In the laboratory many meters beneath, the ceiling in the lab began to crack and fall slowly, then faster, as the weight of the ceiling became the source of damage rather than protection from it. Just then, another B-2 dropped two conventional AGM-130 bombs, each armed with Mark 84 530-pound warheads, and obliterated the small airstrip outside Fordo and the Iran Air 757 that stood near it.

Elsewhere in Iran, two other known enrichment sites buried deep in the mountains were subjected to similar devastating treatment by Air Force B-2s. Iran's radar had yet to show a single attacking airplane, as its signals bounced aimlessly off the angles of the stealthy bombers.

Fallen Timber plus twenty minutes

Fighter/bombers from the *Bush* accelerated toward targets along Iran's east coast. There were no Iranian radars probing for them and causing alerts from the F/A-18s' threat-detection electronics. The land below was newly dark and quiet. The GPS-targeting software was operating normally when the first four of the F/A-18s began their bomb runs at Bandar Abbas. Each aircraft lurched slightly when its CBU-97 one-thousand-pound smart bombs were released from the rails on its wings and began their guided path to destruction of goods and people.

Each CBU-97 held forty separate hockey-puck-shaped projectile bombs called Skeets, that electronically scan an area equal to about two football fields to detect a preset set of images that define the heat signature and shapes of the infrastructure of a military installation. Boats, armored vehicles, trucks, and refueling stations were high-value targets on this mission; people were less important right now. Explosively formed penetrators are fired at anything detected. If nothing is detected, the Skeets self-destruct at fifteen feet above the surface to avoid future civilian casualties and to enhance current ones.

Two minutes behind the first four of the *Bush*'s F/A-18s came another flight of two, carrying more traditional weapons to Bandar Abbas. They were CBU-87 cluster bombs, again one thousand pounds, each with a similar target footprint but loaded with an explosive and incendiary payload designed to discourage resistance and encourage fires.

Behind the F/A-18s, as they climbed and turned to their second target, a reconnaissance plane surveyed and recorded the scene. There were fewer people on the ground running. Explosions among the fuel trucks happened sequentially as fuel spilled from the impact of earlier munitions caught fire. Boats burned at their moorage. A small, flat building exploded suddenly, vaporizing three people who were running to it. More, smaller secondary explosions were seen across the expanse of the base. Trucks were stalled along lanes of docked boats. Some boats were floating amid the devastation, with men aboard trying to push debris away from other boats still moored and unmanned.

"Sierra, this is Moptop," said the pilot, Lieutenant Amy Fleur. Her reconnaissance operator sat behind her, face buried in a vision tube, controlling the images. There was a three-camera unit mounted externally beneath the F/A-18. It was called a Tactical Advanced Reconnaissance Pod.

"Moptop, Sierra, go."

"Target Alpha is afire broadly and going boom. How is your image? No powered movement of boats yet. No active force seen moving. I have film. Ready to move on."

"Image good, Moptop," Sierra responded. "Target Bravo now under attack."

"Sierra, Moptop. Roger. I'm headed that way. Moptop out."

The Iranian islands of Abu Musa, Kish, Qeshm, Larak, and seven others were all under attack at that moment. Shore batteries outside the Straits were given special attention, because they had a straight shot at the US fleet if their missiles were launched.

Tomahawks delivered the Pulse along the entire Iranian coastline in an attempt to disable small boats that could attack the fleet. Known dockage was then bombed, twice.

In Tehran, Air Force F-15s launched from Sheikh Isa air base in Bahrain were swarming toward their assigned targets a few minutes after Tomahawks, launched from B-2 bombers, had arrived. Two bombs were reserved for the Telecommunications Company of Iran, the single hub of all of Iran's communications service.

The Tomahawk used a Pulse blast, electronically shaped to destroy all exposed wiring and circuitry there; its power was sufficiently focused as to be lethal for any workers in the building.

The second bomb, an AGM-130C was dropped a few minutes later by another of the stealthy B-2 bombers that were invisible to the Iranian radar. The guided bunker buster was employed to deal with the rumors that tunnels had been constructed by the Iranians beneath the telecommunications company headquarters.

The use of the B-2s in the early stages of the attack on Iran was designed as a first strike surprise to cripple the command and control structure of the Iranian forces and their government. Headquarters for the Corps Guard and the Quds Force were hit early. All known Iranian missile sites were pulsed by a swarm of Tomahawks followed by AGM-130 bombs equipped with the Mark4 conventional warhead and dropped by Air Force F-15s and F-16s following closely to hit their targets before remaining missile sites could become operational.

CHAPTER 20

FALLEN TIMBER PLUS THIRTY-FIVE MINUTES

"SCHEDULE A PRESS CONFERENCE immediately," President Roberts said. "National TV."

The state of defense readiness, called DEFCON 3, had been used only twice in recent years. Once during the Yom Kippur War and then again just after the attacks of September 11, 2001. Around the world US forces were recalled to duty from leave and home stays. Reserve forces were alerted to a call to active duty. Ships came to battle stations, and civilian airlines were alerted that their pilots and equipment were soon to be nationalized for an undetermined period.

President Roberts interrupted the most popular evening show on US television.

> *"My Fellow Americans,*
>
> *"Iran today declared open war on Israel, with an announcement of a nuclear attack on them and coordinated ground attacks across Israel's borders by their violent allies in Palestine, Jordan, Syria, and Egypt.*

"The ground attacks by Iran's allies are under way as I speak, but the claimed nuclear attack has not yet materialized, for reasons we are attempting to determine. There has been no nuclear blast. Iran has gone silent, perhaps as a tactic. US forces have been mobilized to defend aggressively the Straits of Hormuz and our allies around the Persian Gulf. I have ordered our forces to an alert level of DEFCON 3 in order to be best prepared for any more surprises from Iran and their henchmen. We are preparing for the worst.

"I have ordered to be distributed to you a copy of the Iranian press release that on the Internet declared this escalation to nuclear conflict. When I know more, you will know more."

The press assembled, frantic with questions while speed-reading the press release.

The Islamic Republic of Iran
The Holy City of Qom

PRESS RELEASE

Subject: Annihilation of Israel Infrastructure
Wednesday, 2330 hours, GMT

Three Iranian patriots were martyred today in an act of war by the Islamic Republic of Iran upon the Jewish state. As a result of a small nuclear explosion created by the devout young scientists of Islam, the state of Israel has lost its entire electrical system. Few, if any, of the Jews lost their lives, but the Zionists have today lost their ability to threaten Islam. The electromagnetic pulse associated with Iran's first deployment of its nuclear weapons has destroyed all exposed electronics in the Jewish state.

The long-oppressed forces of Iran's allies—Hezbollah, Hamas, and the Islamic Jihad—have tonight attacked the Zionists across Israel's illegal borders in order to finally reclaim their homeland.

> Other than government officials and military planners, there have not been, and will not be, widespread execution of the Jews. Most survivors will be given opportunities to serve the Shiite victors and to atone for the sins of their fathers.
>
> The Islamic state of Iran has two additional completed weapons and several nearing completion. One of the completed weapons has been deployed to Europe and the other to the Gulf of Mexico. Any attacks by infidels on Iran or its people will cause one or both of those weapons to be detonated, and the infidels there will join the Zionists in living without modernity, as they so richly deserve.
>
> Allahu Akbar

The White House
Oval Office

Roberts walked into the Oval Office from the press conference and slumped into his high-backed green leather chair. He sighed as he leaned back and looked at the ceiling. Kelly, MacMillan, and Brooks Elliot sat across from the desk, with small tables between each cushioned chair. Each had a yellow notepad in front of him.

"Well, we're in it now, God help us," Roberts said. "I gave their draft press release back to them, right up their nose, almost verbatim. Tell me some good news."

"The good news is that the three nuclear sites we knew of are gone," Patrick Kelly said. "Destroyed. They won't be a problem, so Iran may be without the means to produce a nuke. That was a primary objective. Much of the Shiite leadership in Qom is also dead. We have not yet been attacked in the Gulf by small boats with big weapons, as we feared. Their air force and navy have been severely compromised."

"Tell me the bad news," Roberts said.

"The bad news is of uncertainty," Kelly said. "We don't know what we don't know. They have not yet responded to our surprise attack, as they will. They are capable. Things are likely to get ugly soon."

"Mr. Elliot," Roberts said, "I asked you to stay in touch with Mr. Cuchulain. Have you?"

"Only recently, Mr. President," Elliot said. "Once their telecoms went down from the Pulse, he could transmit and receive over our satellite network with little fear of detection."

"And?" Roberts replied impatiently.

"Cooch has been in touch with the group of Republican officers we identified as unhappy and potentially subversive. They have viewed the videos and probably met separately at dinner the night before they met with Cooch. At the end of the dinner among them, they expressed interest in helping with the negotiations but were discouraged by Cooch, as we agreed."

"And the nuance that you two pushed so hard?" Roberts said. "Will Cuchulain be successful in this outrageous endeavor?"

Elliot smiled. "That has not arisen and perhaps never will, as we discussed at some length. None of the events essential to success in this particular scheme have been initiated, let alone consummated. Specifically, they have not yet openly considered regime change and how they will govern if successful."

"And your recommendation, Mr. Elliot?"

"Let the battle plan run, Mr. President," Elliot said. "It's not broken yet and seems to be running as hoped."

"And the Israelis, Colonel MacMillan?" Roberts said. "Are they happy yet?"

"The Israelis are surviving, Mr. President," Mac said. "They seem to be doing well against a huge number of massed insurgents, even though they lost some of their new construction and its workers. They seem to be counterattacking. That's a good thing."

"Maybe they'll see the light," Roberts said. "A potential nuke attack should get their attention."

"Indeed, Mr. President," Mac said. "If they do well against the attacking insurgent masses, we should have some goodwill with them to settle the whole Palestinian problem. We'll not have a better chance anytime soon. At this point, lacking a real nuke attack, it seems unlikely the Israelis will lose."

CHAPTER 21

TEHRAN

JAHAN AND ALEX WERE SITTING AT the kitchen counter, talking about the life-shattering implications for Jahan arising from the attack by the Americans. Jahan's classes had been canceled, and the university was in turmoil. Both his livelihood and his living spaces were at risk. Dust filtered into the apartment from the construction across the hall despite Jahan's placing of a wet sheet around the door. By early evening the sounds were slowly diminishing as troops left the construction of a new office to sleep in their barracks. At dawn they would be back to prepare for an assault on Tehran from a yet-unknown, still invisible aggressor

There was a soft knock at the door. Jahan hurried to it and said, "Who is it?"

"It's your loving brother and I'm tired," Dahir said. "Let me in."

Jahan pulled the still-damp sheet from around the door, then unlocked and opened it.

"Are you here to throw me from my home?" he asked.

Dahir walked in and swatted sawdust from his field uniform, then plopped into the chair Alex had pulled over earlier.

"I'm here to collapse," he said. "I may still throw you out."

Alex stood and went to the refrigerator. He took out a bottle of Iranian white wine and held it up.

"Are we going to sin tonight?" he said.

"If not now, when?" Dahir said.

As Alex opened the bottle, he said, "I got the Kphones set up for you. There is a sheet of paper and two extra Kphones on the counter beside a plastic bag to carry them. I assigned IDs to each of the phones, so all you have to do is enter the ID and press the "send" button. Multiple sends will create a conference call. There are two numbers left, if you can think of who would use them well. You may want to tell all to be careful with their Kphones if they have been exposed to the pulse."

"What do we do about charging them?" Dahir said. "Do you have cords?"

"The Kphone uses induction charging. They induce charges from the electrical-system wiring. As long as there is electrical power flowing through the wiring, they'll stay charged. It works faster if you store the Kphone beside an electrical outlet. There is a charging slot with a mini-USB connection if you need it."

"Got it," Dahir said, leaning back to stretch his chest and shoulders. "As best I can tell, our Republican forces are mostly intact. The Corps Guard has been devastated. How do we get word from our top leadership as to battle orders? Our radios that were near the airport of the air base have been fried. Most of the others are fine. It's been about less than twenty-four hours since we were first attacked. What do you think is next?"

"I imagine the industrial and leadership side of Qom has been vaporized, so battle orders seem unlikely to come from there," Alex said. "Fordo, Natanz, and whatever other enrichment sites that existed are likely gone. I wouldn't think many orders are coming from any of those places."

Dahir got up and poured another glass of wine, then said, "You're just a bundle of joy, aren't you, Alex?"

"What shall we do?" Jahan said. "Our people will need religious guidance."

"More importantly, my troops will need tactical guidance," Dahir said.

"How are you going to figure out who to fight and where they are?" Alex said.

"I guess I'll worry about that when they come," Dahir said. "Right now, I'm worried about my wife and two daughters. I've been trying to reach them all day. I sent a messenger to check on our place, but it is deserted."

"Isn't there a boss where you live? You are housed in government quarters," Jahan said. "There has to be someone."

Dahir nodded. "General Nikahd was able to get orders to me to take over the defense of Tehran, and he has administrative responsibility for the housing for the academy's faculty. Maybe I'll contact him to check on my wife and the girls. Oh, and I got promoted to colonel to lead the Republican effort for the defense of Teheran. Defense from whom is the question of the moment."

"Then why don't you and I find a car that works and go check on your family," Alex said. "I need to get out of here a little while. Your family is probably better off here anyhow. I can help you to pack and move."

Dahir gazed at the ceiling for a few moments, then nodded and walked to the door.

"I'll get a car," he said. "I need some things from there anyhow, even if we decide that a move isn't a good idea. Ten minutes."

DAHIR WALKED BACK INTO the apartment twenty minutes later. Alex was wearing a green canvas vest with multiple side pockets over a mottled green shirt, brown cargo pants, and brown canvas lace-up hiking boots. He stood.

"Shall we?" Alex said.

They walked from the apartment. An old Toyota Land Cruiser, green with Republican markings, was idling by the door with a man at the wheel.

They drove north through the nearly deserted streets of Tehran. The teeming masses seen on the streets and in the shops when Alex had been shopping weren't in sight. Faces could be seen staring at them from apartment windows as they passed.

In a few minutes, they pulled up to the Ghorbani residence. Dahir jumped from the Cruiser and ran inside. In a few moments, he returned.

"It's empty. Three small suitcases are missing."

Alex looked at Dahir and said, "Perhaps your boss can shed some light on this. Is his office nearby?"

"It's not far," Dahir said. "I certainly hope someone there knows what is going on."

They drove another ten minutes north to the regional headquarters compound of the Republicans.

They slowed for the guards at the entrance. The dark silhouette of the prison loomed over the compound.

"Ah, Colonel Ghorbani," a guard in the field uniform of the Republicans said. "Pass, please." He saluted as the other guard lifted the gate.

They drove past the hulking mass of the prison for political and religious prisoners, then went around a small compound of vehicles behind barbed wire. There were several armored vehicles and one medium tank, an old Russian-built T-34. Trucks and cars abounded.

The driver pulled up to a building with the Iranian flag on a tall pole and a green military flag flowing just beneath it. Dahir stepped out and put his cap on, then squared it as soldiers do. He stepped inside, while Alex sat in the backseat and casually thumbed his Kphone.

Ten minutes later, Dahir burst out the door followed by General Nikahd, three burly NCOs, and a young lieutenant.

Ghorbani's face was red as he spoke to the general. "There was zero need to relocate my family from our home. I demand to see them and their quarters immediately. I can't run a defense of Tehran without knowing whether my family is well."

As they passed out of earshot, Alex could see General Nikahd talking and nodding to Dahir as his back hand waved a sergeant closer.

"Follow them slowly," Alex said to the driver. "We may need to help Colonel Ghorbani's family move their things. Our colonel is angry about something, so we shouldn't be far behind."

He bent his head again to his Kphone.

The Land Cruiser moved slowly twenty meters behind the walking group. The group walked to a two-story barracks building with slatted wooden sides and a crumbling roof and into one of four doors on its facing side.

Fifteen minutes later, Dahir Ghorbani was led from the barracks building in handcuffs. His nose was bleeding, and two of the sergeants had blood on their faces. General Nikahd held a handkerchief to his left eye.

"Are you armed?" Alex said. A quick, nervous shake of the driver's head gave Alex the bad news.

Alex stepped from the Land Cruiser as they approached. He bowed and said, "Is there a problem? I am a religious advisor to Colonel Ghorbani and his family."

"Official business of the state," Nikahd said. "Get out of the way."

"But I don't understand," Alex said, stepping in front of them.

"Cuff him," the general said. "Bring him along."

General Nikahd began to hurry with Lieutenant Latifpur toward the low office building. The defense of Tehran would have to be otherwise led, this time by a reliable Shiite patriot.

One of the sergeants pulled a pistol from the holster on his belt and pointed it at Alex. A second pulled a set of handcuffs from his belt.

Alex held his hands out in front of him. They cuffed him and began to march them, side by side, to the office building.

ALEX AND DAHIR WERE shoved into an unused office. The door was shut and locked behind them.

"Well, that was exciting," Alex said. "Are your wife and kids OK?"

"They might have been better off if I hadn't come," Dahir said. "My family was moved from our quarters to be in the protective custody of the Republicans. They are in a one-room barracks setup. One toilet, three beds. My wife has a mark on her face, and the girls are terrified."

"I assume you reacted badly to that," Alex said. "I would have. But here we are."

"I may not even have a chance to kill Masaud Nikahd, our devout general," Dahir said, looking at him. "Your face is getting all weird. Are you all right?"

Alex's face was transforming once again. He could feel the skin around his eyes bunching and his face flushing as his adrenaline level continued to grow. His breathing was loud.

"I'm fine, but what do you suppose is going to happen now?" Alex said. "Is our devout general on the radio to his superiors?"

Dahir smiled grimly and shook his head. "Nikahd prides himself on handling his own problems. He isn't talking to anyone. He is thinking about how to make this situation work to his advantage. He will want to question me and has a set of goons he uses for unpleasant interrogations. I just about threw up at the one I witnessed. Now I'm next."

"Well, what's your plan, tactics master?" Alex said as he reached with his cuffed hands to his wide belt and fumbled with it.

"You're the ex-commando," Dahir said. "What would *you* do?"

Alex sat silent for a moment, then said, "If I had the opportunity, I would kill them all and hope that the word hadn't gotten out before I managed that."

"Fat chance," Dahir said. "The time to do that would have been before we got handcuffed. You just stuck your hands out to be cuffed."

"At least they cuffed me in front. This belt I wear has pockets for all sorts of things. Some of those things are two or three different handcuff keys."

Alex fumbled with his handcuffs, and they came open. He reached for Dahir, and Dahir watched his cuffs come open, speechless.

"Now what?" Alex said.

"You seem to have thought more about this kind of thing than I have," Dahir said. "There are six or eight very nasty men coming in the next ten minutes or so to begin a multiday interrogation. Cuffs or not, we lose. Any ideas?"

"Yeah," Alex said. "Let's kill the guards, the goons, and the general, then pick up your family and go back to Jahan's apartment and talk about what to do next. Maybe have a cup of tea and a snack."

Dahir rubbed his wrists, then took a handkerchief from his hip pocket, unfolded it, and dabbed at his nose. He put it back in his hip pocket.

"It seems to me that we're unlikely to do that, given the numbers we will face. If we try, they're going to beat on you as well. Bad idea."

"Compared to the chance of getting a bad beating," Alex said, "I'm going to go for it."

"You're a Sunni scholar," Dahir said. "Your commando days are over. We wouldn't have a chance. We wouldn't have a chance even if you were on top of your game that way."

"If they come and are unarmed," Alex said, "you take the general first to distract them and then give me some help when you disable him. I'm going for the goons. We'll want a fast exit."

Dahir sat, thoughtful. "And then what?" he said.

"Then we figure out what's next," Alex said. "According to you, there aren't likely to be many who know of the situation outside this compound, You figure a way to go back to your job, with no one the wiser."

"We'd have to destroy the entire compound to make that work. No chance. But I'm going to put some marks on General Nikahd, no matter what."

"Keep your hands close in front of you when they come in," Alex said. "You're still cuffed."

FROM THE HALLWAY OUTSIDE the office door, there was the sound of men laughing and talking loudly as they approached the unused office where Alex and Dahir were held.

The door burst open. General Nikahd walked in and gave Dahir a triumphant smile. His eye was beginning to swell closed. Behind him were Lieutenant Latifpur and a crowd of men in Republican battle dress, one holding a long wooden baton and another pulling on a pair of black leather gloves. When the last of the eight men came into the office, he closed the door.

Nikahd turned to Dahir and said, "So, Colonel. We—"

Dahir launched himself at the general with a roar, punched him in the nose with a straight right, then hit him in the jaw with his left.

As Nikahd fell, the lead interrogator raised his wooden baton with two hands. His hips leaned forward; his chest and back arched to bring leverage to the blow. Dahir's head was the target.

Time slowed down for Alex. He saw Dahir's right hand impact Nikahd's nose. The crimson splash seemed to float gently around Dahir's fist. Alex's training took over, with Dain supervising.

The CIA Special Operations unit had developed seventy-two martial arts routines that dealt with the most common forms of physical aggression. Alex had rehearsed each of them hundreds, perhaps thousands, of times. There was more than one expression of the CIA seventy-two-move martial art set in play in dealing with an aggressive group of eight men. The combination of moves against the crowed mass played out in his instincts as his conscious mind reviewed the situation. It was that mental divide between muscle memory and conscious observation that had been so hard to learn.

Alex drove his body between Dahir and the baton, disrupting the force of the blow. On that path his right heel drove into the left knee of the man with the black gloves, collapsing it with a crunching of cartilage. The force of the kick slowed Alex's forward progress enough that he could grasp the head and left ear of the man with the baton. His right hand grasped the baton wielder's beard. With a convulsive jerk of both hands, he spun the man's head as he emitted a loud grunt. The sound of bones breaking was audible.

Alex dropped the ragged remains of beard and skin as he pushed the man into the crowd beginning to reach for him and pulling their fists back. As the dying bulk hit them, there was confusion and an effort to disentangle to engage Alex.

Two Republicans came free of the pack. Alex drove his left thumb into one man's eye and slashed deeply with his thumbnail, then reflexively flicked his thumb in hopes of dislodging the eyeball. He drove the heel of his right hand up and into the second man's nose. The target of Alex's blow was the wall at the back of the office; the head slammed abruptly into it. The force of the blow drove the broken nose bone into the man's brain. Alex sensed, perhaps saw, two bearded heads at his left. He twisted to grab an ear on either side of them and slammed the two heads together, pulled them apart, then slammed them together again. He dropped a severed ear from his bright-red left hand.

"*Six*," Alex heard Dain say as he moved.

The door to the office came open, and Lieutenant Latifpur slipped out through it, running.

"*Knife, seven o'clock*," Dain erupted.

There was the snick of a knife opening as Alex spun. He let his body flow away from the dwindling mass of men. The knife holder had the blade low and was lunging toward Alex. A second remaining man lunged laterally and was digging in his pocket. Alex kicked him in the stomach as he slid to avoid a knife slash that caught the inside of his arm, opening a deep gash. He grabbed the knife arm as it burrowed past and pulled it up in a spray of his own blood, while his coiled body unwound with a forearm strike to the man's face, breaking the nose and collapsing bones in his face. The force of the blow put the man on his heels. Alex swept the man's feet out from under him with a push of his left foot against the man's ankles. The feet shot into the air. The man landed on the side of his head. Alex kicked him in the throat.

"That's eight, laddie. Get the general."

Alex flowed away from the mass of men to make room for assessment. Everyone was down. Dahir was kneeling on the general's arms and sitting on his chest, pounding the face with his fists and still yelling.

"Let's go, Dahir," Alex said as he pulled Ghorbani to his feet. "The lieutenant got out the door. He'll be bringing reinforcements."

General Nikahd's face was a mass of blood, and he was still. Dahir kicked him in the ear as Alex pulled him to the door and into the hall.

"Let's get your family," Alex said. "There's not much time."

DAHIR BURST INTO THE barracks room. Alex stood behind him at the door and watched for the Republican troops who were sure to come.

Dahir's wife looked up at his face in shock, her face still swollen and red with tears. Dahir's face was still marked with a fan of crimson from his nose and his hands were bright red with Nikahd's blood. The two girls were huddled in the corner, crying.

"Get up and come with me," Dahir said. "There is no time to talk."

He pulled his Yasmin to her feet and went to the girls.

"There's no time for crying," he said. "We're in danger. We must run—and run fast."

They burst from the door. Alex ran down the dirt street toward the office and said, "Follow me."

At the first intersection, they turned and kept running behind Alex. Their staff Land Cruiser was nowhere in sight. After fifty meters or so, the gray stone walls of the prison loomed in front of them. Alex stopped and crouched behind a parked truck. The gate was another hundred meters away and still manned by guards. Sounds of yelling were loud in the compound near the office building.

Dahir breathed hard from the run, as did his wife. The girls were in better shape but stood staring at Alex.

"I am Kufdani," Alex said to the girls. "I'm a friend of your father, trying to help him get you out of here."

He pulled his Kphone from a pocket on his vest and thumbed a few keys.

"Don't mess with that phone right now, Alex," Dahir said. "There is no one to call. We're in trouble. What's our plan?"

Alex slipped the Kphone into his vest pocket and said, "Right now we're going to steal a car and get out of here. I don't like it here much. Let's get closer to the gate, then we'll figure out the next step."

The small group began running again, this time a little slower, with Alex still in the lead. They reached the north wall of the prison and turned toward the gate, then stopped again, this time beside a small lot where two staff cars and several small trucks were parked, all unmanned.

In the distance there was a yell as the Republican forces of General Nikahd spotted them. In a few moments, there was the roar of a tank moving out of the fenced motor pool.

"See if you can get one of these vehicles started, Dahir," Alex said. "Take your family with you. I think we've upset General Nikahd, or at least his lieutenant."

"I hope you brought an antitank weapon, Alex," Dahir yelled over his shoulder as he ran to the staff cars with his family. "That's the sound of a T-34."

Alex watched the street as he pulled his Kphone from his vest again and thumbed it. He looked at the screen and waited.

On the street a group of men armed with pistols and rifles began to run toward them. At the front of the group was a man with blood covering his face and staining his uniform. It was Nikahd.

"Don't kill them," Nikahd could be heard yelling. "I want them alive. They must be alive. All of them."

Behind Alex was the sound of a car starting. Dahir had found transportation for them. The car pulled up beside Alex.

"Get in," Dahir yelled to Alex.

"Not yet," Alex said. "Get out of the line of fire. I'll be with you shortly."

The large group was within fifty meters when the tank turned onto the street and accelerated, its gun turret swiveling toward them.

"About time," Alex muttered. He pushed a button on his Kphone and waited. A few seconds later, there was a huge explosion in the midst of Nikahd's group. As the smoke began to clear on the crater, a second blast caused the tank to burst into flames.

Alex turned and ran to where Dahir had stopped the idling car. As he reached it, the guard shack disappeared in another blast.

Alex got into the passenger seat, blew out a loud breath, and said, "Now then, where were we in our planning?"

Dahir put the car in gear and drove to the exit, where the guard shack had been a few moments ago. He drove out of the compound, around a smoking crater, and south toward the university. He checked his rearview mirror frequently as he drove, and his family sat in the backseat, stunned and still silent.

"We bought some time with those strikes," Dahir said. "Where the hell did they come from?"

"We'll talk about it over coffee when we get back," Alex said. "We're busy right now."

Dahir glanced in his rearview mirror again.

"They'll be coming again soon," he said. "There are four hundred troops in that compound, all of whom will want to kill us—or worse."

"Good point," Alex said. He glanced at his Kphone and thumbed it again.

Dahir concentrated on driving and putting distance between them and the likely pursuit. Alex fumbled with something from his vest, then wrapped his bloody arm in his handkerchief and tied it.

After several minutes the compound behind them erupted in flames from repeated explosions. They continued for several minutes.

"You can slow down now, Dahir," Alex said. "I've had enough danger in my life for today."

Dahir slowed the vehicle and said, "The compound has been destroyed? You caused that?"

"I certainly hope it was destroyed," Alex said. "They were planning to hurt us—or worse."

"That was impressive, but we can't defeat all the Republicans," Dahir said. "They will all be after us before long."

"Oh?" Alex said. "Why will they be after us?"

Dahir started to speak several times, then was silent.

"Everyone who knew about that encounter with Nikahd is dead," Dahir said. "Maybe no one knows."

"Indeed," Alex said. He was comfortable waiting while Dahir absorbed this information. His family had been given a get-out-of-jail-free card.

"What were the missiles? Hellfires?"

"They were," Alex said. "The bombs were probably smart five-hundred-pounders from Air Force jets."

"The Hellfires were from American drones in the area, I assume," Dahir said. "That was handy."

"I'll say," Alex said. "The wonders of playing with a Kphone when you need it."

"Will someone tell us what is going on and where we are going?" Darya, the eldest daughter, said, "and Daddy, you should wipe the blood from your face and hands. It's really gross."

"Hush," Yasmin said. "It's enough that we are away from that awful place and those awful men." She handed Dahir a handkerchief from her purse.

"You should have some answers, young lady," Alex said. "You've been through some difficult times. Your father and I can talk later. We're going to your Uncle Jahan's home at the university, where you will stay for a while. There won't be as much room as you might like, but it's better than where you just were staying. Your father is staying there, too, but he'll have to work much of the time."

"Anything is better than that dump where we were," Darya said.

"But what will we do?" the younger girl said.

"Work on your lessons, of course," Alex said. "And maybe watch some videos, maybe practice your English. I have just the thing to keep you busy. Everything will be fine."

They pulled through the university gates and went up to the ground-level entrance to Jahan's apartment. A Republican guard was standing outside. Alex slipped from his seat and stood close to him on the sidewalk.

"Welcome back, Colonel Ghorbani," the guard said. "Congratulations on your promotion. You had a pleasant trip, I trust."

"Useful, at least," Dahir said. He opened the rear door for his daughters to scramble from the car and look around. Alex opened the door for Yasmin.

The five of them went through the door and up the stairs to Jahan's apartment.

Jahan stood at the door as they arrived. Behind him, uniformed men were scurrying back and forth through the newly built double doors of the new Republican Defense of Tehran offices, as was roughly written on the wall above.

"Welcome, welcome," Jahan said to the three females. "Welcome back to my home. Let's get you settled. I have moved things around in the hopes that Dahir would return with you. You will stay here until this unpleasantness is over. You have three rooms. Kufdani and I will double up in the fourth."

As he led the three of them across the open space toward the bedrooms, Jahan said over his shoulder, "You two have probably been entertained, but I made tea if you want it. The pot is hot. I'll be busy for quite a while here."

"I've been entertained enough for today," Dahir said. "I need to get some work done. Before we left, I had the Kphones sent out to my colleagues. I think I'll see if they are working before things get violent."

Alex walked to the kitchen and picked up the pot.

"Goodness, we certainly don't want any violence," Alex said. "And being able to talk to colleagues after such a boring day should be good therapy."

Dahir stopped at the door and said, "What an interesting discussion this should be. Don't go anywhere. I'll be several hours."

Alex nodded. "I understand that I'm restricted to quarters. I'll be here."

CHAPTER 22

THE WHITE HOUSE OVAL OFFICE

GENERAL PATRICK KELLY, MAC MACMILLAN, and Brooks Elliot sat across from President Roberts, each with a yellow notepad in front of them. The only computers allowed were those of Sheila Molyneaux and President Roberts. She was in an armless chair near the big live-oak desk, facing them, an iPad on her lap.

"Well, gentlemen," Roberts said. "Progress at last? We've spent several billion dollars in the last twenty-four hours and put thousands of American men and women at risk. Assuage my pain."

Kelly said, "Mac watches this twenty-four-seven. I'll let him summarize. Mr. Elliot is hard on it as well."

"We've had a break," Mac said. "And the timetable has likely accelerated from our first guesses. Long story short, there was violence, monitored by drone video. Ghorbani, the Republican officer who was our first choice to subvert, suffered the indignity of having his Republican leadership detain his wife and children. They moved them to a barracks apartment. Ghorbani and Cuchulain were taken prisoner there, then removed in handcuffs."

"This is good news how?" Molyneaux said.

"Quiet, Sheila," Roberts said. "You're just a sore loser."

"The next thing on the video is eleven minutes later," Mac said. "Six men in Republican battle dress were hurrying to the building where they were detained. Eight minutes after that, the door of the building opened, and Ghorbani and Cuchulain were seen running from it to the barracks where the dependents are housed. Ghorbani and Cuchulain got the wife and kids within four minutes and ran out and away from the building, cut down a side street, and hid. Ghorbani ran and got a vehicle from a parking lot beside them. It was quick, so the keys were probably in it.

"By this time, a second drone's video picked up a mass of men running and a T-34 tank pulling out of the motor pool there. Of the eight drones we had hovering around Tehran, waiting to be useful, four were diverted to support Cuchulain and his charges about ten minutes before all of this trouble started. He had a Kphone code that tied to his GPS. He had a second code to shoot the Hellfires from them. The targets were pretty obvious."

"The tanks and the troops were the targets, I assume," Roberts said.

"And then some," Patrick Kelly said. "The code Cuchulain used had been set to direct the destruction of a compound or base. We first destroyed the tank and the troops; then we attacked the base with the remaining Hellfire missiles and recovered the drones. A fully loaded pair of diverted Air Force F-15s did the cleanup bomb attack a few minutes later. Those twenty-three acres are gone. Cuchulain and Ghorbani are back in Tehran at the university apartment."

"Was that extra attack necessary?" Molyneaux said. "We killed a bunch of people for no good reason."

"We'll never know whether it was necessary or not," Elliot said. "The genesis of that destruct code was the feeling that any insurgent effort had to be supported in terms of deniability of their treason until they got traction. Alex's using that code was a reflection of his decision that the effort would be jeopardized if the compound wasn't destroyed."

"And when, pray tell, will we know the reason he pushed that particular button?" Molyneaux said. "Cuchulain must have been under enormous stress. His thinking efficacy must suffer."

"Thinking efficacy?" Roberts said. "Please."

"We'll know soon enough, I imagine," Mac said. "He'll call when he can. But his thinking efficacy, as you call it, is best when he is under enormous stress."

"How nice for him," Molyneaux said.

Elliot nodded. "And for us, we hope."

"Anything else, for now?" Roberts said.

No one spoke.

Roberts shrugged. "We're prepared. We know the most we have to give. I hope it won't come to that."

CHAPTER 23

UNIVERSITY OF TEHRAN JAHAN GHORBANI'S QUARTERS

IT WAS PAST TEN WHEN THE DOOR opened and Dahir Ghorbani walked in. Jahan had gone to bed an hour earlier, exhausted from the stress of the day. Yasmin and the girls had been asleep for two hours, refreshed after their first hot shower in several days; but also exhausted.

Alex sat in one of the three chairs, sipping a cup of tea, waiting. He'd spent most of the past hour on his Kphone, talking to Mac and Kelly. Beyond saying, "Hi," Elliot had been silent.

Ghorbani looked at Alex's teacup with distaste, then slumped into his chair.

"Does Jahan have anything decent to drink around here?" he said. "I'm not in a white wine mood."

"How would I know? If he does, he hasn't shared it," Alex said. "I may be able to find a bottle of vintage port in my luggage, though."

Dahir's face brightened. "Before I arrest you and maybe have you executed, that would be a nice thing. You got this through our customs how?"

"I'm an Islamic scholar on a religious diplomatic passport," Alex said. "Besides, how could you arrest and execute a harmless scholar, even if Sunni?"

Dahir leaned back and closed his eyes. "Get the port," he said softly. "I'll arrest your harmless, pacifistic self later. I'm a little tired right now. The girls are asleep?"

"Indeed," Alex said. "Stress is a marvelous soporific."

Alex walked to his luggage, which Jahan had placed in the great room just outside their new shared bedroom, and dug out a bottle of Dow's 1963 vintage port in bubble wrap. Beside the refrigerator, he cut the foil from the top, then stuck a corkscrew into the cork and opened it. He sniffed the cork and smiled. At the counter by the stove, he opened a lower cabinet door and found two tiny teacups. He poured a little into each and took both teacups to the small table between their chairs.

"Shall we talk, my friend?" Alex said.

Ghorbani pushed himself from his chair and walked to the left-most bedroom door and peeked inside at his sleeping family. With a nod he walked back, sat down, and picked up the teacup of port.

"Why don't you just tell me what is going on?" Dahir said. "Your actions today were those of neither an Islamic scholar nor a Moroccan businessman. You have deceived me."

"Perhaps," Alex said, "but only by circumstance and not by word. I led you to assume that I was no longer an active commando and I'm not. Neither am I an employee of the US government."

"Skip the word dance, Kufdani," Ghorbani said. "You called in Hellfire missiles to protect your escape today, and you destroyed a Republican military compound to protect your story."

"All true," Alex said. "Well, to be fair, it was *our* escape and *our* story, but I won't argue semantics."

"After today," Dahir said, "I'm convinced that I may not be able to beat the story out of you. Why don't you just tell me what is going on?"

Alex nodded, took a sip of his port from the tiny teacup, and said, "My team at Kufdani lucked into an opportunity to convince the US Defense Department and the president that Iran was a candidate for a civil war, rather than total destruction and American occupation. I don't know that Saudi troops and occupation are a serious consideration by the president. He views himself as a more secular, humanist type.

"Since there is little understanding of the political and moral structure in Iran among the Americans, I volunteered and was chosen to be the scout, to see if there was a way to facilitate a relationship with the more liberal views in Iran."

Dahir was silent for several moments. He finally pulled his Kphone from his pocket and put it on the table between them.

"I contacted my colleagues when we returned," Dahir said, "using the Kphone network you so graciously set up. We discussed the American attack and its implications. I finally reported the day's events to them and your role in it."

Alex raised his eyebrows and then his teacup.

"That was fast," he said. "I'm surprised. Are they sending the gendarmes after us or at least me?"

"Not yet," Dahir said. "They seem more interested in your role here and in what use they could make of it in service to our republic. It seems that a large number of Republican assets were spared damage and destruction as a result of your advice at dinner the other evening that they be moved from facilities shared with the Corps Guard."

"That was part common sense and part a result of being personally convinced that an attack was near," Alex said. "Attacking the radical thinkers first, then the more liberal ones is current dogma in many countries at risk of war."

"And what do you think is next from the Americans if you again exercise your common sense and your convictions?"

"As I mentioned the other day, I think they will continue to attack military targets around the Straits of Hormuz. Religious leadership positions and offices have likely been attacked to avoid the clerics stirring up fervor for counterattack. Here in the North, and elsewhere in Iran, there were many attacks in the first few hours of the battle. The Americans will likely assess the battle damage done and use that assessment to plan more attacks. Missile sites and modern antiaircraft installations that protect them are likely the next focus for the Americans. They will get around to the ground forces before long. I haven't seen an Iranian fighter since it began, so I think it is likely that your air force has been rendered ineffective."

"Your cheery optimism continues to warm my soul, Kufdani," Dahir said.

"What do your colleagues think, Dahir?" Alex said. "Did you mention your encounter with General Nikahd and his concern for your family?"

Dahir nodded. "I told them the why and the what of Nikahd and his actions. I also told them to beware of their Kphones, lest they cause Hellfire missiles to rain on their heads. You really must tell me someday how you arranged for them to do your bidding."

Alex shrugged. "There are eight drones now constantly cruising around Tehran, each armed with two Hellfires. They diverted four to me upon my request."

"For a Sunni cleric?" Dahir said. "That's unlikely."

"For the Sunni cleric who convinced them that it was worth protecting a man who hopes to avoid tens of thousands of Iranian dead and an unacceptable number of American casualties."

"I suppose that makes sense," Dahir said. "But you seemed competent at looking out for yourself."

"I wasn't there to look out for myself," Alex said. "I was there to help protect your family and keep you safe."

"Really?" Dahir said. "Why? Why us?"

"It was only about your family to the degree that they divert your attention with their danger," Alex said. "It's mostly about you."

Dahir sat for a minute or so, staring at the ceiling and then at Alex. "OK," he said. "I simply don't get it. Why is it about me?"

"Because your countrymen need you," Alex said. "They are without leadership. You are qualified."

"If we need leadership after the war," Dahir said, "Colonel Tousi will provide it. I will support him, as will my colleagues."

"I'm afraid not," Alex said. "Tousi has colon cancer. He will be weak from the treatments for many months. At best, he will be useful in giving you support and credibility."

"Camel crap," Dahir said. "How could you possibly know that? Does he?"

"He was told just before the attack by his physicians in an e-mail," Alex said. "As far as what the Americans know, welcome to the world of a technological hegemon struggling with its new powers. They know about your group at dinner the other evening and the meetings you've had over many months, including the e-mails you've exchanged. You're viewed as potentially subversive, in fact."

"This is outrageous, Kufdani," Dahir said. "They've been spying on me, on all of us, and for a long time."

"Of course they have," Alex said. "They have access to every e-mail ever sent, every receipt, every newspaper article, and every essay in Iran since as long ago as they choose to look. They fed it into a big system, and the names of potential subversives came spitting out. I've read everything you've ever written, and I'm an outsider. It turns out that gentlemen do, in fact, read others' mail."

Dahir stood and walked to the counter. He poured a large dollop of port into his teacup and turned to Alex, who had his own teacup held up behind his head. Dahir poured an equal portion into it, then walked back to his chair and sat.

He raised the tiny teacup. "Good port," he said.

Alex returned the salute with a small smile. "Says one Muslim teetotaler to another," he said.

"OK, Alex," Dahir said. "Skipping all of the deadly and widespread mechanics of a civil war, why me? Your hegemon sees something here that I don't."

"Your group seems best placed and most likely to succeed in providing new leadership for Iran," Alex said. "You are the group's thought leader. It's that simple."

"What do the Americans expect?" Dahir said. "Capitulation?"

"They don't expect it, and I expect they'd try to refuse it if offered," Alex said. "I certainly wouldn't offer it if I were in your shoes. The American attack was over the nukes and their potential use by Iran to destabilize the Middle East and the world. As I mentioned, I imagine those nuke-enrichment sites are gone, or at least the three the Americans knew about.

"Given that, they'd like to get out of Iran without putting US boots on the ground. If you can make a civil war begin to work, you have a very strong negotiating position."

"Are you negotiating for the Americans, Alex?" Dahir said.

"I'm not, as I told your colleague the other night at dinner. I'm a facilitator."

"And your goals in that facilitation, Kufdani?"

"Beyond helping to avoid Muslim bloodshed and to allow a better education scheme for the Iranian people, young and old, my goals are twofold," Alex said. "First, I'd like to have Iran provide a platform to help promote cooperation across Islam among the Shiites and the Sunnis. Today Iran speaks for the Shiites. It would be useful if the voice was rational and friendly.

"Second, I'd like to see some balance among the power structures in the Muslim world. The Shiites need an ally."

"There will be a vast crater in religious belief in Iran, Alex," Dahir said. "You think it likely that the ayatollah and his ilk have been killed. Still, the people need their religion, particularly now."

"Indeed," Alex said. "And I need mine, whatever its depth might be. I can wait for the details, and so can your people. Religion as the opiate of the masses must be managed."

Dahir walked again to the kitchen and refilled his cup one more time, then Alex's.

"Skip the Marx or whoever coined that opiate phrase about religion. I'll need to sleep on all this, then talk to Colonel Tousi," Dahir said.

"I think you have about forty-eight hours before the return of the American violence is directed at the Republicans rather than the Corps Guard," Alex said. "Use it well."

ALEX SLIPPED OUT OF bed the following morning at first light; Jahan was still snoring on the second bed. Alex picked up his boots and clothes and quietly opened the door to the great room. He dressed, walked to the stove, and picked up the teapot. It was hot, so Dahir had been up early and was gone. Alex ran some more water into the pot and put it on the gas flame, then pulled two ceramic mugs from the cabinet. Yasmin and the girls were likely to be up soon and be hungry.

He took some eggs from the refrigerator and some chicken livers, uncooked from the dinner a few nights before. After cracking ten eggs into a bowl, he poured some olive oil into a skillet, put it over a low flame, and began to chop the chicken livers. Some chopped onions were next, then some spices spread over them. He dumped the lot into the hot skillet, then added salt and pepper.

Before long it began to simmer and crackle. Alex stirred for a moment, then lowered the flame and covered the pan with its steel lid. When the Ghorbani women rose, he would whip some air into the eggs and add them to the bubbling mass in the skillet. He wanted to be sure today was a better day for them than yesterday. A distracted Dahir would be counterproductive. Alex set four places on the wooden counter, poured some milk into glasses for two of them, and set the milk jug beside the eggs. A big splash beaten into the eggs would make things a bit fluffier. He then walked to sit in one of the chairs beside the small tables. He pulled his Kphone from a pocket, pressed a key, then began to record. After a few minutes, he read a transcription of what he had spoken, made a few corrections, then sent it on to Brooks.

CHAPTER 24

FALLEN TIMBER PLUS TWENTY-FIVE HOURS

ON THE EAST COAST OF THE PERSIAN GULF, just beyond the entrance to the Straits of Hormuz and twenty-five kilometers north of the newly destroyed Iranian coastal city of Jask, fifteen men finished their morning prayers and sat eating cold combat rations in canvas chairs along a long wooden dock. Overhead was a roof constructed of the rushes and other plants that grew nearby built over a thick wood-slatted cover.

During the first twenty-four hours of the Americans' attack, they had huddled and prayed, furious and waiting to die, inside a cave that had been found several years before and improved. Several feet of dirt on top of the cave shielded their body heat from discovery. They were apparently not on the Americans' list of targets, nor had they yet been discovered.

During the Yankee attack, the noise was cacophonous and nonstop at first. The crack of bombs detonating could be felt as one continuous assault on the eardrums. Then the sound became more distant as the bombers moved down the coast to attack more targets. The scream of jet engines could now be heard every few seconds.

The distinctive smell of burnt explosives that drifted over them in a cloud of smoke was oppressive.

Along the long wooden dock built parallel to the coastline were six boats, three on each side, with space at the end for the inner boats to turn to the sea. Each boat was about forty feet long and was similar to the cigarette boats cocaine dealers used to avoid the American Coast Guard as they approached its mainland. Many used the design of the Swedish-crafted Boghammar boats that had circumnavigated the British Isles a few years before to win a cash prize for speed in open seas. They were constructed largely of fiberglass. At sea they provided a poor signal for radars that sought their location. Their metal engines gave off a small, clear radar silhouette similar to that of the hundreds of wooden fishing boats that plied their trade in the Gulf of Oman and the Persian Gulf.

Above the deck of each of these glass boats was mounted a long, slim torpedo, a newly installed Russian VA-111, the most modern torpedo in the world. Its greatest asset was its rocket-driven speed. Its destructive power was five hundred pounds of the most advanced conventional explosive in the world in a shaped charge, enough to cripple a multibillion-dollar carrier or destroy a modern missile cruiser.

The fifteen men were a senior group in the Corps Guard Navy, chosen for both their experience and their devotion. During the initial Pulse attack, the radios to be used to coordinate attacks by the flotilla of small, torpedo-equipped boats had been destroyed. In all there had been over one thousand small boats of varying speeds and descriptions in the Iranian inventory along the east coast of the Persian Gulf. When the radios failed and the frequency of attack by American aircraft subsided after five hours, the commander of the main unit sent messengers to assess damage and pass orders for attack. Of the nine fast-boat sites near the one where the men had the cave, only they had survived. A few hours later, a second messenger brought the new battle plan and a fresh radio from a buried supply.

The revised Corp Guard Navy battle plan called for the special unit to carry out an attack with its six boats in an attempt to surprise the US fleet. All were to target one of the three US carriers operating in the Gulf of Oman, firing from a big spread to reduce the chance that one boat's destruction would impair the mission of the others. The commander hoped for major damage to the fleet vessels, which would divert the attention of their aircraft and allow a plan for the remaining boats to attack. If six boats could do damage in a surprise attack, then after the cowardly first strike by the Americans, the 220 remaining boats could provide a devastating blow to the Great Satan's plan, dealt in the fog of confusion.

A period of twenty-four hours from the first strike by the six fast boats was decided to be the tactically appropriate delay for an Iranian second strike, so that American forces would be exhausted from their angry searches and futile retribution. A coordinated Corps Guard attack could thus be launched, based on the experience and success of the first six boats' attack. Messengers had also been sent to several concealed—but within radio range—inland hafar-3 surface-to-surface missile bases that may have survived the Great Satan's initial attacks to allow them time to plan their support of the Iranian retaliatory strike. Each messenger carried a fresh radio and instructions as to when the radios should be activated to coordinate the Iranian attack. Plans would be finalized on the messengers' return and assessment of damage.

A single four-missile strike would be launched at the tanker community on the west coast of the Persian Gulf that had been loading oil from the Saudi oil fields. Two tankers would be sunk, and the blast and subsequent fires would destroy the facilities. In the confusion following that attack, a larger missile strike would be pointed at the fleet and the remaining infrastructure supporting the export of oil to the thirsty, greedy West. The remainder of the small boat effort would be directed at the US fleet after the missiles had done their work.

CHAPTER 25

ARLINGTON, VIRGINIA
FALLEN TIMBER PLUS TWENTY-SIX HOURS

BROOKS ELLIOT MADE HIS WAY TO THE Pentagon and through two sets of security, one at the entrance to the Pentagon proper from its commercial shopping area and the second at the entrance to the offices of the Chairman of the Joint Chiefs of Staff. Joshua Kim stood by the second security desk and introduced himself, then led the way past. Kim was in short-sleeved blues, with the silver leaves of a lieutenant colonel on the tabs of his shirt. Elliot was in his usual preppy attire, a blue button-down cotton shirt, a red striped tie, a blue blazer, worn at the elbows, and gray wool slacks. He wore blue cotton socks and shined brown lace-up oxfords with a pebbled rubber tread.

Kim walked just ahead of Elliot to a table in the corner of a large conference room. It had the expected central long table for group meetings. At one side of the room, beside a coffee cabinet, there were four upholstered wooden chairs with arms around a clean, round wooden table. Kim pointed to a chair, reached for the coffeepot on the cabinet, and said, "Regular? Tea?"

Elliot settled into his chair, pulled his Kphone from its holster, and set it on the table. A thin leather briefcase went beside it.

"Regular, with water please," he said.

Kim reached into a small refrigerator in the cabinet and pulled two bottles of Calistoga water from it. He put them on the table and reached for two coffee mugs, white with the US Air Force logo on them in blue. He poured from one pot into both cups, set the pot back on the electric burner, and picked up a small blue bowl with packets of powdered creamer and the usual sugar packets.

He set all three on the table and sat down beside Elliot with an empty chair between them.

"So, Mr. Elliot," Kim said. "I've read your navy evaluations, as well as some of your papers and some of your press. You've had an interesting career."

Elliot smiled. "As have you, Josh. Call me Brooks." He picked up a thin sheaf of papers from the leather case in front of him and handed it to Kim.

"Shall we address the formalities?" Elliot said.

Kim reached toward the table and handed a thin set of folded pages to Elliot, then dropped his head to read. When Kim got to the last page, he stopped and looked up at Elliot.

"My word," he said. "This last clearance is notable. Your pull exceeds General Moore's expectations."

Brooks grinned at him. "I think it's a nice touch for our conversation and will be generally useful in the future, I imagine."

The laminated page was on the personal stationery of the president. It said,

> The White House
> Washington, DC
>
> The bearer of this letter, Brooks F. T. Elliot IV, upon positive identification, is to be given whatever information and assistance he requests. He is acting on my orders and in the interest of national security.
>
> Roberts
> President and Commander in Chief

Kim nodded, gathering his thoughts. He took a sip of his coffee and said, "You know what I do and all, I assume."

"I do," Elliot said.

"You have more clearances than I do. And you have that magic memo as a trump card," Kim said. "How shall we proceed?"

"First," Brooks said, "fill me in on your take of the first twenty-four hours of Fallen Timber. How much havoc did we wreak against the plan? Give me whys and wheres you think are appropriate. Make me understand."

Kim pressed a few keys on the tablet computer in front of him. A screen dropped from the ceiling and lit up with a map of Iran.

"The biggest change to this war over those earlier," Kim said, "is the heavy and early use of a nonnuclear electromagnetically generated pulse similar to the EMP of nuclear fame; here I'll call it 'the Pulse.' A key part of our battle plan is to disable the infrastructure needed to support a counterattack—their computers, communications, trucks, electricity, pumps, and anything with silicon or copper wiring. We have information that many of the Corps Guard missile installations are not pulse hardened. There's the first big bet.

"The Pulse was delivered by nearly four hundred Tomahawks across Iran. In many cases the Pulse was followed by bombing and/or bunker busting. A key early-tactical objective of these attacks was to cripple Iran's ability to communicate both within the country and elsewhere by Internet. Cities that support Iranian oil field work were pulsed but not yet bombed to facilitate post-op recovery at a reasonable price and to discourage sore losers from making things harder. As you may imagine, the selectivity of targeting required to support the strategic plan is tricky."

Kim took a sip of his water and leaned forward to gaze at a small screen in front of him.

"All surface ships belonging to Iran have been destroyed," he said. "Thirty-seven airfields have been pulsed; aircraft and integral offices have been destroyed and their runways cratered. Their three nuclear sites have been destroyed together with their surroundings, all pulsed hard. Seventy known Corps Guard troop concentrations, a hundred fourteen missile sites known and suspected, and all Corps Guard headquarters have been pulsed and bombed heavily, including the main one in North Tehran. Their Internet center in Qom, their launch centers there, their protective missile batteries, and the offices of religious leaders around it were pulsed, bunker-busted, then bombed. If the ayatollah was home, he's dead. He was at home as best we could determine. The Iranian coastline of the Persian Gulf was hit particularly hard, including Jask and its new naval base south of the Straits.

"The city of Chabahar, farther south on the coast outside the Straits, with its headquarters facilities and missile sites, was also destroyed. Several other cities with large Corps Guard components have been destroyed. Bandar Abbas was the biggest of them; it was totally destroyed as a city and a base to a radius of five miles, with many of its 350,000 people dead.

"We have not yet targeted Tehran or other major cities other than to destroy Corps Guard regional headquarters and troop concentrations there, together with the housing around them to a radius of fifty yards or so.

"The ability of Iran to wage an effective war has been severely compromised, if not destroyed. But they still have an ability to hurt us, we think."

Brooks looked at the screen hanging from the ceiling. "From where?" he said.

"There's the question," Kim said. "It is unlikely that it will be by air power. That leaves boats and missiles.

"We've hit all the sites we've noticed over the years; in many cases a single strong signal detected was enough to add a site to the secondary target list. As more signals were recorded, a site would go up in targeting priority. The coordinates of any decent-sized Corps Guard installation of troops and missiles were in our attack parameters, with some hit twice. They have no blue-water navy remaining, but they still probably have at least five hundred small boats somewhere. We know where we've hit. We don't know where the remainder are. When we find them, we'll kill them."

Elliot nodded. "The trick will be for us to find them before they find us. The whale in the pond is how much damage they can do with what they have left and how the US public will react to that."

"Indeed so," Kim said. "We've gotten a few signals since our initial attacks and sent a Hellfire down their transmitting azimuth bearing to them, without regard to the circumstances of the location where it emanated. One missile site started to power up. It was detected and has since been destroyed with no shot by them. An important addition to our intelligence capability is the widespread use of drones; they are everywhere, watching and reporting. One in three or four is armed."

Brooks shrugged and said, "We should probably stop doing that much civilian damage after the next engagement, at least in the cities. When the Iran forces finally come out to play, they'll use everything they have. After that, we should look to see what is around given targets, such as schools and hospitals. The rebuild costs will be lower and the populace less pissed off after they get over being terrified."

Kim made a note on his tablet.

"One can but hope," he said. "We've avoided Republican targets that didn't have missile sites within them. If the Republicans engage, we have a whole new ball game."

"Tell me what you'd like to discover from me and why," Elliot said. "After we get through that, I may have some questions."

"I'd like to understand the Emilie product," Kim said, "and what it does in the battle scheme that is not immediately obvious to me. It appears to be quite powerful, and I get the feeling that I don't understand it well enough to do my job as I should."

Brooks glanced at his Kphone and thumbed a few keys.

"There is recording equipment active here. If it's yours, I'd like you to turn it off. If not, we should change rooms."

Kim looked startled, then glanced at the near cabinet door. He leaned and opened the door, then reached for a panel and flipped a switch.

"Now?" he said.

Elliot glanced at his Kphone and nodded. "We're good," he said. Elliot took a sip of coffee and leaned back in his chair.

"Emilie, the name we use when discussing her," he said, "is a probability engine, the result of twenty years of work by the smartest person I've ever met. Emilie absorbs vast amounts of data and reaches incremental probabilities of something happening. Her conclusions have been tested for more than ten years as she learns."

Kim's head snapped up. "Emilie is heuristic? She learns from her mistakes?"

"Yes, she's heuristic, thus much of her power," Elliot said. "For this discussion you should accept, as has the president, that her conclusions about Iran are very accurate—call them at the .9 probability level or greater.

"She gives value to increasing probabilities in a given time frame and their acceleration as part of her heuristic behavior. It is routine to give her concentrated geographic and political targets, such as behavior in Iran. The talent in tapping her skills is in asking the right questions and supplying the right data, the more data the better.

"Some of Emilie's power is in her accoutrement. The two most important of those are the Kphone and her encryption skills."

Kim glanced at his Kphone as he picked it up. He raised his eyebrows and shrugged.

"Do tell," Kim said. "We'll talk about encryption later. The signals sensor was impressive. But first I'd like to understand a little more about the Emilie product itself. Who wrote it, what is written in it, and so on? Do I have time to get into the bowels of it and understand it?"

Brooks grinned, then said, "Let me keep this short. Caitlin O'Connor wrote it, and she is the only one who touches Emilie's bowels. She says it is written in quantum mechanics and claims that getting Emilie to translate that into machine language was difficult. She doesn't say 'difficult' often; 'interesting' is how she describes most problems. It took Caitlin five years to finish the generalized interpreter that took quantum mechanics into machine code. I don't think you have the time to get into Emilie's bowels and understand her. If you want a head start, talk to the NSA. They've been trying to understand Emilie for seven years. They've spent about seven hundred million dollars on her so far."

"Got it," Kim said. "O'Connor is far smarter than I am. And richer."

"She's smarter than all of us, and she told the president so not long ago, then convinced him."

Kim smiled and took a big drink of his coffee, then put his hands behind his head and looked at the ceiling.

"And I was afraid that this would be one of those fifteen-minute meetings where I'm told to mind my own business," he said. "Tell me what I need to know. It sounds like any Emilie leverage I have for this engagement would have to be in the as-yet-unexplained accoutrement."

"Quite so," Elliot said, "and we may be a few hours in the telling. First, the Kphone is Emile's user interface. You manage Emilie through the Kphone. The Kphone is a proprietary smartphone with about a thousand times the computing power of a good PC and access to the cloud for memory beyond her many gigabytes. Most of the phone code in her is public domain—some form of Android plus another bunch of quantum mechanics translated. Caitlin's working with Intel to test their new fourteen-nanometer technology for an in-memory solution that would be far faster than the cloud solution she uses today. There's some open-source software in the in-memory computing space, she tells me. She downloaded the open-source code of a small company named GridGain and is ah, enhancing it. Caitlin says they made a good start—high praise, considering."

Brooks walked Kim through the various surveillance controls within Emilie, if access was granted to her. He told Kim how to download the training videos Alex had used in Tehran and search for anything else of note.

"Tell me about the encryption," Kim said. "The NSA is proud of their public key interface, their PKI encryption model. Does Emilie use that?"

"No," Brooks said. "Caitlin says PKI is a joke, one propagated by smugness in the old-timers at the NSA, whose jobs are never in jeopardy. You see, they've spent something over twelve billion dollars on building PKI out. They thought it was clever for them to propagate an encryption system they could readily decode. It's so clumsy that few want to be bothered with it beyond the Department of Defense, which has no choice. The private sector has spent hundreds of millions of dollars trying to work with and around PKI; anything new and effective was killed by the old guard at the NSA. Emilie uses her own encryption, then wraps it in PKI to allow DOD to do their usual secure transmissions. When she doesn't fully recognize the identity of the sender or the recipient, things get unreadable."

"Can you think of some discrete task to give this probability engine that might help with my job?" Kim said. "When the Iranians come, it will happen quickly. They'll throw most of what they have left around the Gulf—fast boats, missiles, maybe even chemical agents, although we've destroyed all of their known chemical-weapons storage sites."

Brooks leaned back in his chair and picked up his water bottle. He was quiet. After several moments, he said, "I assume you have coordinates of every place you've hit. If we feed Emilie that data and any after-action damage assessments, perhaps we can figure out coordinates of the most likely remaining sites that could hurt us."

"How would she do that?" Kim said.

"Emilie could take her synthesis of all the other Iranian data she has—e-mails, phone traffic, radio signals, gossip, et cetera—and integrate it with the new targeting data. Maybe some new and useful information could come from that."

"Interesting," Kim said. "How long would that take?"

"I'll have to ask Caitlin," Brooks said. "I'd guess eight hours for the first pass. Tweaks would be faster after that."

"It's worth a try," Kim said.

Brooks stood. "I'll get after that. Let's talk again soon. I'll tell you about encryption, if nothing else."

Kim stood, and they shook hands. Brooks turned and walked briskly from the room.

CHAPTER 26

TEHRAN

ALEX SAT WITH A MUG OF TEA IN the chair he'd claimed earlier in the great room of Jahan's quarters, dressed again in his loose vest over a green shirt and dark pants. It was thirty-six hours after the first attack by the Americans. Dahir hadn't been seen since dawn. Jahan had gone to check on the state of the university and provide comfort to the needy. The two Ghorbani girls were sitting in a far corner of the room, playing with the Kphones Alex had loaned them. Squeals of pleasure from the girls told him they had figured out how to use the Kphone and were exploring.

He'd have to think about dinner soon. There were still more chicken livers, bought at a bargain price.

The outer door opened, and Dahir looked in.

"Would you join us, please, Kufdani?" he said.

Alex stood and set his mug on the small table, then walked to the door.

A rough conference room had been thrown up at the back of the old storage space. It had a window, a table made up of a door set on sawhorses, and eight rickety government chairs, green with tattered upholstery on their arms.

Alex walked into the room behind Dahir; Colonel Tousi stood and nodded. He didn't offer to shake hands. With him at the table were three of the officers who'd attended the earlier dinner at Jahan's. They remained seated.

"So, Kufdani," Tousi said, "we should talk about your role as a facilitator. We seem to be lacking in guidance from our superiors, if they are still alive."

At a wave from Tousi's hand, Alex sat in one of the chairs, Dahir across from him in another.

"Tell me what the Americans think we are to do," Tousi said. "Are we to surrender before the battle is waged? Are the Saudis coming to enslave us?"

"I can only report what I know," Alex said. "The Americans don't want this war. They attacked to destroy your nukes, or at least your capability to make them. One would guess that this goal has been accomplished, but you would know better than I. If there are more sites, they also will be destroyed."

Tousi was distracted for a second and grimaced, then shifted in his chair and lifted his hips from it.

"What do you propose that we do?" he asked.

"If it were me, I'd make contact with the Americans. Your goal is to make the best deal for the Iranian people in a war you are unlikely to win."

"And what about the devastation this cowardly attack has wreaked on the Iranian people?"

"A good negotiating point, I'd think," Alex said.

"So we make contact with the Great Satan, facilitated by you, I imagine," Tousi said. "What position do you suggest we take, O facilitator?"

"Demand something outrageous," Alex said. "Work from there. Time is on your side."

"And how could you claim that time is on our side?" Dahir said. "With the inevitable follow-up on attacks, victory will be much easier for the Yankees or perhaps for the Saudis."

"Time is on your side for a number of very good reasons," Alex said. "First, the Americans have learned that whatever they destroy they will ultimately have to rebuild as victors. Look at Iraq and Afghanistan and the tens of billions of US dollars that have been spent there in repairing damage wrought by them.

"Second, the balance of power in the Middle East has suddenly been altered by this war in favor of the Sunnis, the mother of al-Qaeda and ISIS. The Americans would like to see the Muslim world go back to an even balance of power so that if all Muslims are to be slaughtered, it's an even fight that doesn't really involve America. The possibility of nukes changes the game. If one side gets them, the others will also and threaten world peace. They'd rather you stuck with killing each other with suicide trucks."

"Is there more?" Tousi said.

"Of course there is more, but those are two points you could use to open negotiations with the Americans."

"Let's talk through this, then see if we can reach the Americans," Dahir said.

Alex pulled his Kphone from his vest pocket and leaned closer.

CHAPTER 27

THE WHITE HOUSE

BROOKS, MAC, AND GENERAL KELLY hurried to the Oval Office from Kelly's office, where Brooks had taken the call from Alex.

In a few minutes, they were sitting around the massive live-oak desk, with Sheila Molyneaux again sitting and facing them beside President Roberts.

"You take the lead, General Kelly. Hand it off to me if it seems the right time," Roberts said.

Brooks keyed his Kphone and put it on the speaker system in the room.

"This is Colonel Tousi of the Iranian Republicans. To whom am I speaking?"

"This is General Patrick Kelly, the United States national security advisor, Colonel Tousi," Kelly said. "Good day to you."

"A better day for you perhaps than for the Iranian people," Tousi said in fluent but heavily accented English. "You attacked without warning."

"A conversation for another day perhaps, Colonel Tousi," Kelly said. "Right now we have a war under way."

"Indeed we do," Tousi said. "It would be nice to stop that war, to cut to the chase."

The game is afoot rather quickly, Brooks thought. The president was leaning forward in his chair, fully engaged.

"The United States has little interest in continuing this war, Colonel Tousi," Kelly said, "but we are in it now. It's not a war we plan to lose."

"Perhaps we should talk about your objectives in attacking Iran," Tousi said. "Your facilitator here, Kufdani, seems to think you have destroyed all of our enrichments sites. Of all your public statements concerning Iran over the past few years, those were the problems that made you most nervous."

"True enough," Kelly said. "Now we worry about missiles and fast boats. You have many of both."

"As you know, we control only some of the missile sites. The Corps Guard controls the remainder. We control none of the fast boats, nor the submarines."

"Do you have a proposal I can take to the president, Colonel Tousi?" Kelly said.

"The leadership of Iran appears to have been killed for the most part," Tousi said. "Iran needs both political and religious leadership at this point in time. We propose to take control of Iran and establish an alliance with the United States. We propose that we lead the cause of Shiite Islam around the globe once this unpleasantness is over."

"That is a noble goal," Kelly said. "We understand how many steps must be taken between here and there. What are the first steps?"

"We will plan our revolutionary efforts in the next few hours. There will be a civil war of some unknown duration. We will today stand down the Republican missile sites as a gesture of goodwill. What will you do for us?"

"The United States will act as your ally in that civil war. Any future alliance will, of course, be subject to intense negotiations."

"And what form will that support from you take?" Tousi said.

"We will provide intelligence and air-combat support on targets you designate, whether in support of a battle or in destroying personnel and infrastructure you designate. When you sort out your new religious structure, we will provide marketing support to get that word to your populace."

"You will avoid the casualties of a ground battle that way," Tousi said. "How do we know that you won't turn on us once we have done your dirty work with the Corps Guard and have Iranian blood running into our gutters and soil?"

"You don't know that, I suppose," Kelly said. "You'll have to decide what is in your best interest going forward, and we'll decide ours. You will excuse us for a moment while we discuss these matters."

The line went dead as Alex put the Kphone on hold.

"Well, that was exciting," Roberts said. "What do you think?"

"I'll stay out of it for now," Molyneaux said. "We'll figure out the political spin as we know more. It's still a minefield."

"I'd say let it run, Mr. President," Elliot said. "It's going our way right now, and we'd like to keep inland Iran busy while we clean up the Persian Gulf. That's where most of our risk is, and ugliness has yet to arrive there."

Mac nodded and was quiet.

"The first missile that is shot at us will be a breach of faith and maybe a deal breaker," Roberts said.

"There are missile batteries in the South that are out of the Republicans control and several in their East," Mac said. "I suggest we shouldn't tag the Republicans with control of them yet. If they start to win, we'll up the stakes."

The phone came back on with some static. "Are you there, General Kelly?" Tousi said.

"I'm here, Colonel Tousi," Kelly said. "What do you have for me?"

"Your facilitator says we can trust you, as of course he would," Tousi said. "We'll give it a try and trust you for now. We would also like you to restore our Internet capability for use in announcing our control efforts as we prepare our new religious position and present it to the people. Stay tuned for an ugly civil war for some time as we work to gain control."

"For now let's work through Kufdani for targeting," Kelly said. "Let him know what is needed. We'll look into restarting Internet capability in Iran, at least in the cities. The news that we are perhaps not enemies but rather allies may have publicity value if it happens, is managed, and is a surprise."

CHAPTER 28

TEHRAN

"THIS IS LIKE LISTENING TO AN opera on fast-forward," Dahir said. "Things are not supposed to happen this quickly."

"The Americans are in a hurry," Alex said. "Their generals have no doubt spent weeks on a carefully timed battle plan for all of Iran. They will resist changes once they engage inland Iran. When the battle in the Gulf is over, they will want to move against all missile emplacements, whether Republicans or not. It might make sense to continue to get your troops and equipment away from Corps Guard installations, since they still seem to be the primary targets for the Americans."

"We have some complex planning to do and a very short time to accomplish it," Tousi said. "You will excuse us, Kufdani."

Alex stood, nodded to the group, and left the room.

CHAPTER 29

EAST COAST OF THE PERSIAN GULF NORTH OF THE COASTAL CITY OF JASK FALLEN TIMBER PLUS THIRTY-SIX HOURS

MANUALS AT HAND, TWELVE MEN began to remove the covers from the engines of their boats. The new thick metal and canvas engine covers had been built as Faraday cages to diffuse a directed pulse such as the Americans had delivered. The final check on the torpedoes was done one more time, the manuals carefully followed. The Russians said the VA-111E, named Hoot by Iran, was hardened against the pulse, as was the radar control unit on each. All was in readiness. The commander of the small unit moved to the edge of the covered roof and raised his binoculars to study the surrounding waters and the air above it. Nothing was in sight.

With a twirling motion of his hand above his head, the eleven men behind him mounted the six boats and stood waiting. When their leader dropped his hand, the engines were started nearly simultaneously. There was a loud cheer as the engines roared. The front three boats moved together out of their shelter and turned right. The remaining three boats worked their way out of the dockage and turned left.

When all were in deeper water, they accelerated toward the fleet, spreading apart as they gained speed. As they reached their cruising speed of one hundred kilometers per hour, the image of the lead US warships in the fleet's protective deployment came into hazy view on the horizon. The three carriers were well back from the lead vessels, deep in the Gulf of Oman.

ABOARD THE *BUSH*, AN alarm sounded in its Combat Information Center, or CIC. The fast-boat movement had alerted a drone circling just outside the Straits, and now it focused on its source. The drones' controllers aboard the *Bush* immediately saw the six boats and their long white wakes. The general quarters alarm sounded for *Bush* and was immediately transmitted to the others in the carrier group. *Bush* was the nuclear carrier closest to the Straits and thus to the attacking fast boats.

COMMANDER JONATHAN SPANE, CAPTAIN of the USS *Dewey*, an Arleigh Burke-class missile destroyer positioned at the eastern perimeter of the carrier strike group, stood on its bridge and said, "Flank speed. Come to course zero seven-five degrees. Sound general quarters."

The call for emergency power was driven through *Dewey*'s engines to its propellers; white water suddenly churned high above the stern as the steam turbine engines spooled suddenly to full power. The claxon of the general quarters call accompanied sailors dashing to their battle stations.

On the bridge, as *Dewey*'s deck tilted beneath his feet from the turn and acceleration, Commander Spane was considering how much to depend on the USS *Ponce* in his portion of the Carrier Group screen. She was an experimental warship, but promising. Spane turned his head to look for *Ponce*. He didn't have any trouble seeing her profile on the east horizon as *Dewey* accelerated.

Ponce was steaming at the coastal edge of the defensive formation. She was a clumsy-looking warship with some of the grace of a small freighter. Spane saw *Ponce* turn her bow toward the fast boats and begin to accelerate to a speed that would best stabilize her for the new weapons electronics to do their job. *Ponce,* in her experimental construction, lacked the sleek eye appeal of a destroyer. She had her superstructure forward and two helicopter decks aft. White radar domes bristled from her superstructure. A large, boxy structure was just forward of the helicopter decks and shielded by the superstructure, with heavy electrical cables running forward from it. A thick, short tube protruded above the bow deck of the *Ponce*, surrounded by a squat steel box.

Spane glanced at his radar and saw *Ponce* slowing. She was stabilizing. *We shall see*, Spane thought. He turned to his duties at hand.

THE FAST BOATS WERE skipping over the tops of the waves, thumping and bumping in clouds of bow waves as they sped. Their wakes were great, white fans of layered turbulence at their edges; there was roiled, but relatively smooth water at their middles. The crew was strapped into each boat, one driving and the other watching the targeting radar for the image of the *Bush*.

After several minutes, the pilot of the lead boat of the most southern group of three boats lifted his hand and shot a flare into the air. As it burst high in the air, each boat was now free to shoot its torpedo when it had an acceptable targeting image, preferably a carrier.

A THERMAL-IMAGING DEVICE ON the *Ponce* locked on the flare as it burst, then on the boat. The squat tube just aft of the bow turned a few degrees on computer command. A thin ray of blue light came from it and hit the lead fast boat at a range of seven miles. The boat exploded.

Ponce was a platform for the US Navy's experimental Laser Weapons System (LaWS). Its system was designed specifically as a weapon against swarming fast boats and incoming missiles or newly launched ones. The large box behind the superstructure was its power supply. A laser beam shot required vast power, which the boxy aft power supply built up; each new shot required forty-seven seconds to recharge the laser's power supply.

A second fast boat was targeted. Just before the laser hit full charge, the boat launched its torpedo. The boat exploded ten seconds later.

Aboard *Dewey*, Spane saw the second fast boat explode and vanish from his radar screen and smiled. Welcome, *Ponce*.

BENEATH THE GULF OF Oman, the USS *California* was cruising at ten knots a mile southeast of the outer perimeter of the fleet when a cry came from the CIC. "Torpedo in the water. Range, sixteen thousand yards; bearing, one seven three; speed, one hundred twenty kilometers per hour. Stop. Speed is now two hundred kilometers per hour."

Fargo came running from the small bulkhead table where he was doing paperwork. "Open all outer doors. Back azimuth, now," he said.

The XO hit a green button above his head and sent targeting information to his first torpedo. "Ready," he said.

"Match sonar bearings. Tube one, shoot," Fargo said. The sub lurched perceptibly as the torpedo was pushed from the sub with a burst of water.

"Torpedo away," XO said.

"Torpedo in the water," the shout came again. "Range, sixteen thousand five hundred yards; bearing, one niner four; speed, one hundred fifty kilometers per hour."

The XO hit the button above his head again. "Ready," he said.

"Match sonar bearings. Tube two, shoot," Fargo said.

"Torpedoes identified as Russian VA-111 Squall modified for export, Captain," said an officer standing by the sonar screen. "They are attacking the fleet. Both of our shots are likely misses behind."

"Come to course zero six zero degrees, close the outer doors, and reload one and two. Come to flank speed for thirty seconds," Fargo said. "Let's get closer to those puppies and close the angle a bit. They're too fast to shoot from here, and they're not shooting at us. Set antitorpedo, high rev, small engine."

ON THE SURFACE *PONCE*'s laser destroyed a third boat before the boat launched its torpedo. There were now four torpedoes in the water, heading for *Bush* and its protective shield of destroyers and missile cruisers.

The *Ponce* radar operators labored to enable a fix on the new lead torpedo as the laser recharged.

ABOARD *DEWEY*, SAILORS SMOOTHLY prepared the Phalanx Close-In Weapons System (CIWS) that provided fleet outer defense against missile and surface threats. It was designed to use a forty-five-hundred-rounds-per-minute rate of fire to destroy threats before they could reach the protected ship. The wakes of two torpedoes were finally visible. They prepared to engage the lead torpedo as it came into range, but then it disappeared with a flash of blue light as *Ponce* found it, destroyed it, then began its recharge.

The sailors on *Dewey* turned their attention to the second torpedo, and the system began to fire the CIWS with a clattering roar. The decades-old computer system controlling the CIWS underestimated the speed of the VA-111 and thus its rate of closure. The shells hit behind it as it went deeper. The torpedo impacted at *Dewey*'s stern, just below the engine compartments, and exploded a half second later, directing its charge in a shaped balloon of destruction. The entire stern of *Dewey* sheared outward in ragged jaws of steel. The orange-and-gray blast roared out a half second later.

BUSH LAUNCHED TWO STANDBY attack helicopters within seconds of the alarm and the call to general quarters. On the flight deck, young men and women in bright vests, each color-coded to particular job assignments, flowed everywhere in a practiced ballet. Launching an airplane was a complex motion of many parts, tasks *Bush*'s crew had done a thousand times before.

No effort was lost. The slam of the steam catapults launching first tankers and then F/A-18s, two at a time, sounded against the roar of engines in afterburner mode, painting the mottled, pulsing air in orange on the blast shields raised behind them.

Full aircraft launch was under way from the other two carriers, which cruised farther into the deep waters of the Gulf of Oman.

The first of the attack helicopters from *Bush* accelerated toward the fast boats. Within minutes the wakes of two torpedoes came into sight, and the pilot, Lieutenant Larry Brooks, dove toward them. The copilot armed the 20mm chain gun in its nose and fired. The shells impacted behind the VA-111.

Brooks wrenched the helicopter sideways to engage the next torpedo. As he lost altitude and wrestled the nose up to the path of the next Hoot, he said, "Walk them in."

The cannon roared again, and the VA-111 streaked into the rain of exploding 20mm shells.

The blasts of nearly five hundred pounds of high explosive igniting its peroxide-and-kerosene fuel supply threw a tsunami of water in the air. The concussive force hit the helicopter and turned it upside down. A few seconds later, it hit the Gulf of Oman nose first.

Sheikh Isa Air Base
Bahrain
US Air Force A-10s were launched from the west coast of the Persian Gulf at the US base in Bahrain, two at a time from each of two runways, every thirty seconds. F-15s and F-16s were moving to ready areas, to be launched when the last of the A-10s was airborne.

In the *California*, the boat slowed from its timed sprint and Fargo watched the VA-111s being tracked on her electronics.

"Open outer doors. Match sonar bearings and shoot."

The boat lurched as four torpedoes were pushed out of its bow tubes. Each began pulsing for a target that met its recently loaded instructions—high speed, fast propellers, and concentrated small-engine mass. The torpedo shot from the number one tube angled up and accelerated as it sensed a target.

Forty seconds later it hit one of the two remaining VA-111 torpedoes. The concussion from the explosion of two large warheads simultaneously moved the other three US torpedoes off their paths and blinded their sensors for a moment. The one closest to the blast slowed and pointed its nose at the bottom of the Gulf, its electronics gone awry. As the other two recovered, each sensed a target gone by. They continued on their programmed paths and soon found a single speedboat running from the fight after it had launched its torpedo—a high-rev, high-speed, small-engine target. Each torpedo hit the fleeing fast boat within a second of the other. The boat was gone.

The VA-111 fired by the second speedboat, riding the tactical benefit of surprise, had time to go deep and was under and past the protective screen of the carrier group. It traveled at 220 kilometers per hour in its protective, friction-cheating cone of bubbles. It soon sensed *Bush* and directed itself at center mass.

It impacted, penetrated, and then exploded just under the flight hangars, in the shaped-bubble force that had hit *Dewey* earlier.

USS *Dewey*

Commander Spane struggled to his feet on the bridge. The blast had thrown everyone to the deck and blown in one window aft of the elevated bridge, opening a slice in the helmsman's right shoulder. Spain held a grab rail and looked to the stern of his ship.

Firefighters fought furiously against the spreading flames as the deck continued to tilt to the stern beneath their feet. From the bridge Spane gave a final glance at his ship as it began to sink into the Gulf of Oman; then gave the order to abandon ship. He vowed to himself that they would recover what remained of the crew who'd been killed or badly wounded with no hope of care.

Of the 175 sailors who served *Dewey*, at least fifty were dead. They could count noses once they were in lifeboats and away from the suction pulling anyone nearby beneath the surface by thirty feet or so as the remains of Dewey and more than fifty of her men slid beneath the sea.

USS *George H. W. Bush*

Bush's hangar deck was on fire. Firefighters leaped over smoking, twisted steel, dragging their equipment behind them to save fuel supplies. *Bush* was still making way, her reactors still driving steam down to the propellers. Most of her planes had been launched, making the job slightly easier for the firefighters.

Watertight compartments were sealed routinely at the sounding of general quarters. They were keeping the seawater from flooding the ship; the gaping hole below the hangar deck was open to the sea but contained. Bodies of sailors were seen on the decks and unseen below the damage.

On the bridge, damage control was being managed as often practiced but never before performed in earnest. The *Bush* was hurt but not out of the game.

The Pentagon
Office of the Chairman of the Joint Chiefs of Staff
Fallen Timber plus thirty-eight hours

Elliot again walked into the conference room of the chairman behind Josh Kim. General Moore was elsewhere, monitoring the war with more than a few other generals in a war room with large display screens and computers at every desk. Orders could be coordinated and executed there in real time.

In the conference room, a single summary screen displayed symbols over a map of the Persian Gulf area.

"It sounds pretty bad, Josh," Elliot said. "We lost *Dewey*, and *Bush* is in trouble but still in the fight."

"Looks like maybe five hundred dead, twice that in wounded between the two of them," Kim said. "We'll know the actuals before long."

"What's the plan?" Elliot said. "You have the first pass from Emilie on targeting. Will you need more?"

"I won't know until we get the after-action damage assessment from this next round. We're moving some ships around. We'll need a new set of coordinates to work from. I'll forward them to you as I get them."

Brooks sat down and looked up at the screen, symbols moving dynamically around it. "I think I'll watch the show," he said. "This should be interesting."

"Best seat in town," Kim said. "And you have the magic memo. You can do what you choose."

"Yeah. Do you have coffee?"

CHAPTER 30

TEHRAN

ALEX AGAIN SAT AT A BATTERED DESK chair around the makeshift table in the new Republican office in Jahan's apartment building. He gazed across the table at Tousi, Dahir Ghorbani, and three of the Republican lieutenant colonels and a major from the original dinner group.

"We have completed an initial version of our plan," Tousi said. "In terms of positioning, we have established titles and so on. I am to be defense minister. Colonel—now General—Ghorbani will be the supreme commander. Imam Jahan Ghorbani will be the new grand ayatollah and in charge of our religious affairs, both with the Islamic Republic of Iran and with the Shiite community at large. Work is under way to develop our message to our people."

"I will assume the role of Iran's negotiator with the Americans," Dahir Ghorbani said. "Colonel Tousi will be my key advisor."

"Congratulations," Alex said. "I am at your service. How may I help?"

"We want an assurance," Dahir said, "that America will defend our shores from Sunni attack as we deal with our civil problems and thereafter, as is appropriate for an ally of the United States. Sanctions will be lifted immediately. There will be a requirement for extensive US funds to rebuild our society. You may wish to advise me as to how to facilitate such a position. We have prepared an initial list of Corps Guard sites you may not yet have attacked. There are a number of hidden ballistic missile sites, thirty-four in all."

Alex nodded. "If you send them to me, I will pass them on."

"We have decided to go with a communications blitz to announce our new government. The activation of Internet capability will allow us to communicate at once with the middle class in the cities. They are the portion of our populace most displeased with the tone of our government in the recent past. We have prepared speaker trucks and will send the plans on to our various elements we have identified when we again have Internet. Only the computers near the American targets seem to have been disabled, although they are of little use to many without phones and Internet."

"Good," Alex said. "I'll find out how long it will take to enable the Internet here and maybe get it started. A few minutes to operation should be a good target. I imagine it's a matter of dedicating satellites and supporting communications drones to the problem."

"That's fine," Dahir said. He stood and walked across the room, then back. "Here's the way I see things playing out. First and most importantly, this is neither an insurrection nor a civil war. This is a restoration of civil order by the Republicans, now under my command. Jahan will prepare religious pronouncements, *fatwas*, in webinars and educational videos that describe our new view of the Nation of Islam. Religious training under the auspices of the Department of Islamic Philosophy at the University of Tehran will be initiated under the grand ayatollah's supervision. How to get that message to the peasants is still being evaluated, since you mentioned that the cities would likely get Internet first.

"Second, resistance to our new order will be considered treason and be dealt with accordingly. New Republican commanders will be named, and others will be put on notice that they are being watched."

"I like it," Alex said. "You want this whole change in management to be a nonevent."

Tousi smiled, then grimaced. "Spoken like a businessman, Kufdani, but exactly right. We want there to be a loud sigh of relief when we announce a new government."

"We'd like to announce that we have entered negotiations with the Americans," Dahir said. "Can you facilitate that?"

"I think so," Alex said. "It, of course, depends on the message."

"Then work with me on the message, Kufdani. It needs to be done now."

"Let me make some notes and do some checking," Alex said as he stood. "I'll be next door when you finish up here. I think someone there wants to talk with me."

ALEX WAS AGAIN IN his chair, talking to an excited Jahan, who'd walked into the apartment a few minutes ago, after discussions with his colleagues in the Department of Islamic Philosophy.

"We can do this, Alex," Jahan said. "This could be a great time for Islam."

"*You* can do it, Jahan," Alex said. "You and Dahir. This is your chance to bring all of Islam together for the common good. The Sunnis were winning, but now you Shiites are back in the game. Persians will come flocking back, and the removal of the sanctions by the Americans will unleash a flood of creativity here."

"Is that why you came here, Alex?" Jahan said. "Was the lecture series I arranged for you just an excuse to get you here to do this while the Americans attacked?"

"It's why I do everything, Jahan," Alex said. "You know that. Think about the words of Allah. Our schism of religion is an abomination in his eyes. I want the people of Islam to come together in order to make a better life for themselves under Allah. Every lecture, every class has that same goal. We teach for a better Muslim life. I hope it works before I die."

Jahan nodded.

"It *is* very exciting," he said. "I will work and pray to make it effective."

DAHIR OPENED THE DOOR and walked into the great room.

"Jahan, will you excuse us?" he said.

"Of course," Jahan said as he stood and walked to the door. "I'm becoming accustomed to being thrown out of my home by my little brother."

As Jahan opened it, he said over his shoulder, "I have work to do, *General*." He slammed the door.

Dahir sat in his chair, closed his eyes and leaned back, then he leaned forward to Alex. "And?" he said.

"Ten minutes on the Internet activation, on your command," Alex said. "I got the list of missile sites from you and sent it on as a gesture of goodwill from you. On the announcing of negotiations, there are a few potential hitches."

"Oh?" Dahir said.

"I argued that your announcement of negotiations would be a good thing, but the president is worried about politics and the image of the United States in the war. I think he'll go for an announcement that we are in negotiations, but he'll want to make the announcement first in a talk to the American people ten minutes before the Internet here is activated. When you make your announcement, you'll get credibility from the American news on the newly available Internet."

Dahir shrugged. "I can live with that," he said. "We need to work out the wording."

Alex pulled out his Kphone, keyed it twice, and said, "Then let's get to it. I'll transcribe."

CHAPTER 31

INDIAN OCEAN
FALLEN TIMBER PLUS TWENTY-SEVEN HOURS

US AIR FORCE MAJOR DUNCAN Routh was playing bridge in the ready room for ten cents a point. He was eleven dollars behind in the game when he spread thirteen cards in his left hand for a first look from a fresh deal. He had seven spades to the ace, king, and ten. He had the ace of diamonds and five decent side cards. His bridge partner and copilot, Cam Greene, had dealt the hand and opened the bidding with one no trump; she was a good player.

Routh smiled to himself. He'd be ahead of the game within ten minutes. Bridge hands like this didn't come along very often when one's competent partner had shown a strong opening hand.

The crew alert sounded with a loud warble. The card game was over. House rules said that when they were called to mount their ancient steeds and earn their salaries, the hands were thrown in to be played another day by survivors, if any.

Routh was excited. They had been given an unusual heads-up over this one. Their planes were heavy, loaded earlier and awaiting a call; final targeting information would come by satellite to the B-52s' onboard computers. With the payload they carried, it wasn't a training mission; they were flying to Iran.

When he watched his crews load the bombs, Routh had known. If

General Moore's boys in the Pentagon came out to play a serious game, they brought their favorite toys. The AGM-130 was the favorite bomb of the United States Air Force. The Mark84 warhead was its playmate, mounted on the top of one of the ever-evolving series of AGM-130 bombs. The Mark84 warhead was called the "Hammer" for its power and blast radius, a name tag earned in the Iraq wars. Its explosive was tritinal, a mixture of TNT and aluminum powder that greatly increased its power beyond that of TNT alone.

Routh smiled to himself. You can't tell a killer by its casing. It's like calling LeBron a good dribbler. Yeah, swell—what else can he do?—lots.

Routh and company left unsaid that a few aviators might not pick up cards for the next round of bridge. It was about three thousand miles to Iran at a speed of 450 miles per hour. A seven-hour flight was routine for these crews. Being shot at was not.

The B-52s routinely flew from the US air base in Diego Garcia, an island in the central Indian Ocean. Combat missions had been flown from there by B-52s of the US Air Force since the first Gulf War. Getting the B-52s off the ground was a well-rehearsed ballet. Sixteen air force pilots ran from their ready rooms to waiting buses. Crew members were picked up nearby. Within twenty minutes, eight B-52H bombers had started their engines. The youngest of those B-52s had rolled from its manufacturing line in Wichita, Kansas, in October 1962. There had been no fiftieth birthday celebration for any of the planes, although a few of the crews back then had used the occasion to send sympathy cards to their flight commanders. Many of the B-52s had been flown from Guam to Vietnam and back for the first fifteen years of their existence, dumping tens of thousands of dumb bombs with hopes that some would hit their target. Few did.

The takeoff roll was long and bumpy, shaking the controls in Routh's gloved hands. The planes weighed nearly half a million pounds each at takeoff; their wings bowed toward the runway with the combined weight of fuel and ordnance. Each B-52 was loaded with ninety AGM-130s that had been fitted with special JDAM targeting hardware bolted to their tail fins. Many of the effectiveness improvements in the AGM-130 were in its guidance. The JDAMs, Joint Direct Attack Munitions, could accept a GPS coordinate for a target fifteen miles away and guide the bomb to within five feet of the coordinates stored within it.

Routh engaged his autopilot as they climbed slowly and finally reached cruising altitude; it got better gas mileage than he did flying it.

East Coast of the Persian Gulf

Fallen Timber plus thirty-one hours

A swarm of US Unmanned Aerial Vehicles (drones) held west of, and above, the Iranian coast. Some were equipped with Hellfire missiles. Many more were surveillance drones, feeding grid data to the network on any activity sensed. A radio transmission could generate a Hellfire shot within thirty seconds of detection if the target was in range of the Hellfire; if not, the drone was sent posthaste in on the bearing of the signal until the target was in range. If the signal was from a handheld radio, its owner lived for the time being. If a drone detected radar or anything connected to a missile battery, a Hellfire was launched. In the computer network, it was noted as a site hit by a Hellfire on a single signal of a certain type. The site could be revisited at another time—soon.

Colonel Joshua Kim watched the battle evolve on the screen in General Moore's conference room. There were four field-grade officers with him, each with a set of responsibilities within the complexity of the battle plan that had been completed, staffed, and war-gamed twice. There were redundant very large computing facilities driving execution of the battle plan's software. Kim's plan was based on optimizing the use of bombs and other ordnance based on an evolving electronic picture of where threats had been detected, colored by the recorded US responses. Kim's goal was to hit primary targets once, hard, and then begin to use prioritized data from damage assessment by reconnaissance planes, satellite signals, and the database of suspected target sites to designate new targets in near real time. The Persian Gulf was a target of great political significance and thus of great strategic importance. The battlefield nuance, upon which Kim would later be judged, was in the geography of his response—don't lose the Gulf, but don't lose the country of Iran while you are concentrating on the Gulf.

THE FIRST OF THE A-10s launched from Sheik Isa Air Base in Bahrain dove from the north and down the coastline toward the Iranian coastal city of Khorramshahr. It leveled at an altitude of four hundred feet at 350 miles per hour. Captain Leroy (Buck) Rogers kept his hands lightly on the controls, one finger on his flare and chaff-release button as the computer guided his airplane to successive targets. A red light showed up briefly in the heads-up display mounted in his helmet's visor. A half second later, the Gatling gun fired a one-second burst. Soon the light was blinking every second or two as a rain of 30mm explosive fury sought targets. In what seemed like just a few moments, Rogers saw the "ammo exhausted" light come on in his helmet visor.

Rogers pulled his A-10 west and away from the coast to return to Bahrain and reload. A new set of target coordinates would be loaded into his onboard computer when he next approached the Iranian coast.

"Elmer did good, guys. Trust him," Rogers said over the radio.

Elmer was the name the A-10 jockeys had given the still-experimental weapons system that joined an autopilot with firing a seven-barrel Avenger Gatling gun in one-second bursts of seventy 30mm explosive shells on a target, impacting in two-foot increments. The A-10 was noted as a tank killer when it flew over columns of Iraqi tanks during the first Gulf War and fired an explosive round through their lightly armored roofs. One round was usually enough to kill all within a tank; three hits were more usual. The A-10s on these attacks used the high-explosive incendiary round, rather than the armor-piercing one. It penetrates the target using kinetic energy before the incendiary charge ignites, smothering the crew in flames, detonating ammunition, and destroying the target.

The Air Force establishment had been trying to kill the A-10 program for several years, based on its cost and old technology. Kim had convinced General Moore that they should continue funding it.

"General Moore," he had said, "the A-10 is one hell of a tank killer. But it's also old, slow, and vulnerable, which makes our pilots vulnerable. If we made an A-10 without pilots, old and slow wouldn't be a problem; it would be new and faster with no pilot to lose. First, we should see if we can control its firepower without a lot of pilot involvement. I also hate to see three rounds used where one will do the job; computer control should manage that problem."

THE STRING OF SIXTEEN A-10s followed Rogers down the coast, a half mile apart and attacking on slightly different paths. As the fourth A-10 began to attack his run just below the city of Bushehr, a thin stream of smoke rose just behind him.

In the pilot's helmet an alarm blinked brightly and "Shahin" showed on it, designating the missile as a modern infrared, heat-seeking missile, mass produced in Iran since 2009. He stroked the chaff button to dump a cloud of reflective aluminum strips as he broke off his run and turned north to present the smallest possible heat signature to the missile as the chaff blurred his heat signal and the just-released flare burned brightly and hot behind it. He guided slightly west to get out of the attack lane and allow the rescue helicopter a safer pick-up lane if it needed it.

The A-10s low altitude and slow speed worked against it as its pilot took emergency action to avoid the heat-seeking Shahin missile that flew through the chaff and burst just below the A-10. The airplane rolled slightly to its left as smoke came from it. The canopy blew off, then a seat with the wounded pilot on it shot straight up.

The plane exploded a second later, enveloping the pilot in flames and obviating the need for a rescue helicopter.

Three more A-10s were downed that day. One more pilot was lost.

The Air Force F-15s and F-16s following the A-10 attack had grid coordinates downloaded for each site that had fired a handheld heat-seeker missile, sent from the computers on the A-10s and confirmed by drone surveillance. No more shots came from any of those, as a 250-pound bomb fell on each target, newly reprioritized by Kim's targeting system. The fighters flew much faster and higher than the A-10s, depending on JDAM controls on their bombs to put them precisely on target.

While they finished their targeted bombing runs and returned to Bahrain to refuel and reload, the Navy's F/A-18s from three carriers, nearly six hundred in all, attacked new coordinates along the long stretch of coastline south of the air force's targets.

CHAPTER 32

FALLEN TIMBER PLUS THIRTY-FOUR HOURS

AS ROUTH'S LEAD B-52 APPROACHED the target area, new targeting was sent yet again to the JDAMs from the encrypted satellite data as the battle plan was updated, morphed, and reached for new targets. There was no computer flying their airplanes, but their bombs were ready to be precisely guided by the latest targeting data. There were no anti-radiation missiles fired; most of the big sites had been Pulsed and were likely struggling to get power. The bombs' targeting had recent history driven by the electronics marvels of Josh Kim's electronic battle plan.

The targets had been computed as inland rather than on the well-beaten coastline. Two swaths of targets were from one to fifteen miles inland from the Gulf coast. In each there were targets that had shown a radio signal at some point in the recent past and had been prioritized as to its value to the bombing-solution mission. There were drones watching and listening as the B-52s opened their bomb bays and dropped their JDAM-guided bombs.

Each flight of four B-52s dropped 360 five-hundred-thirty-pound bombs on carefully selected targets along a five-hundred-mile path. Every inland location within fifteen miles of the coast that had generated a radio signal of interest within the past two years was targeted. The bombs, as designed, would collapse a tunnel within twenty feet of the surface, rupture any lines for water and fuel, and kill anyone within a thirty-yard radius of its impact. Most of the 720 bombs killed goats, cattle, plants, or people without helping the war effort. But they hit where they were aimed, at a point where once a dangerous radio signal had been detected and recorded.

Eleven of the bombs struck Corps Guard missile sites awaiting their chance to be useful, devastating them and taking them out of the battle. Twenty-three bombs struck regional headquarters sites where Corps Guard warriors awaited their chance to be deployed. The remaining seven hundred or so bombs fell on struggling farms and businesses to kill innocent people and animals. The mass of the B-52 attack seemed like overkill, except for the damage that could have been wrought on American sailors by a single anti-ship missile battery.

Major Routh turned and leveled his airplane for the long return flight to Diego Garcia. The seven others followed, lighter now and still unfired upon.

PONCE WAS IN THE MIDDLE of the Persian Gulf. Four Arleigh Burke-class missile destroyers joined her. After the first fast-boat attacks, she was sent through the Straits to be positioned for missile strikes launched from Iran's southern interior and to deal with any further fast-boat attacks. Drones armed for missile defense had been deployed to the air force north of the Persian Gulf for several hundred miles with overlapping areas of responsibility.

The *Bush* was now at the rear of the three carrier groups, limping. Both of the other two carrier groups had sailed deeper into the Gulf of Oman. Half of *Bush's* aircraft had been recovered at the US Sheik Isa Air Base in Bahrain. *Bush* took on the remainder, weakened but still in the fight.

JUST OUTSIDE THE CITY of Marvdasht in southeast Iran, twenty-one men prepared their Shahab-3, medium-range missile battery, for action. There were five missiles on a mobile launcher. The coordinates of the targets were loaded and approved. Three cities in Saudi Arabia were on their target list, plus one in Bahrain and one in Qatar.

A US satellite detected the first of the missiles when its radar guidance was activated. Digital map coordinates were sent to the network, and twenty seconds later a Hellfire missile was launched at the firing site from one of the armed drones. There were no friendly forces in any of the areas being monitored, so the approval sequence for counterfire was electronic.

Ponce was the first ship to detect a missile. In the time it took to track the missile and compute a firing solution, another missile was launched. The thin blue beam shot from *Ponce*'s laser turret burned a hole through the first missile, small in front and not much larger in the back, It flew for ten more seconds, then exploded.

In far-eastern Iran, a team operating a battery of S-300 Russian-supplied ground-to-air missiles finally restored electrical power to their site. They had moved to their current location a few days before the attack and had not yet brought their battery online. There had been no attack on them. The Corps Guard crew ran their diagnostics on the missile system and found everything to be within tolerances.

Not far away, a pair of Air Force F-16s were flying a routine surveillance mission, looking for missile sites. The radar of the S-300 battery came on and lit up a bright, blinking warning in the helmet visor of the pilot. It showed "S-300," the most dreaded of the Russian-supplied Iranian ground-to-air missiles. The F-16 pilot armed an anti-radiation missile, and when the targeting beep sounded, he shot it at the radar. Before it arrived, the first S-300 missile was shot at the F-16.

Its pilot responded with a hard right turn away from the direction the missile was traveling to minimize exposure of hot engine exhaust to the missile's sensors. He punched out his chaff and flares, one after the other. The S-300 flew through the chaff and the flares, focused on its internal guidance, and exploded beside the fighter. Smoke poured from the wounded F-16 as the pilot nursed the plane toward safety. The anti-radiation missile fired by the wounded F-16 had destroyed the S-300 radar, yet its location was in the fire-control system of the second F-16. The second unloaded its bombs on the site and turned to escort its wounded mate to safety.

Elsewhere, a second battery of ground-to-ground missiles was launched, then a third, all from the eastern borders. A drone got one, *Ponce* got three, and Aegis missile cruisers got two.

Forty-one fast boats were launched along the coast. Destroyers, working closely with a swarm of attack helicopters, got them all before they could arm their weapons.

Within three hours, there were no more hostilities under way by the Iranians.

CHAPTER 33

TEHRAN
FALLEN TIMBER PLUS THIRTY-SEVEN HOURS

IN THE CONFERENCE ROOM, DAHIR GHORBANI, as the new leader of Iran, prepared for his first discussion with General Kelly.

Alex sat with Colonel Tousi and the three lieutenant colonels who had attended each meeting. A young Republican major named Fallani, who'd been a late invitee to the original dinner among them, also attended. Dahir was at the head of the table in camouflaged battle gear with new general office markings sewed on its collar tabs.

"Good afternoon, Colonel Tousi," Kelly said. "You are well?"

"My health is none of your concern, General Kelly," Tousi said. "Our supreme commander, General Ghorbani, would like to talk to the president of the United States."

"I can handle discussions at this point, Colonel Tousi," Kelly said. "Good afternoon, General Ghorbani."

"Good afternoon, General Kelly," Dahir said. "You will connect me to your president, please."

"As I told—"

"My hearing is adequate," Dahir said. "I have no wish to talk to an underling. I am the supreme commander of the Islamic Republic of Iran—the head of state. I would talk with yours."

There was a moment's silence; then Kelly said, "If I may put you on hold for a few moments, General, I will attempt to get him on the line."

The line went on hold.

FORTY-FIVE SECONDS LATER, PRESIDENT Roberts came on the line.

"General Ghorbani, this is President Roberts. Congratulations on your appointment as supreme commander."

"Thank you, President Roberts," Ghorbani said. "We are ready to initiate our efforts to re-establish control of our forces. There are a number of things I would like to discuss before I make such a dramatic step. You have destroyed much of our country, and perhaps worse, you have vastly enabled our Sunni enemies. We must discuss necessary reparations and policies before any announcements are made."

Ghorbani articulated a long list of demands, created with the help of his facilitator. The White House had anticipated and discussed some of them. In the discussion that followed, they reached agreements on the major points.

"If I may suggest, General Ghorbani," Roberts said, "we have accomplished much. Most importantly we have agreed to agree on major issues. These things take time to get right. There are a great many tedious discussions and negotiations to be addressed. Each of us has competent help to assist in these tasks. Shall we each get on with our business and allow our selected subordinates to continue?"

"A good point, Mr. President," Dahir said. "Thank you for your time. I assume we shall speak again soon."

"We shall indeed, General Ghorbani," Roberts said. "Thank you for your time and for your goodwill."

AS DAHIR TURNED FROM the Kphone, he said, "Well, gentlemen, we're in it now. We'd better get to it."

Major Fallani leaped to his feet, his right hand coming up from his trouser leg.

"You are a godless monster, Ghorbani," he yelled as he lifted a small automatic pistol at Dahir. "You defy the word of Allah."

Dahir came to his feet and turned away from Fallani, his right hand raised in defense.

Alex yelled to distract Fallani as he grabbed and threw in one motion the knife that usually hung at the back of his neck. One shot sounded as the Republican officer on his left leaped from his chair toward Fallani and jostled Alex's aim. The thrown knife opened a long gash across Fallani's cheek, then clattered against the wall. Another shot sounded as Colonel Tousi lunged to his feet and reached for Fallani. A loud grunt was heard.

Ghorbani slumped to the floor with his arm in front of him, bumping the table as a long fountain of blood gushed from his arm. Fallani was wrestled to the ground by two of the staff officers, as Colonel Tousi fell limply among them.

Alex lunged to his right and slid to his knees in front of Dahir. "Call an ambulance," he yelled. Alex dug into his vest pocket with his right hand, pulled out a thick vial, stuck the top of it between his teeth, then pulled up the sleeve of Dahir's battle dress to bare the arm. There was a long, deep furrow up the forearm from above the wrist, past the elbow and exiting behind the bicep. The edge of the artery was visible by the wrist, untouched. A mass of blood poured freely from the furrow to the floor.

Alex squeezed the edges of the wound near the wrist with his left thumb and three fingers, then ripped the top from the vial with his teeth. In the bloody gap that remained between his left thumb and three fingers, he squeezed a thick gel of fluorescent green on the wound and all around it as he held his grip for ten seconds, then moved his hand up on the wound and did it again, then again. The gel was a clotting agent approved only for veterinary use, but Mac had seen a YouTube video that showed it working during a sedated pig loinectomy and was having it evaluated for battle. The vests of many US warriors now held a vial of that gel.

Alex had a predator's visage on his puffy face. He smiled around the cap of the vial, then spit it out.

"It works," he said, then released the wound and pulled up his sleeve to show a bright-green line on his arm to the lieutenant colonel standing above him. "This was from the slash I got yesterday. Let's let General Ghorbani rest until the ambulance comes." He stood slowly and said, "May I have a look at Colonel Tousi?"

CHAPTER 34

THE WHITE HOUSE

THE FOLLOWING AFTERNOON, PRESIDENT ROBERTS again interrupted television for a preannounced address to the nation from the East Room at the White House.

> *My Fellow Americans,*
>
> *Your government has agreed with the Islamic State of Iran on a armistice path that I hope will forever end all hostilities between us.*
>
> *The Iranian government has agreed to end all efforts to enrich uranium, to cease any efforts to create a nuclear weapon, and to cease supporting terrorist activities around the world.*
>
> *The United States has agreed to support the efforts of the new Iranian government to suppress elements of their society that have been active in efforts to create nuclear weapons and to create terrorism in the Middle East and around the world.*

As an incentive to Iran to fully suppress their rogue citizens from terrorism, nuclear and otherwise, I have agreed to several other conditions. Upon verification that they have gained full control of their society, we have further agreed to lift all sanctions and to assist the Iranian nation in rebuilding their society.

Our military efforts in Iran will be limited to supporting their government with air and naval power and intelligence, with no use of US ground troops there, and to helping defend them from aggression if required, using those same US facilities.

Too many American men and women have been killed and maimed in the Middle East to no good end. The goodwill of the American people has repeatedly been abused. Those whom we hoped to help have turned on us again and again. Allies have morphed into enemies. Today, marked by this agreement with the Islamic Republic of Iran, the policy of the United States has changed.

The United States will no longer act as the world's policeman.

We will instead support with our arms and our money those forces whose interests and goals are in concert with ours. If there is to be a change in governments abroad, we will support only those forces whose interests we determine to be in concert with ours. If forces that reject our policies come to power, we will deal with them from our bases. In our policies, we have a bias toward democracy.

I call this the Colaris Doctrine in honor of our secretary of state, who provided much of the early thinking for its creation.

We are at peace.
Good night, and God bless America.

Roberts had his stockinged feet up on the desk in the Oval Office. Molyneaux sat back in a chair across from it, drinking a glass of white wine.

"I suppose that Colaris Doctrine thing wasn't good politics, but I made that decision," Roberts said. "Sorry."

Molyneaux smiled. "Right now, Mr. President, who gives a shit? Your approval numbers are already skyrocketing."

"Yeah," Roberts said. "I think we dodged another big bullet."

"If it gets messed up," Molyneaux said, "it's her fault. If not, you were being presidentially magnanimous. What do you care what name they call a win that happened on your watch?"

Roberts nodded and took a big sip of the malt scotch his steward had so graciously provided and leaned back in his chair.

"Whodda thunk that the Hardy boys could pull this trick off?" he said. "A preppie and a killer."

"Food for thought," Molyneaux said.

"Think about the killer," Roberts said. "You need some spice in your life. The preppie is taken."

Chesapeake Bay

Fallen Timber plus eighty-two hours

Josh Kim sat with his bare feet up on a small wooden table. He wore faded Air Force Academy shorts and a gray T-shirt. There was a glass of red wine beside his feet, half empty, and an almost full bottle of Calistoga water. A small charcoal grill, lit behind him, made appealing noises. Yo-Yo Ma was playing his cello through very nice speakers. He closed his eyes and leaned his head back.

"Nice boat," he said.

Elliot had owned the forty-eight-foot sailing vessel, *Old Fashioned*, for more than twenty years. She was anchored in a small cove on the east side of the Chesapeake Bay. A slight westerly breeze moved her slightly in the water, tugging at an anchor. Other than antennae sprouting seemingly everywhere from masts and booms, she looked like she was a rich man's toy. Between them, Mac and Alex had ensured that satisfactory communications were an integral part of *Old Fashioned*.

Elliot was in a wooden-and-canvas chair playing with his Kphone. His bare feet rested on the other side of the table, a red wine glass beside them.

"Thanks," he said. "Since you failed to file for overtime during your latest little effort, you should get some downtime. Spin your head a little differently while things are still fresh. Talk to me."

"So what do you think?" Kim said. "What does the president think? The pinkos are going to be coming out of the woodwork, looking for fresh meat. There are a bunch of dead and maimed civilians around. Gotta be a bunch of good photo ops for the press."

"Roberts, Kelly, and I all think General Moore pulled it off," Elliot said. "Few casualties, enemy broken, new government that shows promise. The new government was a stretch goal and may be coming true."

"Good," Kim said. "I was surprised at how little they had to throw at us on their counterattack. It was over in three hours."

"When the press or whoever coined that shock-and-awe tag, they had no idea what it was."

"Yeah," Kim said. "Now they will, and I'm in the line of fire."

"Yeah, I envy you," Elliot said. "Maybe they'll come after me."

"Probably not," Kim said. "They won't figure out your link to all of this for months, maybe years. I'm a full-bird colonel in the United States Air Force. I should be easy press meat. You know the type—in shape, politically astute, and politically correct. One twenty IQ or so. They will try to shred me."

"They might come up fifty points short," Elliot said. "But in return for dealing with the nuisance of the press, you get to articulate a message of your choice with regard to national defense. I wish it were me."

Kim took a big sip of his wine and rolled it round in his mouth, then swallowed. "Yes, indeed. I'm glad it's to be me and not you. One event like this in my lifetime—a culmination."

"Why don't you keep me around to kibitz?" Elliot said. "I love this stuff, and I'll be up soon enough."

"Really? What did you do now?"

Elliot laughed just as he swallowed some of the Bressler 2008 they were drinking. It burned his nose and put pretty, new patterns on his paisley shirt.

"This is damn good wine, Josh. Better in my mouth than in my nose, though."

"Thanks. I buy it every year," Josh said. "On a friend's advice, my wife and I went to a tasting at Bressler Vineyards up in St. Helena in the Napa Valley. It turns out the vintner is an MIT guy who made the rounds on the technical side of the Internet in Silicon Valley in his earlier days. We stayed for dinner. Good wine, good conversation. He knows a lot about networks."

They both took a deep sip of wine. A speedboat went by; its wake rocked the boat.

"They took fifty missile shots," Kim said, "all within a half hour of each other. *Ponce* got seventeen, some at very long range. The drones and the air force took care of the rest. We could have handled maybe twice that. The Israelis got two with their Iron Dome. The navy pounded the coast again. I'm not sure there is a rifleman alive there, let alone anything dangerous."

"Interesting," Elliot said. "What are you going to do now?"

Kim grinned and took another sip of wine. "President Roberts approved an emergency-funding order for fitting *Ponce*'s Laser Weapons System to our Arleigh Burke missile destroyers. The *Dewey* was scheduled to be the first fit after *Ponce* finished her evaluation. *Ponce* was experimental. She done good."

"That was fast," Elliot said.

"I wrote the order before the war," Kim said. "I thought there was a chance that it would be handy, All of a sudden, boom. No finance hassle in the euphoria of victory. The Joint Chiefs just want to get their hands on the laser technology. The contracts are in place from the *Ponce* test, so things could evolve quickly. The air force will get an A-20 drone contract; we've seen good results with A-10 computer-controlled fire missions and we know how to build drones. The army is pissed; they didn't get jack."

Brooks stood and opened the cooler. He pulled out the Bressler and poured a quarter measure into each of their glasses. He sat back down.

"So," Kim said, "You're avoiding the question. What are you doing that would excite the press and the pinkos?"

Elliot laughed. "Hell, the pinkos are almost out of issues, so they'll make a lot of noise about the injustice of something we do. With the speed of the Internet, the appetite for new news is getting substantial, so the press will be rabid."

"When you do what, Brooks? What?"

"Put the US teachers' unions out of work over ten years or so and make the teachers happier. Fix the Middle East. Make a ton of money. There will be broken eggs from our efforts in visible abundance."

"All at once?"

"It will be visible soon," Brooks said. "I imagine Iran will have a new educational system before long that exposes our weakness in primary education. We should talk about it sometime."

A melodic tinkle from his Kphone told him the fire was at the appropriate temperature to cook steaks.

"It's time. I'll get the steaks. You get the rest of the stuff from the cooler. Be careful with the potato salad; it's messy."

CHAPTER 35

TEHRAN

DAHIR HAD VIDEO-RECORDED THE announcement of a new Iranian government and broadcast it on the newly enabled Internet forty minutes after the speech by President Roberts. Yasmin had told him he was dashing in his Republican dress uniform with his contrasting white bandage and pallid face.

Yasmin also declared that Jahan in the background was suitably solemn and wise in his new grand ayatollah attire. His first fatwa on the new definition of Allah's will had been distributed in leaflets that supplemented his Internet video presentation that followed Dahir's.

Sound trucks were blaring the message around Tehran. Several thousand Corps Guard officers were arrested and detained. Republican officers of questionable loyalty were asked for their support or their parole, all under the gaze of Allah. Two of the faculty members in Jahan's department were arrested.

"What are you going to do about your Quds Forces?" Alex said. "Their people are all over the world stirring up trouble, supporting terrorism, killing Sunnis and nearly everyone else. They are accustomed to making trouble abroad. They could do it here."

"They will be a problem," Dahir said. "I haven't thought too much about them yet."

Alex shrugged. "Throw them at the Islamic State of Iraq and Syria—or whatever they are calling it. ISIS is the current buzzword for them.

Harass their new Sunni radical leadership, which is killing Shiites all over the place and is too violent even for al-Qaeda. Get the Quds Forces at arm's length and hug them to the breast of Allah against the godless Sunnis."

Dahir leaned back and grinned. "I like it."

There was silence as both pondered what the other had said.

"I wonder what the United States would pay us to quietly engage ISIS," Dahir said. "As you point out, I have Shiite troops trained and available to make trouble for the radical Sunnis. Busy hands are happy hands."

"I love it! You are indeed the right supreme commander."

"I could use some advice as to how to . . . ah, facilitate that negotiation with President Roberts," Dahir said.

"Off the top of my head," Alex said, "you should get what you can get from the Americans now and then slowly work into the Quds deployment issue. The goal would be a huge number not openly tied to using Quds as mercenaries. You ask for the works to rebuild infrastructure—all of it . . . roads, power generation, telecom, oil. Use any success you have with the Quds forces against ISIS, or the new Khorasan group in Syria, to up the ante. A few billion dollars goes farther here than in the US Department of Defense. We just have to figure out how to move it from one US pocket to another. It might make sense for the Americans to bring it up. I may be able to facilitate that."

Outside their windows there was the sound of masses of people entering the streets of Tehran and the university grounds, cheering.

Darya and Arian were leaning out the window, waving. Yasmin leaned against the window jamb, watching and smiling. Alex rose from his chair, then Dahir. They walked to the window and looked out, then turned and walked back to sit in their chairs.

"It appears that the Ghorbani brothers have pulled off a coup.

Congratulations."

Dahir smiled. "At least our odds have gone way up. I'm sad that Tousi is not around to see it."

"That second round went through his lower intestines and bounced around a little. Small caliber rounds do that. I didn't know how to fix it," Alex said. "Where the hell did Fallani come from?"

"It seems that our departed leader, General Nikahd, didn't trust us and sent a spy to keep an eye on us. Fallani proved to be interested in talking, bragging even. He was almost successful in destroying us, and proud of it."

"Almost," Alex said. "I think my role as facilitator is ended for now. Maybe I'll get to do a lecture or two."

"What would you think appropriate as a token of our Islamic nation's appreciation for your role now that it is ended?"

Alex smiled. "I wish you would consider revamping your *madrassa*, your public school system, so that there is a good education given all to your people as a long-term catalyst for the rebuilding of Iran. Kphones can be purchased for you by the Americans for this purpose if you ask, I'd guess. I have technology that would enable success."

"Inshallah," Dahir said. "I'll try to help Allah's will along. Jahan should know how to get that started. You can advise him."

"Inshallah indeed, Supreme Commander," Alex said.

CHAPTER 36

***OLD FASHIONED* SAILED UNDER THE** looming mass of Gibraltar and not long after tied up in midafternoon in Tangier harbor at a pier, beside a Kufdani Industries freighter. Brooks, LuAnn, and Mac had sailed her from Annapolis to Tangier. As they approached the dock, big plastic bumpers on cotton lines were dangled over *Old Fashioned*'s shiny hull to allow it to snuggle up to the dock without getting too familiar. At first nudge on the bumpers, Mac threw a line to Alex to tie her up. Brooks threw another line to Jerome. Mac wore gold Under Armour shorts and a white polo shirt with the Marine logo on the left chest. He was dark from the sun, relaxed and looking fit, with a flat stomach and corded arms.

Alex, Caitlin, and Jerome climbed up the gangway and aboard, each carrying a small bag. Dock workers began to load provisions and luggage. After seventy minutes, they cast off, set the sails, and pointed the bow in the direction of Greece, east by northeast.

As they left the protection of the harbor, seldom seen shadows from Gibraltar angled east in the clarity of low humidity. An unusual breeze was blowing the dirty shore air to the northeast and sucking clean air in from the Atlantic. What remained was Gibraltar's looming mass shading froth-tipped water and hundreds of small boats. Many boats with sails were beating and reaching for vacation or vocation beyond the northern tip of Africa. *Old Fashioned* was heeled over a few degrees and bouncing.

When they had cleared the crowd, Alex sat back in a chair while Brooks tended bar and Mac watched from the captain's chair. Mac kept half an eye on the vista beyond the bow and the occasional eye on the electronics console, where several radars reported on computer screens. His drink would come last.

Caitlin, LuAnn, and Jerome were standing near Brooks, waiting for their drinks to be served and talking casually.

"Caitlin and I are going below to unpack and do girl things," LuAnn said as she was handed her drink by Brooks. "I'm sick of being a sailor. I'm from Texas."

Caitlin grinned and said, "Yeah, why don't you guys have a circle jerk about the Iran war and how it went. Get all of the booms and bangs out of your systems. I have the clearances to hear all of that shit, but I don't really give a rat's ass about how it was done. It was never that hard if one thought it through. It's over. We should get on with our mission to transform the Middle East. Let's try not to fuck it up. This one was messy."

Caitlin walked with her drink to the ladder and went below. LuAnn waved her fingers over her head and grinned, then disappeared down the ladder.

Mac was handed his drink as Brooks moved from the bar and took the helm. Mac chose a chair between Alex and Jerome.

"What's up with the hard body, Mac?" Alex asked." "You look great."

Mac grinned. "Plastic surgery."

"Good for you, pretty boy," Alex said, grinning as he picked up his glass. "I was a math guy and I like numbers, you may recall. Let's consider the math of what you would have had to do in the way of a workout, if you hadn't had that surgery. You look like you lost 25 lbs or so. You can't do plastic surgery on muscle the way you can on skin. At 3,500 calories to the pound that would have been in the neighborhood of—

"Doesn't matter," Brooks interrupted. "Suppose, just suppose, LuAnn and I had sat on the captain's deck of *Old Fashioned* for maybe forty mornings for seventy-five minutes each time, watching him skipping rope, him singing the cadence under his breath for an hour of that Marine Hoorah workout shit. Even if we had sat like that, Mac would never admit to doing all that work to be pretty. He just wouldn't admit it. No, sir."

"What you think about Mac's suntan," Jerome asked. "If he grow a beard, he could pass for a brother in Tangier. He be having a fine head of white hair, like we all hope for many years from now. I could fix him up with some of Tangier's finest."

"He still wouldn't admit it," Brooks said

"I just thought it would be fun to see if I could look like a bad ass again," Mac said with a big grin.

Brooks again glanced out the glass past the bow of the boat, then leaned forward a little. "Again? Mac, get a grip. You're our idol when it comes to thoughtful bad ass."

Mac smiled as he brought his glass to his lips. "Thanks."

Jerome raised his glass. "You look great, Mac. You also did a fabulous job at the sneaky, hidden helm of this Iran gig."

"I feel great. I hope I don't get that far out of shape again or have one that ugly again."

Brooks turned his head to Mac again. "Any sense yet of how Colonel Kim will be treated? I'd hate to see him get screwed over during the inevitable post-battle power struggle at DOD. I can't imagine what kind of shit is going on now that they won one."

Mac chuckled. "It was fun to watch that power struggle and how quickly it started. The Air Force brass was trying to figure out how to contain Kim—he got too much power, too quickly. He threatened their power structure that had worked so well for so long. It was time for them to get back to running the complexity of the Air Force and Kim was in the way. They were going to make him the commandant or commander or whatever of the Air Force Academy, since that's where military academics belong. Kim gets an early promotion to brigadier and some medals."

"Kim would like that," Brooks said,

"Maybe, but I didn't like it," Mac said. "He's one of us—a warrior. We need him. His ego doesn't count. I'm a national security guy. Basically, my job is to think about that shit and keep my contacts within earshot. We needed Kim elsewhere. I went to argue things about Kim with Kelly and Moore, but they supported my thinking quickly. I suspect they had already talked about it. The three of us went in to the president and Molyneaux, she of the infallible nose for public opinion and votes. Yeah, she was there, go figure. We argued the case for enabling a fundamental change in our society. Give Kim control of a lot of money and a lot of power and we may be able to cut the cost and raise the effectiveness of our military. They bought it. Together.

"The president decided, with Molyneaux's infallible opinion-sniffer quivering in the air, to promote Kim to three star, once Roberts met with various leadership of the services and DOD."

"Wow," Brooks said. "There must have been hooting and hollering there. How did Roberts sell it?"

"I helped the president a wee bit with his lines. I convinced him to wave the flag.

"So," Mac said, "President Roberts was with sixteen general officers chosen from the office of the chairman and the chiefs of the various services. He opened with a brief monologue.

"'I am your commander in chief,' Roberts said. 'I will form and reform the government as I choose within my powers. You, gentlemen, are within my powers and I am here to command you. I need your help in making a hard, but necessary situation easy. With the support of General Kelly and General Moore I am promoting Colonel Joshua Kim of the United States Air Force three grades to lieutenant general with full expectations that he will be chairman before I retire. I will task Kim to come up with a plan to modernize the cost and shape of our military. He will report to General Moore.'

"So," Mac said. "Within two minutes, four guys, ten stars total, got relieved when they wanted to argue things. The rest said, 'Yes, Sir.' The squids might have said, 'Aye, Aye, Sir.' I'd guess they were all happy, deep down, to have a clear set of marching orders. Getting things through the Congress was now less political for them and Roberts had volunteered to be the bullseye for the Congress to shoot at."

"Cool," Alex said. "What advice did you give Roberts on how to sell it to the military bureaucracy and the troops?"

"I'm known as a tough guy," Mac said. "I'm an experienced government executive and a stern commander, up for no bullshit. I told the president to pick guys like me. Of course we're tough. We're professional warriors. We work for the commander in chief. We swore to it. It's that simple. We'll get the word out to the officer corps loud and clear. We don't expect much resistance. The president stuffed up our noses how poorly the budget is being managed. Nearly all of us knew it."

Jerome snorted. "It's just what DOD's limp-dick, candy-ass, desk-bound bureaucratic darlings deserve. Did they really think the warriors were going to sit around forever and watch the bureaucrats play, or bloat, or whatever verb they use for what they do? How much pushback is there?"

"A lot of resignations, but we expected that. Good stuff. High rank openings. It should work."

"One hell of a win for you," Alex said. "Congrats."

Mac smiled again and nodded his thanks. "How's your education thing going?"

"Good, we think. We'll get something big out of Dahir Ghorbani, somehow. Billions, much of it from the US, I hope. Dahir will sort it out when he gets a chance. We have an experiment underway in the Rif mountains in Morocco that is quite promising. Big bucks funding mass education—Kufdani Industries will put in a billion dollars and the king will put in fifteen plus some tax rebates if they come true. We own the business model to manage the product and recover our investment. Fair's fair."

"I imagine we'll get our billion back with some extra," Brooks said, "But back to the war. What happened with the Israelis, other than they won? The Palestinians are fairly quiet with their outrage and the Israelis seem quiet, maybe even contemplative in their public comments."

Jerome chuckled. "This one's going in their history books and their Torahs. The Israelis say they think they killed something like fifty-five thousand combatants, with quite a bit of collateral damage to civilians, but they haven't told the UN much, other than they are traumatized and unsure of casualties on either side. They've asked the US to help rebuild their society from the damage done by the Shiites. That's called chutzpah, or some such."

"The Israelis are hurt and confused by the talk of nukes from Iran to be used to annihilate their society?" Brooks asked.

"Yeah, go figure," Jerome said. "Guns Epstein did good. I don't know how many of the attackers were Palestinian, but Hamas took a huge hit. The Israelis strafed, bombed, and sunk over a hundred boats, most loaded with fighters heading to the beaches from the sea. Thousands more, hordes of men, came storming across the Syrian border. As many came over the other borders. All ran into depths of wire, with final protective fire locked and loaded. I'm told that the bodies were ten deep on the reinforced wire and stacking up fast. Attackers were bunched and pushing. The Israeli heavy weapons were used from the back of the attackers' mass to the front. Coochmores, advanced Claymores, compliments of our Islamic scholar's earlier designs, were shooting ball bearings down a programmed vector in all the escape routes from the fields of fire. They had good motion sensors. There were a few buildings destroyed away from the action. The Israelis are being accused of up to ten assassinations elsewhere around the Middle East."

"That's a lot of dead radical leadership," Alex said. "There has to be a political pony there. Maybe the UN can actually fix the Palestinian problem with this leg up."

"One can but hope," Mac said. "Colaris is rounding up her troops to sell a permanent solution to the UN. I think she likes the credit she's getting for the Colaris Doctrine. It's hers now."

"So, Alex," Brooks said. "What's going on with the kids, Karim and Salima?"

Alex smiled and leaned back in his deck chair. "The kids are a work in progress. Karim has enormous physical talents. He has worked well with Tang, who is enthusiastic about his progress, mostly. You know how hard it is to get Tang excited."

"Mostly?" Mac asked.

"Uh, huh, mostly," Alex said. "Karim isn't a killer. He doesn't have the instincts. He catches bugs in the air, examines them, and then releases them."

Jerome smiled and said, "But the four of us squish the bugs we catch. They're annoying. Still, Karim can shoot and hide. The kid can really run. He has patience. He'd make a good sniper, except for the missing killer gene."

"Salima has been Caitlin's project," Alex said. "They swim, work out with Tang together, and study. Salima is Caitlin's magic slate. She's trying to figure out how fast children, both Salima and Karim on different schedules, can reasonably learn, when the child doesn't have much exposure to how fast she or he should be able to learn. Neither Karim nor Salima had formal schooling until now. So far, the answer is both surprising and encouraging. Caitlin is having a ball."

Caitlin's head popped up from the ladder hatch. "OK, kiddies. Put them away. Boy time is over. Give me the summary in five words or less."

"Five words?" Alex said. "We all done good. Next?"

The End

AUTHOR'S NOTES

PULSE

I aspire to become a competent storyteller. On that long path, I work at getting my facts right and then telling my story with as little departure from fact as I can manage.

Much of my research for *Pulse* was by Internet. Google knows all but gives it up reluctantly.

Wikipedia also knows much, particularly about weapon systems. DOD and its vendors, such as Boeing, as well as the press, do a good job of keeping Wikipedia things up to date. The VA-111 torpedo used in *Pulse* to target *Dewey* and *Bush* is real, but I used a description that blended the VA-111 export version sold to Iran with the higher-tech Russian home version. You can Google nearly all weapons systems described and check them out. Fiction? Your call, as always.

Some folks I respect say that I should discuss which, of what I write, is fact and which I have created as fiction. Here's my take:

In the novel *Pulse*, of the three most important pieces of technology used, two are new to Cooch fans—the non-nuclear EMG pulse and the high-tech drone.

Non-nuclear EMP has been demonstrated by Boeing for DOD. There's a good video at https://www.youtube.com/ watch?v=0m-jua2e8Y7k or Google: Boeing Utah EMP champ

The Pulse as presented has a destructive affinity for copper and silicon and is deployed in a human crafted shape. There are many variables in the strength of a given pulse, including height when fired or deployed.

The size of the blast is the biggest energy variable. I ignored most of that as too complex for me to tell, so I had the Pulse do what seemed reasonable, if perhaps not entirely accurate.

The third important technology is Emilie, Caitlin's big data system; she was around for Cooch book 2, *Patriot and Assassin*. Emilie is a star. Her capabilities as told within *Pulse* are well within the bounds of current and future product in the big-data space. The constraint for big data growth, in my opinion, is speed in handling incremental great gobs of relevant data. In Memory Computing (IMC) firms such as Grid Gain will solve much of that problem with their IMC driving software. Rumors abound that Intel is about to announce fourteen nanometer architecture with 10nm nodules that will greatly enable IMC.

Drone capabilities as told may be exaggerated, or maybe not. But descriptions are close to accurate and well within the bounds of current technology. When I am looking for military gadgetry for my stories, I ignore the timing gap between publicly demonstrating the military science under contract and deploying a product to the warrior. Science fiction has morphed to science fact with drones deployed in combination with the Pulse. We are in the early days in the reality of this weaponry. Stay tuned.

The military high-tech drone is used heavily in the second half of *Pulse*. It delivers sophisticated surveillance and real-time communication systems, EMG pulse, and missile fire. I don't differentiate between the various makes and models of drones and ignore handheld drones since there is no ground combat in *Pulse*, by design. Again, this is a synthesis of what is known and what is discovered. I don't know of a single drone that can do everything mentioned, but I felt that too many folks hadn't been keeping track of how much the Tomahawk has morphed under its outer shell and what that could mean for effectiveness if drones could shoot one.

JDAMs exist and are described from current literature, once again greatly morphed from the first design many years ago.

The political descriptions within Iran are fairly accurate, i.e., accurate for some readers but not others, depending on their views of politics and life. I bundled the radical forces of Iran under the Corps Guard tag and all of the traditional forces under the Republican Guard tag. Reality seems far more complex, with many different units that are mentioned, particularly with the Corps Guard forces. It's fiction, and was easier for me to write and carry my story in this way.

Much of my research was in the form of my ongoing habit of reading periodicals such as *Foreign Affairs*, written by prominent scholars. For example, there was an interesting discussion of the recent history of the Iranian nation that came in an article written in *Foreign Affairs* in mid-2014. I haven't used it yet, but it's that kind of writing that I seek out for verisimilitude in my writing.

I have become a bit of an Enlightenment junkie in the past decade or two. I'm a student rather than a scholar, but I enjoy the story and its possibilities as a model for bringing technology enhanced education to the Middle East. One of my best sources for this kind of research has been the videos of the Teaching Company. In particular, I commend the lectures given by Professor Daniel Robinson of Oxford University on The Great Ideas of Philosophy. The discussion on Voltaire's thinking and Goethe's subsequent comments was based on one of Robinson's lectures. Caitlin's comments on Newton were inspired by another of those lectures. For the basics in Islam, I commend the course by Esposito, Great World Religions: Islam.

All errors are mine, of course, rather than a fault within sources.

READING GROUP GUIDE

1. In what way did reading *Pulse* change you? Did reading the novel give you a different view of the world from what you had before reading it? In what way?
2. What do you think was the author's most important message to his audience in writing *Pulse*?
3. What scenes gave you the greatest insights into Cooch and his character and why?
4. What do you believe is Cooch's strongest character trait? What motivates him?
5. What was your impression of the opening scene in the book in the Petit Socco in Tangier? What kind of impression did the author's description of the run-down neighborhood leave on you?
6. What is the source of Cooch's moral compass and desire to educate those in the Middle East?
7. How did you feel about the situation in which the thugs harassed the two children? Discuss the dichotomy in Cooch's character in that he showed extreme kindness in saving the children, and yet the means he used to save them were extremely violent.
8. Cooch doesn't have a life partner and mentions being worried about being in his sixties and not having a mate or children. Why do you think he has not found a love match? Will Cooch eventually find a permanent partner?

9. Were you surprised to find out he had children? Could you visualize him ultimately ending up with Hala? Discuss why you think he might or might not commit to her.
10. What male character did you identify with most and why? What female character did you identify with most and why? Do you think the male and female characters were developed equally?
11. Which character did you feel was the easiest to know and why? Who would you want to spend an evening with and what would you like to discuss with that person?
12. What did you think about Dain, the voice inside Cooch's head? Can you relate this entity to anything in your personal life? Where do you believe the voice originates?
13. Discuss your impressions of the extremely advanced weaponry that plays a part in *Pulse*. How did you feel about the capabilities of the Kphone and the drones that were described in the book? Discuss whether you find these advanced forms of weaponry exciting or frightening or both.
14. What was your impression of Dahir and the others inside Iran who were ready to ally with the United States? What did you think about the ability of the computer, Emilie, to select Dahir specifically? Did you find it interesting at how easy Cooch made the whole operation seem? How did you feel while the attack against Iran was taking place? Was it exciting, frightening, surprising?
15. Can you imagine *Pulse* as a film? Who would play the role of Cooch, and which female character would be given prominence? Who would play that role?
16. The last line in the book suggests there will be a new adventure for Cooch, Caitlin, and the others. Where do you think or hope that adventure will take them?
17. If you were to sit down with Cooch over a cup of mint tea or a drink, what would you most like to ask him?

AUTHOR'S Q & A

1. Have you always wanted to be a writer? Could you comment on your path to becoming an author? Did you have the plot of *Pulse* developed to the end, or did the novel unfold in terms of plot as you wrote it?
   I started as a reader and was always interested in writing. As I aged, I began to read books about the craft of writing and then I gave it a try. It's hard. The plot unfolded as the characters moved within it.

2. What made you decide to begin the book in Tangier? The description of the neighborhood was very evocative. Why did you choose to set the opening scene in a neighborhood where the scent of offal and sewage are overpowering? What was the inspiration for the two children and the thugs that harassed them?
   I like Tangier and its opposing textures. The first scene was to be one of violence so I took my memories of animals and garbage and worked them in. I needed a setup for an early violent scene, which is how I like to start thrillers. I figured out the kids as a trigger. They have moved on to boarding school in a later book. Thugs are easy; it is the creative, evocative killing of them that is fun to write.

3. Cooch is a unique person. How did you decide to create a child who was the product of a Marine and a Moroccan? Why did you decide to have Cooch be an Islamic scholar?

Marines are easier to describe than army. More pizzazz for the most part. I've always been interested in Bedouins and Tangier, and thus, Moroccans. He needs credibility as an Islamic scholar to make the argument that the Shiite/Sunni schism is stupid. He has to be able to move around as a scholar, not as an American.

4. What was your favorite scene to write and why?
I really liked the Muslim feminism scene with Hala and the subsequent evolution of his mother telling him about his children. Great fun to write. I read five books on Muslim feminism first. That was fun, too.

5. Could you expand on the source of your inspiration for some of Cooch's extremely powerful moves such as when he grabs eyeballs and squeezes them?
Pop! I knew a guy once with very strong hands. He was formidable with them. So I gave Cooch those and figured out the martial arts moves.

6. Why did you decide to give your character the surname Cuchulain?
Alex's surname is for the Celtic warrior god. I like to write about the Irish—they're colorful and wild. Dain is the Celtic god of violence, dragged along in Alex's head to put nuance on violence.

7. Could you comment on Cooch's extreme violence when he is engaged in battle?
Cooch was trained in violence and it is part of him. He was trained to kill, not to capture or defeat an opponent. He practiced these skills for eight years. In violence is when he feels most alive.

8. Could you comment on what seems to be your extensive knowledge of weapons? Would you please talk about the Kphone and where you got the inspiration to create a phone with such powers?
I was an Army infantry officer and was active for over five years, and in the reserves another eight. They teach you a lot, so it was easy to keep up when I got out of the reserves after those thirteen years. The phone is a reach to the future, where vastly more power is inevitable. The big data

aspects of the Kphone are underway today. I lived in technology for a long time, so I keep up.

8. Is Caitlin based on anyone you know? Why did you decide to have a woman be the smartest person in the room?
   Pulse *is laden with strong women—the secretary of state, the president's chief of staff, Caitlin, and others. I want to attract female thriller readers. Things are a changin' for women in combat. Being captured by Muslims is uglier for them. It will morph.*

9. Is it significant that the only person that we know Cooch has children with is Hala? Is the fact that she is a moderate Muslim of significance? Why has Cooch never married?
   That she is a modern Muslim is key. She will develop the pre–K-6 student support starting in the Rif and moving on. Those are Alex's only kids that he knows of—I haven't decided. He's in love with Caitlin and has been for years. She has no interest in monogamy, or in being married. I haven't told the world yet.

10. Alex comments that there is little understanding of the political and moral structure in Iran among Americans. Can you comment on your knowledge of why we don't have this understanding and why Cooch believed that there were forces inside Iran that would want to have a relationship with the US?
    We portray Islam the way we portrayed the Germans and the Japanese in WWII, as monsters to be hated reflexively. There are 1.5 billion Muslims; we should learn how to make nice. For Muslims, the US is the world's military hegemon—getting along with us is important; witness Iran today.

11. How do you see the intersection of technology and weapons? Will the closeness we feel via social media eventually eliminate the need for war or will it simply make war and violence even more absurd?
    The latter. Iran is the best bet for helping establish an uneasy peace in the Middle East in Pulse. *Until they loosen the grip of their theocracies the peace will be uneasy, for reasons explained. It's fiction.*

ABOUT THE AUTHOR

Shooter, soldier, entrepreneur, philanthropist, venture capitalist, vintner, and now author.

Robert Cook is a United States Army Vietnam veteran, who attained the rank of Major and holds the parachutists badge, the Bronze Star Medal and the Army Commendation Medal.

Cook was named the Ernst and Young Entrepreneur of the Year for the Metropolitan Washington, DC Region in 1987.

Mr. Cook is an active philanthropist. He endowed the Robert E. Cook Honors College of Indiana University of Pennsylvania that was recently covered in Donald Asher's book, *Cool Colleges for the Hyper Intelligent, Late Blooming and Just Plain Different.* www.iup.edu/honors.

Mr. Cook, originally of Altoona, Pennsylvania, holds a BS in Mathematics from Indiana University of Pennsylvania and an MBA from the George Washington University.